GUNNER'S LEAP

TIM NEWTON

Published by 10 streets publishing

Paperback ISBN-13: 978-1-9162722-0-0
.epub eBook ISBN-13: 978-1-9162722-1-7
.mobi eBook ISBN-13: 978-1-9162722-2-4

"You put sweet FA in, you get sweet FA out"; words of wisdom from '81… thanks Pops Xx

PROLOGUE

Lucas, Rick and the HSG

On the 1st of February, 2014, after twenty-one year's loyal service, Staff Sergeant Lucas Roxby's military career sadly - but not unexpectedly - came to an end. And, after an unending quest to find alternative employment yielded nothing but a string of dead ends, the normally outgoing sergeant began to feel that, like many who'd served before him, he was destined for the scrap heap.

But then things changed.

During the late afternoon of the 21st June, 2015, after a nervy second interview, Lucas finally landed a viable offer of permanent employment. The role, described simply as Field Technician, was with North West based salvage and recovery company, the Hanlon Stuart Group. Based in Warrington, the HSG were well-established, privately owned, and had an enviable reputation for offering a range of specialist services across the globe.

"He's got an old school vibe," HSG's CEO, Ray Stuart, said to himself as he watched the rangy retired royal engineer head back to his car, "…I think he'll work out nicely."

As ever, Ray's gut instinct proved uncannily accurate. From the get-go, the fit was right, and Lucas settled quickly. Taking to the work like the proverbial duck to water, the tenacious ex-sapper was soon thriving in his new role and when, four months in, he was teamed with one of HSG's longest serving field agents, things only got better. Lucas's new partner, ex-shipyard fabricator Rick Kruger, was a straight talking South African with short blond hair and the meanest right hook this side of the Stellenbosch. While Rick could always be relied on to give his all, he was viewed by some as difficult to handle. But Lucas, never one to be fazed by hearsay, quickly realised the duo's instant chemistry was likely to get results, and he wasn't wrong!

Now almost two years down the line, the brief for the pairing's latest assignment was simple: The Book of Martyrs recovery - as explained so succinctly by Ops Director Gerry Hanlon - consisted of nothing more than a short trip to the US to retrieve a package. The package in question was a misappropriated first edition of a renowned work of sixteenth century religious propaganda known widely as Foxe's Book of Martyrs. This rare copy of historian John Foxe's inflammatory classic was to be collected from an address in Mesa, Arizona, and returned directly to its rightful owners in Scotland.

"You get all that, Roxby?" the director barked after completing his instructions. "This one's as easy as it comes, son. It's a straightforward collection, so you've got four days max - OK?".

Lucas smiled. "In and out in flash, boss," he said. "We get in, pick up, then get back before you know it."

"Right answer," Hanlon replied. Then, pointing a telling finger, added, "And don't forget, even though it seems a simple one, I still want daily reports, and I want them in on time – understand?"

After several seconds of deliberate silence, Lucas finally nodded his acknowledgement. Rick followed with a gruff 'Yebo, chief!' and backed it up with a slow-motion thumbs-up. Then Gerry stood up from behind his desk and shooed them out of his office…

***

CHAPTER 1

ARIZONA

As the blisteringly hot afternoon slipped seamlessly into evening, Lucas Roxby and Rick Kruger found themselves in familiar territory. Sat tucked up at the bar in the comfortable lounge of their motel, the two men were working their way through a pitcher of ice-cold beer. Despite the idyllic setting, the mood was subdued and, as they discussed their predicament, Lucas looked the unhappier of the duo.

"Two days down the pan," he said with a despondent shake of the head, "and that's a bad start in anyone's book." The forlorn Englishman stared silently at his reflection from across the bar, "I'm convinced," he added, as he dropped his gaze to focus on the half empty glass in front of him, "that these freaks are just messing with us."

"Based on what evidence?"

Lucas turned to his colleague. "Look, Rick," he said, "I'm telling you the whole thing's a stitch-up, mate." He reached for the beer and took a slug. "I don't care how much paperwork's in place, this crowd have no intention of honouring the hand-back….and that's based simply on the problems experienced so far."

Ex-royal engineer Lucas Roxby was not a man to lose heart easily, but this job was getting to him. Sitting alongside him at the bar, swilling a Jim Beam chaser round in a tall tumbler, Rick Kruger was listening intently to his disgruntled companion. As the blond South African swirled the ice round in his glass he didn't look particularly worried. "You've been wrong before, Sarge," he grinned, "so I wouldn't go getting all dramatic quite yet." He paused. "In my book it's too early to call."

"Well, I don't agree," Lucas snapped. "I think we're done."

Rick looked at his colleague and smiled. "OK, fair enough," he said, "if that's how you see it, then I'm not going to argue with you, but all I'm saying is you never know.... the excuses could be legit."

"Nah...no way - we're just wasting our time, mate – might as well pack up and go home."

Rick Kruger thought the world of his teammate; the lanky Englishman with the odd-ball sense humour was his rock. But at times he could be a real pain in the arse and getting too high on the highs and too low on the lows was a character trait Lucas was unlikely to change.

"Look, I understand," Rick said, nodding sympathetically. "Yes, it's frustrating. Yes, it's a ball-ache, so there's no argument about that." He stopped to inspect the meagre contents of his glass. "But it's not our fault, Rox ... it's nothing to do with us, so if I were you I wouldn't worry about it."

Lucas sighed and encircled his colleague's shoulder with an outstretched arm. Then he laughed. "OK, OK, I'm sorry, Ricky," he said, "but you see, I am worrying about it – and you know I take all this shit seriously...very seriously indeed."

Rick smiled. "You can't tell, Sarge," he said with more than a hint of sarcasm.

Lucas smiled back then started to speak. "I thought..." he said, but then hesitated. "Well, I just thought it would be like it was supposed to be, you know, a straightforward collection job, that's all - but it isn't, is it? Now it looks like it's gonna be a complete waste of time."

It was Wednesday, early evening, and '*The Shooting Star*' was busy. The popular 3-star motel on the outskirts of Scottsdale was set back from interstate 87 and had been the duo's base since they'd landed in Phoenix two days earlier. Now, for the third evening in a row, they were perched on high stools at the bar in the motel's lounge. It had been early - even by their standards - to start drinking, but the Hanlon-Stuart Group's recovery team had a lot to think about.

"Cheers!" Lucas held his glass up. "Here's to a simple job going tits up."

Rick grinned, gave a quick roll of the neck, then raised his own glass in acknowledgement. "Yeah, I'll drink to that," he said, "but we've been here before, haven't we?"

Lucas drained the dregs of his beer then placed the glass back on the bar. "Yeah, we have, Ricky," he said, "but this, this is just one old book for Chrissakes. Fly over and collect, they said. Bring it back to the UK, they said. Dead easy, they said. I don't bleedin' think so."

Rick hung his head. "For God's sake, Rox," he muttered in exasperation, "I told you – don't let it get you down."

"Get me down, Ricky? Are you kidding? I'm not down, I'm just pissed off, and there's a big difference, you know."

"Yeah, whatever..."

Lucas placed his elbows on the bar then cradled his head. "Right. Now, let me think," he said. "What do we do now? What next? What's our Plan B and how we gonna solve this one?"

The ex-sapper wasn't expecting an answer. The rambling questions were rhetorical; Lucas was talking more to himself than to his faithful comrade. But Rick wasn't fazed. He knew his companion well. While the incoherent jabbering continued, the South African sat back, crossed his arms and shook his head. Some things never change, he thought quietly to himself.

***

The trip had started well.

Monday's connecting flight from Atlanta was on-time, incident free and, on arrival at Phoenix, the Arizona sunshine was most welcoming. But their luck wasn't to last: after a routine grilling at passport control, the two men were detained for further questioning. The explanation for their visit was not liked by the border control team. The stone-faced US officials were far from convinced about its legitimacy and demanded more detail. Four sweat drenched hours later, after a distinctly frosty question and answer session – which had included personal background checks and two calls to the UK - they were finally told they could go.

As they were being led back into the terminal building, Lucas turned to their chaperone. "Thank you, Officer," he said as politely as he could muster. "Sorry to have caused you so much trouble."

The giant of a man from the Border Force eyed him suspiciously. "You enjoy your stay, gentlemen," he said. "Stay safe and be good and remember - don't outstay your welcome!"

Lucas smiled. "Not a chance," he said. "Four days and we're gone."

***

Now behind schedule, the two men were eager to find their car hire desk.

"Ricky, it's this one," Lucas shouted as he beckoned his partner to follow him through the bustling concourse. "It's the usual."

The car hire had been pre-booked, and as the duo raced toward the Hertz counter they were relieved to see no other customers waiting. Despite being several hours late, they were still greeted enthusiastically by the branch's animated – and a little too touchy-feely - Duty Manager, Randolph.

After twenty minutes the documentation was completed, agreed, signed, and the car was ready to go. Both men were down as drivers, but it was Rick who would take first slot. While the South African familiarised himself with the controls, Lucas prepared for his job as navigator.

"Don't go getting us lost again," Rick joked. "Remember what happened last time."

Lucas replied with an in-your-face one-finger salute and a smile. "Up yours!" he said quietly.

The hire car was a base model Chrysler MPV cross-over. It was a silver-grey Pacifica LX with no obvious distinguishing marks and looked like thousands of others on the roads of the Mid-Western United States. And whilst there was no doubt it was exactly as HSG's standard operating procedures decreed - plain, boring and innocuous

- Rick struggled to hide his disappointment. "Hardly your top of the range, is it?" he said as he stood in front of the bland grey lump.

"Yet again the company comes up trumps," Lucas grinned. "Another mind numbingly dull car for us to drive thousands of miles in."

Although not enamoured by the charms of the Chrysler, the duo accepted that it was better they didn't stand out. As long as the car had sat-nav, decent air-con, and was reliable, it was fit for purpose. So, with the pre-requisite company boxes ticked and little point in complaining further, they loaded their bags and headed for the exit.

The short drive to Scottsdale was straight-forward and - much to Lucas's relief - the well sign-posted roads made for a stress-free navigation. The Shooting Star Motel, on the other hand, had disappeared from the face of the planet and, when there was still no sign of it after going twice round the block, they decided something was wrong.

"We need help," Lucas said, "or we'll carry on like this all day."

Rick pulled up to the kerb. Lucas lowered the passenger side window and politely asked the first passing local for directions. "Excuse me, friend," he said, "we're looking for The Shooting Star Motel…." But there was no reply; the target obviously wasn't in the mood to help. Maybe it was the accent, maybe Lucas looked intimidating, who knows the rationale? Whatever it was, the man just glared and kept walking.

The second accostee, an Asian woman with a sour face and a killer wiggle, was more accommodating. After several seconds of over-acted head scratching, the young lady confirmed they had been given duff information. The Motel was on the West side of town, not the East. The address details in their information pack stated East Carlton Street but should have read West Carlton Street. Lucas, appreciating the odd administrative error was an occupational hazard, simply rolled his eyes then thanked the woman profusely for her help. Then, and as she remained motionless at the kerb, the Chrysler disappeared into a blur of city traffic.

To their relief, this time it was easy to find. They'd followed sour face's concise directions to the letter and ten minutes later were pulling up in the car park at the front of the large but modest looking motel set back from the main street. It was surrounded by neatly manicured lawns, brightly planted borders and had a line of arrow-straight palm trees running strategically along its roadside frontage. The exterior looked clean, like it had just had a fresh lick of paint, but the garish neon signage – with a psychedelic shooting star depicted in the centre – looked a little jaded. Lucas thought it was probably better suited to an amusement park rather than an hotel but didn't comment out loud.

Check-in was routine; lots of welcoming smiles and lots of questions. Particularly questions about what brings an Englishman and a South African to Arizona.

"You guys sure have come a long way," the smiley blonde at reception said. "Y'all here for the Sci-fi convention?"

All the usual well-meaning innocent small talk but, as ever, the two men remained tight lipped. For most operations they'd have a cover story and for this foray it was nothing too complicated. Their spiel about a simple market research visit on behalf of a UK-based electrical engineering company had been well rehearsed. It worked for the questions at the car-hire counter and now at the motel check-in. When the need for covert distraction arose, the boys from the HSG could smokescreen with the best of them.

They were both allocated rooms on the first floor. The adjoining doubles were on the rear elevation of the main block and were big, roomy and simply furnished but there was a subtle difference; Rick's reportedly had the better view. Despite this minor disagreement over the outlook, they were both happy with the standard of accommodation and the motel's facilities in general. They were particularly intrigued by the aptly named ground floor bar. The '*Meteor Lounge*' seemed more nightclub than hotel bar, but it looked a good place to while away the hours, even more so once they found out it never closed.

CHAPTER 2

Ronnie Stafford

The fact that Ronnie Stafford looked even bigger and uglier in the flesh than on screen had the HSG's CEO, Ray Stuart, seriously rattled. Now, as Ray desperately tried not to let his feelings show, close up - face to face - he was struggling. How anybody could not be overawed by the gargoyle of a man that stood before him was inconceivable. Virtually impossible, he told himself several times over.

Ray's idea from the outset had been to meet with an open mind and play it casual, but that philosophy went out of the window the minute Ronnie's hulking frame loomed before him. "Mr Stuart," the big man said as he thrust out a shovel of a hand. "What a pleasant surprise, I am so pleased to meet you."

Ray stood wide eyed and silent for what seemed like an age. "Likewise," he replied eventually, sounding far from convinced.

"So good of you to accept my invitation," Stafford said. "I was wondering if you would actually show, but, very sensibly you have. Like I say, I am pleased."

The big man gave the impression of being delighted to meet his guest and continued to greet the dumb-struck CEO with gusto. "As I was clear to highlight in my invitation," he continued, with a flash of yellow teeth, "I have seen your company name mentioned on many, many occasions and have heard so much about you personally," he hesitated for a second, "so much so that I thought it was about time

I arranged to meet you in the flesh." He paused again, then smiled. "And now, happily, you are here."

"Well, yes," Ray said trying to regain his composure. "Here I am - I mean, how could I refuse such a polite and beguiling offer? I thought, why not give it a go…you never know, it could be genuinely worthwhile."

"Good for you," the hulk boomed. "Excellent choice, a very smart move…got your interest, did it?"

Ray tried to look his host straight in the eye but was still finding it hard not to stare. "Your invitation was as unexpected as it was intriguing," he replied as calmly as he could, "especially with the little teaser dropped in - that subtle comment about our job in Arizona?" He stopped and nodded slightly. "That definitely caught my attention."

Ron Stafford was a giant of man: while the polite would call him statuesque, the truth wouldn't be quite as kind. He was a successful businessman, a big drinker and gambler, and came with a colourful reputation. In his own way he was articulate, definitely street savvy, and was never seen in anything other than designer suits. But, despite the wealth, his fancy talk, and the smart clothes, he still came over to too many as uneducated and uncouth. Looking like a cross between a punch-drunk back street brawler and WC Fields, his appearance was perversely mesmerising and from the minute Ray laid eyes on him he couldn't help but gawp. The man's overall size was remarkable. With that bull neck, the veined cauliflower nose, and two jagged scars etched into the pock marked skin of his bloated face, the man was a frightening sight to behold.

Stafford was no stranger to being stared at and during this particular encounter he could not fail to notice his visitor's unsuccessful efforts not to. "Handsome bastard, aren't I?" he laughed. "Can't keep your eyes off me, eh, Mr Stuart?"

Ray suddenly felt embarrassed at being caught out so obviously but, thinking quickly, quipped, "Movie star material, Mr Stafford… what more can I say?" The light-hearted comment was appreciated and, as Ray sensed the underlying tension ease, Ronnie led the way to a baize covered table by the window.

The ground floor office was vast. It was a mismatch of green and beige eclectically furnished with a variety of period pieces, albeit none of them appearing to be from the same era as any of the others. "I like classical furniture, Raymond. Do you?" Stafford asked.

Ray shrugged his shoulders. "Not something I've ever been into that much, to be honest," he replied. But Ronnie continued unfazed. "Take this card table, for instance," he said. "It's Victorian, it's great for absolutely everything: meetings, eating, blackjack, poker and.... counting money on. You know what I'm saying, Raymond; all sorts of good stuff." Ronnie chuckled under his breath, adding, "I love it, looks great doesn't it? Just think of the craftsmanship involved in making such a beauty."

Ray half nodded in acknowledgement of the big man's off-beat small talk then sat down as directed in the chair opposite.

"So, now," Ronnie said, as his smile subsided, "time to get down to the business in hand, Mr Stuart." He paused as he smoothed a tiny crease from the baize in the middle of the table, then asked, "Do you have any inkling as to why I ***really*** asked to meet you?"

Ray considered the question for a few seconds. "Err, no, I don't actually," he replied tentatively. "Obviously, since the invite I've thought about it a few times, but nothing springs to mind." He paused, smiled politely, then decided to continue in the same controlled manner, "Other than the fact that our business interests do occasionally cross over, I can't really work out what you'd want from me - or how – and, equally, why you would want to help me or my company."

"You do surprise me, Mr Stuart," the big man mocked. "I was convinced you'd be a little more clued up than that. I thought a man of your calibre and standing - a man with so many international connections - might have some ideas, some preconceived thoughts about my motive... but possibly I'm giving you more credit than you deserve, yeah?"

The truth was simple; Ray Stuart had no inkling why he was there. He'd been surprised to receive the request in the first place but, despite some initial reservations, had decided to throw caution to the wind and give it a go. While he'd never met the man, or ever had any direct business dealings with him, he was well aware of who Ronnie Stafford was. He was also familiar with his operation; he knew where he was based and what services his Company, Excel Export, offered. At least what the legitimate side of the business did.

The invite had come out of the blue. It was hand-written and addressed to 'Mr R. Stuart, CEO HSG Ltd' and had been delivered by courier direct to the yard. In this technologically advanced age this was an unusual approach and definitely added an element of mystery to the rationale behind it.

"Seriously, Mr Stafford, I don't have a clue," Ray answered, "although from the feedback I've had, I would respectfully suggest it's for reasons that would personally benefit you. As we all know, you are not exactly famed for your generosity, are you?"

The big man's eyes narrowed. "That's a little unfair," he said. "I don't know where you get your information from, Raymond, but I can assure you I look after those who look after me – a simple maxim, but remarkably effective."

Ray had been sitting rigid in his chair but now shifted sideways into a more relaxed position. Then, looking the unsmiling giant in the eye, decided it was time to end the charade. "OK," he said firmly, "why don't you stop poncing around and simply tell me what the fuck you really want to talk about."

Ronnie's scowl intensified. "OK, Mr Stuart, I get the message. I'm going to have to give you the benefit of the doubt, aren't I?" He forced a smile. "I'll believe you really don't have a clue about my reasons for asking to meet you."

Ray was no charlatan; yes, he ducked, dived and occasionally bent the truth but that was the nature of his business. "Well, that's good because it's true," he snapped, "so please go ahead and explain."

"OK, then…" Ronnie replied, "best start at the beginning." As he spoke, he spread his huge hands flat down on the green baize in front of him and gave a practiced drum of his fingers. "Which in this case begins with the following question," he paused and looked up. "Are you acquainted with a Spanish company called Ebro Logistical Solutions - run by a man named Miguel Lerado?" Ronnie stared at his guest as he awaited a response.

"*Ebro Logistics*? Yes, yes, I am." Ray replied. "We've done work for them on occasion." He stopped as he trawled the memory banks. "Probably only two jobs though, although I don't recall a Miguel Lerado," he frowned. "We dealt through a guy called Pedro, I think, but his full name and official title escapes me. From what I do remember, he was alright, and Ebro as a company were OK to work for – why do you ask?"

Ronnie continued to stare, "Pedro Grillo, Head of European Operations – is that the man you dealt with?" he asked.

"Yeah, could be – as I said, definitely a Pedro. Although, if it is the same fella, I'm sure his title wasn't that grand.... I think back then our guy was just a plain old logistics manager." Ray was trying his best to recall as much detail as he could about their previous Ebro jobs. He could definitely remember two specific ones and, as he'd just explained, in both cases everything went relatively smoothly and to plan.

"Well you were lucky," Ronnie snarled. "I'm telling you now that bastard man is a two-faced shyster and Ebro is nothing but a front." The suited giant was now riled and the venom his tone exuded was positively toxic. Ray was taken aback by the sudden change of mood, baffled as to why the giant was suddenly going off on one about a little-known Spanish logistics company. But after several seconds of silent deliberation, he responded, "I find that hard to believe," he said. "Sounds like crossed wires to me. Are you sure we are talking about the same company and the same people?"

There was no immediate response from Ronnie. He just glared. After a brief, awkward stare-off, Ray decided to continue. "What you're telling me sounds nothing like the outfit we dealt with," he said. "I'm telling you, they were OK - we did two relatively low-key salvage jobs for them and there was nothing dodgy or underhand about their behaviour. It was all totally legit." He paused, but, with still no comeback, he kept going, "We got well paid for both jobs, and we got paid on time by bank transfer with no fuss or dispute – now, that doesn't seem like the behaviour of a gang of con men, does it?"

Mindful that Ronnie was already wound up and starting to foam at the mouth, Ray had kept his tone forceful but controlled. But it was too late; the blue touch paper was well and truly alight.

"I'm telling you straight, those fuckers are out-and-out gangsters," Stafford bellowed, "and they've stitched me up good style, and I'm talking serious fucking money!" He stopped to brush away copious beads of sweat from his temple. "And that, my friend, is the reason you're here." The big man was now staring wildly at his guest, eyes bulging, and his fat forefinger pointing menacingly toward Ray's head.

Ray was now getting worried for his own safety. "You'd better calm yourself down," he said firmly. "You need to take a deep breath and think about what you're saying for a minute."

"Why should I?" Stafford growled.

"Why?" Ray retorted loudly. "Because I haven't the foggiest idea what you're ranting about – that's why!" he bowed his head. "And, to tell you the truth, I'm more confused now than I was when I walked in here fifteen minutes ago."

The HSG CEO was genuinely perplexed. The whole situation was still making no sense to him and with now only a manic stare from Ronnie, he decided to take the bull by the horns. "First you say you want to get together because you've heard so many good things about my company: good start." He stopped and smiled half-heartedly. "Plus, as an additional enticement, you drop in a hint you might be able to assist with a particular problem we have: still good." Again, he smiled. "Then…then you insinuate I should know the real reason I'm here - which I don't - and then suddenly you're raving like a maniac, blowing a gasket and saying that you've been shafted by a Spanish logistics company, who you claim are a criminal organisation."

Ray stopped, took a deep breath, then put on his best *'bollocks-to-you'* face. "And now you're saying that's the real reason why I'm here." He stopped talking and slowly shook his head. "That's a crock of shit, Ronnie, and you know it. You're going to have to start explaining yourself better than that or I'm just going to fuck off and leave you to it."

Ray Stuart didn't give a toss now about the seething hulk's sensibilities. He wasn't going to pander to anyone's incoherent ranting, not here, not now, not ever. Easing back in his chair, he folded his arms across his chest and pursed his lips. It was time for a proper explanation, or he was leaving.

Ronnie looked deflated at the forcefulness of his guest's response but, realising he was not being unreasonable, moved back in his chair, shrugged his shoulders, then let out a loud sigh. "You are absolutely right, Mr Stuart," he said. "I am making no sense at all. I am letting my frustrations get the better of me. I'm talking in riddles and rambling on like some demented old goat - I apologise."

Ray was surprised by the sudden apology and watched, intrigued, as Ronnie continued to backpedal.

"I shall take a deep breath," the Excel boss promised. "I will calm down and try to keep my emotions in check and then, hopefully, I can explain the situation to you in a far more coherent fashion."

The change was instant. As quickly as he'd got riled in the first place, Ronnie now calmed. Suddenly he was rational and relaxed again, with such an intense mood change that Ray began to have a suspicion the man was bi-polar.

***

The remainder of the meeting lasted just an hour, during which Ray got a clear and thorough brief on the whole Ebro situation. Thankfully, Stafford stayed measured and articulate throughout the remainder of the session and, with no hint of the bombastic wild-eyed demon of before, it was a far less stressful experience. The explanation process took some time, although the critical issues were quite simple to understand.

"Again, Raymond, my humblest apologies for the bad start," Ronnie offered as the meeting drew to a close, "but hopefully now, after a proper explanation, my frustrations make more sense to you – yes?"

"Oh, yes, absolutely," Ray said. "I get the picture."

"Good…and I do hope that we can reach agreement on what's been discussed." Ronnie stopped, smiled, then asked, "When do you think you can come back to me?"

Ray answered quickly. "By close of play tomorrow," he said, "and I know we can sort something out, although, like I said, I have to discuss with my team, which may take a little time but, whatever the outcome, I'll speak to you tomorrow, probably later on."

"Good. I'll be waiting."

As the HSG CEO prepared to leave, the two men stepped away from the table and turned to face each other.

"Thanks, Ronnie." Ray put out his hand. "Thanks for getting us together; it's been a real eye-opener." He smiled. "This could be interesting."

"My pleasure, Raymond," Ronnie replied as his giant paw encapsulated his guest's. "It's turned out better than expected. I look forward to discussing it further."

With that, the two men shook hands enthusiastically. Farewells over, Ray headed down the garishly carpeted corridor towards the main entrance, continued through the double doors and into the parking area where his car was waiting.

CHAPTER 3

Collection Day

Lucas and Rick's itinerary for the trip was tight.

Day Two of only four allocated was scheduled for the main event: the collection. Their target, a rare first edition of Foxe's *'Book of Martyrs'*, was owned by the Presbyterian Church of Scotland (PCOS) and the Scottish order had not seen their cherished book since loaning it out to an international exhibition in Davenport, Illinois over two years ago. How and why the book vanished after the event and ultimately ended up in the hands of an obscure religious order from Arizona was still a mystery to all. But it had.

Initially, the book's disappearance caused a massive backlash. It had then taken the PCOS -and several external agencies - months to track it down. But once located, the negotiations for its return had taken nearly as long as the original search. Eventually, after the final legalities had been closed out, arrangements were made for its journey back to Scotland. As a company in favour with the Presbyterian Elders, the Hanlon Stuart Group was contracted to undertake the seemingly simple collection and return operation.

The 'Divinity of Christ the Redeemer' was the religious order identified as the 'unofficial' custodians of the book and had begrudgingly agreed to use their administrative base in Mesa for the official hand-over. Their nominated contact was a Reverend Gary Coleman and both his landline and mobile numbers had been included on the collection team's job sheet. The meeting was scheduled for 11.00am Tuesday morning at The Divinity's down-town HQ. The brief clearly highlighted they were to make contact with the Reverend the night before.

"I'll give him a call now," Lucas said as he left Rick checking out an information board by the front desk. "I won't be long."

At 8:45 pm from a pay phone in the foyer, Lucas rang Coleman. He tried both numbers several times but there was no answer. All attempts went to voicemail, so the frustrated Englishman left the same simple message on both numbers, speaking clearly and slowly: "Message for Gary Coleman. This is Lucas Roxby of the Hanlon-Stuart Group confirming our meeting at your Mesa office tomorrow at eleven o'clock as agreed. Trust everything is still OK for the handover and look forward to seeing you tomorrow. Thank you. 'Bye for now."

Lucas knew it wasn't a good omen. The faint chime of alarm bells echoed in his head. He felt a nip of apprehension creep in. "Nothing we can do now, Rick," he said to his expectant colleague. "Might as well call it a day…we'll just see what tomorrow brings, eh?"

Rick had other ideas. "Hold on a sec, Sarge," he said, pointing down the corridor. "Don't you fancy a quick pint before hitting the hay?"

Lucas didn't need much persuading. After eighteen hours travelling, he was more than ready for a night-cap. They headed toward the arched entrance of the 'Meteor Lounge'.

Rick showed little signs of tiring. "Yeah," he said rubbing his hands together in eager anticipation, "a few beers will go down a treat."

Lucas nodded in agreement. "Suppose we do deserve it," he answered. "It's been a long day."

It was Monday night. The place wasn't busy, but it seemed welcoming, so they settled at the bar. Lucas ordered two large beers. After an hour chatting while knocking back an extra one or two more than planned, they called it a night. They finally trudged off to find their rooms, agreeing it really was the only way to end a very long tiring day.

***

Despite the time difference taking its toll, Day Two started as expected. Both men were up early, showered, dressed and down to the restaurant before 8.30am. After feasting like kings on the breakfast buffet, they decided to take a leisurely stroll round the motel.

"This is a great spot, isn't it?" Rick said as they stood in the car park admiring the motel's well-kept exterior. "Certainly better than the last digs we got."

Lucas grinned as he thought back to their last job. "I know," he replied. "That was one bad place to stay…thank God it was only two nights."

Rick laughed. "Yeah, but it was two nights you'll never forget."

***

The Divinity HQ was easy to find. So much so they arrived half an hour early. Surprised by the building's striking appearance, the two men double-checked the address. It was the right place, and far from the subdued, humble affair that they'd imagined. Before them stood a gleaming, state-of-the-art office block that looked like the headquarters of major corporation. It gave the unmistakeable impression its occupants weren't short on funds.

"Ricky," Lucas said as he stood outside looking up at the vast, vaulted exterior, "remind me again what this lot do."

"Couldn't tell you," the South African replied, "but whatever it is, I'd say it's making money."

Inside, the lobby was positively palatial. With its high-end finishes and imposing water feature, it looked even more ostentatious than the exterior did. The striking bronze centre piece took the form of a giant pair of praying hands. Jets of water exploded from between the touching fingertips, blasting fifteen feet high before falling back to earth in a spectacular cascade down the fingers of each hand and into an ornate pond at the base. The front desk was of an equally high specification; it was tall, long and all marble in construction, and exactly matched the water feature pond in colour and detailing.

The reception was manned by one uniformed male. He was a short po-faced man of Latino appearance "How can I help you?" he asked curtly as the HSG men approached.

Lucas did the talking. Officially, he was the lead operator and was quite simply far more eloquent than his colleague. Thankfully this arrangement didn't bother Rick; in fact, it made his life easier. He was quite aware his accent could be a bit tricky to understand at times. "So what?" he often said. "I've got a short-fused ex-Staff Sergeant to do all the rabbiting for me."

Lucas explained their 11.00am appointment to the unsmiling man and was quick to emphasise they'd come a long way to attend it. "And we rang last night to confirm," he added.

At the mention of Reverend Coleman's name, the attendant's expression changed. In an instant he switched from dead pan to harsh scowl, then asked Lucas if his calls had been answered. The Englishman confirmed they hadn't, but said he'd left a message on both the numbers given. There was a brief pause, then the attendant looked up. "Gentlemen," he said, "I am sorry to inform you but last night Reverend Coleman was involved in a very serious road traffic accident." The man stopped for a few seconds, seemingly to compose himself. "He was travelling back from a conference in Flagstaff and was involved in a head-on collision…sadly he died at the scene."

The man's droning delivery coupled with his sullen look and the shocking news itself rendered both the HSG men speechless. After several seconds of awkward silence, Lucas regained his composure and, without even a sideways glance at Rick, calmly asked the sour faced attendant, "Does he have a deputy we can see?"

Lucas knew it seemed a little uncaring, but it matched the indifferent icy vibe the man was giving off, "No, sadly not," the man said. "Coleman only has an assistant and he was in the car at the time of the accident. He's now in hospital on life support." Again, the delivery was matter of fact, and again, despite the graveness of the news being dispensed, he showed no hint of emotion.

"Does he have a superior, then?" Lucas asked, also showing little concern in his tone.

The attendant was giving nothing away. He looked blankly at Lucas then at Rick and then back to Lucas. As he drew an exaggerated breath, he gave a slight nod of the head then begrudgingly replied. "Well, yes," he said, "like us all, the Reverend works under Monsignor Dubois." He paused and shook his head very slightly, "But unfortunately he's not available.... would you like me to pass on a message?"

Lucas couldn't help but notice the smirk flash across the man's face as he asked the final question. But, despite his growing frustration, the ex-sapper wasn't going to let the cold, irritating little prick get to him.

"Yes, we would," he answered calmly. "You can tell the Monsignor, or anyone else in authority for that matter, that we've travelled five thousand miles to get here ... and we've arrived at the agreed location at the scheduled time." He stopped and intensified his glare. "And whilst we appreciate that, due to tragic circumstances, our contact is no longer available, we still need to collect our consignment, OK?"

The man held Lucas's stare for several seconds but eventually nodded a faint acknowledgement.

Taking the cue, Lucas leant forward. "As a gesture of goodwill," he said, with his elbows now resting on the counter, "we are willing to give you a twenty-four-hour grace period - time for your organisation to re-arrange things if you like." He stopped, hopeful of a response, but got nothing other than a belligerent gaze. "So, we'll be back here same time tomorrow, and this time we're not leaving until we have what we came for - understand?"

Lucas glared at the obnoxious little man then handed him his business card and offered a final word of warning. "I would advise the Monsignor to ring me sooner rather than later. In the long run, it will save you a lot of hassle and that is no idle threat, if you get my drift," and with that he turned on his heels, gestured to Rick it was time to leave, and without so much as a backward glance left the building.

Driving back to Scottsdale the duo tried to make sense of the situation. Was it a Divinity smokescreen or had tragedy really struck?

The timing seemed almost impossible to believe; on the eve of the final hand-over, after months of protracted negotiation, the sole point of contact for the transaction is killed in a car crash. What are the odds? In their eyes the story was too coincidental to believe, so ultimately they decided it was a stalling tactic, but both agreed it was a bloody serious one.

Back at the Motel, Rick completed the day's field report and emailed it back to the UK. At the same time, Lucas made a call to HSG's operations Director, Gerry Hanlon. Lucas kept it short and sweet but, as soon as he'd finished, his South African colleague wanted answers. "So, what's old Gerry saying, then?" he asked. Lucas looked at Rick, then ditched his scowl. "Well," he said with a casual shrug, "as you can imagine, he's not happy with the delay…but he's not panicking. Says he has no reason to think it's not genuine."

Rick looked puzzled. "I am surprised," he said.

"Well, that's what he said," Lucas replied. "So, he's not going to report anything to anyone at the moment. He simply wants us to try again tomorrow and see what happens."

***

Back in the UK, Gerry Hanlon was sat alone in his office. Ensconced in his favourite armchair, he pushed back into the worn leather and took a long deep breath. Then, as he stared blindly out of the window, he exhaled and pondered the call he'd just received. "Are we worried?" he asked himself. "Should we be concerned, have the wheels come off or is it just an unfortunate hiccup?" He'd no way of knowing the truth but, for the benefit of the field team, he'd decided to remain positive.

The HSG had undertaken commissions for the Church of Scotland twice before. The first opportunity had come via a random introduction to the Presbyterians Elders by a close friend of Ray's sister, and the second had been as a result of that first assignment turning out to be a howling success. So now - on the strength of two well executed jobs - a third had been awarded and Doctor of Theology, Edmond

Reid, the PCOS's eminent spokesperson, had been adamant from the outset that the collection and return of his organisation's cherished *Book of Martyrs* be entrusted to the HSG as it was a company he felt he could trust.

But this third commission differed from the others; this outing involved a unique artefact, an antiquity so entrenched at the core of the Presbyterian's belief that it took on a spiritual significance all of its own. And Gerry, mindful of this revered status plus its eye watering £120,000 price tag, wasn't keen to inform Dr Reid of a problem. He had no intention of causing unnecessary worry and would remain tight-lipped until his team had been given at least one chance to try again.

CHAPTER 4

Sarah Stuart

The sky was black and the rain so heavy that Sarah couldn't see past the bonnet of her ageing VW. Now conditions were so bad she'd decided it was better to stay in the car in the Service Station car park and let it pass over.

Resigned to going nowhere fast, she sat staring blankly at the rain obliterated windscreen. The idea of making a few calls crossed her mind but, realising the clatter of the rain would drown out any chance of meaningful conversation, she quickly gave up on that option. So, to kill time she turned her attention to the small, innocuous-looking notebook lying on the passenger seat beside her. The book was bound in black leather. On plan it measured six inches by four inches and was a good half inch thick. It was obviously well used; the pages were well-thumbed and the gold marker ribbon was tatty and frayed. The book was face down but open, so she picked it up. She then turned it over and spread the pages wider and started to read the neat flowing text across the pages.

She studied the words closely. The book was her own, it was the one she took everywhere with her, the one in which she incessantly scribbled all her work-related thoughts. She wrote To Do lists, she wrote research notes, she listed names, places, dates, phone numbers, she even doodled in it. The book was rammed with thoughts, ideas and theories. It was a warts and all insight into the workings of her professional mind and by her own admission if she ever lost it, she would die. Next to her mobile and lap-top it was her most treasured possession.

The pages consisted of several neatly written lists. One detailed high value works of art which had disappeared and never been found and another highlighted works that had been lost but ultimately found years later. The last entry of the second list caught her eye:

Michelangelo Merisi da Caravaggio: - "Judith beheading Holofernes"; lost for over 50 years then found in a farmhouse attic in Toulouse, France in 2014 – N.B. currently valued at £100,000,000.

She wasn't sure why she'd jotted the information down. Her recollection was hazy. But she guessed it was a result of something fellow art-lover Calvin Lentz had made her aware of; the affable Scot was always passing on titbits of information from the world of art mysteries and she lapped it up. Suddenly her concentration was broken by a sharp ping. She pulled her mobile from her bag quickly and checked the message. 'What now?' she muttered as she squinted at the screen. It was a text from her father:

Team: please make yourselves available today at 4.30pm. Mgmt. strategy mtng (main boardroom) cld be a long one and everyone needs to attend – no excuses accepted. Regards, RS.

As HSG's CEO, Ray Stuart was always formal with his daughter on work-related matters and he'd never been any different. In response, she was equally as professional, and it seemed to work well. To the casual observer, during working hours at least, it was hard to tell they were actually father and daughter - and that's just how they liked it.

Sarah checked her watch: it was 2.25pm. If she was to make it back to Warrington before 4.00pm she needed to get a shift on. No way did she want to miss finding out what the big drama was, so after a quick glance skyward confirmed the rain was easing off, she backed out of her parking space and headed down the slip road onto the spray engulfed motorway.

***

The HSG's yard had developed significantly over the years and was now a formidable set-up. Almost military style in layout, it had a well fenced perimeter, security-controlled access gate, central elevated admin block and various secure storage/workshop facilities dotted around the compound area. But, despite its fortress like nature, from the adjacent approach road it didn't look too dissimilar to other industrial complexes well established around the area and as such it was only close up or inside that anyone took real note.

Once through the double doors of the admin building, visitors were greeted by a large, tidy, well-appointed reception area complete with the usual necessities. It was furnished with a coffee table, two gigantic chesterfield sofas, a water cooler, drinks machine, three potted palms & a large well-worn reception desk. The remainder of the double-storey block was fed by two brightly lit corridors. One went left, and one went right from the reception and both led on to a variety of general open plan office areas. There was also a board room, a strong room, and a recreation area jokingly referred to as the "Green" room provided for use by all employees.

***

The boardroom was a fancy affair. In a deliberate nod to the founding member's naval heritage, its antique timber panelling and brass detailing gave it a heavy nautical feel. The conference table was huge, rectangular, and had a warm polished oak finish that complimented the room's walls perfectly. With seating for eighteen, plus the obligatory overhead projector set up at the far end, it looked nothing short of classy. But this evening the table was arranged for only eight attendees and each place had been set with a gleaming cut glass tumbler, an HSG branded jotter pad and pen set, plus a single page agenda.

As usual, Ray Stuart took his place at the head of the table. Gerry took the seat immediately to Ray's right and Steve Harrison to his left. The remaining attendees were Finance Director Robert Smith, Admin Manager Carol Mellor, her number two Kevin Doyle, and, pen-ultimately Senior Logistics Co-ordinator, Rajesh Khan. Then, last but by no means least, was the final invitee, Sarah Stuart – but she wasn't there.

Everyone was seated and looking to Ray to commence proceedings when Sarah suddenly made her whirlwind entrance. With a flurry of apologies for being late, she headed straight for the empty seat and sat down. The group appreciated she'd done well to get there, so as soon as she was settled the meeting fell silent. Again, everyone's eyes turned to the CEO.

"Well, Ladies and Gents, thank you all for attending," he said, "particularly, in light of the short notice, we do appreciate your efforts to be here, and as you know under normal circumstances you'd be given a lot more notice for a meeting like this."

Ray remained seated whilst he spoke. "But as you are well aware," he smiled," there are no normal circumstances and, as usual, we have a few problems, a few problems we need to discuss, then quickly make a decision how we respond and move forward."

Ray had drafted a brief Agenda for the meeting and for reference each attendee had a copy on the table in front of them. He had also produced a brief report summarising the key details of their situation but did not intend to issue it until later in the meeting. Item number one on the Agenda was simply titled: Arizona mission - operational update.

Ray explained to the group that the US recovery mission was linked to the main topic of the evening and, as such, gave the whole team a thorough résumé of where that operation was up to. During his explanation he asked both Steve and Sarah to input, which they both did enthusiastically. Agenda item two was in bold underlined capital letters, it read **MEETING WITH R. STAFFORD.** This, as far as Ray was concerned, was going to be the hardest part to articulate. Just the background to his morning's meeting alone was going to take a little explaining but it was the obvious starting point.

"Folks, I'm conscious that it's already 5.20pm," he said. "So, before I get really stuck into the Ronnie Stafford stuff, do we need a quick five-minute break? Grab a drink, ring home or use the loo, whatever you want. I did warn you all that it would be a long one… and I wasn't joking."

Ray smiled at the array of serious faces surrounding him, then added reassuringly, "Look, it's not going to be that bad, I reckon we should be finished around 7.00, 7.30 at the latest – can we all live with that?" All heads nodded; it was a given they would stay late, and a quick comfort break was a good call.

Once everyone was back and settled, the CEO continued his marathon explanation. Conscious of time, he kept it pacey but was careful to leave nothing out. He gave the team the background on Stafford and his infamous Import and Export Company. He ran through the strange circumstances surrounding the invitation to meet, where the meeting was held and Ronnie's odd behaviour at the start. He then led onto the Ebro connection: who they were, where they were based and how the HSG had worked for them in the past. Then, before he went through Stafford's personal issues with Ebro, he stopped. He placed his hands on the table and leant forward, "Now listen hard," he said firmly, "this is where the story starts getting a little complex, so you need to focus."

Everyone smiled and subconsciously edged closer. Ray then went on to explain Ronnie's primary beef. He told the entranced gathering that Excel had been contracted by the Spaniards to supply them with a fleet of ten military spec land rovers, which – after a lot of hard work - they had done. Ebro had paid the deposit but now, several weeks after successful delivery, Stafford was struggling to get them to pay the balance, and now the whole non-payment issue had become so critical Ronnie was about to go legal. The big man had got himself into a major state of distress about the issue and was seeking redress via any avenue he felt could help, one being a covert reclaim of the goods.

The CEO was covering a lot of ground quickly, but everyone seemed to follow the tale without too much trouble. Just to be sure, he checked a couple of times along the way. "All following this OK? Any questions so far? Come on, guys, don't be shy, just butt in when you need to, OK?" He grinned as he scanned his attentive audience for feedback.

A barrage of smiles and nods confirmed they were all on board so far. Without further ado, he ploughed on with the story, "So, as I said earlier, our own dealings with Ebro were fairly straightforward and uneventful - but we must remember that the last job we did for them was well over eighteen months ago...and it now appears that in the intervening period, well, certainly according to our new acquaintance, things at Ebro have changed."

Ray was now standing in front of the group, and by his body language they could sense a headline was imminent. "That leads me on to what I believe is the real crux of the issue for us," he said, before pausing for a quick sip of water. "Our precious Mr Stafford is not only adamant that the Ebro organisation has stitched him up royally but also claims that now, in its present form, it's nothing but a front for organised criminality and he believes that some of those illegal goings-on are being carried out in close partnership with a religious organisation from the US of A." He stopped, hoping to heighten the drama. "Yes, Folks," he said eventually, "you guessed it – the one and only...Divinity of Christ the Redeemer."

The assembled team looked puzzled. They stared at their boss, all thinking the same thing: had they heard him right? And, if they had, what type of illegal activity could a religious order from Arizona and an international Spanish logistics company jointly undertake? It sounded bizarre and they wanted to know more.

Steve Harrison was the quickest to start with the questions. "What proof does Stafford have to back up his claims?" he asked. "Does he have anything specific, anything tangible, anything we can verify?"

Ray had expected a barrage of questions and wouldn't be disappointed. Steve's was the first of many which he answered quickly.

"Plenty on the vehicle non-payment," Ray said, "but on the other stuff it's all just hearsay and rumour at the moment."

The R&I Chief's question was immediately followed by a salvo of other queries. With every member of the team chipping in,

Ray battled through the onslaught, firing answers back like some demented political campaigner. But, after five minutes of the frenzied questioning, he held his hands up in surrender and, raising his voice above the haranguing group, shouted, "Look, guys, I understand your surprise. It blew me away when I first heard it too, but that's only half the story – you need to sit tight and just keep listening, OK?"

The group eventually settled down and, when the table fell silent, Ray sat back in his chair and continued. "Right," he said slowly, "so Ronnie Stafford claims that Ebro, under their banner as an International Logistical Solution Provider, are working for The Divinity in various areas of Central America. OK with that simple premise, Folks?"

The group again nodded their understanding, so Ray cracked on, "The services Ebro provides - from what we can glean - are simply described as transport, storage and logistical support. And we're told this assistance is given to at least half the missionary projects The Divinity have around the Central American region." The animated CEO stopped briefly to clear his throat, then continued, "On paper the operation looks to be part of a worthwhile cause and, to many outside observers, it is almost unquestionably legitimate. But this well-meaning humanitarian crusade is a smoke-screen. The projects are apparently a cover for an elaborate drug distribution operation," he paused to look round at his open-mouthed audience. "Simply put," he went on, "it would appear The Divinity, ably assisted by Ebro, are moving tonnes of high quality cocaine from remote regions of South America into central America, then shipping it out from Honduras to the USA and Spain, and - according to Stafford's sources - it is the constant flow of equipment and supplies to the projects that the shipments are concealed in. Seemingly, it's the perfect cover."

Steve Harrison's hand instantly shot up. "Yes, Steve?" Ray acknowledged without missing a beat. "Fire away."

"But surely that's shipments into Central America, not out," Steve said. "I don't understand how, if all this stuff is true, err, how product is shipped out of the country."

Ray smiled at the ex-DI. "Exactly the question I asked," he replied. "But apparently equipment, particularly plant items - you know, generators, pumps, water purification systems and all that kind of gear - is regularly returned to the US and Spain for repair, servicing, maintenance and even resale sometimes and that's how they do it."

Ray was regurgitating Ronnie's explanation back to his team almost verbatim. No need to alter anything or put any kind of spin on it, the big man's description of what he believed was going on, however implausible it sounded, was pretty clear.

The HSG group now sat as if in a trance, digesting what they'd heard. Could such wild allegations be true? Could such an arrangement really fool the authorities? No one broke the silence; they all knew a further twist in the tale was likely to come. What did the dubious Mr Stafford expect to do about the situation and why would it involve them?

Ray stood up again - they were about to find out.

CHAPTER 5

The Watchers

As a native of Arizona, the heat didn't faze him. In all his fifty-eight years Mordecai hadn't known it any other way. The grizzled rough-neck was as much in tune with the harsh surroundings as a diamondback rattlesnake, and the only real difference between the two desert dwellers? Mord Ings was simply way more dangerous.

His latest job for The Divinity wasn't difficult. The brief was straightforward: monitor the movements of two foreign visitors for a few days whilst on US soil and report back as required. In his book it didn't come any simpler. The targets were easy prey. All the key information had been supplied up front, Ings knew who the men were, when and where they were expected, and why they were here. The rest was a piece of cake.

Getting the tracker in the hire car had been the only difficult part, but the Arizonan bad boy had influence in the strangest of places. And, whilst the hire desk manager at Hertz's airport branch was no friend, Randolph Delgado owed Mordecai big time.

"You'll do it, boy," Ings had hissed during his late-night visit, "or we'll cut your balls off." The camp cokehead had been scared shitless and had no choice but to do exactly as he was told.

Leon Tate, The Divinity's Security Chief, had made it clear to Mordecai he was not to physically confront the interlopers. The requirement was purely to observe and report. Once the targets had picked up the right car, he enabled the tracker, checked it was functioning properly, then sat back and kept tabs from a distance. But the old rattler was a realist. He knew it was unlikely to be that simple. There was always the possibility things would change, so from the off he'd made arrangements for a second team to be prepped and ready for instant deployment if required.

That need arose far quicker than even he'd expected. Tate instigated the surveillance up-grade immediately after the HSG duo's visit to the Mesa HQ. He hadn't liked their aggressive attitude or veiled threats and, suspecting they could be a little more troublesome than envisaged, wanted the odds stacked in his favour.

"Listen, Ings," Tate had purred, "that pair will be back tomorrow, so I want another set of eyes on the ground watching them, OK?" He paused as he awaited the redneck's acknowledgement.

"Yes, Sir," came the attentive reply.

"I want it from the minute they arrive," he said. "In fact, make sure your team's here well before that pair of lame brains arrive - understand?"

There was no panic or urgency in Tate's voice, he was not overly concerned about the visitors' presence, he just didn't want to leave anything to chance.

"No problem, Mr Tate, I'll sort it," Ings answered. "Might even call in at the motel myself and check them out, you know, up-close and personal… if you get my drift."

"That's all well and good," Tate had said, "but don't spook 'em, that's the last thing we want."

Mordecai, acutely aware of how powerful The Divinity were, wouldn't dare let his paymaster down. "Of course, Mr Tate," he answered. "They'll never know I'm there…."

***

Ing's visit to The Shooting Star was hardly a surveillance master class; he simply wandered around the place, looking like any other random guest checking out their new surroundings. The motel was not small, but after five minutes of nosing he'd seen most of it and was now left standing at the entrance to the lounge bar. Deciding to give it the once over and without being too obvious in his intent, he casually walked in, sat down at the bar and ordered a beer. The place was quiet. Except for a few huddled groups and the odd miss-matched couple scattered about, it was nearly empty. Obviously, a slow night but, once settled and sipping his Bud, Mordecai eased round to take in the view. He took his time. Slowly but surely, he clocked every one of the nooks and crannies of the place – but, sadly, no joy.

Still, he was confident they were close; he'd seen the Chrysler in the car park so they couldn't have gone far. After drawing a blank in the bar, he drained the remnants of his beer, placed the bottle on the bar, then stood up and turned to leave. As he made his way to the exit, he was aware of two men entering. He watched them walk through the arched entrance and then - as it became obvious they were going to pass within inches of him - the penny dropped. Lucas and Rick, deep in conversation and oblivious to the lean, leather faced yokel coming towards them, just kept talking, brushed past him and headed for the bar.

Mordecai didn't falter. In one casual glance, he studied the pair closely and, despite the opportunity to check out the opposition being only brief, it was enough. His initial impression didn't suggest too much to be concerned about; he'd dealt with a lot meaner looking than these two wannabes. The taller one looked mid-fifties and was doing most of the talking. He was dressed in dark blue jeans and a black polo shirt and seemed quite animated. His companion was younger and shorter but was much more powerful looking. With a square jaw and muscular build topped off with shaved blond hair, the Arizonan got the distinct impression he could handle himself.

Ings was happy with his night's work, it had been worthwhile. On paper it didn't seem like he'd achieved much but seeing his adversaries close up and doing it undetected was all he needed. That one brief moment of contact gave him a faint glow of superiority and some idea of what he was dealing with. So now, smiling smugly to himself, he sauntered across the lobby, out through the main doors and disappeared into the warm Arizona night.

***

The Shooting Star was a no-frills facility, but it was popular. It was big, bright, spotlessly clean and very comfortable. Its corridors, its reception areas and its amenities always felt busy, and with the effervescent reception staff seemingly in constant demand, the place positively buzzed with activity.

Lucas and Rick liked it. They felt happy and relaxed and had already agreed that if they had to extend their stay, they'd be happy remain at the motel. A few days extra in the US wouldn't cause Lucas any hassle. He didn't need to explain himself to anyone back home, except maybe Matt - his younger brother – who, as usual, was looking after his dog.

Rick, on the other hand, would have to ring his wife and explain everything!

***

Back in the UK, Sarah was working late. But by 6.50pm she'd decided enough was enough. It was time to call it a day. As she turned her office lights off and prepared to leave she noticed another light still on. It was at the end of the corridor. She stared down the dimly lit passageway before realising the faint glow was coming from her father's office.

She stood silently for a few seconds. 'Is Dad still here?' she asked herself. 'Is he another fool working all the hours God sent?' Maybe it was a hereditary trait, an inescapable Stuart family character flaw. Maybe overtime was in the DNA. Despite her fatigue, Sarah decided that, if he was there, she'd go and have a chat, so set off down the dark corridor.

Ray was indeed still in his office and was checking over documentation needed for the following day. As his daughter knocked on the half open door, he looked up. "Sarah, my darling," he said with an enthusiastic grin, "what a pleasant surprise! Come in, sit down…I am truly honoured."

She came in, smiling, gave him an affectionate kiss on the cheek, then slumped down in the chair opposite. Once settled, she started to ask about the Arizona mission. In particular, the rumour she'd just heard about progress. The CEO looked affectionately at his babbling daughter and gently shook his head. He loved the way she was so committed to whatever she was doing, never a slacker, never a shirker, always thinking, always on the case.

"Listen," he said, "Lucas Roxby may be a touch unconventional, but he's like you, Love. He gets results," Ray paused and stroked his chin. "Yeah, OK, so maybe he has got a few teething problems, but we're not particularly concerned about it - it'll get sorted."

Sarah smiled at her wise, kind father. "I'm sure you're right," she agreed, "it's just we've put a lot of hard work into setting this up, haven't we?"

"Yes, we have," he said, "but it's early days so I wouldn't worry too much about it for now, OK?" He waited as she nodded her agreement, then asked, "Now, my dear, is there anything else troubling you?"

Ray knew full well that the probe about Lucas's rumoured problem was just an opener. He guessed there was something else his daughter wanted to discuss, and he wasn't wrong. "Well, seeing as you ask, Pops," she smiled," it's the bloody book itself - I want to understand why it's so significant, why have these people been so unwilling to give it back? I mean, it's not theirs anyway, so what's the big deal?" Sarah stopped and took a deep breath, "I want to figure that out…but I need help."

She sat back in the chair, crossed her arms and looked pleadingly at her father. "I've spent a lot of time trying to dig up some proper details about them," she said forlornly, "but it's a bloody slow process… seems The Divinity are big on secrecy and misinformation. In fact, it's a miracle we know anything about them at all." She then slunk down deeper in the chair and put her head in her hands.

"Now, now, young lady," her father comforted, "don't take it too hard, this is the nature of the game we play." He smiled. "It's all a puzzle, it will take time to crack, but we *will* do it, we'll get there in the end…so don't worry." Ray didn't want his beloved Sarah getting overly exasperated about the situation. He appreciated her request for help - it was a rare occurrence and fortunately for her he had a suggestion that might just help. "Sarah, you know Gerry has a meeting with Doctor Reid later this week, don't you?"

"Vaguely," she said looking up. "Why…what's the agenda?"

"Well, formally, it's supposed to be for Gerry to brief the Doctor and his team about progress and confirm an exact return time," he paused and smiled knowingly at his wide-eyed daughter, "but maybe now we use it as an opportunity to gather other information, you know - extra details that may help our cause."

"Like what?" she queried.

"Well, think about it. They're likely to have info that we weren't party to first time round. Stuff they didn't think was relevant to us as purely the collection agents. Could be names, places, reasons. I don't know exactly what, but it's worth a shot – don't you think?"

"Yeah, suppose so," she replied. "Sounds reasonable."

"So now I'm thinking: why don't you go to Glasgow with Gerry? See if you can get a direct insight into their take on the book." He leant forward over his desk. "You know: grill them face to face about its relevance, its meaning, its history. See what reaction you get."

Sarah sat bolt upright, smiling again. For a few seconds she gazed into her father's twinkling green eyes then replied, "Great idea, Pops, you're a star!"

CHAPTER 6

Unchartered Waters

Ray was keen to ring Ron Stafford back within the time scale promised so didn't hang around. He got up early - washed, dressed and fed in half his usual time – and was out of the door like a whirlwind. At that time of the morning the roads were quiet, so he made good progress and arrived at the yard before 7.00am. Whilst it was only an hour earlier than his usual starting time, he was still surprised to see how busy the place was. "Do these people not have a life?" he asked himself as he took the steps two at a time on his way to the first floor.

He knew it would be a long day. There were a host of contract loose ends to resolve plus two client meetings to attend and, on top of the everyday stuff, Ray needed a sit down with Gerry, Rob Smith, and Steve Harrison to review the previous night's boardroom get-together.

The get-together had been a revelation. Even Ray himself had been surprised how well it had gone; he'd hoped for a positive team response and got it in spades. Everyone round that table had had an input - it was a real group effort. Ray loved all that *esprit de corps* jazz, the democratic approach, the team always looking out for each other, the whole being greater than the parts; when it clicked, it gave him goose-bumps.

The CEO summoned Steve and Gerry to his office and it took the three men less than forty minutes to review the arrangement and agree it was a goer. Next stop was the Commercial Director's office. Robert Smith was a stereotypical accountant, a good man but with no obvious sense of humour. Always suited and booted, Rob came over as a full-on dull conservative type. But, whilst he might not be the life and sole of the party, he did know his job. He was thorough, astute, and knew the ins and outs of a balance sheet better than anyone. Ray loved him. He had the greatest respect for the straight-laced Mancunian and knew without a doubt he had the right man overseeing the money side of the business.

The Rob Smith sit down wasn't as easy as Ray's earlier one; HSG's commercial whizz was emotionally detached from the sharp end and, seeing things purely in black and white, Robert never considered the ever-present grey zone. But, despite this handicap, he was often as not the individual who identified potential risks no one else even thought could exist. This tendency to look on the negative side of everything pissed most people off, but not Ray who positively encouraged it. He appreciated the fact that in Rob Smith he had an employee who played the devil's advocate role to perfection.

The meeting lasted an hour. Despite the Commercial Director's usual protracted questioning, Ray was eventually happy he backed the proposal. Comfortable with most of what he'd heard, Robert only had concerns over two minor issues, and - like the true professional he was - he assured Ray he would include some suitable wording in the contract to plug the gaps.

Once the CEO was satisfied his key men were on board, he returned to his office to make the call.

***

"Mr Stafford it's for you, it's Ray Stuart, he's on line three. Do you want to take it?"

When his secretary rang through, Ronnie was sat at his beloved card table leafing through a pile of handwritten ledger pages. The papers were haphazardly strewn in front of him and he was trying hard to find a particular sheet which was presently eluding him, "Oh, yes, Janie, I do," he replied enthusiastically. "Put him through, will you."

Ronnie had been waiting for the call. It was now 4.45pm and he'd started to worry that, in spite of all the promises, HSG's likeable CEO wasn't going to get back to him today. Whilst he appreciated Ray had said late afternoon for the call back, the big man had hoped it would've been a bit sooner. Itching to get going with something meaningful, Ronnie didn't waste time on small talk.

"Ah, Mr Stuart," he said loudly, "I've been looking forward to your call all day…what's the news? Is your organisation willing to help me out? Do we have a deal?"

"Yes, Ronnie," Ray answered, "you'll be pleased to know we have a deal."

Ray, much like Ronnie, just wanted to get straight to the important stuff, adding quickly, "But I must make it crystal clear there are a couple of caveats that we insist form part of the contract, nothing major, no showstoppers, just protection for our interests. I'm sure you'll understand."

"That's good news, Ray; the important thing is the agreement of the principle. I'm sure your extra clauses won't be a problem." Ronnie took a very audible breath then continued, "I know it's early days, but have you had a chance to prepare any kind of contract yet? It would get the ball rolling; we could start a review right now. No time like the present, eh?"

Ray knew full well that it was in HSG's own interest to be the ones who prepared any formal contract documents and Robert Smith, in less than a day, had done a great job with that task. "Better than that, Ronnie," he answered, "we can have a draft over to you within the hour. It's not massive but it's clear and concise and keeps it all legal and above board."

"Excellent, Raymond, absolutely excellent, what an efficient man you are, I'm impressed. Get it over to me as quick as you can. You've got my email, haven't you?"

"Yes, it's on your business card," Ray replied. "I'll get it sent over. Come back to me as quick as you like. Once you're OK with it, we're ready to move." He paused, then added, "And, in anticipation of your agreement, I would just like to say, we look forward to doing business with you."

Ronnie was positive it would be a simple matter of a quick read through, sign it, then all systems go. "Yes, yes, absolutely, Raymond, same here," he replied enthusiastically.

"OK, then… I'll speak to you once you've checked it over. Thanks again, Ronnie. 'Bye for now."

Ray waited for Ronnie Stafford's reciprocal goodbye then hung up. He lent back in his battered swivel chair, looked across his tidy desk and exhaled sharply. Then, focussing on the stern looking face opposite him, he grinned, "Well, Gerry, my old mucker," he said, "here we go again!"

***

At 10.30pm, Ray was still in his office but was now alone. A small reading lamp illuminated his immediate surroundings and the desk was clear except for one sheet of paper in front of him. The one A4 page he'd been studying was an email from Ronnie Stafford. It was a simple, but formal, acknowledgement that the Ebro vehicle recovery contract had been signed and accepted. Ray was impressed. Excel's legal team must have checked over the documentation super efficiently; the response had come back within two hours of being sent.

Now sat silently in the half light, the CEO was in reflective mood. Despite the fact that, hours earlier, he'd given his own team formal approval to proceed, Ray still found himself questioning the big man's under lying motive. Politely declining to help Excel was an option he'd considered earlier in the day, but it was a momentary lapse of faith. Puzzling over why he'd obsessed over the Ebro/Stafford affair since he'd met the man face to face, he was caught in two minds. Yes, he'd warmed to the uncouth gargoyle, but something didn't add up.

Was the reported connection between Ebro and The Divinity the problem? If so, why? In his mind, this rumoured link didn't assist their stateside operation - certainly not immediately - but in the aftermath even Robert Smith had felt the need to comment. "It is possible gentlemen," he'd said, "that this Chinese whisper could be significant?"

The information Ronnie passed onto Ray was no more than a report of an overheard phone call. A snippet of a conversation one of Excel's men had picked up during a recent meeting with an Ebro delegate. The call had been made by Pedro Grillo, a senior executive, a man who should know better than to allow anyone to listen in on his private conversations.

The HSG knew Pedro; he was a man they'd dealt with before. But, since those dealings, it had been reported that the amiable Mr Grillo had done very well for himself. Apparently, he'd moved up the company's management tree and was now tagged with the rather grand sounding title of 'Head of European Operations', although, if Ronnie Stafford's accounts were to be believed, during this meteoric rise up the chain of command the man had undergone a major personality change.

Ray had been surprised by the accusations. During their previous dealings, Pedro had always come over as friendly and co-operative. The HSG personnel working on the Ebro projects had enjoyed working with him, and both companies had been pleased with the outcome of the two jobs.

The conversation Stafford's man overheard appeared to link the HSG to the rumoured Ebro/Divinity alliance. The claim was that Pedro had been heard to tell a colleague about a meeting he recently attended in Phoenix, a meeting with a Divinity big-hitter called Leon Tate. But the real concern was that Pedro had then asked his underling to pull out everything they had on record about HSG and forward it on to him.

Eventually Ray gave up worrying; his head hurt, he was tired, and it was time to go home. He'd made his decision and was sticking to it and what would be, would be!

***

As soon as Sarah found out about the rumoured connection she panicked. The idea that The Divinity may have sourced confidential information about HSG - and had done it in advance of Lucas' and Rick's departure for the US - was troubling. She needed time to think, so headed to her office, put the kettle on, and made a strong coffee. Then, cradling the much-needed caffeine shot, she sat back and thought hard about the predicament.

After ten minutes of silent contemplation she now had a suspicion the radical Franciscans never intended returning the book in the first place. But, she thought, if that was the case, why sign up to a formal return agreement? Or was the signing just another calculated step in a never-ending stream of stalling tactics? And, the most puzzling of all (*why is the Book so bloody important?)* desperately needed answering. She knew it was her job to find out and knew she needed help, but who could assist, where could she turn, where would the answers be?

Sadly, she hadn't got a clue, but that had never stopped her before, and it certainly wouldn't now....

CHAPTER 7

Back to Mesa

The Motel's restaurant was a simple affair, and, with a bright, airy industrial feel, it was another well used amenity. However, despite the obvious popularity, it rarely felt packed and both Lucas and Rick agreed it served the best breakfast selection they'd seen in years.

The food was nothing short of fabulous, and the sassy, smartly uniformed waitresses were friendly and entertaining. Nothing was too much trouble for them, even in the earliest hours of the morning they wise cracked their way through the bleary-eyed punters and relentlessly dished out flirty smiles with a never-ending flow of coffee refills. With such great food and slick, attentive service, the duo knew they'd be hard pushed to find a better place to start the day. But, despite the comfort once they'd eaten, it was time to hit the road. "Come on, Kruger," Lucas said as he finished his third re-fill, "time to try again."

***

The previous day's journey to Mesa had been easy, but today the traffic was heavier and slower.

"What's with the traffic?" Rick asked as they ran into yet another line of stationary cars. "Fuck me, these roads have gone crazy."

"Gotta be road works, hasn't it?"

The South African shook his head. "Who knows?" he sighed. "This is worse than the M62."

Pulling up ten minutes late, they parked on the main street opposite the building, locked the car, then dodged the frenetic morning traffic and headed for the front door. They expected the main doors to operate automatically on approach but today they remained closed. After several failed attempts to open the doors, Lucas shouldered the plate glass. It didn't budge and, as the men peered through the darkened glazing into the cavernous lobby, it was obvious things had changed. They could see the place was deserted; there were no lights on and the reception desk was bare.

"What the hell's going on?" Lucas growled. "It wasn't like this yesterday, so how come all of a sudden it's a ghost town?"

Rick was as surprised as Lucas but could sense his partner's growing frustration. "Try the intercom," he suggested. "They might just be pissed off we're late."

Fixed to the left-hand side of the door was a slim line box. With just one tiny mother of pearl call button placed centrally under a small circular gauze speaker point, it was hardly noticeable. There was no writing or instructions on the box; all that could be seen was a tiny cross-like symbol neatly engraved above the button. Lucas grinned at Ricky as he pushed it. The recorded message was short, sweet and eloquently delivered by a husky female voice: 'At present our offices are temporarily closed and will reopen after the Cirrus Five Equinox.'

"What the hell is that supposed to mean?" Lucas barked as he hit the button again.

The message repeated itself. He pushed a third time and the message played again; much to his annoyance each press got exactly the same response.

"I tell you, Rick, these fucking weirdos are taking the piss," he snarled as he got more and more wound up. "They've deliberately shut up shop because of us, haven't they?"

"Don't let it get you so crazy, Sarge," Rick said soothingly as he pressed his nose up against the glass again. "There may be a perfectly simple solution." He stopped, then turned and looked down the street. "Come on, let's have a scout round," he motioned along the pavement, "check out the neighbours, ask a few questions, and see what we can find out, eh?"

Rick was never one to get too stressed over work matters; he was a pragmatist who simply viewed job-related problems as an occupational hazard. In their twelve months working as full time partners, Lucas had never seen him lose his head – not even once.

"You're right," Lucas said, "we need to remain calm and have a good look around." He smiled as he playfully gestured for Rick to take the lead. "After you, Richard," he added with his trademark grin and, without hesitation, the big south African gave a thumbs-up and walked past him.

***

The scout round revealed little. The Divinity's block fronted the street and was sandwiched between two other offices, but there was no obvious access to the back of their building. The adjoining properties had single leaf personnel doors in the back wall, but The Divinity's was solid. Enquiries at both neighbouring buildings generated nothing of interest. The newer one was unoccupied and had several brightly coloured "Office Space To Let" signs plastered inside the front windows. The other was an older property which, according to the external signage, was split between a law practice and an accountancy firm.

The security attendant at the second building, a heavy-set man with a flushed face and a perspiration problem, was friendly and talkative. But, despite his enthusiasm, he was unable to give any insight into the goings on next door. There was only one thing they found interesting: earlier that morning he'd noticed a three-car convoy waiting outside. All the vehicles had been dark, luxury sedans with blacked out windows and the middle one sported two small flags either side of the bonnet. He'd noticed the cars because they'd pulled up with their hazard lights flashing directly in front of his building. This blatant double parking had prompted passing motorists to show disapproval with the generous use of their horns, but the man had not seen anyone enter or exit the vehicles and the convoy had been outside for no more than ten minutes.

The duo thanked him for his assistance before reluctantly heading back to the car. As they made their way across the street, they glanced back at The Divinity building. Nothing had change; it still looked closed for business.

"Like the bastard Mary Celeste," Lucas scoffed.

Dejected, they set off back to Scottsdale in silence.

***

Watching from above, Leon Tate gave a wry smile. "They've gone," he said as he turned away from the heavily tinted glass. Vincent Dubois's fourth floor office offered a perfect view of the street in front of the building and The Divinity's Security Chief had taken full advantage of the fact.

"Would you like me to do anything further with our visitors?" he enquired.

The Monsignor, seated behind an enormous glass desk, rocked gently back and forth as he considered the question. "No, Leon ... it's fine," he said eventually. "I think for now we are doing as much as we need to. We're watching them twenty-four seven, so let's just wait and see what happens next." He stopped to stroke his neat goatee. "If our annoying little duo decide to pursue the matter further, we will simply implement a more severe strategy for dealing with their approaches."

Tate nodded approvingly at the Monsignor's statement. "Excellent, sir," he said. "We'll leave it at that for the time being, then." With that, he curtly nodded, then left the room.

Leon Tate was of average height, a non-descript looking man who rarely smiled and never stood out from the crowd. In his clandestine role as The Divinity's security advisor this natural anonymity had proved useful and, over the years, plenty of unsuspecting folk had been fooled by his plain, innocuous exterior: failing to realise that, behind the veneer, lurked a ruthless, vicious sociopath was the undoing of many a poor soul.

But within the organisation, his position was shrouded in mystery. Tate's official designation was 'Director of Human Resources'. It was a title that confused many, but helped mask a multitude of sins. More importantly, it was a title that afforded significant power and privileges.

***

CHAPTER 8

The Quiet One

As the evening progressed, the Meteor Lounge started to fill up. And when the Sci-Fi convention crowd descended on the cool, dimly lit bar to talk all things extra-terrestrial, Rick manoeuvred his stool closer to his still muttering partner.

"Yeah, OK, so we need a Plan B," he said as he leant in. "I mean, like you I don't want to stay out here any longer than necessary, but we don't want to go home empty handed either, do we?"

"Not really," came Lucas's lacklustre reply.

"Not really what?" Rick asked. "Not really a Plan B? Or not really going home empty handed?"

"Both, I suppose…"

"Roxy, you gotta pull yourself together! You can't just sit here drinking and talking to yourself."

"I am together," Lucas answered, "and I like drinking."

"But it's getting us nowhere. We've gotta do something positive."

"OK, then. We go back the room, you file the report, and I'll give Gerry another call, bring him up-to-date and see what he thinks we should do. OK?"

"Yeah, fine by me," Rick said morosely as he swirled the final dregs of his Jim Beam around.

Lucas then patted his South African colleague affectionately on the back. "Good man!" he said as he hailed the bartender for the bill.

***

The daily field report was sacrosanct. Company rules dictated it should never be fudged; it must be posted on time and must be as accurate as possible and, as all the HSG field teams were regularly reminded, especially at senior management briefings, the report was an essential part of the company's operational procedure. Lack of detail, bullshit, and cover ups would never be tolerated. It had to be the real deal - the whole truth and nothing but the truth was what ***they*** wanted every time and, in begrudging compliance with company rhetoric, Lucas and Rick reported accurately, whether good or bad. Although, at times, a back-up call was pretty much essential to help those in the office gain a proper understanding.

Rick compiled Wednesday's report with his usual diligence; it was clear in its explanation of the problems encountered but was e-mailed well past the 6.00pm deadline. Whilst Rick sorted the paperwork out, Lucas made the call. He didn't want to be the bearer of bad news again, but it had to be done. Despite the late hour back home, he got through to Gerry almost immediately, and to his surprise he didn't complain about being woken. The call lasted over twenty minutes and the Ops Director got a full update on events since yesterday. Gerry liked detail. He went back over events so far, quizzing his team leader mercilessly as he went. But Lucas didn't mind; like the other field ops he was well used to his boss's abrupt and intense style. Their Director was hands on, always looked for an angle, and was forever trying to conjure an ingenious solution. It often worked; Gerry Hanlon was famed for pulling rabbits out of hats.

The idea of abandoning the job was discussed, but Gerry was adamant it was too early to give up. Lucas, although frustrated by the lack of progress, was happy to agree they should continue in the short term. It was decided the team would extend their stay by three days but would do nothing more until they'd received further instructions. Lucas was happier now he'd passed the baton. Time to let the brass sort it out, he thought to himself before reminding his boss that return flights needed rescheduling.

"Yeah, no problem," Gerry replied, "Jo will do that in the morning - you sort the motel out direct and I'll ring you before lunch... hopefully this time with something meaningful." He paused as the first glimmer of an idea started to form, "Tell you what," he said, "I'll have a word with Steve, see if his squad can dig anything up for us - never know - they might just get lucky."

"Wouldn't that be nice?"

"Well...they've done it before," Gerry said, "so let's see if they can do it again." He hesitated, as if trying to remember something else, but nothing came. "Right, gotta go," he continued, "I'll ring you tomorrow - in the meantime behave yourselves!" and, without waiting for a reply, Gerry Hanlon hung up.

"So, what's happening?" Rick asked.

"Nothing," Lucas said shaking his head. "You heard most of that, didn't you? There's fuck all we can do... the man says sit tight and wait for instructions."

"Great plan," Rick said as he gave a sarcastic thumbs-up.

Lucas's idea of *'sit tight and await instruction'* was always going to be different from that of his Operations Director and, while the next step was dependant on factors beyond his control, he still needed an outline plan to focus on. "We'll hit the road tomorrow," he said as he looked across at Rick. "Might as well, eh...can't just sit here, can we?"

"And do what exactly?" Rick asked.

"I don't know. We'll just go and do a little digging, try and ruffle some feathers...you know, all that type of stuff," he stopped and shrugged his shoulders. "So, breakfast at seven OK with you?"

Lucas was tired and his bed was beckoning so he started to usher his favourite South African out of the room. "Come on, Ricky, time for bobos," he said.

"Yeah, whatever, Roxy," Rick replied as he shuffled out of the door. "See you at seven."

***

Dressed in full clerical regalia, Doctor Reid stood at the head of a long oak table surrounded by twelve of the church's highest ranking officials. The glum faced elders were waiting for an update on their sacred *'Book of Martyrs'*, but the wizard-like synod leader didn't have good news to dispense,

"Gentlemen, please be seated," he said earnestly. "It is with a heavy heart that I bring you news of another problem."

Having received a phone call earlier in the day from Gerry Hanlon, Doctor Reid was far from happy. When HSG's Ops Director told him The Divinity were stalling and that it was becoming increasingly likely they'd no intention of honouring the hand-back agreement, the church leader was deeply troubled by the news. He'd personally battled long and hard to get to this stage and the thought of failing at the eleventh hour was just too much to contemplate. The financial worth wasn't the key issue; the book was so much more than its monetary value - it represented the purity, strength and resolve of their Protestant beliefs – and this particular bespoke edition had been central to the PCOS's history and faith for centuries.

The meeting didn't go well. The assembled Elders were massively disappointed with the news and unanimously demanded an escalation in the forcefulness of the recovery operation. The Doctor could only concur with his team and promised to action the dictate immediately.

***

Sarah Stuart had worked for her father's company for ten years and was now an integral member of the management team. Her role was varied but, often as not, the bulk of her work involved research and intelligence support to the salvage/recovery teams in the field. Sarah wasn't afraid of a challenge; she was a grafter and would turn her hand to whatever task was needed for a successful outcome and Ray was proud of her contribution to the company's success.

The morning after the call from Lucas, Gerry spoke to Steve Harrison about helping the stateside recovery team. Steve, an ex-police DI, had been head of Research and Intelligence at HSG for the last five years and for three of those he'd had the boss's daughter as his number two.

After Steve briefed Sarah, she immediately suggested speaking to Wiseman and Scott. "Calvin might help," she said. "Do you want me to ring him…see what he thinks?"

W&S Associates were an international private investigation firm based in Gibraltar and had been tasked by Dr Reid with overseeing the original search mission. The PI specialists had satellite offices scattered around the globe and their lead investigator, a mild-mannered intellectual named Calvin Lentz, lived less than a mile from their busy Glasgow office. Having dealt with the erudite Jew many times, Sarah had no qualms about asking him for assistance. As expected, he was more than willing to help. He wasn't the least surprised to hear the Mesa based sect were being obstructive. It had taken his organisation and the PCOS's legal team many months to secure an agreement for the return of the book and throughout the whole tortuous process The Divinity had fought every inch of the way and now it seemed they intended to keep on fighting.

Calvin explained that, during the latter stages of the original search, they'd engaged the assistance of Arizona's State Library Service. The ASLS had been extremely helpful and, in particular, the involvement of a senior research assistant named Marion Armstrong had proved to be a Godsend. Sarah was informed Miss Armstrong lived and worked in Flagstaff in Northern Arizona. She was an expert in the field of ancient religious literature and specialised in classic works of the Christian faith,

"She's definitely worth talking to again," he said enthusiastically. "She was fantastic, knew everything about Foxe's works, a very, very knowledgeable lady."

"OK I'm convinced," Sarah said. "I'll get right on it."

When she finally got through to Miss Armstrong, Sarah politely introduced herself and explained the reason for the call. The American research assistant naturally remembered helping the investigation and was curious to know whether the manuscript had been restored to its rightful owners. When she learned they were still having issues, Marion kindly offered to meet up with the field team and help in any way she could.

"Thank you so much," Sarah replied. "I'll tell the guys – they really will appreciate any help they can get."

***

Just before ten o'clock Thursday morning, Lucas and Rick arrived in Flagstaff. It was noticeably cooler than it had been further south, but by UK standards it was still seriously warm. With temperatures in the mid-twenties, a light breeze and clear blue skies, the two men agreed it wasn't far off the perfect summer's day.

During the drive North, Lucas explained the day's plan. He went over the details of the information he had received during the early hours of the morning from Head Office as well as the rationale behind their Flagstaff visit. The ex-sapper was genuinely impressed with the behind the scenes antics of their intelligence team; arranging an instant hook-up with a client-friendly contact from the Arizona library service was no easy task, and his partner obviously agreed.

"All that while I was asleep," Rick remarked. "That's bloody good going."

After a slight detour, the Chrysler pulled up in the gravel car park of a bohemian looking block of shops on the north side of the city. The two men looked around. The lot was deserted except for two figures standing next to a battered blue pick-up. The Chevy Silverado was parked at the far end of the lot, the driver's door was open, the engine was running and two males - both wearing sunglasses and bandannas - were stood either side of it.

Rick parked their car in the shade at the opposite end to the Chevy and let the engine idle. Both he and Lucas looked towards the pick-up; despite the distance between the two vehicles, it was obvious both bandanna boys were watching them,

"What the fuck are those two pricks looking at?" Lucas asked quietly.

Rick shrugged. "No idea," he said. "Maybe they're something to do with who we're meeting?"

"I doubt it. Like I said earlier, our contact's a librarian in her mid-fifties," Lucas stopped as he pointed back across the car park, "and hopefully she's waiting for us in that coffee shop over there."

With a last glance over at the pick-up, Lucas told Rick to turn off the engine and get out of the car. Rick did as instructed and, after locking the car, the two men set off in search of Dylan's Coffee Shop. As soon as they started walking, the bandanna twins got in the pick-up and headed for the car park exit. The battered Chevy turned out of the lot onto the main street and then slowed as it drew level with the HSG men. The passenger - a big hollow cheeked Mexican - lent out of the window.

"Hey, Gringo!" he called out, pointing at Lucas. "A little word of advice, amigo…we think you need to finish your vacation and go home. Arizona can be a very dangerous place," he stopped and spat on the road, then looked up. "Especially if you don't know the right people – if you get what I'm saying?"

The warning was delivered in a slow menacing growl and was finished off with a knowing smile. Then, without another word, the pick-up roared off in a cloud of dust.

Lucas was taken aback and started wracking his brains; who the hell knew they would be here this morning? Who were those guys? And, more importantly, who the fuck were they working for?

"Jeez, Ricky - I think we've started to piss somebody off," he said. "Those boys were fucking serious."

"Gotta be more to this than we're thinking," Rick replied.

Lucas shook his head. "Must be," he said, "but come on, let's go see what Library Lady has to say, eh?"

The coffee shop was as rustic as the rest of the block, but it hadn't put anyone off. Inside there was hardly a spare seat to be had. But in a far corner booth, a four-seater, Lucas saw there was only one occupant. The lone woman was slim with greying blonde hair tied back in a ponytail. Wearing a simple navy dress and horn-rimmed glasses, she sat straight backed, nervously sipping her coffee.

"Could be," Lucas muttered to himself as he led Rick through the busy café. The woman didn't quite match the description the intelligence team had sent but he was sure it was her, and, if he was right, then her name should be Marion Armstrong,

"Marion, Marion Armstrong?" he enquired as he approached the booth.

She looked up and nodded, "Yes, I am," she said quietly, "and I presume you must be Mr Roxby?"

"That's right," he replied, "and this is my colleague Rick Kruger." He paused, then smiled, "May we join you?"

"Of course, gentlemen," she gestured for the two men to sit down in the two seats facing her. "Please do!"

During a brief round of initial pleasantries, the HSG men ordered coffee and pancakes then got down to the real reason for the meeting. Lucas, as ever, took the lead in asking the questions.

"Miss Armstrong," he said, fixing her with a smile, "you work for the Arizona library service and you have more than a passing interest in rare religious books, true?"

"Yes, that's absolutely correct," she replied.

Lucas looked closely at the librarian. "And you know a lot about this Book of Martyrs, don't you? Particularly this first edition we're trying to recover?"

"Yes," she answered. "As I'm sure your colleague explained, my field is religious literature, particularly early Christian printed works." She smiled nervously as she adjusted her glasses. "I got involved when the State Library Service was contacted by Wiseman Scott who asked us to help them track down this particular edition." She paused, then added, "That search, as you're probably well aware, was long and difficult...but, thankfully, in the end a success."

As Marion spoke she began to relax, the pensive look was now fading, and as she started to feel more at ease the words came more readily. "In the world of antiquarian books," she continued, "especially early printed works, you have to stay in the know...you need as many friends as possible. You see, there aren't many of us and we are extremely competitive. Knowing they were tracking a first edition of Foxe's book, well...I simply had to remain in contact with Calvin and his team...." She paused to adjust her glasses for a second time. "I was informed yesterday by your colleague... Miss Stuart, I think it was... that it was via Mr Lentz she got my details. So, if there's anything I can do to help, I will."

Marion stopped talking and looked enquiringly at Lucas. Lucas cut to the chase. "What'd you know about this religious sect, this Divinity crowd?"

Marion's face dropped, "Well... my sister, Kitty, and I have a passing acquaintance," she said, "a lady called Meredith Higham. Meredith is a formidable woman, you see she's a very active charity campaigner and a member of The Divinity's congregation.... and she lives right here in Flagstaff."

"Right...OK," Lucas muttered, "so what's her story, then?"

"Well, Meredith is well-connected and very wealthy," she explained. "She has a huge social network that includes some of the Church's senior associates...and by all accounts a few of its less important hangers-on," she stopped and very subtly cleared her throat.

Lucas smiled encouragingly, "Yes, yes, please go on, Ms Armstrong," he said softly. "We're keen to hear it all - tell us everything you can."

Suitably buoyed, she continued, "Well, my sister and I often attend bridge evenings at the Country Club here in the Old Town and we regularly bump into Meredith there; she's a great one for chatting during the games and some of that talk you would probably call gossip... Well, I certainly do!" she smiled. "It never stops!"

"And...," Lucas said eagerly.

"One of Meredith's favourite topics is the latest goings on at her Church. She does make me smile, though. After anything she lets slip, she always tells us that the information is strictly confidential and we should not breathe a word about what we've been told to anyone…," she pulled a face and looked across the table at the expectant Englishman. "Well, I can assure you, Mr Roxby, that whilst Meredith's gossip makes for good listening at times, my sister and I are always sceptical about how true her stories really are."

Lucas was beginning to like this woman. Listening to her tale was genuinely intriguing but, as ever, he was keen to get to a punch line as quickly as possible. "So, when did you last see this woman?" he blurted.

Marion didn't appear fazed by his obvious impatience, "Well, as it happens, Mr Roxby, we saw her at the Club only a few days ago. It's been quite a while since we last saw her, so she had lots to tell us. She went on and on about numerous subjects but, as usual, the main one involved the latest goings on at her Church. She said a member of its clergy had been arrested here in Arizona - and was being held on, of all things," she paused, "suspicion of people trafficking."

"Sounds a little farfetched," Lucas said. "Are you positive that's what she said?"

"Yes, Mr Roxby, that's exactly what she said – and then she told us it hadn't been reported in the press. Apparently, it's part of some on-going investigation into The Divinity's business interests," she smiled knowingly. "Not a surprise, really, is it?"

"This member of the clergy didn't happen to be a Reverend did he?" Rick asked. "A Reverend Coleman?"

"Meredith wasn't sure who it was," Marion replied. "Her source hadn't confirmed a name." She paused and tapped the table gently, "But she was expecting an update very soon."

Desperate to find out something meaningful to work on, Lucas continued the rapid-fire questioning. "Did she mention anything about a car crash?" he asked.

The librarian raised an eyebrow. "There was no mention of any car crash," she said, "but apparently the man arrested was travelling north from Tucson toward Phoenix, and the vehicle - a big van she described it as – was carrying illegal immigrants…all reportedly Hondurans."

During the discussion it had been Rick's duty to write down notes for reference. He was meticulous on detail and, thankfully, it was always clear and legible. Lucas often joked, "Sometimes it's easier to read Ricky's words than listen to them," and, deep down, the South African knew he really meant it.

After the meeting finished, they exchanged contact details and Marion promised an update the minute anything new came to light. The two men thanked her for her assistance, then stood to leave.

As Lucas and Rick stopped still in front of their new ally, she placed a hand lightly on Lucas's forearm. "Oh, one last thing I should mention to you," she whispered. "It might be important. Meredith said The Divinity's Head of Internal Affairs, a man called Leon Tate, was dealing with the incident personally. She knows very little about him other than he has a reputation as a particularly nasty piece of work, so I would advise caution, gentlemen. Please be careful."

Rick added the name Leon Tate to his neat meeting notes. Then they said their goodbyes again and headed for the coffee shop entrance door, this time without interruption. As soon as they were on the street, the heat hit. It still caught them off-guard. Every time they went from an air-conditioned interior into the outdoors the enveloping surge of warmth nearly knocked them off their feet.

"Jesus, it's warmed up a bit, hasn't it?" Lucas said, looking skyward. "Come on back to the car - quick!"

With that, the two men started a half-jog back to the car and, as they rounded the corner, they were both relieved to see it was still in the shade and thankfully untouched.

***

As soon as they pulled out of the car park, Gerry rang. The Ops Director was looking for the latest update fresh from the coal face so, without so much as a hello, how are you? the duo ran through the details of the trip to Flagstaff, the veiled threats from the two Mexican thugs, and the meeting with Marion. Gerry listened closely then, as promised, explained the official mission view as decreed by Senior Management.

"Well, boys, it's like this," he said. "Doctor Reid has told us to up the ante, they want us to exert as much pressure on The Divinity as we can without actually breaking the law." He took a deep breath then added, "Those old Proddy clan chiefs just want what's rightfully theirs to be returned; they don't want excuses, they want results - OK?"

"Easier said than done," Lucas replied flippantly.

Gerry had his own thoughts as to what could be done, but initially he wanted to hear the view of the team who were hands on with the job itself. "I'm sure it is," he said, ignoring Lucas's tone, "but do you two have any bright ideas on how to squeeze these bastards?"

"No, not straight off," Lucas answered. "This lot are devious, you know, Gerry. They're well organised and they have the upper hand and they are on home turf, aren't they?"

"Tell me something I don't know," Gerry replied.

Lucas didn't respond immediately. "Look, I'll tell you what," he said, "give us a couple of hours to work on it and we'll come back to you later on this afternoon - OK?"

After a brief silence, Gerry responded in his usual brusque tone, "Yeah…OK, boys, but you need to be creative; there's a lot riding on this." The line went quiet for a moment before Gerry decided to continue. "So, come back to me asap, will you," he added, "and, in the meantime, we'll pool our thoughts here and we can discuss options later, and don't fuck around in ringing us back. Understand?"

"Yes, yes, Gerry we understand," Lucas droned.

"Good. I'll speak to you later, then." And with that - *'Click'* - he was gone.

The two men looked at each other and smiled; Gerry's gruff and abrupt style of communication never ceased to amuse them.

CHAPTER 9

Bad Decision?

Gerry was sat in the quirky comfortable surrounds of the works' canteen. He was alone at a corner table nursing a steaming hot cup of tea and was obviously deep in thought. In front of him, on the plastic-coated table, was an A4 jotter pad. It was open a couple of pages in, and his engraved silver pen lay neatly in the crease between the open pages. He was re-reading a series of bullet points running down the left-hand page. The handwritten notes were an agenda, his list of key items for discussion at his imminent get-together with the PCOS team. The meeting was scheduled for the following day, 11.30am at Dr Reid's base of operation in Glasgow. The prominent Presbyterians were based at St. James's, a gothic monstrosity of a church north of the city that looked the perfect backdrop for a vampire movie.

The HSG Director was not relishing the prospect of meeting the Doctor and his Synod. The thought of looking to your client for answers, answers on how to solve a problem they'd employed you to sort in the first place, was not a good one. As a seasoned negotiator, he'd experienced many tough situations facing clients, and this one was going to be particularly galling but, whilst the meeting would cause him a degree of embarrassment, he knew it was likely to be worthwhile. He was pleased Sarah was going with him; he'd chatted with Ray about the idea and was perfectly comfortable with the rationale behind the suggestion. A better understanding of the book's significance would be good for everyone to know.

After he finished the dregs of his tea, he checked over the agenda one last time and, satisfied all the important points were noted, he closed the book. He'd included a short section for Sarah's input but how much they would be able - or willing - to divulge, he really didn't know. Still, one thing was for sure, he was looking forward to watching the tenacious Miss Stuart try to find out.

***

Steve Harrison agreed it was a good call for Sarah to attend the meeting. "I'm sure Gerry could handle them," he said," but now he's got you for back up, it evens things up a touch." Steve was stood behind his chair looking down over the dividing screen at the hunched figure sat opposite. "It might get a bit embarrassing," he continued, "but two's so much better than one – don't you think?"

Sarah looked up from her notebook and pulled a face. "Gerry will be fine," she said. "It's me I'm worried about - I'll probably get carried away with my questioning and piss them all off."

Steve smiled at his worried colleague. "Just play it cool," he replied. "Remember: steady and calm all the way. You never know, you might open the flood gates. They might never shut up about their beloved book."

Sarah sighed, rolled her shoulders and stood up from her desk. "I'm having another drink - do you want one?"

"Actually, yes, I will," he said as he watched her cross the office. "Coffee – white, one sugar, please."

She filled the kettle, placed it on its black plastic base and flicked the switch. The red light blinked on and she focused on it. "Think, that book's over four hundred and fifty years old," she said as she stared at the hypnotic red dot, "four hundred and fifty years... that's a hell of a long time you know, Steve." She paused as she contemplated what she'd just said. "I wonder what secrets it could tell us, what horrors has it been witness to, how much blood has been spilt in its name... gives me shivers just thinking about it."

Steve looked out of the window and loosened his tie, "Gruesome times from what I remember from my history lessons," he said.

Over many weeks Sarah had researched Foxe's infamous work in detail and was now well aware of its significance. Any random internet search would give a basic outline of this religious classic but what she'd discovered from her detailed investigation had truly amazed her. And as she made the coffee she decided to give her boss a quick recap.

"Did you know its abridged title is actually *'Acts and Monuments of these latter and perilous days, touching matters of the Church'*?" she asked, looking over her shoulder to see if he was paying attention.

"Bit of a mouthful," he replied with a quizzical frown. "Not exactly catchy, is it?"

Happy he was listening, she continued, "It first saw the light of day in 1563, and when it came out, boy, did it set the Christian world alight - and I mean *literally* set it alight."

For the next fifteen minutes Steve sat listening avidly as his colleague went on to explain how the book was thought by many to be a work of historical accuracy, but the experts felt that only the more recent events portrayed could be factual.

"It's primarily just a wildly successful and influential work of propaganda," she explained, "purely from the Protestant point of view, of course."

"Of course," he replied with a nod.

He then got chapter and verse on how divisive the book was, how it relentlessly rammed home the dogma that the Pope is the Antichrist, the Church of Rome is deviant, and that the Catholic faith in general is hateful, corrupt and evil. She went on about its graphic details of persecution, torture, and execution, and how it included particularly gory descriptions of the mutilation and murders of high-profile Protestant martyrs during Queen Mary I's reign. Finally, she ended her impromptu history lesson with a simple conclusion, "Steve, it's a very famous book, but it's not a read for the faint hearted; it's about as nasty and inflammatory as they come."

Having not made any real effort to find out what the centre piece of the US recovery operation was all about, the ex-DI was fascinated. He'd assumed it was simply an antique book with a hefty price tag and left it at that.

"Jeez, I didn't realise," he said in genuine amazement. "How come I've never even heard of this classic before now?"

"Because you're a philistine," she laughed, "and you only read trash."

Having no understanding of the book's importance, or ever having considered its significance, Steve realised Sarah might be onto something. Maybe it was nothing to do with monetary value; maybe it was all about spiritual relevance.

"Well, I'm astounded," he said. "Makes you realise how much faith matters to some… gives you a different perspective on life, doesn't it?"

Sarah looked at her boss. "Tell me about it," she answered sarcastically.

"This John Foxe fella must have been some cookie," Steve said as he pondered the situation further. "How long do you reckon it took him to write? Must have taken years. It's a remarkable undertaking when you analyse it properly, isn't it?"

Standing with her back to the window, backside resting against the work top and her cooling mug held in front of her, Sarah smiled.

"Too right it is," she said, "and think, there are thousands of copies of that book around, different editions, different formats. God, you can even download a version of it as a PDF online if you're so inclined," she stopped for a final mouthful of coffee, "but why this edition?" she asked. "Why *this* book? This whole situation is about this one particular book – I bloody know it is."

Sarah had convinced herself there was something very specific about the edition they were chasing; it was part of a bigger picture they were all missing. But, despite Steve's new-found interest, he was in no position to comment or offer help: all he could do for now was pray that tomorrow's meeting brought her a step closer to uncovering the truth.

***

Joanne Knox had just finished sorting a return ticket for Sarah's Glasgow trip when the phone rang. She'd made Gerry's travel arrangements several days before, but now Sarah was going with him it had been a bit of a pain to re-jig. But Jo was rarely fazed and, after one phone call and some skilled negotiating, it was sorted; she'd managed to get Sarah in the seat opposite him on the way up there and the seat next to him on the way back. It was slightly more expensive but nevertheless she'd done well, and she knew it. Happy with the result, she let the phone ring several times before answering it.

"Good morning, Hanlon Stuart Group," she purred, "how may I help you?"

The telephone voice was a deliberate put-on. Jo would keep it up if the caller was a client or an external contact, but if it was someone she knew well it dropped instantly. The call in question was from a supplier, so the voice stayed as she transferred it quickly to the Logistics office. "Connecting you now," she said before putting the phone down.

Up next was sorting flights to Malaga, a return for one, and the one was HSG's beloved CEO Raymond Edward Stuart. Ray had informed his faithful PA a little late about the trip to Spain but did apologise profusely for his tardiness. He explained it was an impromptu ex-client visit he didn't want to miss but couldn't afford to be away from the office for more than twenty-four hours. He'd jotted down his ideal itinerary on a scrap of paper then handed it to Jo, knowing full well that by hook or by crook she would try to make it happen.

CHAPTER 10

Anything Goes

The journey back to Scottsdale was long, hot, and uneventful but it gave the HSG men plenty of time to discuss their boss's latest call.

"Is Hanlon for real?" Lucas asked. "This staying within the law bollocks does kind of limit our options." He stopped as he recalled Gerry's actual words then asked, "Do you think he really meant what he said or was it just another one of his bizarre subliminal messages?"

As he spoke Lucas was looking at the side of Rick's recently dyed hair. Stellenbosch's favourite blond was staring intently at the empty highway ahead but, despite the hypnotic effect of the heat hazed blacktop, he was still listening.

"You know what Gerry's like," he said into the windscreen, "he always tells us to be good little boys. He has to: I mean, that's the official company line, isn't it?

"Suppose so," Lucas muttered. "Got to cover his arse."

"But we know he really means fight dirty and don't get caught, don't we?"

"Do we?" Lucas replied quickly.

"Yeah. It's the same on every job," Rick continued. "Gerry can say what the fuck he likes, but you and I know that in the field we make the critical decisions, it's our cocks on the block, so it's our call."

Lucas grinned. "And that, my friend," he said, "is why we're paid the big bucks, isn't it?"

“Big bucks: my arse!” Rick snorted, sliding his sunglasses on top of his head. “You know what, Sarge, if I had the chance I’d screw these religious freaks over for free – and that’s no joke.”

Lucas was impressed. His right-hand man was seriously up for a fight. “Music to my ears, Kruger! I love it when you get all fired up. Doesn’t often happen, but when it does…”

***

Leon Tate sat behind his expensive mahogany desk staring at a large flat-screen monitor. The email he’d just received was intriguing him, so he read it over again:

> *Mr Tate, your visitors drove to Flagstaff this morning and met with a middle-aged woman who we are currently trying to identify. They are now heading back toward Phoenix on I17. In Flag they were given a gentle warning by two of my associates, nothing overly aggressive, but they will know they are being watched. I will update you later on their movements over the rest of the day. Regards, Mord Ings*

Tate had left nothing to chance: from the moment they touched down on US soil, the HSG team had been under surveillance and it wouldn’t let up until they were ready to leave. But, in the meantime, the Chief was keen to find out who it was they’d met with in Flagstaff and he was confident he’d find out soon: he knew his spies were good.

***

By the time Lucas and Rick pulled back into the car park of the Motel, it was already late afternoon. But, before they got out, Lucas was desperate to get to the bottom of something that was bugging him.

"Leave it running for a minute, will you, Rick?" he asked. "Those two ugly grocks in the pick-up truck this morning, they deliberately targeted us didn't they?"

"Definitely," came the quick reply.

"They were in that car park before we arrived, right?" He paused as Rick nodded his agreement. "They were waiting for us to show, so that was no random happening. That warning was specifically for us, so somebody's watching us, but who is it? And how are they keeping tabs on us?"

It was not a direct question; Lucas was now talking to himself. He knew something was wrong but couldn't put his finger on it. He sat silently for a few seconds staring straight ahead at nothing in particular. Then, swivelling in his seat, quietly said, "Ricky, pull the car up over there behind that little wall, will you." He pointed to a partially shaded spot in the corner of the Motel car park out of view of the main street and gestured for his partner to move the car into it.

"Sure, Roxy, whatever you want," Rick replied, before asking a question to which he already knew the answer. "What you thinking?"

"The car's got to be bugged," Lucas said, gently shaking his head. "Some fucker's tracking us. They know our every move. We need to search this car."

With that, the big South African did as he was asked and manoeuvred the Chrysler slowly into the space indicated. Then, after a quick all-round scan to make sure no-one was watching, the pair proceeded to systematically check the vehicle over.

They found the tracker inside the spare tyre. The spare was in a recessed well in the boot area and, as was normal in many vehicles, the tyre was accessed by lifting up the boot compartment floor mat. The tracker was well hidden, but both were experienced in checking for stash spaces, so it hadn't taken long to find it.

"The little bastards!" Lucas said as he uncovered the device. "Not the work of amateurs, though." He paused to examine the small black box now in the palm of his hand. "That's a high-tech piece, not the usual cheap Chinese shit." Lucas didn't give Rick a chance to comment.

"We'll switch it later, just need a donor car to plant the little sucker in. Then tomorrow we'll swap cars – OK?"

Rick nodded. He was fine with the plan but in his eyes things still didn't add up. As Lucas continued to talk, Rick's mind wandered.

"I fancy something a bit flashier than this lump of shit," Lucas wittered as he patted the roof of the Chrysler, "something with a bit of poke maybe; what do you think?"

Rick, still deep in thought, didn't answer. Lucas wasn't impressed. "Kruger," he hissed, "you listening to me?"

"Err…yeah, suppose so," Rick stuttered as he came back to the moment, "a bit of power wouldn't go amiss, although that's not company policy, is it? But what the fuck?! Now the line's been crossed, it might be more fitting." Rick didn't sound too bothered about changing cars, he had other things on his mind. "You know the question that really gets me about this situation, Roxy?" he asked.

"No," Lucas grinned, "but I'm sure you're about to tell me."

"I want to know when that device was fitted. You think about it… since we've been here there's been no signs of tampering with the car, has there? No dodgy looking people hanging round the car, nothing particularly suspicious. So, when was it installed?" Rick was understandably concerned about this latest conundrum and was keen to continue with his analytical questioning, "And how did those two fuckers come to be waiting in that car park, eh? They were in there before we arrived. I know some of this high-tech GPS shit is good, but it can't read fucking minds!"

Both men knew something wasn't right. Finding the tracker was only part of the puzzle; it didn't answer all the questions. Lucas studied his colleague's pensive face for a couple of seconds, "You think the tracker was in the car before we picked it up, don't you?"

"You know me too well, Sarge?" Rick grinned. "Yeah, I do. I think that little fucker was planted before we even landed. Someone arranged for us to get this car."

Lucas raised a hand and stopped Rick talking any further. "And if that is the case," he said, taking up the train of thought, "then this Divinity crowd are much better informed and much better organised than we are giving them credit for." He glanced over his shoulder. "I'd say we've been played good and proper by a bunch of very crafty bastards."

Lucas then looked at the figure stood in front of him. Rick was standing motionless, legs apart, arms folded across his sweat drenched tee shirt, shades on, looking down at the white, dusty car park. For a few moments, neither man moved or said a word.

Then Lucas broke the silence, "Fuck it, Rick, let's get out of this heat and make the call to Gerry. He's waiting for us to call back, so we'll run through this latest bollocks with him as well," and with that they did a slow 180 then marched off across the car park towards the motel reception.

***

The call to Gerry was another long one. He was pissed off to hear about the tracking device but also relieved and was equally mystified as to how the Flagstaff meet had been known about in advance. All they could do in the short term was agree they were up against a devious, dangerous, well organised institution that needed to be treated with the utmost caution.

Once the discussions on the latest issues had been exhausted, they then ran through ideas for moving forward. Throughout the call Gerry had been in his usual blunt and gruff mood but toward the end he lightened a touch. He went to great lengths to assure Lucas and Rick that behind the scenes there was a lot of company resource working hard to help them get a result. It was meant to boost the morale of the field team, and, in a way, it did.

This latest thought centred on a more detailed investigation into The Divinity's Arizona operation. It was hoped the process would generate some sort of opportunity to exploit, somehow using it to get closer to finding the book's whereabouts.

It was based on a three-pronged approach: first, the team on the ground would watch The Divinity closely and also investigate local contacts at source, and this task – which Gerry was keen to stress was to be carried out in a strictly non-confrontational manner; second, that the company's research team would dig further into The Divinity's structure - particularly its geographical spread in the US and, if possible, its links further afield – as well as being tasked with finding out as much as they could about the rumoured investigation by the FBI; third, via Gerry himself, who would call Calvin Lentz to ensure some form of official correspondence was forwarded on to The Divinity. This correspondence would formally record the problems experienced to date and would request a full explanation for the reasons why. Despite it being his own idea, the Ops Director was not convinced this one would achieve anything. He now believed The Divinity had no regard for legalities, absolutely none whatsoever.

During the call, Lucas was told to expect a list of Divinity contacts deemed worth tracking down. Sarah had begun the process of compiling it straight after arranging the meeting with Marion Armstrong and since then the list had grown. Young Ms Stuart was not one to sit on her laurels so any sniff of association with The Divinity, however remote, had been explored.

***

Having said their goodbyes to Gerry, the two men set about deciding on an alternative vehicle. "Dodge Viper, Pontiac Firebird, Ford Mustang, Chevy Camaro," Lucas read out the list with a big grin. "We're spoilt for choice here, Ricky," he chuckled. "What do you fancy, mate, any preference?"

A bit of American muscle, although a bit clichéd, was too hard for the two self-confessed petrol heads to resist and the Mustang GT was coming up favourite. If they were quick - and pre-booked it - there was one available first thing in the morning in Glendale. Glendale was further out than the airport, but they were not keen to go back to see the limp-wristed Randy. It was a definite that someone there was a Divinity sympathiser.

Lucas made the call and booked the car for collection the following morning. It was a white GT Coupe – a five litre V8 – a seriously poky but thirsty machine. "I'm not arsed about the fuel," Ricky had sneered, "as the company's paying for that, I just want something that flies."

***

After the evening meal, the HSG team was ready for action. Using the descending darkness as cover, they slipped out of a side door into the motel car park and removed the tracker from their car. For simplicity, they'd decided to plant it in another guest's car that was parked up for the night. A black Toyota land-cruiser, parked two spaces down from their Chrysler, was the chosen target. It was a car they knew from the previous night's bar room banter was owned by a couple on a mega East to West coast road trip. "My God, that woman wouldn't shut up, would she?" Lucas moaned. "Why we needed every friggin' detail of their itinerary, I'll never know."

The large, self-absorbed woman had gone on about the trip. She'd babbled that she and husband Al were doing a couple of days around the Phoenix area then travelling to Vegas…blah, blah, blah… then on into California and up the West coast all the way to some unpronounceable little town in Northern Oregon. As Rick had said, "It was an opportunity too good to miss."

As Lucas kept a close watch at the car park entrance, Rick removed the spare tyre cover from the Land-cruiser. Once the cover was off, he slipped the tracker into the space behind the tyre support bracket and wedged it into place. He then slid the tyre cover back over, zipped it up, and replaced the small plastic tie-wrap that stopped the zip from accidental undoing. The job took less than five minutes to complete and Lucas was convinced no one had seen them carry it out.

Once back inside the motel, they headed to their rooms, hoping the promised contact list had been sent over. After a brief struggle to find the Wi-Fi code, Rick checked his inbox and found several emails had landed. Quickly he scanned them and, as promised, one of them was from Sarah. It was titled 'Divinity associations' and was addressed dually to Lucas and Rick, with Gerry Hanlon, Ray Stuart and Steve Harrison all copied in.

As ever, the information was detailed and well-presented although against most of the contact details it was noted that the link to The Divinity may be tenuous. But, despite this major flaw, the list at least gave the field team something to focus on. They printed out two copies of the spread sheet and started to figure out the most logical way to work through the contacts. For a change, it would be a quiet, sober night.

***

Leon Tate was another workaholic happy to burn the midnight oil and tonight was no exception. He had no one to go home to; so, finding himself still in the office, sitting behind his plush desk and checking emails at 9.30pm didn't bother him.

It had been a busy day, during the course of which he'd dealt with various organisational issues. From the mind numbingly inane to the business critical, each item was dealt with in the same fastidious manner. Of significant interest to him was the second of two brief emails from the surveillance crew tasked with watching the HSG men. The Chief was happy to read that, apart from the trip to Flagstaff, their movements appeared to have been limited to staying around the motel. He was especially pleased to learn that his associates had identified the woman they had met. This latest communiqué gave her name as Marion Armstrong. Reportedly she was a fifty-six-year-old literary research assistant who lived in Flagstaff and worked for the Arizona state library service.

Tate was more than satisfied with his days' work and particularly Mordecai Ing's contribution to it. The man really was very useful, he'd thought to himself. Rarely lets me down. In fact, Tate couldn't recall a time he actually had.

CHAPTER 11

Nothing Wrong

The likelihood the trip to Spain would yield little of interest was a real possibility and Ray knew it. Setting up the meeting with Ebro had been easy and he was sure the pretence of being in the area and wanting to drop in to discuss future business opportunities had sounded convincing.

His approach had been low-key and neutral, deliberately steering clear of any high-pressure tactics that might arouse suspicion, and the response from the Spanish had been muted. He'd received a two-line email back confirming that a meeting with Pedro Grillo had been arranged for 10.30am on Thursday the 24th. It gave details of the office address and some simple directions from Malaga airport, and that was it.

***

Jo Knox had worked her usual magic; the travel arrangements were faultless and, as ever, Ray was grateful. The Wednesday afternoon flight from Manchester to Malaga was stress free, as was collecting the hire car and making the fifty-minute drive up the coast to Nerja. The Eclipse Hotel was a small boutique affair; with lots of marble, an abundance mirrors and wild splashes of silver over a plush maroon décor, it was a touch of class. It had a prime seafront location, boasted impressive views and, from what he could glean, only ever got rave reviews on Trip Advisor. Check-in was efficient and friendly with no pretentions or faff and the room was nothing short of heaven.

With time to kill, the HSG chief decided on a leisurely stroll along the promenade. He had plenty of time to take in the local sights and sounds and, as he'd hoped it would, it led to the door of a highly recommended restaurant. The eatery did have to be a good one as anyone who knew Ray well would testify; when it came to eating out, Raymond Stuart was one seriously fussy bastard.

Thankfully the Mission Steak House didn't disappoint. After a well-done sirloin, Ray knocked back the last of his Rioja, dropped the waiter a generous tip, then ambled back along the prom towards the hotel. Once inside, he headed to the terrace bar. He grabbed a seat at a small corner table, ordered a large brandy, and started to check through his emails. He scanned his inbox and, after seeing nothing new of significance, he let out a gentle sigh of relief. Suddenly his concentration was broken by a sharp-suited waiter delivering a gargantuan Courvoisier. But the distraction was momentary; no sooner had he nodded a quick thank you to the smiling young man, than he was back to the screen. After double-checking his latest messages, he took the time to differentiate between those that required a response and those that could be left or - even better - deleted. After a couple of brief courteous responses to the ones he'd deemed important enough, he took a last lingering look at the Mediterranean, drained the remnants of his brandy, then headed off to bed.

***

The Ebro meeting was at their Motril office. Motril was their main operational base in Spain and was only an hour's drive down the coast from Nerja. Ray deliberately checked out early and wasted no time in getting on the road. With a handy start, the HSG CEO was hopeful of a quick scout round before the meeting. You never know, he'd thought to himself, might just get a sniff of something useful.

The town was set back from the coast and in parts was very plain and industrial in appearance. The faceless buildings of its sprawling industrial centre all looked the same to Ray and, as a consequence, he lost his precious scouting time trying to find his way round the mass of uninspiring utilitarian facades. But, eventually, the mist cleared, and he found what he was looking for.

Relieved he'd found the place, he parked up and headed for the main entrance. Once through the patterned glass doors, things began to change. The inside was a little flashier, a little more bespoke, more like he'd imagined it would look and, to his great relief, the receptionist spoke perfect English. The olive-skinned twenty-something was not only fluent in his mother tongue but was so efficient she was delivering his coffee before he'd even taken his seat in the waiting area.

"Senor Grillo will be with you shortly," she smiled sweetly as she ushered him toward several armchairs, "but in the meantime please make yourself comfortable, Senor." Ray smiled back, thanked her, and then settled down to drink his coffee.

Fortunately, he didn't have to wait long: the affable Spaniard was punctual and, in his open- necked shirt and a smartly tailored suit, he looked the epitome of Mediterranean charm. "Raymond, you old sea dog," he boomed, "how good to see you again… you are looking well, my friend. Must be nearly two years! How are you keeping? How's the salvage business treating you?"

The greeting was warm, a lot more so than Ray was expecting, and it seemed sincere. As he stood up to meet his host's out-thrust hand, he couldn't help but reciprocate the bonhomie. "Pedro, you don't look too shabby yourself, young man," he said with genuine sincerity. "I hear things are good for Ebro at the moment - and you. Well, you have come up in the world: you've gone big time, from what I gather from your latest title."

Pedro smiled. He had indeed enjoyed a somewhat meteoric rise in status during recent times but was keen to play it down. "Raymond, it is quite true," he said, "as a company we have grown significantly over the last couple of years and I have been fortunate enough to benefit from that; just lucky, I guess." Ray was surprised at how good it felt to see him and, as he followed the still smiling Spaniard down the bright glass corridor, he felt a little rush of excitement.

The meeting went on for nearly two hours, all very informal and loose, with the amiable nature of the banter being a constant throughout. Ray gave a full run-down of the HSG's current operations, bar two obvious ones, and listened avidly as Pedro gave him chapter and verse on Ebro's recent growth spurt and his role in it. They reminisced about the two jobs they'd done together. Ray took great delight in reminding Pedro of the time he got so drunk at the end of job party in Cadiz he'd passed out in the taxi, then been dumped by the driver to sleep it off in a bus shelter. You couldn't argue with the logic, they'd laughed: on that basis alone, it must have been a good night.

The two hours flew, and in the end both men agreed it had been good to catch up and they would definitely stay in touch. As they parted, Pedro reaffirmed the point that, whilst there was nothing on offer for HSG at the moment, the minute the next salvage need arose they'd be in touch.

"I assure you, Raymond," Pedro said, "you will my first port of call…and that's a promise, my friend."

Ray left Ebro's office in a buoyant mood. It had been a worthwhile visit and he was now viewing it as one of his genuine marketing missions.

Keeping up regular contact with ex-clients was shrewd business logic. It was a logic Ray Stuart had long embraced, and this re-connect with Ebro had been both productive and enjoyable at the same time. He was happy, but was now left with an obvious conundrum: what to do with the Ronnie Stafford issue? He wracked his brains. What the fuck is the man's beef with the Spaniards? Surely, he's got it wrong, he thought. It can't be like he's saying, can it? It just didn't stack up with what he'd just sat through. With that thought fixed firmly in his mind, Ray pulled onto the coast road and headed back to Malaga.

***

Having just returned to base after a tiring day, Gerry and Sarah were now sat with Steve Harrison in the office discussing the events of their meeting with Dr Reid.

"I couldn't believe the whole set-up," Gerry said. "I mean, it was straight out of a Hammer House of Horror film, wasn't it, Sarah?"

"I don't remember those films, Gerry," Sarah answered playfully. "Obviously, I'm far too young. But I know what you mean, it really was a strange experience from beginning to end." She shuddered and clasped her shoulders as if to emphasise the eerie nature of the encounter.

"Go on, then, tell us all the gory details," Steve said, fascinated. "How bad was it?"

The coffee flowed as Gerry and Sarah gave Steve the low-down on their trip. Of particular interest was the bizarre meeting with the PCOS's Great and Good. As Gerry regaled his listeners, he left nothing out. His description of the dilapidated gothic monstrosity they'd met in, the dust, the gloom, the history - and the smell - all got the treatment.

"Jesus, I tell you, Steve, the place stank," he said. "I don't know what that smell was, but it was rank - almost like dead bodies, but not as acrid, or as vomit inducing," Gerry was grimacing as he spoke, "but I tell you, it was bad enough to seep into our clothes. We could still smell it on the train home – it was vile."

"What did they say about it?" Steve asked. "The smell, I mean."

"They never mentioned it," Gerry replied. "Didn't seem to bother them and we were far too polite to say anything; we just got on with the meeting."

Over the course of the next half-hour Steve Harrison got his chapter and verse, and to say he was intrigued was an understatement.

***

The HSG Directors had wisely agreed to hold off sending any personnel to Spain until Ray's 'staged' contact with Ebro had taken place. Both men knew the informal chat, if it actually happened, could throw up something that would alter their ideas for helping with Excel's Ebro-related problems. And, after what Ray had just seen and heard, it certainly did that. It cast serious doubt about Stafford's claims in the first place and, as he cruised down the coast toward Malaga airport, he couldn't wait to ring Gerry and gave him the great news, the news that as far as he could ascertain Ebro were still very much a kosher outfit and that Ron Stafford was most likely delusional.

Gerry picked up the minute he saw Ray's name on the screen, "Raymond… what news?"

"I'm in the airport now, mate," he said. "Spent two hours with our old mucker, Pedro Grillo. What a nice guy! Even nicer than I remember - he even asked after you."

"How very thoughtful of him," Gerry said dryly. "Did he give anything away - any clues, any whiff of impropriety – anything that could back up Stafford's claims?"

"Nah…. there's nothing dodgy going on over here, far from it; from what I can see it all looks good. Ebro are on the up, business is booming, that's all. Nothing feels wrong, in fact it's the opposite – we should look to get back in with these guys…and I'm serious."

Gerry was not surprised at his partner's report. His own recollections of previous dealings with Ebro were all favourable. A decent firm: efficient, cooperative, and prompt payers. What more could you ask for?

"OK, so we're in for another round of head scratching, then," he replied. "The Ronnie Stafford story continues to mystify us all, eh?"

"Sure does… but hey, we like a challenge, don't we?" Ray paused but got no immediate response. "So, we'll go through it all tomorrow when I'm back in the office. I'll be in around eight, OK? See you then, Gerry."

Gerry didn't answer for a second, then sheepishly queried, "OK, but aren't you going to ask how we got on?"

Silence.

"Oh, shit…. Sorry, Gerry! Fuck me," Ray blurted, "I'd completely forgotten about your meeting! How'd it go? Any help, any insight?

Did Sarah get any answers?" Ray had been so wrapped up in his own schedule that the Glasgow head-to-head had come and gone without his even realising it.

"Very weird, Ray, I mean seriously weird...but it's given us some insight. So, we've got a bit to talk about. For now, safe journey, see you in the morning, bud, and don't be late!" Before Ray had a chance to respond, Gerry hung up.

***

High on a mist shrouded ridge in the Canary Islands, SKYCHECK's observatory - tagged officially as La Palma SC 4/4 Bravo - was quietly going about its business. In the centre of the darkened control room, two large monitor screens glowed and gently hummed. As the green screen reflections danced a gentle two-step over the surrounding equipment, all was as it should be. But at 2.30am the tranquillity was disturbed. Main Screen One started to bleep. It emitted a low-pitched intermittent pulse at first – ten second intervals at the same volume each time - but then both volume and frequency intensified. Alerted by the increasing noise, a bleary-eyed technician slipped through the glass panelled door and headed to the monitor. He leant in to take a closer look at the bleeping screen. "What do you know?" he mumbled to himself. "Finally.........it makes a move."

CHAPTER 12

A Damsel in Distress

Lucas and Rick indulged in their usual breakfast routine and The Shooting Star buffet didn't disappoint. But, with a lot of miles to cover and keen to get on the road early, the two men bolted sausage, scrambled eggs, hash browns and didn't hang around for coffee refills. Then, as they made their way across the car park, the duo looked over at the black land cruiser and, relieved to see it parked in the same place they'd last seen it, just kept walking.

The drive to Glendale took less than thirty minutes. They arrived at the rental outlet just as it was opening up and, based on the universally accepted 'first come first served' premise, they would be the first punters of the day. They were right, but for whatever reason customer service in the Glendale branch wasn't delivered quite as enthusiastically as it had been at the airport. It was a much more restrained approach, and both Lucas and Rick found the down-to-earth style far easier to deal with. No bullshit small talk, no fake smiles, and no daft questions – being treated in a straightforward, professional manner made a refreshing change.

With a cursory once-over, the Chrysler was inspected and handed back, damage free. Then the Ford's paperwork was filled out, checked and signed. The pair were happy with the Mustang and agreed the white V8 looked nothing short of drop-dead gorgeous.

"I'll keep driving, Sarge," Rick said, itching to get behind the wheel. "You can just sit and navigate."

"Why?" Lucas queried.

Rick smirked, "I'm in the swing of it now, so it makes sense. Plus, if I remember rightly, you're a bleeding liability on the other side of the road."

Lucas said nothing. He couldn't tell if his partner was joking or not. Rick could be pretty blunt at times and maybe he was actually serious.

Once the documentation was complete, they paid the deposit and up-front hire charges by company credit card and that was it - they were done. Minutes later, the Mustang rolled out of the small, packed car park, turned right onto the main drag, then headed north towards Flagstaff.

After picking up the car, the plan was simple: the duo would work through the contact list based purely on the most geographically efficient way to do it and, whilst there was no doubt the team back home had worked hard behind the scenes, under close scrutiny it was obvious most contacts on the list weren't worth the paper they were written on.

The R&I team had already highlighted the tenuous nature of some entries, but Lucas and Rick had taken their thinking further. They'd decided that most of the other contacts were all in the same 'waste of time' category. In fact, when the list was heavily filtered, it only had three worthwhile leads to track down - and one of them was Marion Armstrong herself. So, with such a short list, the pair agreed the first port of call would be the furthest away.

Flagstaff was a two-and-a-half-hour drive away but, based on the previous day's journey, they knew it could be bettered. Marion had phoned Lucas during the evening to tell him she'd already spoken to Meredith and wanted to meet again. So, the mild-mannered librarian was first on the day's itinerary, whether she liked it or not. Their second stop would be the Flagstaff General Hospital, both agreeing it wise to find out if there was any official record of Reverend Coleman or his assistant ever being admitted. It was unlikely, but they still felt it worth checking out. If nothing else, it could help prove the RTA report was just a cover story.

***

Marion's late-night call had been brief - but illuminating. She'd had an update from her socialite friend but was quick to confess to making the first move. She explained she'd phoned Meredith almost immediately after their meeting. Ringing her under the pretext of discussing a forthcoming bridge club charity evening, Marion had eventually managed to swing the conversation around to The Divinity arrest story.

Widow Higham, as ever keen to dish the dirt, confirmed the church member arrested in Flagstaff wasn't Reverend Coleman. The man detained was in fact another stalwart of the organisation, a Father Dominic Williams. Although she admitted she'd never heard of Father Williams before, her source confirmed he'd just returned from an outreach project in Honduras. By all accounts, Father Dominic was a real life Missionary.

Part way through the conversation Marion told Lucas she had another call waiting and had to go. But, before hanging up, said she could meet again the following day if that suited. Lucas jumped at the chance and asked her to text an address and a convenient time as soon as she could. "Will do, Mr Roxby, I'll send something later," Marion responded cheerfully. "Bye for now, see you tomorrow."

Lucas liked the woman. She appeared genuine, seemed keen to assist, and currently they needed every bit of help they could get.

***

Behind the wheel, Rick was like a man possessed and, as the V8 beast rocketed its way toward Flagstaff, the two men discussed the day ahead. But, whilst the bleached-blond South African was happy, his partner wasn't. Lucas was getting concerned about meeting up with Marion again. Despite her promise to text, nothing had come through. No address, no time, no contact at all. He'd tried to ring several times during the journey, but it kept ringing out, not even going to voicemail.

"Probably having a lie-in after a wild night on the town," Rick joked, but the flippant comment wasn't appreciated.

"Don't be a dick," Lucas snapped, "there's no chance a woman like that goes out and gets wrecked, she's more likely to go flower arranging than hit the bottle...so less of it."

"Bit touchy there, Sarge," Rick said quickly. "Protective of our dowdy little book worm, are we?"

Lucas half-smiled but said nothing. He needed to think. Not only was he worried for Marion's safety, but also the impact it could have on the job. She could be the key to cracking The Divinity and without her they had very little else.

Lucas knew Marion was in her fifties. Yet, despite the frumpish, spectacle-wearing librarian look she sported, she looked younger. During their meeting at the coffee shop he'd studied her closely. She was slim, well-groomed, and certainly not unattractive, and in a strange way he'd been drawn to her. Suddenly he caught himself questioning his motives. Was this overzealous concern for her reputation and welfare borne out of company loyalty, or was he developing some sort of weird crush on her? Eventually he reassured himself she wasn't his type and, well, he'd only met her the once...

"Fuck it, Ricky!" he said. "I'm ringing Sarah, see if she's got a home address," he paused waiting for a response, but none came. "If we don't hear from her before we get to Flagstaff, at least we can go and check out where she lives. Got to do something, haven't we?"

Rick knew by Lucas's tone he was concerned. "Yeah, Sarge," he answered. "Just get me some directions."

Their contact information had not included a home address for Marion. Whilst she was at the top of the list, only her place of work and her cell phone number were given. Some other details were added. One note explained the connection she had to the operation. It highlighted she'd assisted Wiseman and Scott's initial investigation for the PCOS, then went on to mention the W&S contact was Calvin Lentz and his Glasgow office number was also listed. But no sign of Marion's home address appeared anywhere.

***

Sarah was surprised how much she'd been able to find out in just a few hours. Social media was one of her best research sources but, still, she never ceased to be amazed by how much information people around the world published about themselves. She loathed self-promotion; in her eyes it was the scourge of modern society. But in her job the forensic analysis of social media platforms was the best way of snooping on individuals and companies alike and, from what she discovered, Widow Higham was well into self-promotion.

Meredith was serious currency in the world of the Arizona State glitterati. She was a woman who knew everybody and everything worth knowing and, by all accounts, her fingers were in every worthwhile cause across the northern half of the state. And if she wasn't the patron of the enterprise, she would definitely be on the committee or a major financial contributor. Meredith was the widow of an old school Tulsa oil baron and her beloved Lee had made a fortune from the black gold. But, after his untimely death, she had decided to up sticks and move from the family home in Oklahoma to the healthier climes of Arizona.

After settling into a stunning house in the Southern suburbs of Flagstaff, she got to work ingratiating herself with every worthwhile social network she could find. The enthusiasm of the woman knew no bounds, and neither did her wealth. As a tenacious networker blessed with an abundance of natural charm it didn't take her long to have an impact and, within four years, she had her feet well and truly under the top table of Arizona's movers and shakers.

Sarah was impressed. With what she'd unearthed, she thought the woman deserved nothing short of sainthood. But, as she regularly liked to point out, the nagging question with social media accounts was always: could any of the profile be true? Was she really as wonderful as she'd led everyone to believe? 'Unlikely' was always Sarah's stock answer.

As she sat in front of her laptop finalising the report, her concentration was broken when the desk phone rang. Without looking away from the screen for even a second, she reached for the handset. "Hello, R&I office," she answered in her usual dead-pan manner.

"Sarah, it's Lucas," came the faint voice, "how you doing, kid? How's everything going? Any breaking news, any joy with our extra research yet? Anything meaningful to report, anything at all?"

Lucas sounded upbeat, but she could tell from his rapid-fire questioning he was in no mood for idle chit-chat. As ever with Lucas Roxby, whenever he needed information, he needed it instantly.

"Yes, Lucas, don't worry: I'm on the case," she answered. "As requested, I've done you a little report on Meredith Higham, it'll be over in five minutes. She's some lady, you know!" She paused for a breath and was just about to continue when he beat her to it.

"That's great, Sarah, much appreciated," he said, "but what I need ***right now*** is a home address for Marion; have you got one on file? It's pretty urgent."

She knew from his tone it was important and was quick to reply, "Yeah, I've got one, do you want me to text it?"

"Yeah, right now, please," he replied. "We've lost contact with her and need to find her sharpish, so be quick. Thanks, kid, gotta go, bye for now," and, with one echoing click, he was gone.

She smiled to herself; the fast and the furious wasn't in it.

***

The address came through within minutes of his call. 'Good girl, Sarah' he muttered to himself as he punched the nine-digit zip code into the sat-nav. Then, as the robotic voice took charge, the display showed the house was ten minutes away.

"Better move it, Ricky," Lucas said. "I'm not getting a great feeling about this one."

Rick didn't answer; he just kept his eyes front and gunned the big V8 in the direction the hollow metallic voice told him to.

***

The street was eerily quiet. It was late Friday morning and, whilst it might be normal to be this deserted, the HSG team didn't like it. The house number given was 245 and, as they got closer, counting down the house numbers on their approach, at 253 they slowed. A dark coloured pick-up was parked just up the street ahead of them. Lucas's heart sank. They recognised it immediately. It was the battered blue Silverado that had been waiting for them in the gravel car park the day before. But this time it was empty.

"Oh fuck, Rick, it's our gang banger friends from yesterday, looks like they're paying our librarian a visit too. Shit! Stop the car before we go past the house, but don't slam on.... then back up and park up around the corner."

Rick's reaction was instant. He slowed quickly but silently to a stop. Then, after a quick glance in his rear-view mirror, reversed steadily back down the street and sweetly swung round the first corner he came to. After tucking the car in tight to the kerb, he turned to Lucas. "How'd you want to play this?" he asked.

"We've got to go in fast," Lucas replied. "Who knows what they're doing to her."

Just as Lucas finished talking, his mobile rang. It was lying in the console between the driver and passenger seats. He grabbed it and checked the number calling. "Fuck, its Marion!" he blurted in surprise, then hit the green button. "Marion where are you - are you OK?"

There was a brief silence followed by a surprised sounding voice, "Yes, Mr Roxby, I'm fine, thank you. Are *you* OK? You sound very agitated - what's wrong?"

Lucas didn't waste time on an answer. "Marion, where are you? You're not at home, are you?

"No, Mr Roxby, I'm not at home. Why do you ask?"

Lucas couldn't hide his impatience. "Look, Marion, we have a problem and I need to know where you are."

She drew an exasperated breath. "Well, if it is really that important for you to know, I stayed at my sister's last night, and this morning I've played a little golf." She paused briefly. "I'm just setting off from the club now and should be home in about an hour, if that's alright with you?"

The tone of her response made it perfectly clear she was not impressed with the Englishman's blunt, aggressive approach. Lucas knew she wasn't happy but was quite sure that when she understood the full story, she would forgive him. In the meantime, he couldn't believe how relieved he was to hear she was OK. He smiled at his quizzical looking partner, then continued the call.

"That's good to hear, Marion," he said. "You're safe and well - that's the most important thing, and I'm so sorry for worrying you." He paused to compose himself, then added, "Err... I don't mean to spook you further, but I need to ask you not to come home just yet, please. We have a little issue to deal with at your house first - OK?"

"I beg your pardon?" came the curt reply.

Now that he knew she was safe and out of immediate danger he was much calmer. "No need to worry," he said, "just give us an hour and I'll call you back with the full story – we will get it sorted."

Marion was far from convinced, but begrudgingly decided to do what he'd asked and just pray that things weren't actually as bad as she was now imagining. Once she'd mumbled goodbye and put the phone down, Lucas focused on the next priority.

They could have rung 911 and reported a burglary, then let the Arizona State troopers do their job, but they didn't. At this stage they weren't keen on getting the authorities involved. It would cause too many complications; complications that could hamper their efforts to find the book.

After a brief discussion they agreed to deal with the intruders themselves. They were no strangers to confrontation, but the big fear was guns. The Arizonan love of firearms was obvious; it was an 'open carry' state and, wherever you went, that underlying gun culture was inescapable. Both men understood it was part of western history and had no problem accepting it. In their eyes, it only became an issue when you confronted a man with a gun when you didn't have one yourself, something they may just have decided to do.

Leaving the Mustang parked in the side street, they approached the house on foot. After only twenty yards from the car, they rounded the corner into Marion's street. As soon as they had a clear view of the road ahead, they stopped in their tracks. The blue pick-up had gone. They looked at each other for a second then, without a word, continued their cautious walk along the pavement up to 245.

As they got close to the open front gate, Lucas instructed Rick to take the lead and head up the path. Rick acknowledged with a nod, then ducked down into a crouching run and moved rapidly up to the front door. He checked the flimsy door. It was locked, with no sign of attempted entry. Rick gave the thumbs-up and then indicated he should check out the back of the house. Lucas, knowing immediately what Rick meant, headed up the side path of the neatly appointed bungalow toward the back yard. He slowly worked his way along the path, hugging the wall, peeking through windows as he went. He saw nothing of concern until he turned into the rear yard. The back elevation of the house had a large set of glass panelled doors, and one had been forced open. The perpetrators had jemmied the lock of the end panel of the door set, forced it open, and created a gap just wide enough for a man to squeeze through. Lucas popped his head in. It looked clear and nothing appeared disturbed. Cautiously he stepped in. To his relief no one was home; whoever had got in had gone. There was no mess, no obvious damage to anything apart from the rear patio door. Deep down he knew the unwelcome visitors had not come to steal - they'd come to find someone.

Once Lucas was sure the house was secure, he rang Marion and explained the situation. She didn't take the news well but, despite her concerns, agreed to head home straightaway. Lucas reassured her they'd be waiting and would stay as long as was necessary to sort out a plan for dealing with the problem. "Be quick, Marion," he instructed, "and please be careful, we need you back in one piece."

He put his phone back in his pocket and turned to Rick. "She's not gonna be happy," he said. "This is our fault and she'll know it."

Rick pulled a face. "Yeah, don't worry, Sarge, we'll put it right… we have to."

It was going to be a nervous wait; they wouldn't relax until the unassuming librarian was back, standing safe and well in front of them.

CHAPTER 13

The Rattler Wakes

Tate ordered Ings to meet him. He told him the organisation wanted to add another job to his list and it was urgent. It was a task better explained face to face, he'd said, but made it clear meeting at his office was not an option. The Security Chief suggested the baseball stadium outside Mesa was anonymous enough. It had a large, crescent shaped car park that, apart from game days, was usually quiet.

"We'll meet by the south perimeter fence," Tate said, "opposite the right field gate at 10.30am - do not be late."

Mordecai might be many things but tardy he wasn't. Being late for a meeting with a man as important as The Divinity's Security Director just wouldn't happen. So, arriving fifteen minutes early, he parked up and got out to wait. As he leant against the pick-up, baseball cap drawn down smoking his second cigarette, a black sedan cruised into the car park.

At exactly ten thirty it pulled up next to him. The windows were impenetrable; nothing inside was visible. But Mordecai knew Tate wouldn't be driving. He guessed Tate's usual chauffeur, Juan, would be at the wheel. The wild eyed Mexican was a street-smart hard case, who not only drove for the Director, but also doubled as personal security.

Seconds after the engine cut, Juan's wiry frame emerged from the driver's door. Cautiously, he checked out his surroundings then walked round the car and opened the rear door. The Chief got out and grimaced in the glare of mid-morning sunshine. As he moved toward the grizzled red-neck, Juan closed the door quietly behind him.

"Ings, we have another problem that needs attending to," Tate said as he drew closer, "a problem we want you to sort out for us."

Squinting into the sun annoyed him. Abruptly, he turned about face, reached into his jacket pocket and pulled out a pair of wire rimmed sunglasses. Then he turned back to face Mordecai as he put the round mirror shades on.

"Ah, that's so much better," he said. "I can see you properly now, always a help, don't you think?" he paused for one final adjustment. "You are monitoring our unwanted visitors 24/7 and I am happy with that arrangement. We feel they can do little to hurt us at this moment - but there's obviously no guarantees – so, until told otherwise, do not let them out of your sight.... you hear?"

The weathered outlaw was standing bolt upright, listening intently to the stern, well-dressed man before him. "Of course, sir," he replied, "we'll carry on as long as you need."

Tate forced a faint smile, "Yes, Ings," he said. "Very good, now onto this other little matter...a matter that causes me a great deal of annoyance," he paused to look skyward. "How do I put this – I suppose you could say we need you to fix a weak link in our chain...no, actually that's not quite right - what we really want is for you to remove a weak link in our chain. This link needs to be removed permanently; it needs to vanish – with no chance of reappearing – do you understand what I'm saying, Mr Ings?"

Mordecai knew precisely what was being asked and it wouldn't be an issue. He'd made good money out of permanently removing weak links - it was a side of the business he could always charge a premium for. "Crystal, Mr Tate," he answered, "just need some basic details."

The Divinity man moved a step closer and reached into his inside pocket again. This time he removed a single plain brown envelope. It was tightly sealed with no markings on it. He held out the envelope. Mordecai closed the gap further and took it without a moment's hesitation.

***

The cramped bathroom was mould ridden, and the feeble looking shower only had two settings: lukewarm and cold. But it wasn't just the bathroom that was a problem. Everything about the dingy apartment was causing the Reverend discomfort. The small shabby abode was not his permanent residence, but for nearly two weeks it was all he'd had to call home and it was a situation he was rapidly tiring of. The Monsignor told him his exile was temporary, purely a precaution. 'Use it as an opportunity for reflection and prayer,' he'd said. He even suggested he would come back spiritually fitter and stronger as a result. Deep down, Coleman knew it was all bullshit.

He'd had no contact for several days now. Usually, one of Tate's underlings rang through every day or so to check he was still there and keeping his head down. But now nothing for three days and this blatant lack of concern for his welfare was not appreciated. For almost two weeks he'd been completely isolated, spending most of his time watching TV or sleeping. It was a mind-numbing existence and he was sick to death of it. He wanted out.

The cleric had contemplated ringing Tate direct, but knew this would be considered over-stepping the mark. The man was just too important to talk to the likes of him. His best chance for contact was via one of his deputies and Clayton Carr was the most likely to be sympathetic. Young Clay, albeit a trusted and loyal servant, was only a runner for The Divinity's Security Chief. But beggars can't be choosers, so he'd have to do. The call to Carr went unanswered. Coleman left a message. "Clayton, it's Gary Coleman, I need to see you. This situation is becoming intolerable. We need to reconsider my position, seriously we do. Ring me back the minute you get this message, please."

Exasperated, he sat back down on the battered leather sofa, the place he currently spent eighteen hours a day, to contemplate his options. His thoughts were suddenly interrupted by a gentle knocking on the apartment door. He looked up at the heavily bolted entrance but remained motionless. The knocking stopped as quickly as it had begun. Total silence. The Reverend was puzzled. In the last two weeks he'd had no visitors. Only a chosen few were supposed to know where he was. Fearing the worst, he sat quietly, hoping whoever it was would simply go away if he didn't answer.

A faint voice came from the other side of the door. "Gary, it's me, Clay," it said, "let me in, will you."

The nervous cleric stared at the door for a second before getting up and tentatively moving toward it. "Sorry - who is it?" he asked as he got closer.

"It's Clay – Clayton Carr," the voice said calmly." Come on, Reverend, open up, will you? It's time to take you home."

***

Ings was obsessive about sticking to his client's brief, especially a client of The Divinity's standing. They were not an organisation he intended to let down, not now, not ever. Mr Tate had been very particular in his instructions. He wanted a daily surveillance update, it didn't need to be elaborate, but it did need to be accurate and Ings had stuck to the instruction faithfully. Since touching down on Monday afternoon, the HSG duo had never been far from his prying eyes, and from that moment on he'd been sending the details of their every move back to The Divinity Chief at least twice a day

Mordecai had been pissed off they'd found the tracker; not as dumb as they look, he'd thought at the time, but after their next move he was confident they'd never outsmart him. Not in a million years, he had sneered after he got the news about the car swap. Those boys might have the nous to find the GPS kit, but in his eyes their choice of replacement vehicle looked wildly amateurish. It wasn't rocket science; a white Mustang GT was much easier to spot and follow than a bland Chrysler SUV.

Since the start of the surveillance, Ings had kept his updates short, sweet and factual. He was economical with the truth to suit his own means so hadn't reported the visit to Marion Armstrong's house.

As a man of devious means with an extraordinary network of state-wide connections, it took him less than 24 hours to ID the woman in the coffee shop. In the search for Marion's identity, he was particularly indebted to the Arizona State Library service. This noble organisation, despite its many systems and procedures, was woefully inadequate in protecting its employee's personal data.

Once a home address had been verified, Ings decided they needed to have a quiet chat, so instructed two of his Phoenix crew to pay her a visit. The visit was to suggest politely she stop talking to strangers from overseas and, in his briefing, Mordecai explained that it was a low-key affair, no strong-arm stuff - just a subtle warning.

As instructed, his two associates arrived in the quiet Flagstaff suburb and parked their battered pick-up outside the target's house. No one would be suspicious of two ragged Latino workmen going about their business. So, with a rake, a wheelbarrow, and a couple of hoes strategically placed in the back, the gardening contractor cover looked convincing. And, as the two grizzled Mexicans ambled up Marion's front path in their well-worn high-viz vests no one took a blind bit of notice.

There was no car on the drive but, undeterred, the pseudo-gardeners rang the doorbell. After several long blasts went unanswered, they guessed she had a car and was out. At that point it was time to report back. But they didn't; the headstrong duo decided to check the house over.

Waiting out of view for the unassuming librarian to arrive home was not a bad idea but busting open the rear patio doors and helping themselves to a look inside was. Just as the two intruders were in the midst of nosing around, they received a phone call from the man himself. "Santi, it's Mord," he said. "Have you found her?"

Despite his poor English, the goon still managed to explain to his boss exactly what they'd done. Mordecai was furious. "You dumb fuck," he snarled, "I told you if she wasn't there to ring me, so why didn't you?"

The Mexican didn't have an answer - he just started mumbling an incoherent half-hearted apology. Ings cut him short, "The two of you get in that truck and fuck off right now, and I mean now.

Those two boys are only a couple of minutes away, so disappear, you understand me?"

The half literate Latino could not fail to understand his master's vicious tongue and fired an immediate 'Yes, Boss' back. Then the two gangbangers made their way out of the property as quickly as they could.

Ings was keen to avoid direct contact with the HSG team. He felt any face-to-face confrontation at this stage was more likely to cause a prolongation of their stay and could even be a catalyst for intensifying their resolve. He was no fool; he was well aware the best outcome for The Divinity was that the visitors simply gave up the chase and left empty handed and, if he could swing it, he would make that happen.

CHAPTER 14

A Time for Action

The last thing the HSG duo expected to see was a glamorous vision in figure-hugging jeans, stilettos, and a tailored jacket strutting toward them. As the two men exchanged quizzical glances, Lucas asked quietly, "That can't be Marion, can it?"

But it was Marion, and the librarian's look couldn't have been further removed from the one she'd sported the previous day. As she walked up the drive, the two men stared. "It is!" Rick muttered. "It's your ***dowdy*** little book worm."

Marion's Honda had pulled up on the driveway within an hour of Lucas's call and, understandably, she was upset. Fearful her house had been trashed, she jumped out of the car and made a beeline for the Englishman.

Instinctively, Lucas moved to greet her. "Miss Armstrong, I'm so glad to see you," he said in his best soothing tone. "Are you OK?"

"No, not really Mr Roxby," she glared. "What on earth is going on…what have they done to my house?"

The agitated librarian was desperate to know exactly what had happened and why she'd been targeted. Lucas, aware that demanding to know 'what the hell was going on?' was not unreasonable, tried to alleviate her fears.

"It doesn't seem as if anything's been disturbed inside," he said, "nothing broken, no noticeable damage, hardly a scratch…but it's your house, so you'll know best."

Marion continued to glare. "I most certainly will, Mr Roxby," she replied coolly.

With that, the two men escorted her into the house. Once through the front door she started a rapid, systematic, room by room inspection. After a frantic ten minutes confirmed nothing seemed out of place and nothing obvious was missing, Marion sat down at the kitchen table. She was relieved but still upset. "What did they want?" she asked. "What were they after? Is this because of you two and that book?"

She looked accusingly at the two of them as she spoke. But, still distracted by how good she looked, both men just stared back blankly.

"Unfortunately, it does," Lucas finally replied. "The intruders were in a pick-up truck, a beat-up Chevrolet that we've seen before." He stopped for a second as he sat down opposite her, "We saw it yesterday," he continued. "It was driven by two mean looking Hispanic guys, who we think had been waiting for us."

"And?" she barked abruptly.

Her annoyance was obvious, but Lucas wasn't fazed. He simply smiled politely and continued, "As we were on our way to meet you, the truck pulled up next to us," he stopped again, this time to look across at his partner for back up, "then the passenger shouted over to us - didn't he, Rick?"

"Very pleasant, he was," the South African answered sarcastically. "He offered us some advice."

"And the advice was very specific and very clear," Lucas explained. "In a nutshell, he was telling us to go home…and he appeared deadly serious."

Marion sat unsmiling, waiting for further revelations, but this time Lucas offered nothing immediate, so Rick took advantage of the awkward pause.

"We can only guess," he said, "that they're connected to The Divinity…either part of the organisation or hired hands – and we think there are others." He pulled his best sympathetic face and shrugged his shoulders, "and now it seems they're interested in you as well."

Rick had tried to make it sound less menacing than it was, but he was struggling. They all knew it was a shitty situation, and it only seemed to be getting worse.

As the three of them sat round the modest dining table discussing their predicament, Marion's mood mellowed. Once Lucas was sure she was back on side, he asked why she hadn't sent him the details of their meeting.

"Mr Roxby, I do apologise for my lack of communication," she said, "it was not deliberate by any means.... it was just unfortunate. You see, at my sister's cabin there is a real problem with cell phone signals; most networks have coverage problems, and I'm afraid the last twenty-four hours have been particularly bad."

Lucas was happy enough with the explanation and left it at that. The big question now was what to do next? After a quick chat about options, all three agreed not to call the police. They decided Rick would carry out a running repair to the door, Marion would go back to her sister's cabin for a couple of days, and Lucas would ring home.

Rick made a decent job of fixing the busted patio door. He eased the damaged panel back onto its runner, levered it back into its closed position with a screwdriver, and then wedged it tight. Fortunately, the glass had only cracked slightly during the entry; once back in place and secured from the inside, the temporary job was solid.

While Rick had got on with the repair job, Lucas made two calls. The first was to Gerry and the second to Sarah. Both calls were brief. Gerry's was just an update: no dramatics, just the facts. And the other one, to Sarah, was even shorter. Firstly, he thanked her for getting Marion's address to them so rapidly and explained they'd found her OK, then asked for assistance in a little matter that had been playing on his mind. It was an odd one even by his own reckoning.

"Sarah, I know this sounds a bit bizarre," he said, "but what's your star gazing knowledge like? Do you know anything about astronomy? Have you ever heard of 'Cirrus 5'?"

Sarah was surprised by the questions and had to double check she'd heard him right. "Did you say Cirrus Five?" she asked. "What the hell's one of those?"

"Yeah that's it, Cirrus 5," he replied. "Not quite sure what it is, that's why I'm asking, but it could be important. All we know is it's something to do with astronomy."

"OK, Lucas," she answered. "Leave it with me...is that it?"

"Yeah, that's all for the moment. Ta, kid. Just see what you can dig up and get back to us, OK?"

But before Sarah could answer the line went dead. She looked at the receiver in disbelief then shook her head. Over the last couple of years, she'd had many off the wall requests from the unconventional Mr Roxby - but this one was even weirder than normal.

***

In preparation for the stay at her sisters, Marion packed a small suitcase, put it in the car, then went back inside to explain Meredith's latest news to Lucas and Rick. This time it included more detail than she'd given in the phone call of the previous evening. Once happy that the duo was up to speed, she wrote a note with the address, basic directions, land line number, and email details for her at the cabin. "And, gentlemen, please make sure you let me know the minute anything changes – and I mean anything at all, OK?"

"Of course, absolutely," Lucas smiled, "as soon as we know more I'll ring you."

Once the house was locked up, Marion said her farewells and headed to her car. As she got in, the two men checked out front for signs of undesirables. All appeared clear but as a precaution they decided to follow her for the first few miles.

After reversing down the drive onto the quiet suburban street, she waved sweetly, then set off. After a few hundred yards she checked the rear view and was reassured to see the white Mustang right behind her. Whilst Rick drove, focused on keeping the yellow Honda in sight, Lucas scanned front and back for signs of prying eyes. After ten minutes yielded nothing suspicious, it was agreed to do another couple of miles then peel off. Five miles further down the freeway it was still looking good, so Lucas rang Marion. He gave it two rings then terminated the call. The twitchy librarian, startled by the ring, didn't attempt to answer. Two rings only meant all clear and goodbye. After checking the wing mirror to confirm she'd understood correctly, she watched the white Ford slow down and pull off at the junction she'd just passed. Now she was on her own.

As they double-backed over the freeway, the HSG team watched the yellow Honda for as long as possible but very quickly it disappeared into the distant haze. It was now out of their hands. So, with nothing more they could do, Lucas went back to his well-thumbed road atlas. "Next left I reckon," he said after a few seconds of deliberation. "Stay in this lane, then turn at the lights."

Rick nodded his understanding and did as instructed. Then, despite his obvious concentration on the road, the big South African couldn't help but comment on the stark change in Marion's appearance. "I can't believe that's the same woman," he said. "The Marion we met in the coffee shop didn't look like that, did she?"

Lucas had been as taken aback by the radical change in her look as much as his colleague, but it was Rick who had the most to say on the subject. "Yesterday in that ill-fitting navy thing," he went on, "no make-up and wearing specs, she really did look like a straight-laced fuddy duddy, didn't she?" He paused for a second, then, shaking his head, added, "But today, in that get-up.... fuck me, she looks ten years younger; hair down, face on, no glasses, tight jeans and smart jacket. She looked gorgeous."

Rick was unusually animated, and Lucas couldn't help but laugh at his partner's obvious awe. "Yeah, Ricky, she looked stunning," he replied. "I really did think it was someone else at first! I mean, when she came storming up that drive I was thinking Who's this babe?"

Rick laughed, then their lively discussions continued all the way to Flagstaff General Hospital.

***

The hospital visit proved a waste of time. The A&E staff had been pleasant and helpful, one even telling Lucas that she loved his English accent. But it came to nothing. All they were able to say was that nobody going by the name of Gary Coleman had been admitted recently and also confirmed they'd not actually had any major RTA admissions in the last couple of days.

They thanked the reception staff for their assistance and headed back to the car. The result wasn't a surprise, but it backed up what they'd thought in the first place and now they could report with confidence that the explanation given for Reverend Coleman's no show was spurious.

Rick spotted the Dodge van first. It was parked a fair distance away from their car, but there was something about it that made him look twice. He stayed quiet until they were back in the Mustang. "Lucas, see that black van over there," he said, "does it look familiar to you?"

Lucas peered in the direction his partner was subtly indicating. "Which van? I can't see a black van," he said as he squinted out the window. "Oh, yes, sorry - the one in the corner, the one with the red pin-stripe up the bonnet?"

Rick nodded. "Yeah, that's the one," he said. "I'm sure I've seen it before. Could be wrong, though.... or it could be coincidence?" He paused. "Look, just humour me, will you? Keep your eyes on it...and, as we leave, see if it follows us out, OK?"

Rick eased the Mustang out from its generous parking space and started to make his way to the exit barrier. He deliberately went the long way around, the way that didn't take them past the Dodge. As the barrier rose to let the Ford out, Lucas spotted the van starting to nose out of its space and turn toward the exit. "It's moving off," he said. "Nice and slow, mind, but you might be right, Rick; it could be clocking us."

"Yeah," Rick said, then nodded gently, muttering, "I've definitely seen it before."

"OK, so we just keep going, head back to the motel as planned, nice and steady... and see what happens."

Rick smiled at his partner. "You got it, Sarge," he said. "Nice and steady all the way."

Their itinerary for the day had been seriously disrupted by the break-in. They'd lost several hours as a result so the final call of the day would have to wait. But the long journey back to Scottsdale gave them ample time to work out if the black Dodge really was a problem.

Rick didn't break any records. Sticking to the speed limit in the US was painful, but they were in no rush. The van followed but it kept a discreet distance back. So much so, that at times neither of the two men could make it out in the mirrors. Even on the occasions when he twisted round in his seat to look directly out of the rear screen, all Lucas could see was a dot on the horizon. "Whoever it is they're awfully subtle about it," he said. "Are we sure they're actually following us?"

"Definitely," Rick answered confidently.

Lucas, now slouched down in his seat, stared through the passenger window into the wing mirror. "Could be a figment of our imagination," he said, "you know… paranoia running wild and all that imaginary bad guy shit."

But Rick had made up his mind. He was one hundred per cent sure the van was dubious. "I tell you, it's following us," he said. "They're pros, they know exactly what they're doing." He glanced over at his partner, "Just watch this."

With that, Rick put his foot down. The speed of the Mustang increased rapidly. Briefly, he held it at 90 m.p.h. then started to decelerate.

"Check out back," he ordered. "Now see what happens." Lucas screwed round again in his seat and looked out of the back window. Initially he saw nothing, but then - as if by magic -the black boxy outline of the van appeared back on the horizon.

"Fuck me, you're right," he said, "it's back – they must be keeping a set distance. How the hell do they do that?"

Lucas was now beginning to believe the Dodge was following them. As soon as they sped up and gained ground it did exactly the same.

“You can easily do it on roads like this,” Rick explained. “They’re big, empty, long and straight – a two-man team up front: one’s spotting, the other drives. I reckon that’s what we’ve got here. It’ll be different in a built-up area,” he added with a manic grin, “let’s see how close they get then, eh?”

The explanation made sense. If the passenger had binoculars or a similar aid it could work a treat. As Lucas looked toward the horizon and saw the Scottsdale city outline come into view, he caught himself thinking, I bet old Kruger’s right.

***

CHAPTER 15

Lost Souls

Due to flight delays, Ray got very little sleep and didn't arrive at the office until 9.00 a.m., but as soon as he pulled up outside he knew Gerry was in the building. Seeing his partner's Land Rover in its usual spot and his office windows open, he wasted no time and bounded up the stairs to the first floor to find him. Sticking his head through Gerry's open office door, he found it empty.

"Gerry, where you hiding?" he shouted.

"Down here, Raymond," came the echoed reply. "I'm in the kitchen getting a coffee. Do you want one?"

Ray followed the voice down the corridor into the kitchen and found Gerry standing at the window. He was stirring his first espresso of the day and broke into a big smile the second his friend came through the door.

"Raymond!" he beamed. "How the devil are we this morning? Feeling refreshed? Any more news from Española?

"I'm afraid not," Ray replied, "nothing more than I told you on the phone. Ebro look right, feel right, and I reckon they are right. It's that simple." The CEO smiled then changed tack. "More importantly though, what about your meeting with Dr Reid? How'd it go? How'd Sarah do.... any revelations?"

Gerry raised his eyebrows and tutted. "You're going to love this," he said, "but first grab a drink and follow me. I'll get Sarah and Steve up here now so we can go through it together." With that, Gerry headed off down the corridor back to his office.

Once all the usual cheery greetings were over, the foursome settled down round Ray's big desk and got on with the Dr Reid meeting debrief. Gerry told the tale stripped down and at speed and felt no need for embellishment. Steve and Sarah had heard the full version once already and Ray, well, Ray was sharper than Gillette's finest. During his explanation, Gerry brought Sarah in on a couple of key points for emphasis and her enthusiasm clearly highlighted that her earlier frustrations had now eased. As he rattled through the finer details of the meeting, Steve Harrison nodded a lot, Sarah smiled a lot, and Ray sat statue-like, taking note of every word.

"So, my friends," Gerry said, grinning broadly, "in summary it seems that Dr Reid and his Synod are a bunch of weird ancient throwbacks," he shook his head, "who live in their own little world and are quite happy for us to use any means possible to get their property back." He stood up from his chair and walked over to the window. "Simply put, they don't give a monkey's chuff what we do as long as we get that bloody book back to them pronto."

"But the real significance of the book's importance?" Ray asked. "What was said about that?"

Sarah couldn't resist her father's question and, before Gerry could respond, jumped in. "They're saying it's not only a first edition, but a first edition that was printed specifically for them.... for the original Presbyterian Church Covenanters, and it has been in their possession on Scottish soil from day one."

Ray, far from convinced, pulled a face. "Day one? That's a long time ago, isn't it? We're talking 1563 here, aren't we? So, you're telling me that they've had that one book for over 450 years?"

"Correct," Gerry said, "that's exactly what they're saying... and they reckon they can prove it." He turned back from the window and continued, "When they say it was bespoke for them, they mean it; they're claiming it contains references that other editions of the time, or even since, don't. They wouldn't go into any specific detail, but they got quite agitated just mentioning it."

“So, where does all this leave us, then?” Steve posed the question directly to Gerry.

The Ops Director was now back behind his desk. “A little wiser, maybe,” he replied, “not that it helps much.” He then took a few seconds to look at each attentive face in turn. “But we have a client who is still backing us and still wants us to do a job for him, so, as I see it, we just keep going.”

After mulling over Gerry’s unconvincing rhetoric, Ray felt disheartened. He just couldn’t see a way forward. What else could they do, he asked himself. With no help from Dr Reid’s team, and nothing but bad news coming out of Arizona, to him the Book of Martyrs recovery would soon be dead in the water.

“Keep going?” he asked scornfully. “Doing what exactly?”

Gerry could feel Ray’s negativity but didn’t let it show. “Come on, Raymond,” he said encouragingly, “just remember the old cliché, will you: it ain’t over ‘til the fat lady sings.”

***

Once the Glasgow briefing was over, Sarah and Steve had headed back down to their office and left the two Directors sat alone round Gerry’s desk. Despite being intent on discussing a host of other pressing company issues, the two men returned time and time again to the BOM’s hunt and its myriad complications.

“It can’t just end like this,” Gerry said, now sounding as deflated as his partner. “There’s gotta be something we can do.... total failure’s not really our style, is it?”

“I don’t know,” Ray said shaking his head, “maybe it is time to simply cut our losses and call the boys home.”

“I suppose we could,” Gerry replied, then with a hopeful smile added, “or maybe we just hang fire a little longer, eh?”

The two-man brain storming session continued for another forty minutes. The animated discussions were interwoven with questions and ideas about Ebro, Excel, Ronnie Stafford and everything else currently driving the two old sea dogs crazy but, as they were about to break for lunch, a flustered looking Sarah came charging into the office.

"Dad, Gerry, sorry to disturb you guys, but I think you'll want to hear this!"

Sarah was ushered into the room and without ceremony sat straight back down in the seat she'd occupied only two hours earlier. Unable to contain her eagerness she started to gush, "Just had a call from a friend of a friend of mine," she said at speed, "the guy works for an Astronomy mapping and recording institution, they're called SKYCHECK.... apparently well known in the business and they've got observatories scattered all over the world." Sarah gulped for air, then raced on, "That Cirrus 5 question Lucas asked me the other day has been bugging me, like I told you, Dad...just sounded so random and weird, I thought he might just be taking the piss," she paused again for breath. "Anyway, I made a few enquiries just to test the water, and bingo! One of them paid off."

"So, go on then," Gerry prompted, "what the hell is Cirrus 5?"

"It turns out," she said, "Lucas's question wasn't that weird or random after all. Cirrus 5 is a red dwarf, a low mass star from the Centauri constellation and guess what?" She had now calmed herself and was looking excitedly at her father.

"I can't begin to imagine, my dear," Ray laughed, "but please do tell.... put the old folks out of their misery, will you."

"Cirrus 5 crosses the earth's orbit regularly, but only when certain atmospheric parameters are right can it be seen," she paused for breath, "and the intervals between recorded showings are long, and I mean long ....in fact, to be precise, it last happened 113 years ago."

"So, what are you saying?" Gerry asked, his impatience obvious. "What's this got to do with Lucas, or the Arizona fall out? Why should we all be excited by some random star, for God's sake?"

"Well, when conditions are right, apparently, it shows as a spectacular shooting star, and the next time that's expected to happen is...." she paused for what she hoped was dramatic effect, but it wasn't appreciated as both men just glowered. "It's in two days' time," she said, looking like the cat that got the cream, "can you believe that? Only two days' time."

"So?" Both men chorused.

She rolled her eyes in mock indignation. "Now," she continued loudly, "listen to this even more wildly coincidental fact. It's going to appear directly above the Mid-Western United States. Apparently, the astrological world is in meltdown over the whole thing. All these revved up stargazers can't wait; a real once in a lifetime show, they reckon. The internet sites, chat rooms and all the other geek forums are going crazy...and they're saying the best place to see it from," she paused again for a further attempt at drama, "is going to be the high ground around South Western Utah! How amazing is that?"

Ray and Gerry looked at each other. They were not quite sure of the significance of this bizarre news, but knew it had to be linked. It must be; it was far too much of a coincidence. 113 years is a long time to wait but now it appeared it was here again. Ray shook his head gently, "Gerry, how time flies, eh?"

Gerry didn't answer immediately; he looked from Ray to the still grinning Sarah, then back to Ray, "So what the hell does this mean to us, then?"

***

Next day delivery was one of Jo Knox's pet hates. Parcel tracking apps, unrealistic time slots and arsy drivers always got her riled and today's was no exception. Just as she'd put the phone down from complaining about another missed deadline, an obnoxious parcel delivering oik with no hint of a smile on his face - or an apology on his lips - turned up at reception. But the ever-efficient Mrs Knox didn't have the patience for poor customer service at the best of times, so this morning Mr Sourpuss was getting it both barrels. "Why do you fellas always complain and never apologise?" she launched, without even offering a basic 'good morning - can I help you'.

The man's jaw dropped. "Hold on a minute, Love," he said, "I haven't said a word."

Jo raised an eyebrow and continued the attack. "All I ever hear," she stormed, "is moan, moan, and moan...and, if it's not the number of deliveries you have to make, it's the traffic or the weather or how flipping hard everywhere is to find. It's painful to listen to, I mean, bloody painful."

"Excuse me," he said raising his hands up in protest, "there's no need for that... we work bloody hard, you know. *You* want to try doing this for a living, see how you like it."

The indignant looking man in ill-fitting overalls was not impressed with the attitude, but Jo didn't care. "I could do it with my eyes closed," she said. "It's hardly rocket science, is it? Right, there's your signature, so goodbye," She glared at him for a second, and then, in her best patronising voice added, "I said goodbye, OK, so off you pop.... go on - chop - or do you need help finding your way out?" The orange clad driver stood in disbelief. But he was given no chance to respond. All he heard was a click of Italian leather then, like magic, she vanished back into the office.

Jo had been told to expect the parcel mid-morning. At Sarah's insistence, Calvin had paid an additional fee for guaranteed a.m. delivery but 'unusually' it arrived an hour and a half late. In Jo Knox's book that was par for the course.

When Sarah heard the light knock on wood, she was sat hunched over her desk. As she looked up it was obvious she was pleased to see the smiling face at the door.

"Package for Miss Stuart," the grinning PA said, "express delivery – well, maybe not quite express!"

"Better late than never," Sarah replied. "I take it that's the stuff from Calvin?"

"Sure is, Chick. Sender's details: Wiseman & Scott, Glasgow. Look!" Jo turned the parcel over and pointed, "It's plastered all over the back."

Sarah took the package from the PA's grasp and got straight down to opening it. Her serrated letter opener ripped through the padded

Jiffy bag like a slaughter man's knife through flesh and, in a flash, with no mercy, no hesitation, it was done. Gently she shook the contents out onto her desk. "Yup, Mrs Knox, I think that's them," she said as she carefully inspected the two old notebooks lying on the desk. "They certainly look the part. Now all I've got to do is read the damn things."

***

Ronnie Stafford stood outside the smart two storey block. All dapper suit and venom, he was intent on kicking arse and only had one backside in his sights.

"You little bastard," he shouted, "get your skinny bag of bones down here now, you hear me, dickhead?" His bellow was so ferocious it splattered the shiny new door intercom with saliva. The incandescent giant was in no mood to consider the other residents of the chic upmarket development, he didn't care: the blinkers were on, he wanted blood, and he was going to get it.

"What's wrong, Mr Stafford?" a weedy voice crackled from the speaker. "Why are you shouting?"

"You either come down here now or let me come up, I don't give a shit which.... you know exactly why I'm shouting, so fucking move it!"

"You need to calm down, Mr Stafford, I've done nothing wrong.... so, so you better leave or I'm calling the police. I mean it, you know," the weedy voice bleated on, but this just incensed the seething hulk even further.

"Go on then, ring them! Get the law down here right now! See what they have to say about the shit you've been pulling. It's your call, you can take a kicking or do five years for embezzlement, I don't fucking care which.... just open this door now!"

After a few seconds of silence, the door lock release buzzed, and Ronnie - despite his size - was across the hall and up the stairs to apartment 2B in seconds flat.

***

The first phase of the sought-after development was twelve months old and fully occupied. Phase 2 was quietly under construction and already sold out, but Phase 3 - with an already burgeoning waiting list – was only at concept stage. It was a prime location. Smack in the centre of Cheshire's uber chic green belt. It was quiet, smart, and classy – a spot much sort after by those with money and secrets.

Over the years, Excel had invested in property. Ronnie had wisely used bricks and mortar as the foundation for his company's pension plan. And it was probably fair to say these days Excel generated more income through its property portfolio than through its basic I & E work, a fact the big man was keen to keep a lid on. Phase 1 of "Elm Park" had been a particularly shrewd investment. Two one bed apartments bought off-plan had almost doubled in value in less than two years. On completion, one had gone straight to the residential letting market, and been snapped up instantly. The second – apartment 2B – had been kept for incidental company use.

For the last five months, 2B had been used to house a young Irish accountant named Owen Carroll. Carroll had joined Excel from a large accountancy firm in Dublin. He'd been looking to gain experience in specialist mainland UK businesses and the opening advertised at Excel for an Assistant Account Manager appeared to be just the thing he was after.

Part of the Excel job offer included six months' accommodation, all at the company's expense. It was to give the successful candidate time to settle in and ultimately source their own place to stay. Ronnie himself hadn't done any of the interviewing: Maurice Brown had been tasked with that. But if Owen Carroll got the thumbs-up from his long serving accounts manager, then that was good enough for him.

Although now, in the lounge of the luxury apartment, holding the scrawny Irish weasel by the neck, Ronnie wished he'd never seen his face, never mind read his bullshit CV.

"How long have you been dipping, eh?" the big man bellowed. "Come on, you slimy little bastard, tell me! Tell me when you started, and at what point did you think, I know let's rip the fuck out of these nice people? Come on, when?"

"I d-d-d don't know what you're talking about...." Carroll stammered, "I've done nothing wrong."

Ronnie couldn't control his rage anymore. The jabbering wreck dangling from his enormous hands had bitten the hand that feeds and that was a cardinal sin. Incensed, Stafford narrowed his eyes and stared his quarry down. Then, in a lightening move, he released his throat hold and slapped the young Irishman full on across the face. The force of the blow sent the gasping accountant crashing to the floor, knocking over chairs and a side table as he went.

As he moved to stand over the prone figure, Ronnie snarled, "I ain't finished with you yet, you piece of shit!" Then, as he lifted Carroll from the floor by his lank greasy hair, he smiled, "You've got to pay for your crimes, son, so you're going to help Uncle Ronnie put this right....do you hear me?" For emphasis he yanked hard on the gelled mop and screamed, "I said, do you fucking hear me, dickhead?"

"Y-y-yes, Mr Stafford," came the pitiful reply, "I hear you."

CHAPTER 16

The Rattler Strikes

Lucas and Rick felt like they'd been in Arizona forever and the slow drive back to Scottsdale was only compounding the illusion. Sticking to speed limits wasn't their preferred MO but they'd agreed that they would, and they hadn't wavered. And now, exactly as Rick had predicted, when they reached the first signs of urbanisation the black van moved closer. Although still a respectable distance back, the van - to suspicious folk like them - was a definite tail. The Dodge was still too far away to make out how many were riding up front, but they'd seen enough.

"These dicks," Rick said, "they'll know where we're staying, won't they?"

"Course they will," Lucas answered, "that's probably where you've seen the van before: parked outside the bloody motel."

The ex-sapper was riled; it had been a long, frustrating day and it wasn't over yet. "Pull in at the next food place. will you," he said, "let's see what these pricks do when we stop for a piss and a bite to eat."

Rick grinned, "OK, Rox, suits me fine – I'm starving."

Two miles on they found a suitable stop. 'Diablo's Bar & Grill' was a large, two storey Tex-Mex restaurant sporting an array of garish red devil signs. It had a large parking area to the front and, judging by the amount of activity, it was doing a roaring trade.

"Yeah, this'll do nicely, Ricky," Lucas said as they pulled in and followed signs for the rear over-spill car-park.

Seconds after they'd slowed to turn, the Dodge sailed by. Once the van disappeared out of sight, the HSG men went inside. Whilst Rick headed for the toilets, Lucas went to the counter. The agitated Englishman ordered two double chilli burgers, large fries, and mega Cokes from a spotty squint-eyed teenager who looked puzzled for a second, then, without a word, got to work. In a blur of well-practiced agility, she'd whipped around the serving area and, in the blink of an eye, the food appeared like magic before him. Impressed by the super-efficient service, Lucas mumbled a brief thank you, paid, then looked round for an empty table. After a quick scan identified a corner two-seater, he crossed the restaurant and sat down. As he dished out the super-sized portions Rick joined him.

"That was quick," he said as he pulled back a chair, "proper fast food."

"Fucking amazing, mate…must have been all of twenty seconds and I was done."

Rick grinned appreciatively. "So, what do you reckon the van gang have done?" he asked but, before his partner could respond, he answered his own question. "Probably gone round the block," he muttered, "pulled up somewhere close, then settled down to watch the car… well, something like that."

Lucas wiped his mouth with a napkin and nodded; it was the obvious course of action. After eating the food almost as fast as it had been served, Lucas decided it was time for a comfort break so, as he disappeared off to the Gents, Rick cleared the table then made his way to the rear foyer.

"Go out the front, Ricky," Lucas said as he emerged from the rest room, "we'll cross the street, go for a wander and see if we can spot them before they spot us, OK?"

Rick gave a thumbs-up. "OK, lead on," he said.

The front parking area was much bigger than the one at the rear and it was packed. The two men loitered in the lobby before venturing outside and, from this handy vantage point, studied the mass of parked cars out front. A minute later, with no sign of the black Dodge, they made their move. Once through the front door, they negotiated a steep set of steps onto a central walkway then headed away from the restaurant. The walkway was paved, at least ten feet wide, and ran the full length of the car park straight onto the main drag. They didn't rush. Ambling casually side by side toward the road, they kept a watchful but subtle eye on their surroundings. Once on the main street, they crossed over and started to walk back past the restaurant, but now on the opposite side of the road.

After 150 yards, Rick caught sight of the van. "Roxy, check it out," he said, "over there: can you see them?" Rick was pointing across the street. Lucas followed the direction of his out-stretched arm and could just make out the top of a black van. It was in a retail outlet car park adjacent to the Tex-Mex emporium.

" Jesus, you've got good eyesight," he said. "Are you sure it's the right van?"

Lucas wasn't convinced, but Rick was. "I tell you, that's them," he replied. "Come on, let's get a little closer: time to introduce ourselves."

The two men continued their walk up the opposite side of the main street. Once a good distance past the Dodge, they crossed back over the busy road and started to double back.

"If we're lucky and they have no idea we've rumbled them, we stand a chance of catching them cold," Lucas said, "but if they've twigged, then it could be a whole different ball game." Rick didn't comment, the adrenalin was flowing, and he was past caring.

"Are you listening?" Lucas asked, turning to his colleague.

Rick stopped and smiled. "Of course I am," he said, "but you're just stating the obvious, so I'm not wasting my breath," and with that he was off again, weaving his way through the sea of parked cars toward their target.

The van was nose first in its parking space. The passenger door was ajar, and the engine was running. It was a panel style van with the two rear windows blanked out. As the two men approached from behind, they were conscious that the only way of being spotted was via the wing mirrors.

"Ricky, move up the line and come in on a forty-five: I'll do the same this side."

Lucas gestured to Rick to move up the right flank; again, Rick nodded and obeyed. As the HSG team drew closer it became evident the van was in a good vantage point. Even from twenty yards away, they could see clearly into the rear car park of Diablo's and the white Mustang was centre stage.

As Rick closed on the Dodge, he could clearly see someone in the passenger seat, but the man seemed oblivious to the approach. He had the window down, his arm leaning out, and was talking loudly to the driver, eyes front. Still unnoticed, Rick leant on the roof of the car in the next space and waited for a second.

"You fellas looking for anyone in particular?" he asked.

The passenger, a young skinhead with heavily tattooed arms, span round to see where the voice was coming from and, surprised to see the loitering South African, did a double-take. "What the fuck's it to you, cock-sucker?" he snarled as he started to open his door.

Rick stood his ground. "It's everything to me, dickhead," he answered. "You've been following us for the last couple of hours, so what's your problem?"

Rick was staying as calm as he could but knew it was about to get nasty. Desperate to confront his tormentor, the meathead was now making his way round the adjacent car and, as the driver leant over to see what was going on, he straightened and prepared to get out. Just as his hand touched the handle, Lucas hit him. It was a perfect right hook. Delivered through the open window, it caught the driver square in the jaw and connected with a resounding thud. The man's head snapped back. Teeth and blood sprayed out over the inside of the windscreen, then he slumped forward, out cold.

The skinhead was caught in two minds. Realising his colleague had just been taken out, he stopped in his tracks. He was only yards in front of Rick but the big South African didn't wait. At the exact moment of the hesitation, he launched himself headfirst. Bang! Another perfect connection. Not expecting a full dive flying head butt, the blow knocked the younger man clean off his feet and sent him sprawling backwards. As he hit the floor, Rick pounced again. Fuck the niceties, he thought as he went in for the kill. The skinhead tried to gain his bearings, but Rick kicked him hard in the groin twice, and that was enough; he wasn't getting up for a while.

As Lucas appeared from around the back of the Dodge, Rick was standing over the groaning body. "Fuck me, that hurt," he said as he rubbed the bright red mark above the bridge of his nose. Then, looking across at Lucas, he asked, "What we doing with these sad sacks now?"

"Lock them in the van," Lucas said, "then sling the keys and go."

After a brief scan round confirmed no one had watched the altercation, it took them seconds to open the rear doors and throw the battered and bleeding pair in. Once they were safely inside, they locked it.

"One sec, Rick," Lucas said, "before we go let's check the van over - might be something that connects us with these two."

"Like what?"

"Don't know exactly… just have a quick rummage through the front, will you - see if you can find anything."

The two men took a side each and proceeded to inspect the door pockets, the dash, under the seats, and the glove compartment. Twenty seconds later, Lucas looked over triumphantly at his partner. "Well, looky here, big boy; guess what I've just found?"

Rick looked up to see Lucas waving a scrap of paper at him, "What is it?" he asked.

"Looks like intel on us," Lucas grinned. "Scribbled notes about The Shooting Star: address details, shit like that, oh... and here's a description of the Chrysler we had." He paused as he read it over, "Yep, these boys were definitely after us…time to go."

Rick didn't need telling twice; he slammed the passenger door shut and started to head in the direction of Diablo's. Lucas did the same to the driver's side door. Then, with two short beeps and a flash of hazards, locked the van. He glanced round quickly then launched the keys skyward toward a lush landscaped area that divided the two car parks. "It'll take them a while to get over this little run-in," he said as he caught up with Rick, "just enough time for us to check out and disappear."

The HSG duo had no intention of hanging around. The Mustang swung out of Diablo's like a bat out of hell and sped off in the direction of The Shooting Star. Things had changed; the rules of engagement had been established and Rick was first to air his thoughts. "Pair of bastards deserved that," he said. "Who d'you reckon they're working for?"

"Got to be The Divinity," Lucas answered, "although I'm sure they're not regular members, looking like that – not a hope in hell."

Rick flicked his head from side to side as he checked his mirrors. "They started it," he said. "That baldy prick was definitely out to give me a kicking; he just wasn't fast enough, was he?"

"Not a chance," came the reply.

Glancing back at his colleague, Rick grinned, "Once you took his oppo out, he faltered… and that was a big mistake."

"Teamwork, Ricky," Lucas said with a thumbs-up, "just good old-fashioned teamwork."

***

Fifteen minutes later they were back at the motel. The early evening rush was in full swing and the place was a hive of activity. People were coming and going; there were check-ins, check-outs, suitcases, cars, and taxis everywhere; hopefully, the perfect cover for an unnoticed departure.

The two men raced to their rooms and, within minutes, were packed and ready to go. Back down in the lobby, Lucas stood in the queue at reception whilst Ricky loaded the car. Lucas didn't have to wait long. He gave the receptionist the excuse that they'd been unexpectedly summoned back to the UK so had to cut their visit short and leave immediately. The motel staff were sorry to hear the tale but very understanding and, as expected, he got the full spiel about coming back soon and all the rest of that good old American customer care bollocks. As the reception team waxed lyrical, Lucas listened impatiently but then stopped them short, saying they'd loved their stay and would definitely be back, but really had to go.

"Yeah, yeah, thanks again, Guys, see you next time," he said, before racing off toward the rear entrance.

The Mustang was in the car park. Rick was sat in the driver's seat. The bags were loaded, and the engine was running. All he was waiting for was Lucas to jump on board and they'd be away. Whilst he sat there, the South African hadn't stopped checking his surroundings. The events of the last few days - particularly the last few hours - had got him a touch paranoid and he was now starting to see bogey-men shaped shadows everywhere. By now the sun had faded and dusk was rolling in but, as the car park lights hadn't kicked in yet, the place was bathed in a ghostly half-light and, with every passing minute, Rick's ability to see clearly lessened. As he drummed his fingers nervously on the steering wheel, he muttered to himself, "Hurry up, Roxy.... for fuck's sake, hurry up."

***

Mordecai's pick-up pulled into the car park adjacent Diablo's and stopped. Now searching for his two young associates who'd called him twenty minutes earlier to explain they had a problem, he was incandescent. How the hell had his boys been spotted, he thought, and not just spotted but taken out, and taken out properly? Now he knew the interlopers were tougher than he'd given them credit for and that incensed him even more. Two of his key men stomped and dumped in the back of their own truck; Jesus, someone was going to have to do some serious explaining.

After circling for a few minutes, he spotted the Dodge on the far side of the lot. The shopping outlets were closing; most of the day's punters had gone home and the car park had quietened down. He parked up next to the van, went to the back doors, and banged on them hard. "Anyone home?" he growled.

There was no sound for a few seconds, then a tentative voice asked, "That you, Mord?"

"Of course it's me, you dipshit," he snapped. "Who else is going to come and save you pair of useless fuckers? Now, where's the keys?"

The muffled voice came again. "I don't know," it whimpered. "If they're not in the ignition, then they've got them."

Mordecai went to the front, but the doors were locked. "Those mother-fuckers" he muttered, "I'm going to kill the pair of them myself." Still cursing, he went to the back of his own truck, dropped the tail gate and hopped onto the bed. In the back, built off the floor just behind the cab, was a lock-up tool chest. The grizzled red-neck undid the heavy brass padlock, popped the lid, and reached inside for a crowbar.

After he prised the back doors of the Dodge open, he glared inside – and what a sorry sight it revealed. Both men were propped up against the back panel, battered and bruised, each looking pained and sheepish in equal measure.

"You idiots," he screamed, "I can't believe you let this happen! How the fuck did you get jumped? You were supposed to be doing the following!" He glared at the forlorn specimens in front of him and shook his head.

But there was nothing he could do so, begrudgingly, he helped the injured men out of the van and shoe-horned them into the back seat of his pick-up. Then, keen to get away from the scene as quickly as possible, he decided to leave the van and come back for it in the morning. As the pick-up pulled out of the parking lot, Ings thought about his next move. Patching up the walking wounded wouldn't be a problem but telling Leon Tate he'd lost the HSG team would be.

***

Lucas jogged across the motel car park, flung open the door of the waiting Mustang, and jumped in. But before he could utter a word, Rick was moving off. "What took you so long?" he asked as his partner scrambled to shut the door. "Feels like I've been sat here forever, waiting for you."

Lucas, well aware of how critical the situation was, could only apologise, "I know, I know," he said breathlessly, "sorry, there was a bit of a queue and then they went through the full rigmarole about how sad they were we were leaving and all the rest of that shit - you know how it is, don't you?"

Rick smiled; he did know, but he was on edge. Twice in one day they'd come across people wanting to cause them harm and he didn't like it much. "Where we heading, then?" he asked.

"Just give us a minute, will you."

"Well, it's already half eight and I'm bolloxed," Rick said, "so don't make it too far, alright?"

Lucas knew it was late, but they had to get away from The Shooting Star. It was obvious they were being watched so it was vital they find a new base; a base far away from the prying eyes of The Divinity and their vicious mercenaries. "Head toward Glendale," Lucas said. "I'm sure we can find something there, or if we spot anything decent on the way, pull in and we'll stay one night then weigh up what's best in the morning. That alright with you?"

Rick nodded his agreement and gunned the V8 beast north out of Scottsdale heading for the sanctuary of highway 101.

***

It was now 9.00 pm and, as he parked up in the floodlit car park of The Shooting Star, Mordecai was still seething. He knew his quarry had most likely left. Their surprise assault on his surveillance team had given them just enough of a window to do it, but he had to be sure and, under the circumstances, felt it best to do it himself.

With no evidence of the white Ford Mustang anywhere in the car park, he checked over the remaining motel grounds and even the adjacent side streets. After the extended search yielded nothing, he headed inside. At reception he politely asked about contacting two guests he'd met the other night in the lounge bar. "Two really nice guys," he said, "a tall Englishman and his South African colleague."

"Oh, sir, I'm so sorry but your friends have just checked out," the receptionist said, "probably no more than thirty minutes ago"

Mordecai feigned disappointment. "That's strange," he said, "I'm sure they said they were staying here for a couple of days."

The blonde put on her best customer facing smile. "Yes, sir, they were booked in until Sunday," she said sweetly, "but unfortunately they've had to cut their stay short."

Remaining in fake polite mode, the devious red-neck continued his enquiry. "Well, Miss, that's a real damn shame," he said as he looked down at the pretty blonde's name badge, "a real damn shame...Ellie."

"Yes, sir, that is very unfortunate," she said, attempting to sound concerned.

"Why did they leave so abruptly?" he asked, "Nothing serious, was it?

The receptionist was now starting to feel unnerved by the lean leather-faced figure standing in front of her. "No, sir, nothing serious," she replied. "I believe it was purely business related." Then, holding her smile, she debated what else to tell him, "Called back to the UK," she said eventually. "Boss's orders from what I was told."

Mordecai pulled a thoughtful face. "Maybe you have a contact phone number for them, do you?" he asked, then he held her gaze and tried to sound sincere. "It's really, really important that I to speak to them again," he said.

She hesitated, something didn't feel right and she couldn't disguise it. "No," she said a little too harshly, then - realising her slip – switched back to a more polished professional manner, "I'm awfully sorry, sir, I'm afraid not," she smiled weakly before adding, "all I am at liberty to say is that they've checked out and are heading back to the UK. In fact, you could probably catch them at the airport if it really is that *important*."

Ings knew he'd been rumbled. He stood rigid at the desk and glared at her; stubbornly she stared back. The frosty silence lasted no more than a few seconds then, without another word, he turned full about and strode off. As she watched him head for the door, she took a deep breath and felt an ice-cold shiver race up her spine.

CHAPTER 17

Who Can You Trust?

Babb was surprised to see Marion back so soon but, despite the reason for wanting to stay seeming a little vague, she was more than happy to have Big Sis round for another couple of days. "Sure, stay as long as you want," she'd said, "we'll have some fun."

North Peak National Park - fifty miles north of Flagstaff - was a sought-after location and Babb had loved it from the moment she'd laid eyes on it. Her cabin was small but, nestled in a peaceful forest oasis, it was picture book perfect. Surrounded on three sides by the rugged beauty of Arizona's most imposing mountain range, every visitor agreed it was a simply idyllic hideaway.

Babb was six years younger than Marion and divorced, but the ex-Mrs Teller positively thrived on her newly single status. Even before the ink was dry on her decree nisi the settlement cheque was destined for only one thing: the stunning little cabin. Marion, impressed with her baby sister's desire for change, was the first to encourage her to make the dream of Wild Mountain living a reality. She knew it would be the perfect fresh start. But also, slightly selfishly, knew she'd benefit as well - and she hadn't been wrong.

***

After finishing supper, the two sisters retired to the comfort of the lounge and cracked open a bottle of wine. After one glass of chilled pinot, Marion started to feel more relaxed and, as the alcohol glow kicked in a little more, she felt the urge to tell the story of The Divinity and the Book of Martyr's recovery.

Babb was surprised. Well aware that to most the work of a literary researcher was pretty unexciting, her big sister didn't usually talk about her job, but tonight was different. As the tale of the long, complex hunt unfolded, Babb sat enthralled.

Marion left no stone unturned. From her first contact with Calvin Lentz on the initial search, right up to the events of that morning's break-in at her home, she explained every twist and turn, and Babb couldn't get enough. "Go on, Sis, this is great," she encouraged.

Marion was not one to over dramatize and never felt the urge to make out she was something she wasn't but telling the story of the hunt in full made her realise just how beguiling a tale it was and, as she talked, Babb absorbed every morsel. With so many questions popping into her head she could hardly contain herself.

"Meredith Higham," she exclaimed excitedly, "yeah...that name does sound familiar, although if you and Kitty play bridge with her it's most likely one of you mentioned her previously to me – could that be it?"

Marion looked at her sister and thought hard. "I don't know, maybe I have," she said, "I can't remember – but she is quite a lady, I can tell you that much." Marion paused for a sip of wine, "You could have heard of her through other circles; she's popular, does a lot of charity work... and I mean *a lot*."

Babb nodded. "Could be," she said slowly." It'll come to me, I'm sure, just let me think on it. More importantly, though, this Lucas guy - what's he like - is he genuine? Can you really trust him?"

Marion couldn't help but smile as she answered. "Yes, I think he is," she said. "Mind you, he does get very forthright at times, almost rude actually, but I think it's only because he cares, so I can forgive him for that." She paused momentarily and smiled, "And yes... I do believe I can trust him."

By the time the two sisters retired for the night, there was nothing about The Divinity, the HSG, or John Foxes' controversial classic that hadn't been deliberated. Now Babb knew as much as her elder sister did about the saga and she was hooked. To her the whole thing really did sound rather exhilarating.

***

The Glendale Ramada was not a patch on The Shooting Star, but it was cheap, cheerful, and both Lucas and Rick got a good night's sleep. They happened upon it by pure chance. It was simply the first reasonable looking place they'd come across on the forced retreat from Scottsdale but for a 'one night catch your breath stop-over' it did the trick.

Yesterday had not panned out as expected; so much happened in just one day that it seemed unreal. So now, sitting in the bustling breakfast room washing down bacon and eggs with a strong coffee, was a good time to start discussing options. As ever, Lucas was keen to ensure they got their priorities right.

"First job is the report for Gerry," he said, "but I won't ring him; we'll just send it over with a basic explanation as to why it's late." He looked at Rick and pulled a face, "Best not go into too much detail about our altercation… he'll only start worrying even more."

Conscious it was 7.30am Saturday morning, both men were surprised that no one had chased them for the previous day's report. It was now well past 3.00pm in the UK - plenty of time for someone to notice it hadn't been posted and start pestering.

"I can't understand why we've had no contact," Lucas said. "Obviously, there's more important things to worry about than us."

It was less than twenty-four hours since the last update call and maybe he'd been so positive during that brief exchange that Gerry was confident everything was under control. If so, Lucas thought, more fool him!

Back in the room, Rick compiled the report; Lucas proofread it, made a few amendments then sent it off. The report covered the surveillance issue and the decision to move hotels. It explained that Miss Armstrong was proving useful but kept the details of the break-in and her temporary relocation under wraps. Their run-in with the black Dodge was also mentioned, but it was played down to no more than a suspicion of being followed. "So much for the company's 'whole truth and nothing but the truth' mantra," Lucas said as he clicked send.

Once the report had gone, Rick checked his email. Hardly any had landed since he last looked and certainly none of any importance – except for one. One from Sarah received during the night was titled, 'Meredith Higham – Additional Info'.

Rick scanned it quickly. "Looks like Sarah's been busy again," he said. "She's sent more on the Higham woman...more detail, all good stuff by the looks of it…and, ohh, you're going to love this," he paused as he looked up from the screen, "you ready?"

Lucas was all ears. "Yeah - fire away!" he smiled.

"Well, it would seem the woman is much more than a fringe associate. In fact, reading this I'd say she was more akin to a full Board Director than a passing acquaintance."

Lucas looked confused. "How d'you mean?" he asked.

"Well, from what Sarah's saying," Rick stopped as he read ahead, "seems this Meredith one is a full blown ambassador for The Divinity; apparently, she's a leading light for their fundraising activities, and one of the big players behind the Central America outreach projects." He paused and looked up from his computer screen, "If everything Sarah is saying here is true, then Meredith the gossip has been playing games with our cutesy little librarian - but why would she do that?"

Lucas didn't know the answer. He was as puzzled as Rick and, as he eased himself down into the room's cheap plastic armchair, he ran a hand through his hair and sighed, "What the hell's going on with these people?" He smiled, "Shit, all we need now is for Marion to confess she's a Divinity High Priestess and we've cracked it!"

Rick grinned. "Yeah, it's mad, innit?" he said. "We've got ourselves into a right old load of bollocks. All this hassle just because we came for one old book." He looked directly at his partner then shook his head. "I'm starting to sound like you, Sarge, all this 'really should have been simple' whingeing, but, mate, I tell you: I'm starting to agree with you. Seems like every passing hour takes us further up shit creek."

As the two men sat quietly mulling over their predicament, the room's TV caught Lucas's eye. It had been on in the background all the time, but he'd taken little notice. Now it was showing a local news bulletin and, intrigued, Lucas leant forward. "Hey, Rick, check this out!" he said.

As he turned to the screen, Rick grabbed the remote and upped the volume. An attractive, dark haired female reporter was talking to camera at the side of a deserted highway. The yellow highlighter banner running along the bottom of the screen looped the headline: Church Minister Slain In Desert Car-Jacking, and the reporter went on to explain that a Catholic cleric from the Tucson area had been found shot dead at the side of a desert road west of Phoenix. The local police believed the minister had been the victim of a robbery. They found traces of two cars at the scene, but no vehicles were found in the vicinity and the victim had nothing of value on him. He'd been shot twice in the chest and left to die in the dust. The news correspondent quickly went on to add that the police estimated the murder had taken place sometime late afternoon or early evening of Friday, and that the victim had been identified as a Reverend Gary Coleman.

Unable to believe what they were seeing, the two men stared at the TV open mouthed.

"After what we just said," Lucas said, "I mean, can you fucking believe that? This shit is getting weirder and weirder by the minute!" He was now pacing round the small room in an agitated state looking at his bemused colleague. "Ricky, we've got to move again. We need to find another base – these people are not messing around, are they?" He took a deep breath, "It's no coincidence the guy we're supposed to meet is now dead, is it?"

"Not a fuckin' chance," Rick replied.

Lucas stopped pacing and stared out the window frantically rubbing his chin, "In fact, when you think about it," he continued, "this is the second time we've been told the Reverend's dead; that's twice in five days, Ricky."

"Yeah," Rick said, "but this time I'm getting the feeling it's true."

CHAPTER 18

The Same Old Song?

"Thanks for the call, Calvin. It's not good news for any of us, but the update is appreciated." Gerry Hanlon sighed, "What a bloody nightmare…"

"Yes, Gerry, it's a difficult situation, I'm afraid," Lentz said apologetically, "and I don't really know what else to say about it at this moment in time."

"It's not your fault," Gerry replied, "we appreciate you're only the messenger - there's not a lot more you can do, except maybe send over official confirmation of what's happened when you get a chance." He paused, "It would help with our paperwork."

"Yeah, no problem," the Scot said. "I'll sort it now."

"Well, really, that's it then, Cal… nothing more to say other than thanks again for being so prompt with the call."

Gerry said his goodbyes and put the phone down. It was not a call he could have anticipated; it was not a call he wanted. In fact, it was the last thing he bloody needed. Shaking his head, he picked up the handset again and dialled. "Ray, its Gerry. Better come down to my office, you won't believe the latest from the States."

"Oh - what now?"

"It's not good," Gerry answered. "I think we've got some re-organising to do."

"Two seconds," Ray answered, then headed down the corridor in double quick time. As the CEO hastily grabbed the chair opposite his partner, he expected the worst. "So, what's the story, Gerry?" he asked. "What's happened now?"

Gerry took a theatrical gulp then started to explain, "I've just had Calvin Lentz on the phone telling me The Divinity have just issued an official statement." He rolled his eyes. "A statement claiming that one of their key members, a Reverend Coleman, has been murdered in an armed robbery... and that the items stolen from him include a rare and valuable first edition of the Book of Martyr's."

Ray's jaw dropped. "You're kidding me," he gasped, "but hold on a sec... we've already been told this guy was killed in a car crash earlier this week, so how can he die twice?"

"Who knows, but apparently this time it's for real," Gerry said, "been all over the local TV news and in the press, so it's definitely genuine. Their man Coleman has been shot dead. Arizona state police discovered the body late yesterday at the side of a road west of Phoenix."

"Dear God," he replied. "We're dealing with real psychos here, aren't we?"

"I think so," Gerry said. "It's getting well out of hand."

HSG's CEO was now seriously concerned about the team in Arizona. "Lucas hasn't said anything about this, has he?" He didn't wait for a reply. "What did the last report say? Did it mention Coleman? Have they been issuing their daily reports on time?"

Gerry frowned. "They were, up until Thursday," he answered, "but that was late...and we haven't had yesterday's yet, so we've no idea how much they know." He stopped as he thought about their most recent communiqué. "That last report made no mention of Coleman, all it really said was they'd had a run-in with a couple of heavies.... and had found a tracker in the rental car, that was about it."

Ray now looked even more worried. "Shit, I hope they're OK," he said, "better give them a bell and check. What time will it be there now?"

Gerry looked at his watch. "Well, its 4.00 pm here, so for them it'll be 8.00am, I'll ring in a minute and find out what they're up to and what they know."

As the two men sat silently contemplating their next move, they were interrupted by Steve Harrison. The R&I chief appeared unnoticed at the open office door and knocked gently on the wooden surround. Gerry looked up, "Hello, Steve, didn't hear you sneaking up on us – what's up?"

The smartly dressed ex-cop looked flustered. "Sorry to disturb you gents," he said, "but we've just received the Arizona team's latest report and it makes for worrying reading – looks like we could have some major issues brewing out there."

Gerry and Ray looked at each other and in almost perfect unison scowled, "Tell us about it!"

***

Lucas couldn't wait to get on the road. The Ramada had done them proud for one night, but it was time to go, time to find another base. So, with bags packed and the bill settled, it was time to decide on which direction to head. Rick, as ever, looked to his partner to decide. "Where next, Roxy?" he asked. "Where do you fancy?"

Lucas's head was still spinning, but after a few seconds he finally responded, "At this rate I reckon we'll soon be heading home, so let's not stray too far from the airport, eh? Why don't we head toward Phoenix, check out the old town with all its Wild West history stuff… and just wait for a call."

Rick didn't mind either way. He just shrugged his shoulders, grunted a less than enthusiastic, "Sounds good to me," then ambled off toward the car.

***

When he got the news about the reverends carjacking, Calvin Lentz had been at home hunched over his overflowing desk. The call had come directly from Dr Reid's legal advisor, Reece Woods QC. Mr Woods, as the man ultimately responsible for the return deal, was the first point of contact for any formal Divinity correspondence, so, immediately after informing Dr Reid of the situation, he'd passed the news on to Wiseman & Scott.

Calvin was shocked but not totally surprised at the latest news. Throughout the whole return saga his team had been convinced The Divinity was a dubious organisation, but this was a step too far and they were all aghast at this latest twist in proceedings. Surely the bigoted deviants hadn't murdered one of their own as cover for breaking the return agreement; could the book really be worth killing for?

***

Dr Reid was equally as shocked at the revelation and immediately summoned the Senior Council for another meeting. Two years of hard work disappearing down the drain in one barbaric act was something they would not accept without a fight. The Synod leader was now conscious the disastrous news put a different slant on the assurances made during his meeting with the HSG representatives. Things had radically changed; Gerry Hanlon could huff, bluff and promise all he liked, but The Divinity had played a trump card. It was game over – or at least that's what they wanted everyone to believe…

CHAPTER 19

Coming Home?

Concerned about the very public demise of Reverend Coleman, Dubois demanded an explanation. It was in total contradiction to his explicit orders and, although for now the authorities believed the brutal murder had been motivated by robbery, he still wanted answers.

When the news broke, Tate was summoned to Dubois's office and The Divinity leader didn't waste time on niceties. In no mood for small talk, he launched straight into lambasting the Security Chief. "What part of 'be patient' did you not fucking understand, Leon?" he snarled.

The Monsignor towered over his subordinate. Staring down, eyes brimming with menace, the evil overtone palpable, he continued to rant, "Come on man explain yourself, why did it happen, why, in God's name, did you contradict my orders?"

Tate stood his ground. He knew Dubois could be a vicious sonofabitch; he was a fire brand with an unpredictable temper and an acid tongue, but from bitter experience he knew how to appease him. "Monsignor, I must apologise profusely," he grovelled. "The last-minute change was my call - a deliberate strategic switch." He took a deep breath and bowed his head, "You see, it suddenly became apparent - excuse the pun - that we had a chance to kill two birds with one stone, an opportunity I felt too good to miss."

With that, Tate fell silent, clasped his hands in front of him, and stood motionless, awaiting a response. Dubois watched his Security Chief closely then, without a flicker of emotion, spoke. "Well, do tell,

Leon," he prompted. "Tell me what was too good an opportunity to miss, and why wasn't I informed before it happened?"

The smaller man lowered his head, licked his lip, then looked up and began to explain. The change of plan had been decided at the last minute by him, and by him alone. It had suddenly dawned on him that if the loss of the Reverend was more public, it would get splashed across the TV news and in the local press, then facts could be manipulated. Facts that would become the ideal cover for the disappearance of the Book of Martyrs. They could easily prove Coleman was the appointed custodian of the book. So, the story was simple. During one of his many cross-state business trips, the Reverend gets stopped. He's robbed at gun point on a deserted stretch of highway; shot dead, dumped in the desert, and everything else, including the book, vanish. It's an appalling crime, so it's reported widely in the media, and suddenly it's very hard for those chasing the book's return to dispute the facts. They have no real alternative but to accept it's gone, certainly in the short-term anyway.

The Monsignor, now sat back behind his desk, listened intently to the articulate explanation and only when Tate had finished did he push back in his chair and stroke his goatee. "Well, Leon, I simply don't know what to believe," he said calmly. "Did your red-neck Neanderthals fuck up again and you've covered well.... or maybe you simply are a devious little motherfucker who's done us all a favour." He stopped and then, for the first time in the exchange, appeared to smile. "I really do hope it's the latter, Leon, I really do."

***

Now Dubois had calmed, the two Divinity men went on to discuss the police investigation. The Monsignor wanted every detail; he needed to check the story was tight, there could be no gaps and no omissions. Tate didn't hide anything. He briefed his leader on exactly how the disposal had played out and repeatedly told him his operators had left no loose ends. They'd done a tidy job, he said, and was confident that under close scrutiny it would all stack up. He also explained the issue of a formal statement: The Divinity's own news feed confirmed the sad loss of their cherished colleague and had expressed dismay at losing him under such tragic circumstances. The statement contained a brief explanation of how he'd been attacked whilst on Church business and went on to make it clear that this fact made it all the more difficult for them to come to terms with. "It couldn't be sincerer," Tate said. "It's a heart-breaking message."

In his eyes, the statement was a shrewd bit of propaganda, a master class in misinformation. It backed up every angle of their story and would go a long way to stopping some of the inevitable awkward questions in their tracks.

Dubois reluctantly agreed. "Ok, Leon," he said, "we'll leave it like that for now."

***

Lucas and Rick were floundering; they'd just left Glendale and, in the absence of any firm plan, were heading in the general direction of Phoenix. As they passed the first 'Old Town' tourist sign Lucas's mobile rang. "This'll be base calling," he said, holding the phone at arm's length and squinting at the screen.

He wasn't wrong; he thumbed the green button. "Hello, Gerry," he answered, unable to hide the hint of devilment in his voice. "Long time no hear."

There was a noticeable pause, then Gerry's dulcet tones kicked in. "That you, Lucas?" he barked. "Are you OK, is Rick with you, where the hell are you and - more importantly - what the fuck is going on?"

Lucas turned to Ricky and grimaced, "Let's put this on speaker, eh, Ricky. This is going to be interesting." He fumbled with the phone for a second, then asked, "Gerry… can you hear me, hello… are you there? We've got you on speaker now, OK?"

"Yes, I'm here," Gerry answered, "and, yes, I can hear you, and I hope that's the both of you."

Rick answered first, "Yes we're both here and both still in one piece."

"Thank Christ for that!" the Ops Director said, sounding genuinely relieved. "I've been worrying myself sick about you two; no calls and no report for nearly 24 hours. Then we get one, but it's late and light on detail. Then, to top it off, we're inundated with reports this Coleman fella has been shot dead." He drew a long, exasperated breath. "What the hell's going on, boys?"

As they continued toward the old town, Lucas and Rick took it in turns to bring their concerned chief up to speed. This time they left nothing out; he got the full story, warts and all.

"Jesus Christ, this is worse than I thought," Gerry said at the end of their explanation. "These people are absolute nutters, pure and simple - deranged, brainwashed psychos all of them - capable of anything." There was a brief silence before he announced, "So that's it, we're calling it a day; we want you back ASAP, you hear me boys? You're coming home, and I mean right now."

***

Mordecai hadn't been able to fathom the rationale behind Tate's last-minute change of heart over Coleman. The initial brief had been clear. No fuss, no mess and no trace - but with one phone call all that changed. He may have been surprised by the U-turn, but it didn't bother him much, "A job's a job," he'd said. "If *the man* changes his mind on how he wants it done, well, that's his prerogative."

Despite the last-minute alterations, it had gone well: the poor, unsuspecting cleric did as he was told with no histrionics and didn't have a clue his lonely journey along that desolate, sand-blasted desert road would be his last. Ings was confident the Reverend's removal had gone to plan but was now troubled by the fact he had no idea where the HSG men were. He'd failed in his primary task; he'd lost the target, his ace surveillance team had been rumbled, seriously out-foxed, then stomped, and now - to add insult to injury - he'd arrived at The Shooting Star just minutes too late to catch the interlopers checking out. “Mother-fuckers,” he muttered to himself as he stormed out of the Motel. “Pair of Goddam mother-fuckers.”

They’d out-smarted him again - a fact Mordecai was now beginning to resent with a passion.

***

Marion was intent on making the most of her unplanned stay. After a short morning hike - which had still taken three hours - the sisters returned to the cabin to eat. A chicken and dill pickle salad was followed by ice cream then a large, leisurely iced tea out on the deck. Marion was enjoying herself: it was an enviable lifestyle, one she could quite easily get used to, and when Babb went back in to tidy up she stayed outside to savour the peace and tranquillity.

As Babb cleared away the lunch plates she noticed Marion’s mobile on the kitchen breakfast bar. “Marion, you’ve missed a call,” she yelled to her sister. “Looks like it’s from this morning, do you want me to bring the phone to you?”

“No, it’s OK, B,” she answered, “just leave it there…it won’t be important, most likely just Bill looking for an update - I’m sure it can wait.”

She finished her tea, then eased back in the stretch fabric lounger she had nestled in. As she closed her eyes and gently exhaled, she thought about the missed call. Suddenly it dawned on her it could actually be important; as things were, it was more likely to be Mr Roxby than the library. Hurriedly, she went into the kitchen.

Checking the phone, she saw there had been two missed calls. As suspected, one was from her ASL colleague, Bill Stanton; the other she didn’t recognise. The caller on the unknown number had left a message. Intrigued, she pressed the little blue arrow to listen to the voice mail:

> *“Marion, its Meredith Higham – I need to speak to you on a rather personal matter and it really is quite urgent. So,*

if you could please ring me straight back on this number it would be appreciated, many thanks, hope to speak soon."

As she listened, Marion frowned, so much so Babb became concerned, "Are you alright, Sis? You look awful worried, what was that about… nothing serious I hope?"

Marion didn't respond immediately. She just shrugged her shoulders and played the message again but this time on speaker so Babb could hear it. "That's odd," she said when it finished, "why's Meredith desperate to speak to me about a personal matter - what on earth would that be about?"

Marion was puzzled and now looked to her sister for an answer. Babb was quick to respond, "I'm not sure, Sis," she said, "but you've got to think it's something to do with this Book carry-on, haven't you?" Babb was sure there was a connection; she'd listened very closely to her sister's tale - and to her - a call out of the blue at this stage from the much-discussed widow was far too coincidental not to be related.

"Yeah - could be," Marion replied, "so let's find out."

She dialled the number. It took a few seconds to connect then rang five or six times and went dead. Nothing but a faint click, then ominous silence. Immediately, she tried again but this time it didn't even connect. She tried a third time but again no joy. Now it appeared the number was unavailable, and permanently by the sound of it.

"How weird is that?" Marion said as she looked blankly at her phone. "Maybe I should try the other number I've got for her - what do you think?"

After agreeing it couldn't do any harm to ring on the number she'd used previously, Marion scrolled down her phone's contact list and stopped at the entry: *Meredith (Bridge).* Then she took a deep breath and pushed the call button.

Hi, this is Meredith, I'm sorry I can't take your call at the moment – but please leave your name and number and I will get back to you as soon as I can.

The message played almost the instant she'd released the call button. Is that normal? she thought to herself. Then her anxiety level began to rise. "Something's wrong, Babb," she said, wide eyed, "I just know it is..."

For a couple of minutes, the two sisters sat in the lounge talking but both were at a loss for ideas. After a further five minutes of unproductive brainstorming they decided to call Lucas and see if he had any suggestions.

***

Disillusioned after their mammoth call with Gerry, Lucas and Rick pulled in for fuel. But as the car stopped, the phone rang again. As he recognised the number, Lucas's stomach tightened. "Hello, Marion," he answered, "are you alright? Is everything OK?"

There was a brief pause, then she replied, "Yes, thank you, Mr Roxby, I'm fine - are you?"

"Yes, Ma'am, we're fine thanks...I think. What's up?"

"Well, you see, Mr Roxby... I'm a little puzzled and rather concerned over something that occurred this morning, and, really, I need your advice."

"Yeah, no problem. Just tell me what happened, and I'll do my best."

She quickly went on to explain Meredith's voice mail message and her failed attempts to get back to her. Keen to stress that it was odd Meredith would ring her directly - especially with a request like that – she repeatedly told Lucas it was out of character. "It's not like her, not at all."

Lucas listened as the sweet voiced librarian explained her concerns. He did not interrupt, he waited patiently until she pitched the inevitable question, "So what do you think she wants, Mr Roxby, any ideas?"

"Marion, have you listened to any local news today?" he asked calmly. "Watched any TV bulletins this morning?"

"No.... nothing," she replied. "Why do you ask?" As she spoke, Marion was gently shaking her head as if subconsciously reinforcing her answer about not seeing any TV reports.

Lucas continued, "Well, I think the call you got is related to a carjacking that happened last night out in the desert west of Phoenix... it's been all over the local news this morning."

Marion didn't say a word. For a second she digested what had just been said, "A carjacking.... what do you mean, Mr Roxby, what relevance would that have to Meredith's message?"

***

It took Lucas ten minutes to explain his theory on Meredith's message and, whilst Marion was aghast to hear that Reverend Coleman had been murdered, she couldn't fathom the link. "I'm telling you, Marion, these people are dangerous," he said, "and we've got to be careful. To me it looks like they've just killed off one of their own to throw us off the scent....and you can't play much dirtier than that, can you?"

Marion didn't answer the question. "So, Mr Roxby," she said, "are you saying Meredith was ringing to tell me about Reverend Coleman's murder?"

"I'd guess she was," he replied, "but maybe she also wanted to know if you knew anything about the circumstances surrounding it." He paused. "My feeling is there's more to that woman than you think."

"In what way?"

"I'm not sure," he said, "but maybe she knows you have a connection to the book."

"A fanciful suggestion," she replied abruptly. "Why on earth would she think I know anything about the book and, even if she did, why would she believe I need to know about a murder in the desert?" Marion's tone said it all; she was not impressed with the errant Englishman's ideas and wanted him to know it.

"Look, Miss Armstrong," he said, "I'm not trying to cause offence." Lucas was now back to formal titles, which was something she'd never dropped. "I'm just saying that this woman may know a lot more about you than you think." He stopped to clear his throat. "You talk quite regularly with her at the Country Club, don't you? So surely you say something about yourself, even if only occasionally – work, hobbies, men.... it can't all be one-way traffic, can it?"

"Mr Roxby," she bristled, "let me put the record straight here, I am a private person, my business is my business and my conversations with Meredith Higham are pure small talk - nothing more, nothing less - period. If she wishes to run off at the mouth and tittle tattle about all and sundry, then who am I to stop her? As I've said in my earlier conversations with you, my sister and I just sit there and listen.... We simply smile politely and nod in all the right places."

Now pacing around the rest area of the gas station, Lucas struggled to hide his bemusement. The woman really was an intriguing mix. On the surface a straight-laced, demure librarian – but underneath the façade he was beginning to think she was part firecracker.

"OK, OK...," he replied, "let's call a truce. I'm sorry for upsetting you, it was not my intention at all." He paused, awaiting a response, but she remained silent, so he continued, "Moving forward, I suggest you keep trying to contact Mrs Higham. Go visit if you have to. She made the first move, so see where it leads, but, like I said, be careful how you go and please keep me updated on anything you find out."

By now, Marion had cooled and accepted his climb-down graciously; she even thanked him for his thoughts on the matter. With the conversation over, Lucas walked back toward the car and, careful not to touch the baking hot roof, stooped down at the passenger window to look through at Rick. The big South African was sat slumped in the driver's seat playing happily on his phone.

"We can't go back yet," Lucas said, "there's still stuff to do." Rick looked up from the screen as his partner continued, "And anyway, if we do pack up and leave it means we failed, failed before we even got started, right?"

Lucas was desperate for Rick to agree but didn't give him a chance to answer. "I'm not having it!" he said, as he gave the Mustang's roof a quick slap. "Out manoeuvred by a gang of zealots and their yahoo heavies is no way to leave a job."

The plug had been pulled, the operation was over, and they'd been told to come home. But the thought of returning empty-handed was weighing heavy. Lucas wasn't ready to quit, he was sure there were still things they could do and loose ends they should tie up. Fuck 'em, he thought, I'm staying.

The ex-sapper wanted to stick with it and now all he needed was his partner to see it the same way...

CHAPTER 20

U-Turn

Whilst Sarah's Cirrus 5 revelation got the ball rolling, it was Calvin Lentz's later email that sealed the deal:

> *Gerry/Ray/Sarah,*
>
> *Just a quick note to let you know we've had another communiqué from The Divinity and in this one they are apologising for the loss of the PCOS's book! They've also offered to meet with your collection guys. They claim they would like the opportunity to explain the circumstances face to face before they return to the UK. Sounds a strange one to me and, as you are well aware, I've never trusted them, so please give me a ring to discuss as soon as you get the chance.*
>
> *Best Regards,*
>
> *Cal.*
>
> *P.S. Hope Sarah got the inventory books OK.*

***

The first of Gerry's afternoon calls to the States had been brief and to the point. As the timescales were tight, he gave Lucas a rapid lowdown on the Cirrus 5 situation, explained it was predicted to show within twenty-four hours, then gave him the news about The Divinity's bizarre offer.

"Ring us back ASAP," Gerry said finally. "The two of you decide if you want to meet them – OK?"

"No problem," Lucas replied. "Ring you in twenty."

It now looked like they were staying, so a happier Lucas hurried across the forecourt to tell Rick. "Let's meet the bastards," he said, "it could be the perfect way to get back in."

Rick had been sat straight backed, arms-crossed, and scowling throughout Lucas's explanation. "You can count me out; they either want to knock us off…or more likely convince us their crock-of-shit story is true, then make sure we get on a plane."

"Probably," Lucas said nodding, "but you never know- those nice people might be offering to make up for the problems they've caused us."

"Not a bleeding chance," Rick spat, "and you know it - one way or another they just want to know we've gone, it's as simple as that." The South African was adamant it was a bad idea and it was obvious from the glare he wasn't likely to change his mind.

"Don't worry," Lucas smirked, "I'm kidding - I don't think for one second they actually want to do anything positive for us."

"Good," Rick said. "For a moment there I thought you were going soft on me."

"I know I have my moments," he replied, "but that wasn't one of them."

Rick looked relieved. "So, what are you saying?" he asked.

"What I'm saying is that attack is the best form of defence, so I reckon we say yes but go with the intention of trying to use it to our advantage - you never know, they might just let something slip."

Rick didn't look convinced but was mulling over options. He always listened to Lucas's ideas and usually agreed instantly with him, but this time it was not that simple. "OK, I'll play along," he said eventually. "You tell Gerry it's a goer, say yes we're willing to meet and let's see what the fuckers come back with. But then…" he paused and looked at Lucas hard, "if we don't like what they're proposing, we just don't show. That keeps our options open… right?"

"Yeah, yeah, OK, that'll do me," Lucas replied. "I'll call Gerry back and tell him to make the contact, see what they're offering – I'll just say we think it's worth a shot."

With that, Lucas got up from the cafeteria table they'd hogged for the last two hours and headed back outside to ring Gerry.

***

After the earlier call with Gerry, Lucas had been pleased but now coming back in after a second chat with the Chief, he seemed even more upbeat. "Result! Ricky, the stay of execution has been confirmed."

"You knew it was coming. How long did he say this time?"

"Another three days," Lucas grinned. "Total U-turn or what?"

"Chuffed, aren't you?"

"Are you kidding? What with this weird comet shit to look forward to and a meet with our favourite cultists, what's not to like?"

"Look, Sarge, don't get too carried away," Rick said, wagging his finger. "It's just an extra couple of days, then its home time, OK?" The South African was quick to play this latest development down. "Anyway, after another three days of this shit I'll definitely be ready for home. Any longer and my Mrs will file for divorce… again."

"Yeah, yeah, I know, Rick, but don't worry, you'll be back home soon, mate, but in the meantime we've got a job to do, so let's get back to the car and you get us the hell out of Dodge, OK? Ha, yeah, literally!" he laughed.

***

Just as Gerry and Ray were starting to think their unexpected and long Saturday at work was coming to an end, Jo rang through again. As they'd been finishing off their second call of the day to Lucas, Ron Stafford had been looking to speak to Ray as a matter of urgency.

"Did he give any details, or was that it?" Ray queried.

"That was it. He was very brief, didn't say a word about what it concerned…just said it was urgent and could I get you to ring him back ASAP."

"Thanks, Jo, I'll add it to the list."

It was 5.25pm on a sunny Saturday afternoon and the HSG Directors were still sat in the same positions they'd occupied for most of the day.

"Good job the air con's good in here," Ray said. "If we'd done this in my office we'd have expired by now." The CEO had not been joking, it was still 24 degrees C outside, and they'd been stuck in Gerry's office all day.

"What first?" Gerry asked. "Do you ring Ronnie, or do I ring Calvin?"

"Toss for it."

Gerry liked the suggestion and grinned as he prepared to flip a shiny new pound coin. "Heads, you ring Ronnie; tails, I ring Calvin…. OK?"

"Fine by me," Ray gave a wry smile. "Flip away!"

The two men watched the pound coin rise and rotate. As it span, it caught the late afternoon sunlight filtering through the window. Then it fell back to earth. And, as it landed on the back of Gerry's left hand, the fingers of his right slapped down over it. "What do you reckon, then?" he asked.

"I don't care," Ray said, "just show me."

Gerry proceeded to turn his hand back slowly from over the coin. "Tails it is!" he said, before reaching for the phone. "So here we go… I ring Calvin - you sit and listen."

Gerry got the easy draw. The call to Calvin Lentz was straightforward, all he had to do was confirm they were willing to explore The Divinity's offer to meet and then it was over to W&S to set it up, it couldn't be simpler.

"OK. Gerry," Calvin agreed, "if that's what you want me to tell them - I'll get it sorted."

Ray got the short straw: the call to Ronnie was difficult. When he finally answered, the big man sounded well-oiled. Veering wildly from psychotic ramblings to stammered apologies, all interlaced with a handful of incoherent muttered threats of vengeance, it was not an easy conversation to have.

"Look, Ronnie," Ray said as calmly as he could, "best thing is you come in and see us first thing on Monday to talk this through.... can you get here for, I don't know, say 9.00am? I know it's awkward but obviously the sooner we work out where we're going, the better, OK?"

Ray's tone sounded like he cared and, in reality, he did. During his recent dealings with Ron Stafford he'd actually grown to like the man, maybe only a little, but there was something there. Yes, they'd got off to a wobbly start and, yes, he could be as fierce as he looked, but surely he wasn't as bad as people said. So what if he was an overweight gargoyle with crooked yellow teeth, a gangster lifestyle, and a volatile disposition? Something between Ronnie and Ray had clicked.

"Yeah, yeah, you're right," the voice wavered. "I'll come to you Monday, 'bout 9.00am's good. Should be with-it by then, and no drink. Thank you, Raymond, bye for now."

Gerry was unable to contain his astonishment at the call's surreal nature. "What the hell was that all about?" he asked.

Ray shook his head. "Sounds like our man might have had a change of heart. Maybe things aren't quite like he thought, eh?"

"Can't wait for that one – yet another bombshell?"

By now, Ray looked visibly drained and his business partner was obviously feeling the same way. "Right, Raymond - that's it!" Gerry said. "I can't take any more of this Saturday working bollocks, so let's call it a day and if anything breaks I'll ring you."

Ray managed a weak smile, "Couldn't have put it better myself!"

***

Since her last, rather terse, conversation with Lucas, Marion had tried to contact Meredith several times, but each attempt had failed. Like the earlier calls they rang out briefly, then ended with an ominous click. Now it seemed going round to visit the Higham house was the only positive thing she could do. "Babb, you fancy a ride out? See if we can call in on Meredith and find out what's happening?"

Babb pulled a face, "Do you actually know where she lives?"

"No, not exactly," came the truthful reply, "but I know the street, well, the area really," Marion paused, "but it's a big house so I'm sure we'll be OK."

Ten minutes later, the little yellow Honda was heading South, aiming for the exclusive suburbs of Flagstaff and, as the sisters frantically discussed how they should go about finding the right house, Marion was hopeful. "I'm sure we'll find it, B," she said, "we've got to do something haven't we? I mean, I can't just sit on your deck sunning myself and drinking iced tea all day, can I?"

"You could," Babb replied, "but I'm sure this will be more interesting."

"I wouldn't bet on it," Marion chuckled.

Babb sat perched on the passenger seat like a meerkat sentry and was now desperate to help, "Do you know what kind of car she drives?"

"Good thinking," Marion said, "and you know what? Yes, I do. Meredith drives a real nice convertible. It's a Mercedes, a fancy looking thing: she showed it off to Kitty and me one day in the parking lot of the club. It's like a powder blue colour with cream leather seats." The pony-tailed librarian suddenly looked pleased with herself for recalling this key detail. "If we can find the car, then we can find her!"

Marion had a rough idea which street Meredith lived on and, apart from one minor detour, it didn't take the sisters long to find it. Cedar Drive was a long sweeping tree-lined affair and the ancient yellow Honda crawling slowly along it - checking front drives and forecourts for signs of a blue Mercedes soft top – looked decidedly out of place. But suddenly, from nowhere, a black limousine appeared and came careering round the bend toward them. "Oh, my God," Babb yelped. "What's his problem!?"

Marion instinctively swung her car as close to the kerb as possible and, as the sedan roared past like a freight train on a deadline, the

Honda was left shuddering in a swirl of road dust. "Dear Lord" Marion exclaimed," why on earth would someone drive like that? That's just plain crazy…for a second I thought he was going to hit us." As she glanced in the rear-view mirror, the blacked-out car was already disappearing into the distance, its two small wing flags flapping furiously as it sped away. "Let's keep looking, B," she said, undeterred, "we're near the end of the road, surely we must be close." She paused, then as an afterthought added, "I do hope that crazy car's nothing to do with Meredith. You don't think it has, do you, B?"

"I wouldn't have thought so," came a reassuring reply.

After another fifty yards, Babb started pointing wildly to a house across the street. "Over there, Marion, look there's a blue Mercedes convertible, through those railings! Do you see it, out front there - is that Meredith's?"

Parked on the gravel drive of a swish retro styled villa was a powder blue Mercedes Benz convertible. Marion slowed, then carefully turned the car round to allow a closer look. As they pulled in kerbside, they caught a glimpse of the car's interior trim and, from where they were sitting, it looked very much like cream leather.

***

Lucas had agreed with Gerry that in preparation for a meeting with The Divinity they'd head back toward Mesa, find another hotel, and lay up and await further instruction. Gerry promised to email Sarah's Cirrus 5 info to them – he thought some intellectual reading would help them while away the hours and might even keep them out of the bar.

"What's the next move, then?" Rick queried.

"Like the man said, find another hotel and wait for a response about a meet…. unless there's anything else you want to do." He paused to look at Rick. "What you thinking?" he asked.

"Don't know really," Rick said. "I just feel we should be doing more – all this hotel hopping and waiting round for a call from Gerry shit does me in. The whole job has just, well, stuttered really." For the first time during their time stateside, Rick looked like he'd lost a little of his famous resilience.

"Sounds like you're not happy, Ricky. What's up, mate – you homesick?"

"Maybe a little," he said slowly, "but more so, I'm fucking pissed off with always getting the run-around."

Lucas looked pensive. "Ok, so what you want to do about it?"

"I don't know, Sarge, but we've got to do something. I can't sit on my arse any longer. We've gotta make things happen," he paused. "I wanna go home soon, Rox, but not empty handed. The more I think about it, the more I want to take the book back with us."

"OK, that's fair enough," Lucas said, "and I understand completely where you're coming from, but something needs to give." He stopped and gave his partner a knowing grin. "Alright then," he muttered, "let's think - what else can we do?"

Lucas smiled again then reached for his road map; after studying it for a second he glanced over at his disconsolate colleague. "We'll keep heading East. Mesa's not far away and that'll have shedloads of good motels. But before we look for a stop-over, let's swing by the HQ again – see if it's open for business yet – what do you reckon?"

Rick didn't have to say a word; the manic grin and a slap of the Mustang's steering wheel was response enough.

***

Mordecai's underworld network knew no bounds. Over many years the unscrupulous degenerate had made solid contacts in all corners of the US and could count some of Arizona's finest criminal minds as his allies. And all of those connections could be relied on to help him out, but most only if the money was right.

The White Warriors MC had a fearsome reputation. The back patch motorcycle club, operating across most of the Mid-West, had six chapters and an infamous nomad contingent. That gave sixty-five active members in total which, in any one's book, was quite a force to call on. The outlaw biker club was one of Mordecai's biggest allies. He'd seen them grow steadily over the last few years and had played his part in nurturing that growth. For all his assistance, mainly guns and crystal meth shipments, the club were grateful; now his brothers-in-arms were more than willing to help track down his problem duo.

The club had nearly half their number dedicated to the task. Twenty-eight two-wheeled assassins were cruising the highways and byways of western Arizona looking for a latest model white Mustang GT containing two Caucasian males. The brief was simple: if you spot a match, get close and check out the occupants, and if they turn out to be a lanky Englishman and a stocky blond South African, incapacitate them. But remember, don't kill them - just keep tight hold and ring it in.

Along with the White Warrior brotherhood, Mordecai had an assortment of other sleaze bags on a state-wide look out for the two HSG men. All it needed now was a bit of luck and he'd be back on top. Those pricks don't realise who they're fucking with, he muttered to himself, and of that fact he was absolutely sure.

CHAPTER 21

The Painted Desert

There was no doubt in Marion's mind they'd found Meredith's house, but the question now was what to do about it? The blue Mercedes was not the only car outside the house but still the well-appointed villa looked ominously quiet and, despite no signs of life, the sisters were drawn to the front gates. With both leaves wide open it seemed to be daring them to venture up the long, shrub lined drive.

"Do you think anyone's home?" Marion asked.

"With two cars out front," Babb answered, "I'd say yes."

Marion looked over at her sister. "Come on, then, let's go knock. You never know, old Meredith could be safe and sound on the back veranda sipping iced tea and enjoying the sunshine." With that, she caught her sister's arm and proceeded to coax her up the neatly raked gravel toward the front door.

As her newfound enthusiasm took a sudden dip, Babb attempted to resist. "Are you sure we should be doing this?" she stalled.

"What's the harm?" Marion replied, yanking her sister forward. "I'm sure it's the right house....and remember, she was the one who was desperate to speak to me. Come on, don't chicken out on me now!"

As Marion led the way to the front door, the only sound they heard was the crunch of gravel from their own footsteps. The noise was distracting, so much so the pair failed to notice that, behind them, the electric gates were slowly easing back into their closed position.

At the end of the drive they cautiously ascended a small flight of steps up to the front door and stopped. The gargantuan door offered the sisters a variety of options: a sculpted chrome knocker, a bell-pull, and an intercom panel. Choices, choices, Marion thought as she plumped for the stylish bell pull. She gave the braided chord a gentle tug and listened. A bell peel chimed loudly and cleanly and seconds later could still be heard echoing through the cavernous house before fading back to silence. As they waited nervously at the front door, Babb turned for a quick look around. She glanced admiringly at the manicured lawns, the colourful borders and the patterned stonework of the front wall. Then she focused on the ornate ironwork of the main gate. As it dawned on her that the gates had closed, her enthusiasm took a further dip. "Jeepers, Marion!" she gasped. "Look! The gates have closed. I didn't see them move, did you?"

Marion turned away from the door to check out her sister's concerns. "No, I didn't, I never heard a thing..."

Before Babb had a chance to respond, the right-hand leaf of the huge panelled door cracked open. Moments later, a tall grey-haired male sporting an insipid smile stepped into view. "Good afternoon, Ladies," he intoned. "How may I help you?"

"W-w-well...err, yes, hello, there," Marion stammered, "we're actually looking for Meredith, Meredith Higham. This is her residence, isn't it?"

As the man met Marion's gaze, he dropped the smile and seemed to take a little longer than he should to digest the question. "Yes, it is," he said reluctantly, "but unfortunately she's not home at the moment; she's away on business."

Marion feigned disappointment. "Oh, what a pity!" she said.

The man silently stood his ground; it was now her turn to think hard about a response. She had several burning questions but got the distinct feeling this was not the right time to ask them. Smiling her sweetest smile, she went for the simple option. "Is she away for long?" she asked before going all out and adding, "Is she contactable whilst she's away?"

The man edged forward. Closing the gap between him and the sisters was a subtle intimidation gesture that he tempered slightly by returning the lack-lustre smile, "Ladies, unfortunately I am not at liberty to disclose any of Mrs Higham's personal information. All I can say is that she is expected to be away for several weeks, so if you would like me to pass on any messages, or your contact details possibly… I am perfectly happy to assist."

He held the smile, but Marion thought it looked like a real effort. "No, actually it's OK," she replied, "we were just in the neighbourhood, just passing you see, we only dropped in on the off chance. I'm sure we'll catch up with her some other time, so thank you for your help, Mr….?"

The librarian was already starting to back away as she pitched the question. The man again considered his response for too long. "I'm… Mr Kavanagh" he finally answered. "I am part of Mrs Higham's backroom staff; I look after her domestic affairs while she's away on business trips."

"How lovely, good for you!" Marion blurted without really thinking about what she was saying. "Well, thanks again, Mr…. Kavanagh, nice to meet you, err – so, goodbye… oh err, and one other thing - could you let us out of the gate, please?"

Marion and Babb smiled awkwardly as they turned to head back down the drive. As they scurried off the man called out after them, "Yes, no problem… goodbye, Ladies, sorry I couldn't have been more help – safe journey, you go easy now."

It took great restraint from both women not to run full tilt down the drive. They wanted to get away from the house, away as fast as possible, and unscathed.

***

As the little Honda high-tailed it back west towards Babb's cabin, the sisters couldn't stop replaying their encounter with the unsettling Mr Kavanagh over and over again.

"My God, that was one of the creepiest men I've ever met," Babb said, "and I've known some weird ones in my time."

"Oh, my Lord, B, I know exactly what you mean!" Marion exclaimed. "What an odd man! That was all very strange, wasn't it? Now I don't know what to think." She frowned and shook her head. "Is he for real? Does Meredith really have a Mr Kavanagh looking after her house while she's away?"

"I don't believe it for one minute," Babb replied. Then, suddenly thinking the worst, added, "Wouldn't surprise me if poor old Meredith's been chopped up into chunks, wrapped in cling film and stuffed in the refrigerator! That man was bad news, really bad news."

Marion was watching the road ahead. "I doubt it's quite that *bad*," she said slowly, "but something's definitely not right."

"More than not right," Babb replied vehemently. "Did you see those blood-shot eyes? My God! The bags, the stare, and that weird lop-sided smile; he was vile! I tell you, Sis, that man is pure evil."

Marion was confused. Yes, they'd both felt uneasy standing at Meredith's door, and yes, something didn't ring true about Mr Kavanagh. But could it all be genuine? Maybe they'd got the wrong end of the stick, maybe she did have staff look after her house while she was away. As they got closer to home, the bemused sisters finally consoled themselves with the fact that they'd attempted to do something positive. Against the odds they'd found Meredith's house and tried to make contact but failed and now, other than call Lucas again, what else could they do?

***

In Phoenix, Mordecai got the break he'd prayed for. A White Warrior prospect riding near the old town had spotted two guys in a latest model Mustang. The white V8 had been at a service station rest area and its occupants matched the description given in Ings' own underworld version of an APB. As he listened to the rest of the call, all the relieved red neck could do was think, 'Thank the Lord for second chances!'

The sighting was called in by one of the Warriors leaders, Mike Connolly. 'Ironman' Connolly, as he was affectionately known, just happened to be a close friend of Mordecai's and, fortunately for the grizzled old rattler, the Ironman was the type of man who would do everything he could to help a brother in trouble.

Connolly explained how the white Ford was now headed East toward Mesa and Tempe with the tenacious young biker following at a discreet distance. "We got another four of the boys heading out of Phoenix now," he reported. "They'll be on the interstate in minutes and will catch the kid up in no time." The biker chief was in confident mood. "So, don't sweat it, Mord, we won't lose them."

"When you get the chance...take them out," Ings instructed, "but don't go killing any one yet, you hear?"

"Yeah, yeah, Mord, we understand," Connolly replied calmly. "Everyone's briefed, we stomp the fuckers a little, throw them in a van, and keep 'em fresh for you - right?"

"Yeah, and as soon as they're ready for collection, ring me. I'll come and get them myself. Those two pissants are gonna regret the day they crossed me... and that's a Goddam promise."

Somewhere at the back of Ing's mind Leon Tate's orders were playing over and over like a broken record, but he chose to ignore it. The desire for revenge was stronger - much stronger – and, after all, it was personal now.

***

Having visited The Divinity's HQ twice already, Lucas and Rick knew this third visit would have to be subtler. This time there would be no parking directly outside, no banging on the front door and no threats.

"Just a quiet look round," Rick said, "see if they're back open for business, maybe drop in and ask to see the big cheese." He smiled. "What did that miserable git say the boss man's name was, the one the Reverend reported back to?"

“Dubois, I think,” Lucas replied. “Yeah, Vincent Dubois. Not one you’d forget, really, is it?” The ex-sapper was rubbing his stubble and pulling a classic thoughtful face. “In fact,” he added, “didn’t he mention he was a Monsignor? Yes, that’s it! The top man’s full title was Monsignor Vincent Dubois and I bet old Dubois is a real deviant…. probably got every fucker scared shitless.”

As they got deeper into Mesa, Lucas started checking out the side streets. He was searching for an out-of-the-way parking spot a discreet distance from the building, The Mustang had turned right into a likely looking street when he saw what he wanted. “Pull in there, Rick,” he said pointing ahead. “This’ll do, we’re close enough, should only be a few blocks from here.”

The narrow one-way street was quiet. It was lined on both sides with tall, retro style brick warehouses but, despite the clear blue skies above, it felt dark and gloomy. It had well-worn parking bays marked up the full length of the right-hand side with a handful of vehicles randomly dotted along it. Rick pulled into a mid-street spot and eased the Mustang to the kerb for the snuggest of fits. He turned the ignition off and, as the big V8 growl died, it was immediately replaced by another distinct engine noise.

Both men heard the V-twin rumble before they saw them. Riding side by side up the centre of the street, two motorcyclists approached. As the bikes got closer, both accelerated hard past the Mustang and, when the deafening engine roar blasted through the car’s open windows, its occupants winced.

“Jesus, that’s loud.” Lucas yelled over the roar. “There’s just no need for that, is there?”

“I tell you,” Rick said, “I fucking hate bikers.”

As the HSG team watched the motorcycles head up the street, the Harleys stopped on the bend at the top and pulled in on the opposite side to the Ford. After a brief exchange of words, the two riders moved in perfect unison like synchronised gymnasts, each taking their right hand off the throttle and performing a one-eighty head swivel to look back down the road. As the bikers stared blatantly in the direction of the white Mustang, Lucas sighed, "Jesus Christ, Ricky, I don't believe it! Here we fucking go again!" He shook his head. "Those two couldn't make it any more bloody obvious if they tried, could they?"

Both men knew without doubt they were back in the cross-hairs. "What's with this lot?" Rick replied. "Do they always employ street gangs to do their dirty work?" He paused. "Do you reckon it's some sort of standard cult M.O?"

"Aah, shit," said Lucas, "look behind you.... there's another two, err, no, sorry three."

Rick peered into his wing mirror and, sure enough, three more menacing looking low-riders had positioned themselves about seventy-five yards back down the street behind them.

"We're sitting ducks. We got two top, three bottom - that's five of the fuckers boxing us in...and we've got about ten seconds before they come in for the kill. Ah, fuck it, Ricky!" Lucas spat. "Let's just go for it!"

Both men knew it was make or break time and they hoped they'd just opted for make.

"OK, Sarge," Rick muttered as he turned the key, "hold tight!"

The Mustang jumped back to life, then Kruger hit the gas. With the force of a sledge-hammer downswing, Rick's size nine sent the big V8 squealing up the street. As it gained traction the car twitched and snaked like a launching missile and controller Rick had picked its target.

At the first sound of screeching tyres, the three-bike rear guard started to race up the street. The front pair, realising what was happening, kicked down their side stands, dismounted, and reached to their waistbands but they weren't fast enough.

The Ford caught the first warrior with a glancing blow and sent the leather-clad lump flailing backward into his bike. His partner wasn't so lucky. He took the full force in the legs, rendering his bike riding days well and truly over. As the second goon rolled over the top of the car and bounced down the blacktop behind them, the two men checked their mirrors simultaneously. "Two down, three following," Lucas observed dryly, then he looked out at the cars bonnet and grimaced, "Kruger, we're going to have a major damage bill at the end of this trip."

The wild eyed South African didn't respond. Now positively overdosing on adrenalin, Rick was totally focused on escape and was stopping for no one. Immediately after totalling the two lead bikers the junction appeared, but the Mustang didn't slow. Rick yanked the wheel hard right and slid the car beautifully onto the main road just controlling the tail slide well enough so it didn't take out any off the oncoming traffic.

"Jesus H Christ, Kruger, that was close," Lucas sounded genuinely impressed and relieved at the same time.

"We should outrun these pricks once we get onto the highway," Rick grunted. "They'll stay with us round town, but this monster will leave them for dead on the open road."

Only two of the remaining White Warrior trio were in pursuit. The young prospect had dropped back to attend to causalities, but the two following were close.

"Best chance we got, then, is the interstate back up to Flagstaff. We know that road…long and fast, well, if no one's watching that is." He was talking down into his trusty road atlas perched across his knee, thinking hard about somewhere to lay low.

"I-17?" Rick queried.

"Yeah…that's the one."

"Maybe we need a weekend stay with Marion's kid sister," Rick suggested. "You know, a secluded mountain cabin could be a good place to hide, don't you think?"

"Sounds alright to me, but let's make sure we ditch this pair of psychos before we go inviting ourselves over to anyone's for the weekend."

"Yeah, OK," Rick grinned, "leave it to me."

As they weaved north out of Mesa, the two Warrior riders tried their damnedest to get alongside the Ford. But Stellenbosch's favourite son was up to the challenge and pulled out every dodge in the book to ensure the bikes never quite managed to draw level. And it worked; once out of the city and onto I-17, the Harley-riding pursuers began to lose ground, and Rick kept his foot down.

***

The next call Mordecai got from Mike Connolly was not such good news. Slouched in the driver's seat of his pick-up, drawing the last lung full of smoke from a cigarette, the grizzled redneck now pondered the infernal question, how the fuck had those two done it again?

Ings was incensed but, worse still, the latest casualties of the chase weren't even his own. The White Warriors were now two men down and he was struggling to quell the biker boss's rage. The Ironman wanted answers.

"Who the fuck are these guys?" Connolly roared. "You just said collection agents, Mord, nothing more."

"I know… I'm fucking sorry, man."

"Sorry don't get you shit," the biker chief screamed. "Those two aren't your Goddam normal collection dudes, no way. Getting out of that street was no beginner's luck – those fuckers knew what they were doing, that's for sure."

"Jesus, Mike," Ings said, "tell me about it! Those cocksuckers! I mean, I thought first time was just a fluke, but it wasn't," he drew an exasperated breath. "I've underestimated them, and, I mean, big time."

"Yeah, you sure have," Connolly snapped, "and I tell you, Bro, it's going take a lot more than you thought to stop them. We should've just wasted the fuckers there and then; if we hadn't needed to wait for you, they'd already be history."

Mordecai knew the biker chief was right. The interlopers might be a lot smarter and resourceful than he'd given them credit for, but even they wouldn't have been able to escape a straight-up drive-by assassination. Five armed White Warrior hard core in that quiet Mesa side-street could easily have dispatched the infuriating duo. But no, again he'd given them room to manoeuvre, and now he'd reached boiling point. Next time they weren't getting a chance. Next time would be third time lucky for him, and he didn't give a flying fuck what Leon Tate would have to say about that.

CHAPTER 22

Bum Steer

As soon as Marion got back to the cabin, she called Lucas.

"Oh, hello, Ms Armstrong," he answered as cheerily as he could. "What timing! I was just about to call you…. are you psychic?"

She paused as she considered the question, "Maybe I am Mr Roxby. Is everything OK?"

"No, not really; we've had another run in with The Divinity's hired help. Well, we assume that's who they are."

"Oh, dear Lord, are you hurt?" she asked, sounding genuinely concerned. "Is Mr Kruger OK?"

"It was a close call, but we're OK, thanks," he was still trying to sound cheerful. The other guys, maybe not so much, but it was a 'them or us' kind of situation you see, and then…well, we had to leave in a hurry, if you know what I mean."

"Well, err...yes, I would think so, that sounds dreadful, but I'm glad to hear you're both OK. Where are you now?"

"Not far away, actually," he replied. "We're on Interstate 17, probably ten miles south of Flagstaff."

"Oh, good," she said cheerfully, "I really could do with seeing you. Babb and I have just got back from Meredith's house and…," she paused, "unfortunately she wasn't there, but a rather strange man was."

"A strange man? Sounds intriguing, I can't wait to hear about this. Where do you want to meet?"

The line went silent for a second, then he heard a faint muffled conversation from the other end before finally Marion spoke again, "Why don't you come over to the cabin? It's a great location. Not that easy to find, mind, but we can talk you in. What do you say, Mr Roxby?"

Lucas smiled. What a stroke of luck! The ideal hideaway offered to them on a plate; an offer he couldn't refuse. He glanced over to Rick, gave a thumbs-up and a wink, then turned back to look out the passenger window of the thundering Ford.

"Yes, that's a great idea, Marion, sounds really good. But are you sure it's OK with your sister? We don't want to impose or cause any hassle."

"Absolutely no problem, Mr Roxby, no problem at all." Lucas was relieved as it sounded like she really meant it. "So, to get here," she continued, "right, well, yes… just stay on I -17 and run right past Flagstaff, then just west of the city find state Route 180 and follow it north. At junction 5a you'll see signs for North Peak National Park, come off there and follow the green signs all the way. When you get to the park's outskirts, ring me. Did you get all that, Mr Roxby?"

"Yes, thank you. We'll ring you when we're close," he glanced at his watch, "we're probably only an hour away - if we don't get lost, that is - so hopefully we'll see you then."

"Yes, OK, Mr Roxby, bye for now," and with that she hung up.

As soon as Lucas put his mobile back in his pocket, he turned again to face his partner, "Jesus, Ricky, I can't believe that, can you?"

As ever, Rick was concentrating on the road ahead. "Unreal, Sarge," he replied with a faint shake of the head, "but, hey, maybe the tide's turning."

***

Sat at home, hunched over her well-worn kitchen table, Sarah was looking at a small battered book laid out in front of her. She wasn't normally at her sharpest on a Saturday morning, especially not before eight o'clock, but this one was different. On this one, despite Friday night's usual indulgence, she was up early and eager to get on with a bit of obscure research.

She was quite happy to admit that the task in hand had been created by her own over-active imagination. It was nothing more than a hunch - pure speculation – more than likely just another flight of fancy. But, whatever the rationale behind it, it had caused a fitful night's sleep. Tossing and turning, mulling over one wild theory after another, she'd analysed every permutation she could conjure. But so far nothing; she'd drawn a blank. Disappointed, frustrated, and with no sign of an imminent eureka moment it was time for Round Two.

The fact nothing made sense was annoying. She had no idea how to justify her theory, never mind prove it – it was simply a feeling she couldn't shake. The notion that somehow the approaching appearance of the C5 comet was connected to their Book of Martyrs hunt just wouldn't go away. She was convinced there was a link, but for now it was like trying to put a 500-piece jigsaw together with only five pieces. With nothing tangible to work with, it was time to consider things from another direction.

Hoping Calvin Lentz's ancient leather-bound notebooks could offer some help, Sarah was prepped and ready to read. And, whilst she knew it was unlikely, Sarah had always been a fan of the long odds outsider.

She and Calvin shared a love of art history, particularly the unsavoury side of it. Tales of larceny, treachery and fraud in the world of classic art was a passion, and the two of them were quite happy to admit they were anoraks when it came to matters of famous forgeries. Both readily admitted to spending endless hours researching accounts of art thefts for fun. Stories of audacious burglaries, ransom demands, and famous works of art vanishing, sometimes forever were, in their eyes, nothing short of addictive.

During the original book search, Wiseman & Scott had assembled a veritable library of reference material on Foxe's classic. Much of that information was of little or no significance, most being purely inconsequential background research stuff. But within the catalogue of documents had been two small leather-bound ledgers. Both were no bigger than an A2 notebook and both were in a dilapidated condition. The less battered of the two was simply titled *'Assets of the Parish 1793"* and the second book's title was indecipherable due to what Sarah could only presume was years of wear and tear.

Calvin explained that, during the original investigation, both ledgers had been at the bottom of a wooden archive box. The box was full of bundles of long forgotten church records and had been given to his team by Dr Reid himself. The issue of this ancient documentation was to assist W&S prove the PCOS's claim to legal ownership of their first edition, which - after some serious analysing - it did. Calvin explained that the only church records from the box not assessed were the two notebooks, but he was quick to point out this was simply due to the necessary provenance being established from the other records provided. At the time, he said, the two ledgers had been subject to a cursory glance only, and since then they'd lain undisturbed in a filing cabinet in the Glasgow office.

Calvin wanted Sarah to see the books. He felt it was something she'd be interested in; during a recent discussion he'd suggested she should give them a once-over. And now, in the kitchen of her cosy little flat, that was exactly what she was doing.

'Assets of the Parish 1793' was first on the table. The binding was leather and was well-worn. It had a hint of its original green showing through in patches and the faded gold leaf title was neatly etched across its front cover. The spine was completely shot so the tatty little book lay perfectly flat when opened and turning the pages was akin to thumbing through a loose-leaf file. Sarah smiled at the meticulous hand-written entries. They were all in perfect flowing copperplate script. Christ, she thought, this must have taken months to write - what dedication, what effort...just for a glorified list.

Next to a cup of cooling coffee she'd placed her own precious notebook. It was open and ready to record anything she discovered. Slowly Sarah began to work through the entries. Immediately she was taken in by the level of detail each contained. Everything was recorded. From altar cloths and candle holders, right through to tapestries and crucifixes, it was all there. But even more impressive was the identifying description accompanying each item. It was a truly exquisite inventory – almost a work of art in its own right.

Two hours in and bingo, she found the entry concerning Foxe's Book, which clearly stated the author, date of issue and its importance. It had a clear and thorough description adjacent to it and, as she read it several times over, the words painted a mental picture, an image so vivid she felt she could almost touch it. No possibility of mistaking its first edition status here, she thought. The book's size, number of pages, cover decoration and colours were also detailed, as was the bespoke nature of its issue and, oddly, a reference to something she couldn't fathom - the '*JLG*' honour inclusion of 1792.

She scribbled a page of notes, took half a dozen photos with her phone, then ploughed on through the ledger all the way to the end. After four hours and ten minutes it was done. She'd read it cover to cover and what a way to spend a sunny Saturday morning! Hunched over your kitchen table reading a 275-year-old church record book wasn't everybody's cup of tea. She knew some people would simply say she was a sad boring cow who should get a life. But did she care what others thought? No, she didn't, and - if the truth be known - she never had.

But for now, time had run out. She had plans for the afternoon, so analysing the second book would have to go on hold for a few hours. A date with Diamond Dave awaited and that was something she didn't want to miss. Who was it said she should get a life?

CHAPTER 23

Cabin in the Woods

The very notion of having gentlemen callers had sent Babb Armstrong into a tizzy and, whilst she'd readily agreed to the suggestion Lucas and Rick visit, it was just that everything, well, everything had to be, as she liked to put it, "fixed just right for guests."

"Come on, Marion," Babb fussed, "you say they're about an hour away? Well, we've got just enough time to get the place looking right, then," she scowled then gestured toward the door. "You do the hall and lounge – I'll do the rest...come on, chop, chop!"

Marion looked a little perplexed at her sister's attempts to spur her into action, "OK, B, but...why the panic? I wouldn't worry too much about Mr Roxby and Mr Kruger... I think they'll be quite happy with the way the house is - I wouldn't say they were your usual types," she smiled at her sister. "They're the kind of visitors who wouldn't be picky about the lived-in look, if you get my meaning."

Babb was indignant, "Don't be silly. Every guest in my house gets the same treatment – you know how I am, so no arguing, let's just get on with it, please." It was obvious she wasn't going to compromise her standards for anyone, however undiscerning they actually were, so to keep the peace, Marion bit her tongue and did exactly as she was told.

By the time Lucas's '*we're close*' call came through, the already well-kept cabin had taken on the look of a developers' show home. There wasn't an out of shape cushion or an unwashed dish in sight; the place positively gleamed and the smell of 'spring Jasmine' was overpowering. A little over the top, Marion thought to herself, but so what? At least Babb was happy.

"Yes, Mr Roxby, I know where you are," she said nodding thoughtfully, "that's exactly right. Sure, yes...just by the blue Pine Woods sign at the ranger station, yes, excellent, well done!"

"Am I going straight up the stone road?" Lucas asked. "The one to the left of the timber building," he stopped talking for a second as he peered ahead. "We're following the Pine Woods arrows - is that right?"

"Yes, that's correct," she replied," but be careful, that road is rough and gets very narrow in parts, but you should be fine - just mind that fancy car of yours.... You really do need to take it easy, you hear." Marion took a deep breath before issuing her final instructions, "So then, after about a mile, it splits in two, OK? You need to take the left-hand fork; Babb's cabin is just up that track... she's the third up on the right, is that clear enough for you?"

"Yeah, no problem, that's great," Lucas said sounding decidedly unconvinced. "One last thing, though, have these cabins got numbers or some other type of identification mark?"

"Oh, yes, sorry," she said, "They don't have numbers but they do have names – Babb's is called 'Mountain Breeze' – the name plaque is just at the bottom of the drive, you can't miss it, so we'll see you in about ten minutes then. OK, Mr Roxby, bye for now."

The duo followed Marion's directions closely and even tried to heed her warning to drive carefully. But, despite Rick's attempts at taking it steady, he still managed to clatter the car's underbelly several times on the pot-holed road.

"Like I said, Kruger," Lucas grimaced, "the damage bill at the end of this job is going to be a monster."

Rick didn't comment; he just chuckled as they bounced the last two hundred yards toward the cabin.

"I think that's it," Lucas said gesturing up ahead. "Yeah, 'Mountain Breeze', this is the one. I suppose we just pull up the drive and.... that looks steep!"

Before Lucas could say anymore Rick swung the battle-scarred mustang into the cabin's rough-hewn driveway and, with one last metallic crunch, the car bottomed out then shot up the slope in a whoosh of dust. Pulling up sharply next to Marion's little yellow Honda, Lucas was quick to show his annoyance. "Cool it with the rally driving, will you? Why fuck the car up any more than necessary?"

As Rick shut down the rumbling V8, the front door opened and out into the late afternoon sunshine stepped the two sisters. A smiling Marion appeared first, followed closely by an apprehensive looking Babb.

"Welcome to Mountain Breeze, gentlemen," Marion said, her greeting warm and friendly. "Mr Roxby, Mr Kruger, I'm glad you found us so easily. You *are* clever... do come in." She turned and gestured toward her sibling, "This is my sister, Babb, known to some as the ex-Mrs Teller, and I've told her all about you both," Marion smiled sweetly again at the two men, "and she has really been looking forward to meeting you, so come say hello."

The two men were quick to oblige and enthusiastically greeted their host with a genuine feeling of gratitude and relief. "This is fantastic," Rick enthused, "I absolutely love it - what a great spot.... how long you lived out here?"

Babb, despite appearing a little coy, was thrilled by the South African's interest and more than happy to answer. "Well thank you, Mr Kruger," she gushed, "I'm pleased you like it so much, and well...yes, I've been here almost two years now and truly it is an amazing place to live - genuinely a little slice of heaven," she paused as she surveyed her surroundings. "Wonderful isn't it?" She smiled, "I don't know why it took me so long to make the move, I really don't. I'd dreamed of living somewhere like this for a long time... I suppose it just took me longer than expected to make it happen."

"Better late than never, though," Rick grinned.

"Absolutely, Mr Kruger, absolutely," she said, then moved a little closer to him. "Can I say your accent is really rather wonderful, it's very...err...very distinctive – I just love it!" Babb, now flashing her best flirty smile, was on a roll, "So, gentlemen, please come in and make yourselves comfortable!" As she spoke, she caught Rick's arm and proceeded to lead the way to the front door. "And what can we get for you two to drink, then?" I've got coffee, juice, soda or a cold beer if you'd like…or maybe be even an iced tea?" She turned to her sister, adding brightly, "I make a mean iced tea, don't I, Marion?"

Marion couldn't help but smile; her sweet little sister who, five minutes earlier had been a bag of nerves, was now schmoozing her guests like a true pro and seemingly loving it. "You sure do," Marion replied, "probably the best iced tea this side of the Arizona state line…. so make no doubt about it, gents - you need to try one."

"OK, then," Lucas said, "iced tea it is."

The foursome settled around the patio table. Then, sipping on Babb's famous iced tea, started to discuss the sister's visit to the Higham house. The two men listened intently as the endearing pair told the tale of the hunt for Meredith's house and, after Marion had explained their near miss with the speeding limousine, the gate shutting, and ultimately their strange encounter with Mr Kavanagh, Lucas couldn't wait to ask questions.

"So, this guy, this Mr Kavanagh," he said slowly, "he told you he was an employee of Mrs Higham, yes?" He paused as he waited for some sort of conformation and, after the sisters nodded simultaneously, he continued, "So… do you think he's a local house sitter type or do you get the impression he's more than that?"

"Well, Mr Roxby, I don't think he's an employee at all," Marion replied. "In fact, I don't think he should actually be there."

"I totally agree," Babb said firmly. "Something just didn't ring true about the man. I didn't like him one bit. We couldn't get away quick enough, could we?" Then, to further reinforce her sister's feelings of unease about Mr Kavanagh, Babb added, "I'd bet my last dollar he doesn't work for Meredith."

"OK, ladies, we get the point," Lucas replied. "You think the man's an imposter who's up to no good, but what's his motive? Who's he working for and why was he there?" Lucas let his questions hang for a second then in a theatrical hushed tone asked, "Do you think he works for them - The Divinity, I mean?"

Marion looked at her sister, then at Rick, then back at Lucas, then asked, "Why would we think that, Mr Roxby?"

"Well, we've had some more information from our team back home," he said. "They've been digging deeper into widow Higham's affairs and have come up with a few surprises," he paused and grinned slyly. "Want to hear what they're saying?" he asked.

"Please do tell, Mr Roxby," Marion replied. "I'd love to know... well, we'd both like to know actually, wouldn't we, B?"

"Sure would," Babb agreed, so Lucas pulled out his phone and flicked back through the recent emails. After finding what he was looking for he turned to the expectant sisters.

"Here you go, ladies," he said. "Listen to this...this is what's come through in the last 24 hours from our team in the UK, OK?"

Both sisters nodded, then Lucas began to read out extracts from Sarah's latest report on Meredith Higham. He went through the claims she was a senior ranking Divinity official and the inferences she was involved in shady business dealings. He explained how the research team suggested The Divinity's outreach projects were actually cover for various forms of illicit activity which they were guessing was drug related.

The sisters listened closely as the tall, scruffy Englishman read aloud to them. Both let out little gasps of amazement at each revelation and accusation he unveiled. "Well, I find all that rather difficult to believe, Mr Roxby," Marion said. "It doesn't make sense. I mean if it were true, why would she tell us different, why make out she only had a loose association when in fact she was a big wig? What would she hope to gain from that?"

Marion's question immediately got Lucas thinking. "Maybe she didn't want anyone from the outside to know how heavily involved she was?" he suggested. "Then this fringe associate busy-body persona she projected could purely be a charade - you know, a cover to help her deflect any awkward questions about her involvement ...maybe," he paused. "I don't know, it's just a thought."

Rick was puzzled as to what his partner was driving at. "What do you mean, Rox?" he asked. "What would that achieve?"

"Well, what I'm saying is, if she's near the top of The Divinity food chain then maybe she doesn't want anyone to know it. It could be important to her. Or is she," he stopped and shrugged, "is she just a genuinely shy, private person?"

Marion was sat bolt upright, arms crossed and now looked perplexed. "Steady on, Mr Roxby," she said, "you're stretching it there; the Meredith Higham I know is not the shy and retiring type - not from where I've been sitting anyway - and if in reality she is, and this has all been an act, well then all I can say is the woman is an exceptional actress, and deserves an Oscar."

"I think the woman's had everyone over," Lucas said. "She's not what she seems…not to anyone; she's a chameleon and she's playing us all – and that includes The Divinity."

"Hold on a sec… now I'm really lost," Rick said. "What are you trying to say this woman is up to?" Rick's head was starting to spin; he knew Lucas was switched on but sometimes his off-beat theories took a little explaining before they sank in. "She's an undercover," Lucas grinned. "The whole situation's been deliberately orchestrated. I'm telling you, the woman's been set up to infiltrate the organisation, she's some sort of government informer - I bet you a tenner on it."

Lucas's left field speculation was greeted with stunned silence. But after what felt like an age, Marion snapped to life. "Are you out of your mind, Mr Roxby?" she said, looking utterly affronted. "Do you really believe a plump, grey haired sixty-five-year-old gossiping socialite is an undercover federal agent?"

Before Lucas could respond, Babb let rip. "I don't even know the lady," she snapped, "but I tell you, I've never heard a more idiotic suggestion in my life."

"Yeah, come on, Roxy," Rick said. "That's a bit farfetched even for your wild imagination."

Lucas held both hands up to the others round the table and smiled. "Think what you like, folks," he said, "but at this moment in time that's my theory and I'm sticking to it. I just can't get any other scenario to make sense," he stopped and looked at the three staring faces. "So, go on, prove me wrong."

***

Sarah's date with Diamond Dave had unfortunately been cut short so she got back home earlier than expected. Nevertheless, he'd still been thrilled to see her, they'd chatted for nearly an hour and he seemed happy enough. To her mind that was a good result in anyone's book. But now, with no other Saturday plans to speak of, it was time for her to get settled back round the kitchen table and check out the second of Calvin's little ledgers.

Number two was in an even worse state than the first and she knew handling it would be tricky. At every touch, it was in danger of disintegrating further so the task of trying to read it from cover to cover was going to have to be approached with real caution. The book was wrapped in a close-fitting waxed cotton pouch which no doubt had been meant to protect it through the ages, but now it served no useful purpose, so she carefully cut it away and placed it in a plastic carrier bag. Then she spread a clean linen tea towel across the table and placed the book squarely in the middle. The job now, before even trying to open it, was to study the front cover. Like the other ledger, the cover binding was all leather but reduced to a peeling flaking mass of grimy brown.

Hoping to detect the remnants of a title, Sarah ran her fingers lightly across the ancient hide. Sadly, there was nothing; front, back and spine, the decaying leather gave no hint as to what the book was, or its origins. "A big help," she muttered to herself.

After taking a small butter knife from her cutlery drawer, she sat down at the table. Then, like a surgeon making the first incision, she carefully inserted the knife directly behind the front cover. Once the blade was in handle-deep, she gingerly opened the book at its first page. As it came slowly to the upright position, she took hold of the cover with the thumb and forefinger of her left hand then exchanged the knife for a small pencil torch. As the beam illuminated the page, she stared at the flowing longhand script now visible.

The writing was similar in style to the first book. Again, it was a neat copperplate style, but this time the entries were not uniform. The ink colour alternated randomly between black, blue, and green, and some parts of the narrative had faded completely. Scanning the first couple of pages, Sarah realised the book seemed more diary like than anything else. Maybe a travel journal she thought, but, whatever it was, it certainly wasn't the asset register that notebook number one had turned out to be.

To speed up the reading process, she placed a small unopened can of Heinz baked-beans underneath the front cover. This arrangement held the book open in the perfect position for her to leaf through the pages. Now, grasping the little torch in her left hand, and still using the butter knife with her right, she made good progress. The ancient paper was stained on every page and some pages had actually fused together. The extensive damage she reasoned was due to contact with water; either it was fully submerged at some point in time or maybe just periodic exposure to the elements had taken its toll. But she'd never know the truth; it was all just guesswork.

With nothing she could do about the swathes of missing text, Sarah simply worked her way through, page by page, deciphering whatever little she could see. As the painstaking analysis progressed, she made notes of anything of particular interest. The odd date was legible, as were some place names, landscape descriptions, and references to what appeared to be members of a travelling party.

After several hours of scrutiny, phase one of Sarah's task was done. As best she could, she'd read every legible word in the entire book and made eight pages of notes. The only downside was tired eyes and a dusting of decomposing leather particles over her table but, thankfully, the towel had caught the majority of them.

Now she was convinced what she'd read would go some way to solve the puzzle she was obsessed with. Whilst there was no direct mention of Cirrus 5, or any other known galactic entity, one passage did refer to *'A rainbow tail of fire'* and another to *'a time of the great light'*.

Sarah was now armed with a list of intriguing references - most of which currently meant nothing to her - so it was time to seek help. But, first up, she wanted to review her notes, then she intended to summarise everything she'd gleaned into a single explanatory document. It needed to be something simple, something that clarified the book's likely purpose and made sense of its timeline and content. So, operating on her usual 'there's no time like the present' philosophy Sarah started typing. Punching "Ute Territories 1791" into her favourite search engine she settled down to yet another wild Saturday night on her own. And then, as the first entry appeared on screen, the determined twenty-eight-year-old felt a faint nip of adrenalin tingle through her veins.

***

As the wind whipped the tops of La Palma's *Roque del faro* mountains, the small control room of SKYCHECK observatory SC 4/4 Bravo started to buzz with anticipation. As the early shift scrutinised data from the previous night's recordings, the sense of expectation was palpable. Pawing over a series of glossy still photographs laid out in front of him, the hunched figure of astronomer Fernando Vega was nodding gently. "Welcome back, my friend," he whispered slowly to himself. "One hundred and thirteen years is a long time, but you are here, and now we will all get to see the comet with the rainbow tail."

***

CHAPTER 24

Warrior's Revenge

The black limo stayed outside the Mesa HQ only long enough for its passengers to alight. Once the small huddle was deposited safely on the sidewalk, the black sedan slipped back into a blur of downtown traffic and disappeared in seconds.

As the group - two men supporting an unsteady grey-haired female - made their way toward the front door, it slid open. The faint whoosh heralded the appearance of two uniformed figures. "Get the chair, Richie," the taller of the supporting men shouted at the uniforms, "and move it."

Instantly the older guard turned smartly on his heels and disappeared back inside. He returned several seconds later pushing a gleaming chrome wheelchair and appeared out of breath. "OK...come to me," the tall man said beckoning for the chair, "that's it – hold it there, help me get her in it...yeah, that's right, you settle yourself in there, my dear." With that, the two men gently eased the lifeless looking woman into the attendant chair. Once in, the same man took the lead. He propped the lolling head back into an upright position, then gestured to the security guard to move the wheelchair inside. "Right, that'll do, Rich," he said impatiently. "Let's get her up to the second floor, quick! I'll get Abi to check her over." He glanced round the lobby then beckoned the group to follow. "Come on, get a move on, will you."

On the command, the group started to make their way across the lobby. They hurried past the giant praying hands and, as the wheelchair squeaked across the polished marble floor, they headed straight toward the waiting elevator. At ten-person capacity the lift wasn't particularly small, but with the two men, a laden wheelchair and the overweight, heavily breathing, Richie, it suddenly felt cramped. Once the doors slid shut, the second guard returned to the front entrance and locked it. Then, as he headed back the reception desk, he checked his watch. The cheap Tag copy showed 1.30pm. "Jesus Christ," he muttered as it dawned on him how fine they were cutting it. Today was a special day for The Divinity organisation and, despite recent setbacks, nothing was going to spoil their long-awaited celebration day. Well, nothing of this world, he hoped.

***

Tate decided to take the stairs to the second floor; he knew the exercise was good for him but, more importantly, he could never resist the chance to wander through the building's opulent interior. He didn't rush: drinking in the splendour of its blatant decadence always gave him a thrill and today was no exception. As he made his way silently along the lushly carpeted corridor, he passed through the empty reception area, then on to the visitor suite. When he reached the partly open door of room 102, he stopped. Fully expecting to be greeted by another problem in need of resolution, he pushed the door open and walked in.

"We brought her straight here, sir," the taller man said, snapping to attention as Tate appeared, "exactly as instructed."

The Security Chief didn't answer. He stood silent and expressionless as he looked at the unconscious form slumped in the wheelchair in the middle of the room. Eventually he turned to the tall man and asked, "What about Leonard?"

"Again, Mr Tate, as you instructed. He's stayed at the house,"

"Good. Did the meddling bitch say anything?"

"Well, no, not really," the man replied. "The shot worked a treat, knocked her out much faster than expected," he paused, shrugged his shoulders and pulled a face. "So, we just got her into the car and came straight here."

Tate nodded his approval. "Anyone see you?" he asked.

"No, sir! It's a quiet neighbourhood, there was hardly a soul around," he stopped briefly as he recalled the day's earlier events. "Saw maybe two cars on her street, that was about it."

"Excellent, gentlemen," Tate said, "well done." Then, with a furrowed brow, the Security Chief turned his attention back to the sorry looking, grey haired lump in the chair. "Well now, my dear," he sneered, "I wonder what delights we have in store for you?"

***

The desire for retribution was strong but Mordecai was no fool. The old rattler knew control was king; it was a lesson he'd learnt the hard way. 'Men blinded by rage make mistakes' was a mantra he used many times but, as usual in the real world, it was easier to talk the talk than walk the walk.

Based on Mike Connolly's latest rant, Ings guessed the HSG pair would now be well past Flagstaff. The two tenacious bikers had last seen the thundering V8 disappear over the horizon on I-17 somewhere before Rock Springs. Which meant the infuriating duo could be anywhere in Northern Arizona, and that presented one hell of a challenge. To hunt down two sharp-witted fugitives in such a vast expanse of territory would take a stroke of luck, a stroke of genius - or a full-blown miracle – so the likelihood was, it wasn't going to happen.

After watching the last plume of smoke disappear out through the pick-up's window, Ings flicked the remnants of his cigarette skyward in a looping arc, then reached for his cell phone. "Santi, its Mord," he said as it connected. "Where you at?" He listened as the gruff Mexican confirmed his location. "OK, OK," he said impatiently, "Right.... now I want you to go back to that library woman's house, the one in Flag – you remember where it is, don't you?"

"Of course, Señor," came an indignant reply.

"Check it out again," Ings barked. "See if she's back home," he stopped and quickly lit another cigarette, "and if you see those two cocksuckers in the Mustang don't hesitate...you hear me? This time just ice the fuckers, OK?"

"Yeah, yeah, no problem," Hernandez answered, "I'll call later when we have news." Mordecai clicked off with no goodbye. He thought about the Mexican gangbanger's 'can't speak English' act and he realised that's exactly what it was – an act.

Next call up was the Dodge Ram team. His two young charges were still smarting from their run-in with the interlopers but, like the man himself, both were keen to avenge their misfortune and hoped it would be sooner rather than later. "Curt," he rasped, "It's Mord." He fell silent for a moment as he looked out across the parched desert before him, then eventually asked, "Where are you now boy, you got Jay with you? You in the van?"

"Sure am, Boss," Curtis answered. "Me and Jay-bird are on the road...we'll be at the yard in about twenty minutes," he drew hard on his cigarette. "So, what's happening, what we doin'?"

"You and Jay stay at the yard," Ings ordered. "I'll be over in an hour, then we're heading to Mesa...we got a collection to make."

As a reminder of his altercation with the South African Barrel, AKA Ricky Kruger, Curtis Danford was sporting a neat line of butterfly-stitches across the bridge of his nose plus matching purple under-eyes. Being hit with the force of a Tomahawk missile was something the young tearaway wasn't going to forgive in a hurry. "Is it them two dick-sucking bitches?" he asked hopefully.

"No, it ain't," Ings snapped. "You just gotta bide your time, Boy, you'll get your chance... so don't worry about that shit now." He cleared his throat, then, with all the finesse of a rabid camel, spat out of the window. "No... tonight's another little removal job for Mr Tate," he said, "and you all know what that means, don't you?"

"Gloves, shovels, and silencers – right?" Curt replied.

"You got it, Boy," Ings said, happy his young guns knew what was expected of them. "You and Jay be ready to roll as soon as I land, OK?"

"We'll be ready, Boss," came the eager reply.

***

Sarah's summary document didn't even run to a full page, but it made interesting reading. After much analysis she'd concluded the second of the ledgers was the remnants of a diary, a diary that charted part of a long-forgotten odyssey.

It was clearly a travel log and the journey it recorded had been undertaken by a small group of Protestant missionaries in early 1791. It was most likely some type of Pilgrimage but, with so much text missing, Sarah couldn't decipher the traveller's ultimate goal and, as it recorded a six-month period with no evidence of a conclusion, her guess was it was volume one of a two book series or even possibly one of three.

The missionary party had comprised of at least four men, but Sarah could put names to only two of them. She'd clearly identified a Francis James McLeod and a Jeremiah Gunner but their companions would sadly remain forever nameless. It was clear, though, that these two key men and their associates left the Western isles of Scotland late February 1791. They departed on a ship bound for Philadelphia on the 25th and, after a tortuous crossing, arrived safely in the Americas on May 15th. The ledger went into great detail about their feelings of relief at landing in the Americas; in the words of Jeremiah Gunner their ultimate safe passage was recorded as *'a miracle of deliverance from the forces of Satan'*.

Sadly, from there, though, Sarah could not decipher how they'd then travelled onward to Santa Fe but that's where she gleaned they ended up. There was a description of a short stay in the 'ribald' township of Santa Fe before starting out with a prospector's expedition on the 21st June. The party joined a mule train heading out west along the Spanish trading trail towards California and she guessed the rationale for travelling with the gold miners was simply safety in numbers.

The details after that got even sketchier. But, despite the smudges, smears and blanks, she'd pieced together the bones of a story. The party was aiming for a newly built mission chapel high up in the

Blackheart Mountains of the Ute territories and, if she'd interpreted the threadbare clues correctly, then one purpose for their visit was to bless the new venture with *'a book of great enlightenment'*. Further investigation confirmed that those Ute Territories were now officially the US State of Utah and, by happy coincidence, there was a thirty-mile-long mountain range that nestled between Iron County and Spencer County in its South Western corner called the Black Mountains.

But Sarah would never find out what happened to those men after August the 8th 1791. The ninth was the last date to be recorded in the ledger and, unfortunately for her, whatever final narrative had been written below that date heading had been obliterated.

Her frantic Google Earth search and local map analysis revealed nothing. She could find no mention or record of any kind of chapel anywhere in that particular mountain range of South West Utah. From the last ledger entries legible she was able to confirm they'd reached the much-mentioned chapel on the morning of the 7th of August. A description of bright lights and a rainbow of fire in the sky was recorded for the evening of the 8th of August, - "*a sight of a most magical delight*" - on the journal's penultimate page, then overleaf nothing but a single faded date followed by stains and ancient water marks.

***

"It's got to be a previous sighting of Cirrus 5," Sarah babbled excitedly down the phone, "it's too coincidental, Dad. 1791 - do the maths!"

"Hold on, child," Ray said sternly, "relax a minute, will you, and just tell me slowly where you've got this crazy notion from?"

Ray Stuart wanted his daughter to calm down and start again at the beginning. It was getting late on a Saturday evening and he had better things to do; watching match of the day, then heading to bed instantly sprang to mind.

"It's easier if I come to you," she replied. "You'll understand it better then."

"What? Now?" he protested. "At twenty to ten on a Saturday night you're going to come round here and explain your crack-pot theory to me?"

"Sure am, Pops," she chortled. "Is Mum still up?"

***

Twenty minutes later, Sarah arrived at her parent's house still charged with the thrill of the mystery she was trying to unravel. And now desperate to get her father's thoughts, she raced into the kitchen, sat down at the monstrous table and proceeded to spread her research out in front of her. Based on past experience her father was likely to view her theory as nothing but a load of old hocus-pocus, so she needed all the evidence she could muster to change his point of view.

"Look at the date here and the descriptions," she beamed as she pointed to a sheet on the top of the pile. "Now, cross reference that to the Cirrus 5 information we got from my friend's friend at SKYCHECK, and, for that matter, all the posts online now it's in the news, and what have you got?"

Ray, bamboozled by his daughter's onslaught, rubbed his eyes, then slid his glasses down from the top of his head and settled them onto the bridge of his nose. He then took a long, exaggerated sip of his second late night cuppa and looked closely at what his beloved daughter wanted him to read.

After a couple of minute's scrutiny, he sat back and sighed. "OK, yeah, we've got a connection," he said. "Not a dead cert by any stretch of the imagination but I agree… there's something there."

"You see what I'm saying though," she was triumphant. "You get it, don't you, Dad?"

"Yes, my dear, I see your argument," he said firmly. "This comet, this Cirrus 5, which apparently is the hottest news on the planet, is due to appear in the next day or two," he paused, "and the best vantage point to witness this spectacular light show - the supposed giant tail and its rainbow colours - is reportedly over the South Western United states, specifically in south west Utah, yes?" Ray smiled as he looked at his wide-eyed daughter. "Which just happens to be the same general area of the chapel mentioned in the PCOS journal you got from Calvin," he shook his head gently. "Some coincidence, eh?"

"Yes, it is, Dad," she nodded, "and you're doing ever so well."

"Well my dear, I'm so glad you're not being patronising!" Ray gave his daughter an old-fashioned glare before carrying on clearly and slowly as if working it out as he spoke, "This last happened one hundred and thirteen years ago according to your research, right? So that showing was recorded as sometime late summer of 1904 and, if you assume the interval's the same, then before that," he paused for a quick calculation, "it was 1791, is that it?"

"Spot on with the maths, Pop," she answered, genuinely impressed with her father's rapid grasp of the idea.

Ray rolled his eyes in wonderment. "So then you're telling me," he said, "that you've got a genuine hand written eye witness account of that 1791 showing and it's right there in that tatty little diary - the one in front of you, the one now messing up my kitchen table - is that what you think?"

"You got it, Pops, that's exactly what I think," she grinned. "Too much of a coincidence, isn't it?

"Well, I'm not sure," Ray said slowly. "Not exactly scientific, is it?"

"Come off it!" she replied tartly. "I mean it ties Dr Reid and his church's history to the right area of the US and to an extremely rare cosmic event that The Divinity appears to believe significant."

"That's pushing it, my girl," Ray laughed. "Talk about tenuous connections and poetic licence; it's borderline crackers, in fact the whole lot of it sounds bloody ludicrous."

Sarah, crestfallen by her father's scathing assessment, wasn't about to give up. She shook her head, put on her best teenager's scowl, and hit back. "There's more chance of winning the Euro twice on the bounce than this being coincidence," she said fiercely. "I'm telling you, Pops... there's something in this - I just know it." She sat back, arms crossed, glaring at her father for a few seconds, then turned to her perplexed, dressing-gown clad mother and asked cheekily, "Any chance of another cuppa, Mum - that last one was bloody lovely?"

Ten minutes later, Ray rang Gerry and, while mother and daughter chattered non-stop in the background about who's going where at Christmas, Ray – still sat at the table and now on his third cup of tea - briefed Gerry on Sarah's latest theory. After listening to the quick explanation of what Ray thought was a mind-boggling suggestion, Gerry was stuck for words as he tried to take on board exactly what it was he'd just been told.

"Jesus, Raymond," he eventually said, in a voice high pitched with incredulity, "this shit gets weirder and weirder by the day, doesn't it?"

"You're telling me! It does."

"And she's adamant that the facts are right…It's not a case of two and two making seven, is it?"

"Maybe four and a bit," Ray answered, "but not seven. I've checked it over, and like I said to her, it's far from a cast iron connection, but who knows it could be a possibility," he sighed, "so I can't decide whether it's actually worth pursuing… but at this stage can we afford to rule anything out?"

Again, Gerry remained silent before answering. "OK, well that's a difficult one," he said after a little thought, "but anyway… I've tried Lucas and Rick about five times in the last couple of hours and I'm getting zilch, nothing by phone or email…Jesus, they're such a pair of dipshits."

Ray shook his head gently. "So, as we speak, no one knows where those two are?" he asked. "Is that what we're saying?"

"Correct," Gerry replied, "but I'll keep ringing, and I'm sure eventually I'll get through to one of them. Can't do much else, can I?"

"OK, so…when you do get through, what are you going to tell them?"

"Firstly," Gerry snorted, "I'll ask them if they're OK."

"Yes Gerry, *obviously*, I know that bit," Ray replied. "I mean, if they're up for it, do you think we should send them to look for this chapel?" Gerry was again slow to answer and this time the silence was long enough to make Ray think he'd lost the connection. "Gerry, are you still there?" he asked.

"Yes, yes, I'm here. I'm just thinking. OK, if they're willing, yes, we'll send them. I mean, at this moment in time, it's the only hint of a lead we've got, isn't it? Sod it: why not?!"

Gerry's reply sounded far from convincing but in the absence of anything else tangible, he was willing to give it a go. Ray, on the other hand, was far more sceptical.

"OK, Gerry, it's your call," he said, "but I think we're clutching at straws…but, hey, if nothing else the boys will catch a great light show!" he laughed.

"When's it supposed to appear?" Gerry asked.

"According to everything I've read, early hours of Sunday morning. US time, that is. So, we won't see a thing here because it'll be daylight, but whatever happens we'll know about it late tomorrow morning."

"Doesn't give them much time then does it?" Gerry said. "Less than ten hours," he stopped for a second to think about the current situation, "and when you think about it we don't know where the fuckers are… they're not answering their phones and we haven't even got a proper location for this mythical chapel, have we?" He was now sounding totally pissed off, "So in truth, I'm not holding out much hope of anything at this stage."

"Look, like you said, all we can do is keep trying," Ray encouraged, "so keep a cool head, just forget about going to sleep for a while and keep on ringing them until you get through."

"Thanks, pal," Gerry said sarcastically. "What a fabulous prospect," and with that the despondent Irishman knew it was time to go. "Right then," he said, "I'll say goodbye for now and get on with chasing them…. I'll ring you the minute I've got any news, OK?

Ray, now happy in the knowledge his partner was on the case, wished him well. "Good man, Gerry," he replied, "have fun."

CHAPTER 25

The Black Mountains

Whilst the cabin's setting was picture perfect, for a reliable mobile signal it was almost useless. Out in this idyllic wilderness Lucas and Rick had abandoned all hope of using their own phones. With both constantly showing the no signal icon, the only viable option for communication with the outside world was the cabin's landline. Lucas looked to his host. "Babb, can I use your house phone please?" he asked. "I need to report back to the UK," he smiled apologetically. "It could be a long one, but I'll pay for the call, obviously."

Babb smiled sweetly. "You go ahead, Mr Roxby," she said, "be my guest and you take as long as you like, it's not a problem."

It was now late afternoon Arizona time, but back home Lucas reckoned Gerry would still be OK to talk. I mean what else would he want to do at just after midnight on a Saturday night – sleep?

"Hello…," the voice answered warily, "who's calling?"

"Gerry, it's me Lucas, sorry for not ringing sooner," he said, trying to sound sincere, "but things have gotten a little crazy over here. I need to fill you in."

"Jesus Christ, Lucas," Gerry growled. "I've been trying to ring you for hours. Where the fuck have you been?"

"We're out in the sticks," he explained. "Well, actually, we're at the foot of some mean looking mountains about fifty miles north of Flagstaff. Mobile reception round here is almost non-existent."

“Whose number is this, then?” Gerry asked. “Where you ringing from?”

Lucas quickly updated his boss; he explained the run-in with the White Warrior hunting party and their subsequent escape north to the safety of the cabin. He left out the fact that they were actually ambushed on their way back to The Divinity’s HQ. Be economical with the truth, he told himself, no point in getting ourselves into any more trouble than we already are.

Sat downstairs at home in his favourite armchair, Gerry listened intently to the ex-sapper’s tale then shook his head in disbelief.

“Well, it’s a bloody good job you rang,” he said. “I tried about ten times, but it just wouldn’t connect,” he took a deep breath. “But now I’ve got you, you need to hear this, right. There’s two things you need to know,” he stopped to double check Lucas was still there. “Are you listening to me, Roxby?”

The Director sounded like a teacher chastising his unruly pupil, but Lucas wasn’t fazed; he’d heard it all before.

“Yes, Gerry,” he answered quickly, “I’m all ears – go on, fill me in.”

“OK first… we got something back from The Divinity about a meet,” Gerry said. “Get this shit: they want to meet you at Phoenix airport. The cheeky fuckers offered to meet you there before your flight home,” he stopped and took another deep breath. “They said it was to ensure ‘no misunderstandings’! Can you believe their fucking nerve? I mean, who the fuck do they think they are, bastard weirdos!” The string of expletives was pretty strong, even for Gerry, so Lucas knew the situation was getting to his boss. In fact, the venom in his tone was so toxic the ex-sapper held the hand set away from his ear.

“When did they think we were going home?” Lucas eventually asked.

“Don’t know,” came the reply. “The fuckers were just pushing their luck…they’re just looking to confirm you two are leaving, that’s all they’re after – they just want rid of you…for good.”

Lucas smiled; Rick had been right. “Well that’s not going to happen,” he said. “Or is it?”

"No way!" Gerry snapped. "You can count on that! Why would we play into their hands? Nah, no chance! We won't take them up on their kind offer, but we might just pretend to."

The gangly Brit knew exactly what his boss was thinking. "A bit of misinformation you mean?" he suggested.

"Yeah, that's the one," Gerry replied. "A little misleading info might go some way to redressing the balance, might even make me feel better." He went quiet for a moment as he considered the idea. "Yeah, if nothing else it'll confuse the bastards," he said finally, "and, hopefully, annoy the shit out of them."

Gerry was now a little calmer and, as thoughts of leading The Divinity a merry dance helped him cool further, Lucas pushed for more information. "OK, so that's point number one," he said. "What's the second thing you needed to tell us?"

"Well, get this: young Sarah's been at it again," Gerry stopped to silently admonish himself for the unintended double-entendre. "In a work sense, I mean, obviously."

Lucas sniggered quietly at his boss's need to clarify the statement. "Yeah, I got that. So, what's she been up to now?

Gerry continued, "Unbelievably, she's come up with a link between this big news Cirrus 5 comet crap and our client."

Lucas remained silent for a second as he tried to fathom what Gerry was suggesting. "When you say our client," he said, "you mean Dr Reid and his old Scottish Bible Bashers, right?"

"Sure do, Roxy," Gerry said. "Now listen to this, it'll boggle your fucking mind…."

***

Ten minutes later, Lucas was running through the copious notes he'd scribbled on the back of a used envelope. During the call to Gerry he'd tucked the phone under his chin and motioned to Marion that he needed to write something down. In an instant she'd passed him a black biro and an old brown envelope to use.

"Well, Mr Roxby, what does your boss have to say?" she asked as she came back into the lounge. "You've written a lot of stuff down, must be important."

Blatantly ignoring the thrust of her question, he asked, "How far is Cedar City from here?"

Marion looked affronted. "What kind of an answer is that?" she asked. But before Lucas could utter anything resembling an apology, Babb butted in, "If that's Cedar City, Utah, then you're looking at one fifty, maybe one sixty, something like that - by car, it's a good three hours."

"Do you mind, Barbara," Marion said glaring harshly at her fawning sister. "Don't encourage the man; it's just down-right bad manners."

Babb pulled a face, "Oh, Marion, don't be such an old stick in the mud. I'm sure Mr Roxby will explain in his own good time, won't you, Mr Roxby?"

Suddenly Lucas held his hands up in surrender. "Look, ladies," he smiled, "before we go on any further, can we *please* stop with all the 'Mister Roxby' palaver; it's driving me crazy," he put his hands down and smiled. "Formal titles make me nervous, you see, so Lucas will do just fine, or Roxy, or even Sarge, if you like; anything but 'Mr Roxby', OK?"

Marion, pretending to be a little put out, turned to look at him then glanced back at her sister. "That's us told, then, isn't it, B?" she said with an impish grin. "OK, from now on 'Lucas' it is!" As she spoke, Babb stifled a grin of her own. She'd known that at some point he was going to have to mention it; she'd seen him wince every time she said his name. Keeping it going while trying to guess the moment when he would crack had been a bit of sport, and she was impressed he'd lasted as long as he had.

"That goes for me as well," Rick chimed in. "I'm just plain old Rick - or Ricky, if you like," he stopped and grinned. "I'm with Roxy on this one, formal titles worry me an' all. You see, the only time I get called Mr Kruger is when I'm in a spot of trouble – and that's not often, believe me," he said with a comedy wink.

Babb clapped her hands together. "Right, that's sorted then," she said. "We are now all officially on first name terms." She glanced toward the ceiling and muttered, "Thank the Lord! Now, who's for more Iced Tea?"

***

Whilst Rick settled down to phone home and report in to his wife, Babb busied herself in the kitchen. As she rustled up some much-needed sustenance, through the window she watched her sister follow Lucas outside. The pensive looking Englishman had retrieved his road atlas from the Mustang and now had it spread open on the table in front of him. He was studying the two pages that showed the South West corner of Utah.

"So, Gerry's wondering if we can find this mythical chapel," he said without looking up, "or whatever's left of it, somewhere round here." He tapped his finger on a spot north of Cedar City. "He wants us to check it out, see if it reveals anything, then report back," Lucas stopped for a second then looked across at a staring Marion. "Sounds a bit of long shot to me, but what the hell, I'm up for giving it a go," he paused, "although finding it won't be easy, will it, I mean, where do you start?"

She smiled. "OK, err, Lucas," she said; this was the first time she'd actually used his first name and liked how it sounded. "This chapel of your colleague's is supposedly somewhere in the midst of the Black Mountains, right?"

"That's right," he said with a nod.

Marion continued, "And we know from this journal's description that it is fairly high up and remote, yes?"

"Yes, that's what Sarah's saying," he replied. "She's studied every detail of the diary, and that's all she can glean." He stopped as he remembered another snippet of information from his conversation with Gerry. "Oh, yeah, that's it's," he said. "Sarah reckons it's close to an ancient trading route that runs through that area, 'The Old Spanish Trail' she called it."

Marion looked thoughtful then grinned. "Right, give me half an hour," she said. "I'll get on the laptop, log in to my ASL account and check our historical records for that area of Utah… see what I can find," as she got up from the table she looked across to the kitchen window and waved at Babb then turned back to Lucas. "So, you just sit back and enjoy Barbara's wonderful hospitality," she said, "and I'll be as quick as I can."

***

After Gerry finished his call with Lucas, he felt relieved. He was happy his 'A-team' were still in one piece and so now, with his mind now kicking into overdrive, he rang Ray.

"Answer your ruddy phone, will you," he muttered as he waited for his partner to pick up, "come on, come on for Pete's sake."

Eventually a groggy sounding voice answered. "Yes, Gerry," it said. "What now?"

"Charming, Raymond," Gerry replied sarcastically, "absolutely effing charming. I did say I'd ring the minute I had an update for you, so do you want to hear it or not?"

The lack of sleep was starting to tell. It had been a long night and it didn't seem to want to end.

"Sorry," Ray replied, "it's just I didn't expect you to come back to me so quickly. I'd actually fallen asleep, but never mind," he stifled a yawn then asked, "so go on then…what's the latest?"

Gerry gave him the full story. He clarified Lucas had been the one to make contact and ran through the team's latest trials and tribulations. He focused on the White Warrior ambush, the call from Marion Armstrong, and the subsequent race to the sister's mountain retreat. He left nothing out and finished off by explaining the field team had agreed to try to put flesh on the bones of Sarah's odd ball theory, despite reservations about it actually being possible.

Ray was now wide awake. "My God those boys are having a bit

of fun, aren't they?" he said. "Reminds me of us back in the good old days, eh, partner?"

"Yeah, those good old days," Gerry mused. "Jesus, Ray, when you think about it, mate, that was nearly thirty years ago."

CHAPTER 26

On the Road

Marion was true to her word and, half an hour after leaving Lucas hunched over his road atlas, she came back outside. But, before she appeared, Rick had joined his colleague at the sun-dappled table and was now attempting to get a feel for the task ahead.

"That doesn't look too bad," he said, studying the map, "we could probably do it in three hours."

"OK...but that's only to there," Lucas said, leaning across and tapping his first finger just above the red dot of Cedar City. "Trouble is, we don't know if that's close - it could be another fifty miles north of there for all we know. Currently, we're best guessing," he sat back, "so I'm just hoping Marion can find out something meaningful."

Just as Lucas finished speaking, Marion stepped out onto the deck. "Speak of the devil," he said loud enough for her to hear him. "Any joy?"

She nodded and smiled. "Kind of," she said as she crossed the fluted timber boarding, "see what you think."

Suddenly both men were drawn to how good she looked. Even today, dressed down in jeans, sweat top and sneakers, with zero make-up and hair scraped back, she had a certain allure. "Gentlemen, there is hope," she announced as she stood next to the table. "It seems there was an old mission house up in those mountains, after all." Then, as she sat down opposite them, she smiled apologetically, "But sadly," she said, "for whatever reason it's not shown on any recent era maps."

"Why's that?" Rick queried.

"Probably because it's long gone, would be my guess," she said, "but all is not lost." She held up a brown A4 wallet and waved it gently. "Fortunately for us, the library records go back a long way, a real long way."

"Who doesn't love the Arizona State Library service?" Lucas said with a goofy grin, "So, go on… what have you managed to dig up?"

Marion placed the folder in front of her, opened it and took out two sheets of paper. She then skimmed both sheets expertly across the table. "Check these out," she said. Rick turned both papers the right way up. One was portrait and one was landscape so when he slid them next to each other, he made a fat letter 'L'. Both men studied the documents closely. "What's that date there, Rick?" Lucas asked as he adjusted his sorry-looking reading glasses. "I can't quite make it out, can you?"

Lucas was now holding the landscape sheet and pointing to the legend in the bottom right-hand corner. "1832, I think," Rick said, then, after screwing his eyes as tight as he could to get it to focus, reaffirmed what he'd just said, "Yeah, 1832."

Marion tapped the table twice. "Both prints are 1832," she said. "They're copies of old railway survey records, we've got thousands of them in our archives… it's the most amazing collection you'll ever lay your eyes on," she sat forward a little. "We've got some of the originals on show in Phoenix and they are stunning, it's a real insight to what the Old West was like in its prime."

Lucas was taken by the level of detail, it was fascinating, and, despite the small print, both extracts were clear and legible. "These are great," he said, genuinely impressed.

"So, this one," Marion said, "is a larger scale map showing the town of Paradigm just there." She had come round the table and was now leaning in between the two men, pointing out landmarks on the first sheet. "And here you can clearly see the trail marked," as she spoke she ran her finger along a dotted line. "It heads up through the mountains…and way over here, see that little crucifix symbol there," she pointed to far corner of the document, "that, I'm guessing, represents your chapel."

The two men were engrossed in her explanation but still couldn't help but be distracted by how good she looked and, now close up, how good she smelt. "OK, so that narrows it down significantly," Lucas said as he tried to regain some focus on the task, "but what about this one, then?"

"Well this is actually from an old survey logbook," she replied. "Still 1832, mind, it's just not from the final map as this one is...see?"

The two men looked closely between the two sheets. "Alright, I think I get it," Rick said. "That's an extract from the finished product and this one's from the back-up info - the sketches and all the other stuff the land surveyors recorded during their field work, right?"

"Absolutely right," she beamed. "This one gives you more detail on the actual location from the trail line...which is what you've got to find, but...," she stopped and moved the first sheet a little closer, "all we know is that it crosses somewhere north of Paradigm here and then heads off north west into the Black Mountains."

Marion pulled back gracefully from between them and returned to the opposite side of the table. As she sat down, she asked, "So then, gentlemen.... what's the next move?"

Lucas sat back, slid his reading glasses back onto the top of his head and crossed his arms. After pondering the question for a few seconds, he answered, "Well, we've got to try and find it, haven't we? Head to this Paradigm town first, then take it from there, waddaya reckon?"

"Not wishing to sound negative, Sarge," Rick said, "but we're going nowhere in that Ford. I don't care how far away we get from Phoenix, it's still a marked car." He shook his head. "If they found us once, they can do it again."

Before Lucas could reply to Rick's objection, a voice from behind suddenly cut in. "No need to worry about that little problem," it said, "you two just need to follow me." The voice was Babb's. Rick and Lucas exchanged bemused glances; they hadn't realised she'd come outside but both were intrigued by her instruction. As Babb scuttled past, the duo stood up from the table and started to follow her. The ex-Mrs Teller wasn't hanging around and, as she disappeared down the side passage, Lucas called after her, "Slow down, will you, what's the rush?"

"Just follow me," she replied. "I've got something to show you."

As the two men navigated the corner of the timber building, they glimpsed her vanish behind the other side of the house.

"Where the hell's she going?" Lucas asked.

"Beats me, Sarge, but just keep going, will you!" Rick prompted cheerfully.

As soon as they'd rounded the far corner of the cabin, they stopped. Babb was now stood facing them with her back against a set of sturdy looking wooden doors.

"Gentlemen," she said grinning like a loved-up mountain cat, "let me introduce you to my other pride and joy," she said, then span round, flung the double doors open and announced, "This is… Ruby!"

Lucas and Rick were gobsmacked. There, parked snuggly in the compact garage was another four wheeled American legend. A true beast of a vehicle: a Jeep Wrangler, Rubicon edition. "My God, Babb, what a machine!" Lucas said as he moved closer for a better look. "Now, that's what I call a four by four."

Rick grinned then whistled. "Jesus Christ," he said, "she's a beauty."

Babb was unable to contain her pride. "Thought you'd be impressed," she said, "and you'll be pleased to know she's fully loaded, gassed-up and totally at your disposal."

Marion joined the others in front of the garage. "Full of surprises my little sister is, isn't she?" Once that divorce came through, I tell you, that was it – she turned over a new leaf and went nuts! No challenge too big, or too small, and that's how it is now, isn't it, B?"

"Sure is, sis," she grinned, "just a pity I left it so long…."

***

Rick moved the Mustang and parked it on the other side of the Honda. During the tight manoeuvre, careful not to damage Marion's pride and joy, he ran over the strip of parched grass that bordered the cabin's tiny parking space.

"That's fine, Rick," Babb said, "don't worry about the grass, it's seen better days," then, as she watched Rick gently ease the V8's nose to within an inch of the cabin, she smiled and gave a thumbs up.

Now with its front bumper almost touching the outer wall, the Ford was hidden from traffic using the access road.

"That looks serious," Babb said pointing to the scrapes and dents in the Mustang's front end. "What happened?"

"Like we said," Rick replied, "another run-in with a goon squad, but this time it was a couple of real unfriendly bikers - tried to box us in." He smiled. "But they're gonna have to be quicker than that to catch me and old Sarge out."

Babb just shook her head. "Seems a dangerous business," she said. "I hope you're paid well."

"I wish," came the deflated reply.

Back inside the cabin, Lucas was in the lounge with Marion. He was rummaging through his travel bag trying to find his wash kit. "Am I OK to use the bathroom for ten minutes?" he asked as his hand wrapped round it. "I could do with a quick spruce up before we leave, I'm feeling a bit minty."

Marion nodded. "Yes, no problem, feel free," she said, "but you know we're coming with you, don't you?"

"What, to the bathroom?" he smirked.

"Funny guy, aren't you Lucas Roxby, real funny," she stuck her tongue out at him. "No, you know exactly what I mean.... Babb and I are going to Utah with you." She looked stern. "We want to help you find the chapel," she said, "if that's OK, mind?"

From the way she said it, the ex-sapper knew it wasn't a request; it was a statement of fact and it didn't surprise him in the slightest. Then, as he finally managed to extract his toiletries from the jam-packed bag, he turned for the bathroom. “I didn’t expect you to say anything else,” he said nonchalantly. “In my book, it was a given.”

***

Rick was as happy behind the wheel of the Jeep as he had been behind the Mustang’s. It was simply another fine example of home-grown automotive engineering that would eat up the miles with ease, but this time - with both on and off road as an option - nowhere was out of bounds. So, with Lucas up front and the two sisters snugged up with the luggage in the rear, they set off on their drive north.

Babb had not exaggerated. The Jeep came complete with all the whistles and bells you could ever want. Plus, it had a full tank of fuel, a front hydraulic winch, extra jerry cans of diesel, first aid kit and a water carrier, to name but a few extra extras. As the lady claimed, it did appear to be ‘fully loaded’.

“Take a left up here, Rick,” Babb said, leaning forward to give instructions into his right ear. “It’s the fastest way to the interstate… gets you onto one eighty and then it’s a straight run north on that for a while.”

“Yes, Ma’am,” Rick shouted into the rush of the oncoming wind.

***

The sleek gulf-stream touched down on the asphalt of Cedar City’s runway 2/20 with only the faint sound of screeching rubber. Then, as the unmistakeable roar of jet engine back-thrust kicked in, it slowed to a trundle and eventually reached the end of the blacktop still positioned directly over the white runway centre line. As the engine noise decreased, it executed a perfect 90 degree turn to the left, then taxied to the farthest corner of the airport and finally shut down outside the dark metallic exterior of hangar number B6.

As the decibel level finally fell to a background whirr, a three-man ground crew raced to the jets side. Within a matter of seconds, the overall clad workers had expertly installed a set of portable aluminium steps and signalled the watching pilot with a thumbs-up. With access securely in place, the rear door clunked heavily and swung open. As Leon Tate looked out into the late afternoon sunshine, he looked relieved.

"At last," he said. "We can go."

The smartly attired hostess didn't know if The Divinity chief was talking to her or not but smiled anyway. "Of course, Mr Tate," she fawned, "and can I say it's been a pleasure to have been of service today. I hope you enjoyed the flight."

"Yes, my dear, it was... fine," came the arrogant reply, "but I expect nothing less."

As a consummate professional, the stewardess ignored Tate's ambivalence; she was well aware of the man's reputation. But it was more than her job was worth to show any hint of disdain for him, so the pretence continued. "Obviously, Mr Tate, thank you," she said sweetly, "and you be sure to enjoy your visit here.... we'll see you tomorrow afternoon for the flight home, is that correct?"

"It's not definite," he replied, "but when our schedule is finalised Clayton will ring and confirm directly with Captain Davis, OK?" She was given no chance to reply as Tate turned abruptly and proceeded to lead his entourage off the plane. The all-male delegation followed their superior in an orderly single file down the narrow set of steps, then across the concrete apron and on toward the open doors of the hangar, and the stewardess couldn't have been happier to see the back of them.

***

In their well-drilled, two by two formation, the eight Harley Davidsons were an impressive sight. The White Warrior's Nomad chapter, fresh from the excesses of the Nevada party scene, were riding East on Route 56 towards Cedar City. And, bringing up the rear of the eye-catching cavalcade, was the club's ever-present crew bus. Their much-appreciated support vehicle was a battle-scarred grey Chevrolet panel van kitted out with everything a modern-day raiding party needed for the road. From critical bike spares to baseball bats, from tools to beer, it stocked just about every motorcycle club essential you could think of.

"Mike, it's Red," the driver drawled into his ancient flip-top phone. "We're 'bout fifteen miles west of CC, where do you want us to meet?"

"We've agreed to hold outside Paradigm," Mike Connolly answered, "so head straight through Cedar onto I-15 Northbound, then up to Para and wait up in the rest area on the north side of town. It's big, you can't miss it," he paused. "Let me know when you're there, OK?"

"OK, Mike, call you later," Red said, then flipped his phone shut.

***

The tourist chiefs of South West Utah couldn't believe their good fortune. The number of calls, enquiries, and requests they'd received about accommodation, camp sites, and hotel availability had reached unprecedented levels and they literally had their lucky stars to thank. The local economy was getting a major boost as every professional, semi-professional, and amateur stargazer in the northern hemisphere descended on their rugged corner of Utah for the much-publicised arrival of the comet known as Cirrus 5.

***

At 9.45pm, when the blue Jeep Wrangler arrived on Paradigm's main street, its four wind-swept occupants didn't look out of place. They blended in perfectly with the excited hordes that'd swamped the town's simple facilities, eager for a glimpse of the much-hyped comet. As they parked up at the top of the street next to a silver pick-up with Colorado plates, Lucas made eye contact with the driver and smiled.

"How's it going friend?" he grinned. "What's the latest on the big show?"

The driver raised an eyebrow. "Say again, partner," he drawled.

"I'm just being polite," Lucas said, now annunciating more clearly. "Just asking for an update on the comet – you got any details?"

"Uh, yeah," the silver haired man said, "best guess they're saying is it'll show round 1.00 am or so," he then shot Lucas a big grin. "You come all the way from England to see this?"

Lucas was amazed; most Americans struggled to identify he was English and, whilst they always twigged he was from overseas, they usually thought he was Australian or Irish. "Good shout friend, very impressive," he replied, then leant out of the window a little further, "and the answer to your question is sort of Yes. It wasn't the main reason for the visit, but as we're in the neighbourhood, you know how it is, we thought it would be rude not to come to see what all the fuss is about."

The man laughed. "Whereabouts in England you from?" he asked cheerily.

"Originally from Lancaster but I live near Warrington now," Lucas replied. "You know it?"

The pick-up driver laughed again. "I know it's a small world," he said, "but can't say I've ever heard of either of them two, but, hey, like that matters much." Then, reaching out his hand, he introduced himself, "I'm JB, JB Collins," he said, "nice to meet you, man. Me and my old lady came over from Colorado Springs yesterday. We're gonna stay around for a couple of days and see how it goes, maybe party a little and comet watch of course." He stopped and pointed upward. "Wouldn't want to miss this baby for the world."

Loving the friendly vibe of JB's chilled approach, Lucas shook his new acquaintance's hand enthusiastically. "Sure, JB, it's nice to meet you too," he said. "I'm Lucas, Lucas Roxby, and this is my good buddy Ricky Kruger," he pointed at Rick in the seat next to him, and then hooked a thumb in the direction of the Jeeps rear, "and in the back here we've got our friends the Armstrong sisters, Marion and Babb from Arizona."

As Lucas made the introductions, his companions all waved appropriately at their new comet obsessed neighbour and then, once the hellos were concluded, Rick turned the engine off, and the foursome got out to stretch their legs. After a quick check on their bustling surroundings, the sisters kindly volunteered to go in search of refreshments and, as they headed off toward a row of shops, Rick ambled round to the passenger side to join Lucas in his continuing conversation with JB.

"So, where's the best view gonna be from?" Rick asked as he got close to the pick-up's cab.

"Well, I never," JB said in mock surprise, "another outta country accent." Rick stopped at Lucas's side and both men now faced the silver haired pick-up driver.

"Don't tell me you're gonna get his right as well, are you?" Lucas asked.

JB was grinning from ear to ear. "Man, that's even easier than yours," he said. "This guy's from South Africa - not a chance in hell of getting that one wrong, I tell you, boys, this is all too easy, way too easy."

The two HSG men looked at each other in wide eyed amazement then started to laugh. This really was a first; both accents right first time. Unbelievable, Lucas thought to himself, what are the odds on that?

CHAPTER 27

Lights Out

As Mordecai swung the pick-up through the gates of Hamer's Plant Yard, Leon Tate's last instruction was playing over in his mind: *This time it has to be subtle, Ings, this one disappears without fuss and without trace, you got that?*

The well-ordered Yard was deserted. Apart from the black Ram parked at the front of the bunk-house, it was dead, so, as Mordecai pulled up next to the van, he blasted the horn, then sat back.

Now, whilst the enveloping dust cloud settled, he checked his phone. It showed one missed call and one text. Both were from Santino and the gist of each garbled communiqué was simple: No sign of the librarian or the Mustang men back at the house in Flagstaff. As he slammed his fist down hard against the steering wheel, he cursed under his breath. "Another fucking dead end," he said to himself out loud, "and another shit-storm to navigate." After a couple of minutes sat stewing, and with no sign of a response to his horn blast, he tried again but this time he held it a lot longer.

After twenty seconds and still nothing, he jumped out the truck and started toward the office door. He'd gone no more than three steps when a troubling thought stopped him dead in his tracks. He turned slowly toward the gate. The gates were open, which was quite unusual in itself, but, even stranger, the dog chains were half buried in the dust. Dog chains lying in the dust wouldn't normally be an issue but, with no sign of a snarling Doberman attached to the end, something was wrong.

Slowly he retraced his steps, opened the passenger door and quietly popped the glove box. The Beretta was nestled in its usual spot and as always it was loaded. Sliding the safety off, he started back toward the building.

"Expecting trouble, are we?" a voice asked from behind.

Mordecai froze. Thinking fast, trying hard to identify the voice, he wracked his brains. Did it sound familiar? Well, if it did, he couldn't place it so, deciding to push his luck, he started to turn to find out whose it was.

"I wouldn't, if I were you," the voice said. "Best just keep your eyes front - you hear me? Then drop the gun."

The grizzled red-neck did as instructed and looked straight ahead; after a several seconds of nervous silence he asked, "Or what?"

"If you don't," the voice growled, "then on a count of three I pull the trigger."

"Who says?" Mordecai asked calmly.

"Never mind who says, boy, just do as you're told.... and do it now."

With no official challenge, Ings figured it wasn't the law that had him in their sights, but since he found himself standing in the open under a blazing sun with what he imagined was a pistol pointing at his back, he made the decision to drop the Beretta.

"Good call," the voice said now much closer, "you made the right choice."

Suddenly Mordecai recognised the voice and began to turn. He didn't even get half-way round before he heard the whoosh. Then the lights went out.

***

The gleaming SUVs were waiting patiently in the cavernous interior of hangar B6. As the jet taxied to a standstill, on cue the drivers headed back to their vehicles. Tate's chauffeur, in the lead car, jumped to attention the second his boss appeared at the hangar doors.

"Señor Tate, your bag please," he said as he motioned toward the black leather holdall.

"OK, you take that," the Chief said, handing over his travel bag, "but I'll keep the attaché." He stood for a second, surveying his surroundings, then got into the back seat. "We're late," he said, "let's get moving."

"Si, Señor," Juan replied as he glanced at the two SUVs behind. Then the Mexican shut the passenger door, checked the boot was closed, and signalled to the two other drivers it was time to go. Seconds later, the three-car convoy pulled out of the hangar entrance and turned left. After passing two brick outbuildings, the cars did another left, then passed through the airport's northern perimeter gate and sped off in the direction of Cedar City.

As the convoy raced west, Tate kept his eyes front but was concentrating on the image in the rear-view mirror. He was studying the handsome young face that sat quietly behind him and, after a few seconds, felt the urge to question him.

"Well, Clayton," he began, sternly, "have you heard anything more from the house?"

"Err...y-yes, sir," the nervous assistant stammered. "Since the two women, there's been a couple more visitors: two workmen and a neighbour. The neighbour was apparently enquiring about a forthcoming charity event and..."

Before he could finish, Tate cut in. "The men," he snapped, "what did they want? Did we get a description, any details?"

Clayton could feel his boss's eyes boring into him and, even via the mirror's reflection, the stare was un-nerving. "Leonard mentioned they were a bit vague," he replied, "said they wanted to know if she was available to discuss some construction work she'd had quoted." He stopped to clear his throat. "Nothing untoward though," he croaked, "he said they were genuine."

"Why'd he say that?" the Security Chief asked quickly.

"Err...well, he told me they were dressed in coveralls, work boots, and arrived in an old pick-up with a stack of timber in the back."

"A perfect cover," Tate said shaking his head. "Check back with him, see if everything's still OK."

Clayton looked ashen. "Yes, Mr Tate," he answered as he reached for his phone. "I'll do it now."

***

As the Bikers van pulled into the northbound section of the I-15 rest area, Red checked his wing mirrors. Happy to see all eight bikes still tight behind, he aimed the van in the direction of a deserted corner of the car park and flashed his hazards. Dutifully, the riders took the cue and followed.

As Red parked up, each of the V-Twins slotted in, one after the other, next to the van, and blipped their throttle. Once they'd formed a neat line of rumbling gleaming Milwaukee chrome, the riders kicked down their side stands, turned off their engines, and dismounted. Then, after shaking off a hundred miles of road dust with a good stretch, the bikers headed for a pair of timber picnic tables shaded by a copse of wind-bent pines.

Once the mob had settled under the drooping branches, Red made for the Chevy's side door and yanked the handle hard. The door panel slid open with a swish and finished with a resounding clunk as it hit its locking catch. The bearded biker looked inside and, with a knowing smile of satisfaction, eyed the array of goodies on display within the interior. Every item was neatly stowed, every item was in good order, and every item had its use. Big Red knew his job; as many of his comrades would testify, he was probably one of the best quartermasters in the business.

"Hey, Red," one of the bikers shouted over, "you fetchin'some cold ones over, bro?"

"Yeah, yeah, dickweed," he yelled back. "Just give me a chance, will ya, for Chrissakes - give a man a fuckin' break."

Red ripped open a bag of ice from a small chest freezer and poured it into a cooler box. Then from the built-in fridge he took out four six packs of Shiner, threw them into the insulated box and closed the lid. After dishing out the refreshments, he left his road weary crew chatting, smoking and quenching their thirst, and moved away to make a call.

"Mike, it's Red," he said as he wandered back toward the van. "Yeah, all present and correct, boss, we've parked up in the rest area north of Paradigm and the boys are just taking a quick break - but we'll be ready to move the minute you give us the word, no problem."

"OK, Red," came the reply. "I don't know how long you're gonna have to sit round, dude... just gotta wait for the call from our friends. Hang tight, bro, ring you when I know more, OK?"

"Yeah, no problem, boss," Red replied. "Like I say, we're ready to roll."

After the call, the bearded biker slipped his cell phone into his pocket and walked back to the eight beer swilling renegades lounging under the trees.

"OK, you sorry looking bunch of mother fuckers!" he boomed. "Listen up," he paused as he glared at the expectant faces, "make sure every one of you is set to go, and I mean like at a second's notice, y'all understand me?"

Unanimously the assembled outlaws muttered and nodded their acknowledgement. "The Ironman will call us the minute we gotta move," Red said, "so be ready, boys. We don't want no fucking slackers, OK?"

CHAPTER 28

The Star Gazers

The sense of expectation in the unusually chaotic town of Paradigm was so intense you could smell it. The streets teamed with every vehicle type imaginable and, as gridlock loomed, the tension mounted. The crazy traffic, coupled with the crowds of excited stargazers that claimed every square inch of free space, made the Utah backwater feel like it was bursting at the seams and then, as the light began to fade, the already charged atmosphere moved up a notch. It now truly felt like countdown had started.

Under the gently flickering lights of Main Street, the HSG men said goodbye to JB. They watched the silver fox and his hippy wife melt into a throng of enthusiastic comet worshippers; the atmosphere was positively electric.

"This is wild," Rick grinned as he watched the passing crowds. "All these people can't be wrong, can they?"

Lucas ran a hand through his unruly hair. "Well, if they are," he said, "I reckon there'll be a bastard riot."

The two men remained by the Jeep enthralled by the surrounding hustle and bustle. Lucas glanced back up the street and spotted two familiar faces. "Here come our favourite yanks, Ricky," he said, tapping his partner on the shoulder. "Some pair, eh?

Rick smiled. "Library Lady and Fully Loaded," he said. "Yeah - helluva combination."

The sisters were back quicker than expected and, much to the HSG team's delight, it looked like they'd been successful. "Two cappuccinos," Marion said, "and a little something to kill those hunger pangs you were bitching about."

Both sisters smiled as they handed over coffee and a stuffed bagel to each of their hungry companions.

"Thank you, ladies," Lucas said, "that's just what the doctor ordered." Then, as he inspected his hand-out closely, he commented, puzzled, "You were bloody quick. I take it you didn't have to go far?"

"Sure didn't," Babb said pointing up the street. "Found a lovely little coffee place just round that corner…and we timed it dead right, didn't we, sis?

"Yes – just lucky I guess," Marion replied. "When we walked in the queue was tiny, then two minutes later it was out the door."

Lucas smiled appreciatively at the sisters but, keen to move on to more pressing matters, he balanced his coffee and bagel on the front wing and reached inside the Jeep.

"That's great, girls," he said, "but now have a look at this." He pulled a large fold-away map from the glove box and spread it out over the hood. "Our new buddy, JB, gave us this little beauty," he said, patting his free gift affectionately, "told us he had two copies of the same one. Just grab that corner, Ricky, will you," he ordered as a light breeze lifted it off the hood.

Rick stretched over and smoothed out the top left quadrant of the unruly map, then Lucas leant on the front wing to continue his spiel.

"This is brilliant," he said, looking like he'd just matched six numbers, "it's got this whole area at one to fifty thou, just what we needed, and we are…," his hand hovered briefly over the map before stabbing his fore finger down, "right there! Slap bang in the middle of little old Paradigm."

Babb was nodding. "Mr Collins seems like a real nice guy," she said. "Obviously a generous soul."

Lucas turned to her. "He sure is," he agreed, "and not only did he give us the map, but he also pointed out a few places of interest."

Lucas went on to explain to the huddle exactly what their new friend had said about the area, such as where to find some of the best vantage points for comet watching, the local facilities, and some thoughts on finding the part of the old Spanish Trail they were interested in.

"He knows a lot about this neck of the woods, doesn't he?" Marion commented. "I thought they were just visiting from Colorado."

"Well, yeah," Rick answered, "the Collins live in Colorado Springs, see, but JB said they do a lot of travelling around the Mid-West and have been in these parts before. Apparently, they love it."

Marion smiled. "Well, we did get lucky, then, didn't we?" she said with a faint hint of sarcasm, "bumping into Mr JB Collins from Colorado was indeed fortuitous – did he say anything else?"

"Only that he's not sure what to expect from tonight," Lucas pointed skyward, "didn't know if the comet would match all the hype, you know. Might not live up to expectation, could be an anti-climax, might be a lot of disappointed people come morning. Just have to wait and see, eh?"

"OK, so what's the plan?" Marion asked. "Where we intending to watch this Lorded spectacle?" She looked at Lucas and pulled a face. "I presume that is what we're actually going to do, isn't?"

"Of course, we're going to watch it," he replied. "We've travelled this far so it'd be a crying shame not to."

Marion smiled. "Good," she said. "I'm feeling quite excited, actually. I think it'll be worth the journey," she looked back at Lucas, "so like I said, where are we thinking of watching it?"

The Englishman returned his focus to the map. "JB reckoned the closest spots to here are these three areas along this ridge line… said they'd all be OK," his finger traced the sweep of the ridges brown contour lines as he spoke. "They'll all be mad busy, but, hey, we knew that would be the case, didn't we?"

"Did we?" Rick said. "I don't remember that bit."

Babb was engrossed in the map. "It'll get cold up there," she said. "We'll need some essentials before we go. For a night under the stars we're going to at least need food and a little something to drink."

No one disagreed.

***

By the time Rick eased the Jeep out of the Grocery store car park, it was dark. The two sisters were packed into the rear seat compartment like sardines in a can and now not only did they have to accommodate three bulging back packs but had two bags of groceries crammed in with them as well. It couldn't get any cosier.

"You girls alright in the back there?" Lucas asked. "If it's too packed, I can still get a bit of stuff in this front here with me if you want."

"No, we're fine Lucas," Marion cooed. "We couldn't fit anything else back here, mind.... but it's OK, isn't it, B?"

"Yes, snug as a bug," Babb answered, "and, Rick, you just remember don't brake too hard now." She giggled. "You don't want some big old grocery bag knock you out, now, do you?"

***

Forty minutes later, the Jeep joined a rag-tag queue moving up a dark gravel road. The narrow track wound its way up to the second of the local vantage points recommended by JB and, as the convoy rumbled its way steadily uphill, it was accompanied by the non-stop chatter and shouts from groups on foot heading up the adjacent trail.

"My God, this is amazing," Babb said in genuine awe. "I'd never have believed so many folks would come out to watch this thing. Look at the traffic, look at the people. My God... it's worse than it was in town. I guess no one's stayed home tonight."

"Just think about it," Lucas said loudly to make sure he was heard over the torquey growl of the engine, "this is only one of hundreds of vantage points – and all of them will be packed. Must be a couple of thousand people here in just this one spot alone. It's crazy."

After a half hour crawl up the steep track, the Jeep reached a large plateau area. Rick followed the lead of the VW camper he'd been behind all the way up and, after a couple of minutes, it pulled over to the left and stopped. He immediately followed suit. Taking their place in the ever-growing line of vehicles parked along the edge of the plateau, Rick checked his mirrors one last time. "Guess this is our spot, then," he said as he turned off the engine. "Time to make camp and get comfy, folks, it's gonna be a long night."

As they all looked out into the clear, star studded sky, it was Marion who spoke first, "If ever there was a night to watch a shooting star," she whispered, "then this has got to be it." And, without over thinking it, she'd pretty much summed up the mood of every expectant stargazer massed on that moon lit mountain.

***

The three SUVs pulled off the main road and approached the gated entrance at a snail's pace. The vehicle carrying Leon Tate still lead the convoy. As a pair of dark clad figures appeared out of the shadows, Juan eased the car to a halt. The first guard approached the car and the chauffeur lowered his window to speak to him.

"Mr Tate's delegation, "he said. "Three vehicles, fifteen personnel in total."

"Passes, please, gentlemen," the black clad silhouette ordered.

"Yeah, here you go," Juan said, handing over a small plastic-coated wallet. "Check it out." While the first guard took the wallet and started to examine it by torch light, gate keeper two slowly prowled around the monstrous SUV checking it over.

"Is Mr Tate on board this vehicle?" asked Guard One as he shone his flashlight directly into Juan's contorted face.

"Man, watch where you pointing that thing," the chauffeur snarled. "You fuckin' blinding me, you moron." The guard immediately dropped the beam away from his face but, before he could reply, the rear passenger window slid down.

"Yes… I am on board," Tate said coolly. "As is everyone else who is supposed to be. Check the passes, your list, and the registrations as quickly as you can and let us through, OK?"

"Will do, Mr Tate," the guard said snapping to attention, "just gotta be sure everyone's legit, sir. You know how it is, just doing our job."

"I know, I know, you're right," Tate replied. "We do have to be careful, we have to be vigilant at all times.... but just remember who's running the fucking show, boy, and who pays the wages. You understand what I'm saying?"

"Yes, sir, Mr Tate," the guard almost bowed as he spoke. "I totally understand." Stepping back from the vehicle, he shouted over to his colleague, "Billy, get those Goddam gates open. Let's get these gentlemen on their way, and I mean right now!"

Guard two jumped straight to it and, seconds later, the convoy was through the entrance and heading up the long, sweeping drive toward the house.

The house was mind-blowing. With all its cool tinted glass and sculpted steel blending into the mountain side, it was the epitome of subtle excess. Invisible from surrounding vantage points, with even low-level helicopter fly pasts revealing little of its existence, it was an architectural master class in environmental synergy and camouflage. It was, without doubt, the jewel in the crown of The Divinity's property portfolio.

The three cars rolled up outside the main entrance in perfect formation and, as the headlight reflections in the glass frontage mingled with the drive's up-lighters, it put on a dazzling show. Once the passengers had been off loaded, Juan led the convoy back round the building to a hard-standing area at the side and parked up. As he walked back to the house, he shook his head in amazement. The sheer scale and luxury of the place was hard to comprehend; although he'd been here many times before, he was still staggered by its decadence. Suddenly, the Mexican's thoughts were interrupted by an approaching figure.

"Hey, Juan, you shit for brains half breed mother fucker, what's happening, man?" The voice came from a grinning, bearded bear of a man emerging from the shadows before him.

"Well, whatta you know," Juan beamed. "The one and only Red Clarke.... what the fuck is your sorry fat ass doing here?"

"Business, my friend," the biker grinned, "always business."

"Yeah...like what?" the Mexican asked.

"Got a full squad on security for tonight's fundraiser," he replied. "Me and eight of the boys." Red stopped to open his cut and flash a holstered .45. "Apparently Mr Tate wants airtight security, don't want no unexpected visitors, just the rich and generous, eh, bro?"

"Cool. Yeah, things are tense at the moment. We got a few issues... so the boss is taking no chances."

"That's what we heard, brother," Red said as he offered the wiry chauffeur a cigarette. "Ings reckons he's spooked by all the shit that's been happening, that's why we're here, see. Just in the background, mind," he paused and smiled, "to keep a watchful eye over things, you know how it is, don't ya?"

"Yeah, Red, sure do, man, makes sense." Juan paused to light the cigarette then, as he blew out his first lungful of smoke, added, "Those two pricks from England really fucked him off as well, you know, and all that hassle with Coleman. What a shit storm! Man, was he pissed."

Reds expression changed to a scowl. "I tell ya, bro," he said, "I hope I run into them two limey cock-suckers. After what they did, we owe them big time, and I mean big time. If they show up again, we just gonna shoot them mother-fuckers in the head... and that's the order from the top."

Juan grinned appreciatively then asked, "Where you headed now?"

"Jus' doing the rounds," the biker said. "The boys are spread out across the estate, so I'll spend the night checking up on them, random visits and calls, coordinator's role, you know the drill." Red waved his radio set in front of Juan just to emphasise the point. "Jus' keeping 'em on their toes," he grinned. "Straight forward gig, man, know what I mean? But gotta stay sharp, bro, gotta stay sharp. You?"

"Back to the house first," the chauffeur replied. "Then me and two other drivers will shadow the group. We'll go from the house up to the chapel and back. Like you, though, Red, we're just in the background, there just in case – and I'm hoping for a quiet night."

"Don't give a fuck whether it's quiet or not," the biker said. "Don't mind if the shit hits. All the same to me, brother, whatever happens we're ready, always ready, know what I mean?"

"Yeah, yeah, Red, I know what you mean. You just the same badass biker gringo you always been, aren't you? You never gonna change, man, never."

"Fuck change, man, can't see the point," the bearded biker smiled, then glanced over Juan's shoulder. "Good to see you, bro, but I gotta run. Lot of ground to cover. You have a good night now, you hear, enjoy the party and stay safe. Catch you later, amigo," and with that Big Red headed off into the darkened grounds of the estate, committed to keeping his mercenary security force focused on the task in hand.

***

Sat alone in the vast dining room of the Mountain House, Vincent Dubois was running through his personal itinerary for the night's celebration. The fund raiser was not his priority, but it was still important although, as they were regular occurrences, he could host events like this in his sleep. The big deal, his main focus, was the annual celebration Mass to be held after the gala and this year it had special significance. It was an auspicious date, it marked a milestone in The Divinity's long history but the number of attendees for this most private of ceremonies was limited. Only true Inner Sanctum would be present and only those carefully selected would participate. That was a golden rule and it always had been.

So now, in preparation for the long night ahead, Dubois pressed his palms flat down on the clear glass table, took a deep breath and held it. While he focused on the sensation of the cooling glass on his fingertips, he closed his eyes, bowed his head then gently exhaled. To an outside observer it would have looked like the man was praying, but if it was to pray then the Monsignor's God would not be listening. Vincent Dubois worshipped only money, and money doesn't listen, it only ever talks....

CHAPTER 29

Bad Company

Despite repeated attempts, there was no response from Clayton's colleague at the Higham house. What the hell is the old bastard playing at, he asked himself as his latest call went unanswered.

But why would there be a problem? Leonard was more than capable, and his earlier update had offered no hint of concern, so maybe he was getting twitchy over nothing. But the reality was, he wasn't worried about his colleague; at the root cause of his distress was the ever-present fear of his volatile boss. At any second, the Chief was likely to demand an update on the situation and having nothing positive to report to Mr Tate was not an option.

Quickly he dialled a fourth time; no joy. Yet again, the phone went straight to voicemail. So, frustrated, the young assistant left another message, "Lenny, it's me again. Come on, for God's sake, ring me back, will you. Tate's on my case – I need to know everything's OK down there, so please get back to me as quick as you can…."

He snapped his phone shut and headed back to the library only to be immediately confronted by his worst nightmare.

"Ah, Clayton," Tate hissed, "what's the latest from Leonard – anything new from the house?"

For a second the younger man faltered. The sweat on his brow ran cold, his pupils dilated and, as he bowed his head to avoid his superior's glare, he could hardly breathe. "Err…no, no sir," he stammered. "I…I have just spoken to Lenny and everything's exactly as it was before –

no more visitors, no calls, so nothing further to report, Mr Tate - all very quiet."

Tate was still in two minds about the winsome young man that stood nervously before him. Will this boy ever make the grade? was a question he often pondered. In truth he didn't know, but when asked if he was committed to the organisation, was he reliable and did he obey every order without question? Then there was no doubt, the answer was a resounding Yes. So, though he lacked forcefulness, guile, and often displayed a vein of sensitivity a mile wide, Tate didn't mind. For the duties he required he believed a sweet sensitive flower was far more use to him than a gung-ho warrior.

The Security Chief stepped closer. "No further visits from construction company employees, then?" he asked sarcastically.

Clayton tensed. "No, nothing at all, sir," he said as calmly as he could. "Like I said, all very quiet."

The young assistant was not a practiced liar, but terror was a powerful motivator. He'd made a snap decision to lie and immediately regretted it; he knew better than most Leon Tate was not a man easily fooled. Initially the Security Chief didn't respond; he simply stood in front of his charge, looking him up and down. As the milliseconds flew by, Carr's unease intensified. His heart rate quickened, his chest tightened, his mind raced, and inwardly he screamed for God's sake just please believe me and go!

Suddenly his prayers were answered. With a rare gesture of appreciation, "Good work, Clayton," Tate said, the atmosphere changed in an instant. Then, with what could have passed for a smile he added, "Right then, you better start getting things ready for tonight." He pointed to a large, gothic style clock on the wall. "We haven't got long, boy, there's a lot to do. So, get a move on," and with that the Security Chief side stepped him and strode off toward the dining room.

As Clayton watched his domineering boss disappear down the corridor, he shouted after him, "Yes, sir, Mr Tate, right away," and then turned to pray his relief had not been too obvious.

***

The squat stone chapel was only small, but the quality of its original features was unmistakeable. From the perfect lines of its hand-hewn stonework to the mosaic tiles of the altar floor it was testament to a skillset long since vanished from the Black Mountains.

Originally built in 1695 by the first missionaries to venture along the old trading trail, the chapel had seen many changes in its time. In fact, local folklore would hint that through its three hundred and twenty-year lifespan it had seen it all. Everything from extended periods of neglect, abandonment and abuse, through to wanton damage and the ravages of time were all there. But, despite the many hardships, it had survived and had still been standing as a derelict ruin when its small high-altitude plot transferred to private ownership in the late 1950s.

Since then the land had changed hands several times and was now part of a luxurious multi-million-dollar chunk of Utah real estate. As a bonus, the visionary development had included an extensive restoration of the ancient run-down chapel that had ultimately ended up within the footprint of its sprawling grounds. As a consequence, The Mountain House was without doubt The Divinity's premier property.

***

For the ceremony the chapel had been lovingly prepared and readied for use, with bouquets of white lilies, gold fringed tapestries, and a black carpeted entrance way, it looked nothing short of medieval. At capacity, the building could accommodate a hundred people but tonight there would be fewer than seventy.

In front of the altar an eagle lectern took centre stage and there, placed on it, was a large leather-bound book. The book was open at a page depicting a cleric burning at the stake and, whilst the wood-cut image was primitive by modern standards, the terror etched on the face of the young victim was as disturbing as it was realistic.

Access to the chapel from the estate grounds was via a sweeping set of steps. The stone stairway was cut into the mountainside and each rise had been reinforced by a thick timber edging finished off with a gravel in-fill. As it reached the plateau, the stairway rounded a jutting boulder then seamlessly merged with the path leading directly to the chapel's door. The classical south facing entrance was an arched slab of solid oak studded with iron rivets and had door handles the size of footballs. The views from east and west were limited to sheer rock faces but, from the rear of the building, looking north across the valley, the scenery was breath-taking. The ground surrounding the chapel was sparsely vegetated and extended no more than fifty feet in any direction and along the full length of the northern elevation ran a razor-wire topped fence. The robust mesh barrier was set back from the leading edge and was designed not only to ensure the security of the estate, but also to protect its occupants from the sheer drop behind it.

Trudging round the rocky overhang at the top of the stairway, an out of breath Red stared into a fluorescent haze that surrounded the chapel. "You two boys OK up here?" he enquired.

The younger looking of the two bikers by the front door looked across. "Yeah, Red, everything's cool, bro," he replied. "Some climb, ain't it?"

"You're not wrong," Red wheezed, "that's a doozey set of steps. Man, if I do that too many times tonight it's gonna kill me." He pulled a pained face as he stood, hands on hips, regaining his breath. After a few seconds he acclimatised and started toward the chapel. "Good job you two boys are a little skinnier than me," he said as he came up close to his charges, "and a little fitter."

"Yeah, more than just a little, gramps," the second biker grinned. "Ten years ago, maybe, you could give us a run for our money, but not now, old man, now you're past it."

Red stepped up and jabbed his finger into the centre of the younger man's chest. "Hey, less of the 'old man', you disrespectful prick," he growled, "and what's with the 'you're past it' shit? I'd still outthink either of you two any day of the week, just remember, boy.

Brains are far more important than brawn, and don't you ever fucking forget it, hear me?"

"Yeah, yeah, Red, whatever, man," Bean grinned. "You do your shit and we do ours, that's cool, that's how it's supposed to be, that's how we like it. Me and Jimbo, we jus' fuckin with ya, you know how it is, bro."

"Yeah – I do," Red forced a smile as he stepped back. "I know you pair are a real barrel of laughs…that's why you got the top job." He turned to face the ancient wooden doors. "Chapel watch," he said as he knocked hard on the gnarled old oak, "and that's real important. This all gotta go without a hitch, so don't fuck it up, boys, you hear me?"

"Don't sweat it, Red," Bean drawled, "we got it under control. Everything's cool, we're good to go and when they come stomping up here we just gonna move back to the fence line and stay out the way. But we'll be watchin' real close, like we supposed to."

"OK, boys, sounds like you got it covered so I'll leave you in peace – for now, anyway," Red paused briefly and gave his two sentries a thumbs up. "There'll be a whole crowd coming up here in about forty minutes, so get the torches lit, get the placed warmed up and looking welcoming. Oh, and don't forget to check that wellhead's locked, OK?"

"Yeah, no problem Red," the Bean grinned. "See you later, old man."

Red didn't bother rising to the bait.

***

As team leader for the night, the burly quartermaster was keen to check on the remainder of his squad before the main event got going. Despite the exertions of the long stair climb, he prayed he wouldn't give himself a heart attack and headed back down the steps as fast as his chunky frame would allow. Once down, he found the last of his dynamic pairings in the manicured grounds at the front of the sprawling estate where long serving White Warrior members Tex Arden and his partner for the night, Eddie Croker, were in discussion with two of the AMS dog team.

"Yeah, man, we've checked it," he could hear Tex saying to the guards as he approached. "It looks fine."

After acquiring the property, the organisation had employed a high-end security specialist for year-round protection to the estate. The company, AMS, provided twenty-four-hour cover which, as a minimum, comprised a two-man two dog team on an alternate twelve-hour shift pattern. But tonight, for such a prestigious event, the standard cover had been increased and significantly reinforced and the addition of the White Warriors nomad chapter – all nine members, all armed, all ready for action - had been at Leon Tate's explicit request.

"We all good here, boys?" Red asked as he approached the four-man huddle. "Tex, everything as it should be?"

"Yeah, Red," a deep voiced boomed out from the group. "We were just checking in with the guys here and they're happy. The dog's ain't fussin' about nothing. We're all cool, bro, all cool."

As Red drew closer, both dogs started to strain in his direction so, whilst he kept a wary eye on the beasts, he slowed his approach. He knew it wasn't the norm for security companies to use Akitas, but AMS did, and these two close-cropped monsters looked particularly menacing. "Hope they know I'm on their side, bro," the burly biker said as he stopped a safe distance back.

"Odin, hold!" the lead handler said firmly as he yanked on the leash of his straining hound. The dog instantly calmed and the second followed suit. Red was impressed. "You got them dogs real well-trained, boys," he said as he stepped a little closer. "Mean looking pair of mother fuckers, aren't they?" He stopped short again as he studied the dogs. "Japanese Akitas, yeah?"

"Sure are, my friend, most tenacious attack dog in the world," the handler said with an obvious sense of pride. "Just one command and they'll tear a man limb from limb."

"Well thank fuck they're with us, then," Red said with a wicked grin. "Any dipshit fool enough to try his luck tonight without an invite won't stand a chance, will he?"

All four men nodded their agreement: with a network of CCTV cameras, gate guards, dogs and nine prowling armed outlaw bikers, it was one well-protected slice of paradise.

CHAPTER 30

The Right Time

After the interruption of Gerry's return call, Ray went back to bed. But before the wily chief exec succumbed to the irresistible lure of sleep, he thought a little longer about the team in the US. And the more he picked over the idea of searching for an ancient mission high in the Utah Mountains, the more it started to sound like a flight of fantasy.

But, then, who was he to argue? The HSG was proud of its democratic ethos and on this particular issue he'd been outvoted. Firstly, Gerry felt it was a gamble worth taking, then Lucas and Rick both said they were happy to give it a go, and finally Sarah - his beloved Sarah – well, she was totally convinced that if they found it, there'd be some clue which would miraculously help. But now, despite bowing to popular demand, Ray had convinced himself it was far too fanciful an idea to believe in. More likely turn up a crock of shit than a crock of gold, he muttered to himself as he drifted off to sleep.

Only after Ray had said his goodbyes to Gerry for the second time, did mother and daughter realise how late it was.

"You're best staying, love," Margaret said as she peered incredulously at the kitchen clock. "It's way too late now – look at the time," she turned back to Sarah. "Go back to yours in the morning, it'll be much easier and safer then." As she watched her off-spring contemplate the offer, she couldn't resist adding further inducements. "Your room's already made up, love," she cooed, "and I'll sort you a nice fry-up in the morning before you go."

At the thought of a cooked breakfast, Sarah's resistance crumbled. "OK, Mother," she said. "You got me… I'm staying."

Margaret smiled across the table. "Good," she said, now obviously relieved Sarah was staying, "your dad will enjoy that. Full English on a Sunday morning with his favourite eldest daughter, how lovely will that be?"

Sarah couldn't begin to imagine his joy.

***

As the night wore on, activity on the Utah plateau increased. The line of vehicles along its northern rim continued to grow: cars, vans, pick-ups, SUVs, motorhomes, and campers of all types and sizes were there. And when the prime front edge couldn't offer any further parking, the endless automotive snake split again. A second wave pulled up behind the first line, then a third behind the second, and so it continued. It was organised chaos but, despite the volume of traffic, everyone played their part. It was courteous, good natured, and all miraculously done without any official traffic management system being in place. The people's stargazing army was making camp for the night and it was a veritable love-in.

"This is pretty cool, isn't it, Rick?" Lucas said. "It's like some sort of weird festival – but without facilities…and bands, and mud."

Rick laughed. "Yeah, it's great, Sarge," he replied. "What an atmosphere! Well chilled - look at all these guys with the fires and the stoves, the tents, sleeping bags, telescopes, camping chairs…my God, some people come well prepared, don't they?"

"Excuse me, Mr Kruger," Babb said in mock indignation, "never mind worrying about other people's set-up. If you just hang on for a second, you'll find we're not exactly short on equipment ourselves, OK?"

With that, she waved a dismissive hand at the now puzzled looking South African then climbed into the back of the Wrangler and started to rummage. "There you go," she beamed after a few seconds of huffing and puffing, "one portable gas stove, some pots, four cups, three fold-away chairs, and a couple of blankets....and that's just for starters."

"My God, where did all that come from?" Lucas queried.

"I told you Ruby was fully loaded," she said. "Back seat lifts... see," she pointed to the void now visible below the rear bench seat. "Awesome storage space, always kept full of camping stuff. You see, out here you never know when you'll need it, do you?"

"You really are full of surprises," Lucas said. "And it seems to run in the family, doesn't it?" He looked between the sisters and shook his head. "You know what, you two haven't turned out anything like expected. In fact, so far you've fooled us on just about every count, you really have." He paused then asked, "Is your other sister this resourceful?"

Marion laughed, then looking at her still beaming sibling answered, "Kitty? Sure she is, in fact, probably more so than we are, isn't that right, B?"

"Oh, definitely," Babb laughed, "way, way better."

Once the general banter had died down, the eclectic foursome got on with setting up their own little comet watchers camp. Babb got the stove lit and the water on, Rick got the chairs set up round the stove, and Marion sorted out blankets, sleeping bags, and something to eat. Whilst the others busied themselves making camp, Lucas decided it was time to go walkabout. "I'll be back in ten minutes," he said. "Just going for a wander, see what's going on, OK?"

"Yeah, sure, Roxy, you just piss off," Rick replied. "We'll get it all set up for you, mate, don't you worry about it." But, despite trying to sound as sarcastic as he could, Lucas wasn't biting.

"Thanks, shouldn't be long," he said as he strolled off into the pulsating mass of vehicles, lights, and campfires.

After Marion watched him disappear from view, she settled in one of the chairs round the stove and, as she wriggled her backside into the green canvas seat to get comfy, she scanned the night sky. "This is going to be good," she whispered to no one in particular. "I'm getting the feeling it really is going to be worth the journey."

"Coffee, sis?" came a voice from the other side of the stove.

"Oh, yes, please," Marion replied. "It's going to be a long night."

Babb lent over and handed her a mug of steaming coffee. Marion took it in both hands, then brought it up close to her face and started to gently blow on it. "Boy, that smells so good," she said. "Thanks, B."

The sisters continued to talk quietly between themselves. Giggling and laughing about their travelling companions and the intriguing little adventure they'd got themselves embroiled in, they sounded like giddy schoolgirls. And whilst it was obvious the ladies were short on a few of life's luxuries, it would take a lot more than the lack of decent food, toilet facilities, and a bed to dampen the spirits of the Armstrong sisters, and that was no understatement.

"What you two laughing at?" Rick asked as he re-appeared from behind the Jeep.

Babb looked up. "We were just saying what great fun this is," she said, "but this one here isn't the camping type, you see, although she's getting into the swing of it now," she smiled. "So, you don't have to worry, she'll be fine, you'll see."

Rick raised an eyebrow. "Yes, OK," he said, "but I won't be worrying, I know she can handle it…." He pointed to the stove, "Now any chance of a cup of that coffee?"

***

Leon Tate knocked lightly on the dining room door. There was no answer, so he tried again, only this time a little harder.

"Who is it?" a muffled voice enquired from within.

"It's me, Monsignor."

"Come in, Leon, perfect timing," the voice said, "I was just about to call you."

Tate pushed the left-hand leaf of the double doors and stepped inside the dining room. At the far end of the room at a large glass table sat Vincent Dubois. The Monsignor remained seated and silent until his visitor had closed the door and started his approach. "What's the problem?" he asked as Tate got closer.

"There's no problem, I just wanted ten minutes of your time to go over tonight's programme…that's all."

"My thoughts exactly," Dubois said. "That's why I was going to call. Sit down and we'll run through it."

At times, it felt like the two men were close, at others it was obvious an immense gulf existed between them. Over the years, Tate had learnt to accept the uneasy nature of their relationship and always trod carefully around his superior. The Monsignor, on the other hand, did as he pleased and nearly always got what he wanted.

"Right," Dubois said sharply, "guests arrive at eight." He stopped to look hard at his Security Chief and for a second wondered if there would ever come a time when his dedication to the organisation couldn't be relied on, but as their eyes locked he realised that day would never come. "After the initial meet and greet everyone is to be ushered into the ball room," he instructed. "Drinks, canapés, general hospitality, we must make a real fuss of all our guests, Leon, and I mean a real fuss, OK? Everyone knows how important they are, don't they?"

"Yes, Monsignor, every member on duty knows exactly how to treat our wonderful supporters and benefactors. They will be treated like royalty; of that you can rest assured."

"Excellent, Leon, that's what I wanted to hear and that's exactly what I want to see – from everyone, and that includes you, OK?"

"Absolutely, sir," Tate replied, "even I will be on my best behaviour."

The two men went on to run through the final guest list, the dinner arrangements, then the after-dinner speakers. The speeches would be followed by a presentation from Father Williams on the latest outreach project progress and then, finally, the annual benefactor award nominations would be presented. The entire evening's programme was geared to ensure maximum guest satisfaction. It was essential that all the one hundred plus invitees went home feeling good as that was the result that guaranteed maximum cash generation for the cause.

The Divinity had honed their craft; they knew exactly what they were doing. Every fund-raising dinner they hosted was promoted as a prestigious event and it worked. The organisation's devotees couldn't get enough of the much lauded black-tie events but, as Dubois vehemently pointed out, at seven hundred and fifty dollars a ticket they really did have to put on a damn good show and - without fail - they always did.

"We need the formal proceedings to be wrapped up by midnight," Dubois said, "and the last of our guests off the premises by....no later than twelve thirty, OK?"

The Monsignor was not asking, and Tate knew it. "Yes, sir, I will ensure all staff understand the timescales."

"Then....," Dubois paused as he looked across to the window, "we head up to the chapel for the main event of the night, our celebration Mass. This year, as you well know, it really is a very important occasion."

"Once in a lifetime experience, sir, something for the history books, I'm sure."

The Monsignor nodded his agreement, closed his folder, and then rose slowly from his chair. "And please remember, Leon," he said, "initially in the chapel it's senior personnel only. The rest stay outside until called, you understand?"

"Yes, Monsignor," Tate replied dutifully, "I understand."

***

Just as Rick started to sip his steaming coffee, Lucas re-appeared out of the shadows. "You lot look nice and settled," he said as he eyed the figures relaxing in fold-away chairs around a glowing camping stove. "Cosy little set-up we've got here, isn't it? I'm loving what you've done with the place."

As all three turned in his direction, Rick put his coffee down. "Well, looky here," he said, "the wanderer returns. So, what's the word on the street, then, Sarge?"

"Its good news, folks," Lucas answered. "We are definitely getting close. I've been chatting to some of the more serious looking groups out there and they're convinced things will start happening around one, so not long now." He smiled then, rubbing his hands together in theatrical expectation, added, "Exciting, isn't it?"

"Sure is," Babb said quickly. "Do you want a coffee?"

"No thanks, but I'll have a beer," he said. "Might as well make a proper night of it." With that, he started rummaging in the Jeep's front passenger foot well. "Where's the beer gone?" he whined.

"In the cool box," Babb answered. "Where it should be."

"And where's that?"

"Over there," she said, "behind the other chair."

Lucas looked hard in the direction she was indicating. In the half-light he could make out a small, white cool box lurking in the shadows. "My God, woman," he said, his tone displaying genuine admiration, "you're a bloody genius, talk about being on the ball - what don't you have in that Jeep?"

Babb sat back, crossed her arms and smiled. "I keep telling you," she said, "Ruby's fully loaded and when I say fully loaded, I mean it. Surely you've got the message by now?"

"Yes, ma'am, I think I've finally got it," he said as a mile-wide grin spread across his face.

"Good," she said, "about time too."

After a few seconds of thoughtful silence, Lucas spoke again, "Can I just say that I'm seriously glad we ran into you two girls and I really mean it." He turned and looked over at his partner. "We'd be lost without them, wouldn't we, Ricky?"

"Absolutely right, Sarge," Rick replied enthusiastically, then turning to the sisters added, "I tell you, ladies, you're a godsend – and that's the truth," and from his tone it was obvious he meant it.

CHAPTER 31

The Rainbow's Tail

By midnight, a soft purple hue had infused the clear starry heavens as far as the eye could see. And now, as expectant murmurs rippled through the mass of spectators, everyone hoped it was a sign of things to come.

"It's looking good, folks," Lucas said. "This could be it; this could be show time."

Finally, the crowd hushed, lights dimmed, and an eerie quiet descended over the packed plateau. With only occasional excited shouts piercing the ghostly calm, everyone looked skyward. And as thousands of eager eyes searched the vast expanse above, Rick whispered into the darkness, "Jesus, this is weird. It's like… it's like the calm before the storm."

The audience were entranced and, when the purple tinge started to pulsate, the crowd positively effervesced with excitement. Then in the distance, from a point above the horizon, an isolated fleck of crimson appeared. Initially the vibrant ellipse elongated, then it widened and began to move across the sky in a low east-west arc. As it continued westward, it effortlessly sliced through the glowing purple backdrop and the resulting two-tone smear prompted the crowd to break out into spontaneous applause. Then, as the stargazing army stood hypnotised by the spectacle unfolding above, the second act got started.

Suddenly, out of the farthest reaches of the eastern darkness, a sphere of spinning white light emerged. For a few seconds it hung motionless over the horizon like a strange Christmas bauble, then it started to move. It followed the trail of the crimson swathe, lighting up the mountainside as it went. Firing shards of white light in all directions, it caught the colourful charge ahead of it and moments later, as white orb and red slash merged, a dazzling trail of colours appeared in the wake of the heavenly union. As the rainbow tail exploded like a fourth of July firework finale, the spellbound hordes, thousands of miles below, went wild with delight.

"Oh, my God," Babb shouted over the cacophony of cheering and clapping, "that is amazing! It's unreal!"

"Unbelievable!" Marion replied with equal astonishment. "And it's happening right in front of us; think, Barbara, we're ringside to a true wonder of nature."

No sooner had she finished uttering her uncharacteristic boxing analogy, than the comet began to lose its radiance. Within only a matter of moments it had faded dramatically, then seconds later it disappeared completely. The spinning orb vanished first, followed quickly by its colourful tail, leaving only a slash of pale crimson stretched across the Utah sky like a healing scar.

"Greatest show on earth," Lucas enthused. "What a spectacle! A touch brief, mind, I mean that can't have been more than three minutes, can it, but it was mind blowing."

All around them, groups of stunned stargazers, some still staring into the now darkening sky, were wildly discussing what they'd just witnessed, and all were hoping for more. But, sadly, it was not to be; the one hundred and thirteen year wait for a glimpse of Cirrus 5 was over.

But no one had been disappointed.

"I knew it was going to be good," Marion said, "and I wasn't wrong; that was insane. I actually can't believe what I've just seen, I really can't."

"Well, after all that excitement I'm ready for a drink," Babb grinned. "Who fancies a shot?"

Lucas's face dropped. "You gotta be kidding me. Don't tell me you've got Tequila stashed in that Jeep as well, have you?"

Babb started to answer, "I don't know how many times I'm going to have to say it…" but immediately she was stopped in her tracks by a vehement protest.

"OK, OK, hold it right there," Lucas spluttered. "I know: fully loaded means fully loaded, sorry I mentioned it again."

With that, the two sisters descended into fits of laughter. Rick couldn't help but join in, and Lucas, appreciating he'd been a fool to underestimate Babb again, eventually followed suit.

Like the other visitors to the plateau that night, the crew of the blue Jeep were in no hurry to leave. It felt right that the crowd make the most of this very special occasion. So, with a C5 after party very much on the cards, Lucas, Rick and the sisters rearranged their chairs in a little circle around the stove, settled back down, and waited for the ever-resourceful Babb to dish out the liquid gold.

"Cheers, gang," Lucas toasted as he raised his glass in salute. "At first light we start our search for Sarah's chapel and here's to hoping we can actually find it."

***

As Tate said a gracious goodbye to the last of the fund-raiser guests, he checked his watch. It showed eleven forty-five. Excellent, he thought, ahead of schedule. Then, as he made his way back to the ballroom, he felt his phone vibrate so stopped to investigate. Slipping the cell from the pocket of his dinner jacket, he checked the text. It read: No show by Ings – the woman is still here, what do you want me to do? DT.

Tate was surprised and read it again. "Why the fuck's he left it this long to tell me," he muttered to himself as he ducked into the first available empty room. Quickly he dialled, then paced furiously awaiting an answer. He didn't have to wait long.

"Hello, Mr Tate," a polite formal voice answered.

Dan Tyler was about to ask his boss how he was but, before he could utter another word, Tate cut him off. "What the hell do you mean Ings hasn't showed?" he growled.

Tyler wasn't surprised. "Well…err, exactly that Mr Tate," he said calmly. "He was supposed to be here at six but hasn't turned up."

"Fuck me, you idiot, that's over six hours late – don't you think you should have let me know earlier about this? Have you tried him direct?"

"Yes, sir, I've tried several times, but no answer, it's always voicemail," Tyler paused as he waited for a response from his boss, but with no immediate comment forthcoming he continued. "Apologies, sir, I should have let you know earlier," he said lamely. "I was convinced he was just running late…. It won't happen again, Mr Tate, rest assured."

The Chief continued to pace up and down the small room. Staring down at his shiny brogues, he searched for a plausible explanation for the no show. "Jesus, what's that red neck mother playing at?" he hissed. "Not like him. Yes, he's a low-life, but he's a damn reliable low-life," he stopped pacing for a second, his mind still analysing the situation. "How's our problem behaving, Daniel?" he asked.

"Quiet as a mouse, Mr Tate. Rohypnol never fails. She's out cold in the visitor suite."

"Anyone with her?"

"Yes, sir, Abigail is checking on her as we speak."

"OK, Daniel," Tate said firmly, "you'll have to hang tight and leave it with me, maybe a couple of hours, so keep that package alive. Well, at least 'til I get there, OK?"

"Yes, sir, will do."

As Tate hung up he shook his head as he thought to himself, that bitch will pay for her sins.

***

By 12:05 the place was ready. The chapel torches were blazing brightly and a perfectly arranged bonfire to the side was begging to be lit.

The tiered pyre, a lesson in geometric perfection and obsessive neatness, was made up of bushels of dry kindling held together with gasoline-soaked cloth straps. The bales were stacked in decreasing layers around a ten-foot cross. The rough wooden centre piece was set into the dry mountain earth and had a large horned animal skull fixed to its centre.

So now, as the shadows from the torches flickered in the breeze, and the sky morphed from clear to purple, the scene for the perfect celebration ceremony was complete.

"These are a weird bunch of fuckers," Jim Bane said as he eyed the bonfire. "These crazies give me the goddam creeps, man. Seriously, they do."

Remy Hilton looked skyward, blew a plume of sweet-smelling smoke into the night air, then handed the joint to his comrade. "Yeah, Jimbo," he drawled, "I'm with you on that one, dude, but, hey, it's not our place, bro. We just here to do a job, you know. Security detail, that's all we are tonight, so let's keep it zipped and just get on with it, OK?"

"Yeah, sure thing, Bean, I was just saying…well, you know what I'm fucking saying, man, don't ya?"

But Jim Bane's inconsequential ramblings went unheard by his young comrade as the Bean's attention was now drawn to the noise of approaching footsteps. "Shhh, Jimmy," he said, "listen…"

Both men stood in silence for a second, then glanced toward the stairway. After a quick double take, Remy turned and pointed in the direction of the chapel's rear elevation.

"Show time, Jimbo," he whispered. "Here they come. Back to the fence, bro, and like we said, we just watching from the side lines… don't want to get in the way now, do we?" The spooked biker didn't need telling twice and, as both men raced for the camouflage of the building's gable shadow, the approaching footfall got louder.

Moments later, the highest-ranking officials came into view and, in a much practiced two-by-two formation, made their way steadily along the widening path toward the front door. Behind the dignitaries came the second tier of The Divinity's finest and then, following their elders at a respectable distance, came the junior members of the order. Finally, bringing up the rear was additional security cover in the form of Tate's personal bodyguard plus two heavily armed drivers. The orderly procession filed through the front doors without a word and, once inside, the senior members and the second tier took their allocated positions.

"Hold it there," Tate barked as he brought his arm down in front of the junior contingent's lead pair. "That's it for now, no more inside. Everyone from here to the back will wait outside," he pointed to series of metal chairs laid out in rows on the flat open area opposite the fire, "and all of you over there, and sit down." The gaggle stood still for a few seconds as they looked over in the direction indicated. "For the time being, take a seat and wait," Tate said firmly, "and every one of you is to sit quietly and patiently until told otherwise, OK?"

As each member of the line nodded an acknowledgement, the Security Chief surveyed the collection of smartly dressed young men closely.

"Gentlemen, this is an auspicious occasion. You are extremely privileged to be part of this celebration, I hope you truly understand that." Tate addressed the gathering in deep, earnest tones. "You are here to witness the love and the spirit of our organisation and to pledge your undying allegiance to its beliefs and codes of conduct. Do you all accept why you are here?"

The solemn looking bunch again nodded and bowed their heads. Not a single hint of dissent emanated from the group. Just as Tate had wanted and expected: total compliance.

"Good, now let's move it," he ordered. "Get yourselves sat down and do it quickly and quietly. Your turn will come soon enough."

With that, the junior members shuffled off toward the neatly ordered chairs and, as they took their seats, all eyes darted between the chapel, the cross, and the menacing Security Chief.

"Juan," Tate shouted as he now turned his attention to the remaining group of three, "I want two watching the steps and one over here at the door."

Juan nodded his understanding. "Sure, Mr Tate," he said before leading his two colleagues to the top of the stairway. After the drivers briefly exchanged words, the chauffeur left the others by the steps and headed back toward his leader. As he approached, Tate was standing outside the front door.

"Hurry up, will you," he ordered, "we're about to start." Instantly Juan quickened his step. "That's more like it," Tate said. "Right, you stay here and do not let anyone in…or out, until I say so, OK?"

"Yes, Mr Tate, as you wish, but what about the back? Do you want that checked as well?"

"No, it's covered," Tate answered. "There's extra personnel looking after that, you should find two of our biker brethren out there," he paused as he squinted into the darkness. "Probably best check in with them, though," he said, "make sure the fuckers are actually there, then let them know the general set-up and numbers etc.… I'll leave you to sort it, OK?"

"Yes, sir," Juan saluted, "will do." Before the faithful Mexican could say another word, the Chief was through the double doors and dragging them shut behind him with an ear-grating creak.

***

On his way back to the house, Red looked up through the trees and, at first glance, mistook the sky's strange purple haze for a fancy outdoor lighting effect. Then seconds later when it dawned on him it wasn't, he scratched his head muttering, "What the fuck is that all about?"

As the perplexed biker made his way round the corner of the west wing, he stopped. There, lying in the middle of the path, no more than ten feet in front of him, was a heavy-duty Maglite torch – and it was still on. The beam was pointing along the floor toward him, but its owner was nowhere to be seen. Red was surprised, so quickly moved out of the glare of the security lights and reached for his gun. Ducking behind a large tree, he checked the surroundings. Staring silently into the cool night air, breathing heavily, he focused on the Maglite and the stretch of path leading away from it into the darkness. Still seeing nothing other than the abandoned torch, he reached for his radio. "Tex, you read me," he said in a low voice.

Several seconds passed with no response. Then the radio crackled into life. "Sure, Red," a voice boomed. "What's up, bro?"

Red almost dropped his handset. The receive volume was set way too high and the Texan's response had probably been heard halfway down the mountain. "Sonofabitch," he cursed as he fumbled with the walkie-talkie's awkward controls. "Who the fuck left it like that?"

Then the radio came again, but this time at a more restrained volume level, "Red, you there?"

"Yeah, yeah, Tex, I'm here," he answered, now having regained his composure. "I think we got a little problem. Where are you now?"

"Front gardens, by the fountain...what's the deal?"

Red briefed his comrade on the situation and two minutes later Tex, Eddie, and the AMS dog patrol team were at the burly biker's side. As they all stood staring at the still blazing Maglite, Red bent over and picked it up. "Don't look like one of ours, does it, Tex?" he queried as he turned the torch off and spun the heavy steel cylinder in his hand.

"Yeah, bro, way too good to be one of ours," the Texan drawled.

Red gave his brother-in-arms a disparaging look then turned to the dog handlers and asked, "Any of you guys use this type of flashlight?"

"Err, well, yeah, buddy, actually we do," replied the lead handler. "That looks like Jonny T's mag."

"Who's Jonny T?" Tex asked before Red had the chance.

"He's one of our supervisors," the handler said, "but I didn't think he was here tonight." He turned to his colleague. "Jonny's not here now, is he, Mitch?"

"Nope," Handler Two answered, "we got extra staff brought in for tonight, last I heard Jonny's doing the day shift tomorrow with Scotty...plus the dogs, of course."

As he looked over the motley crew standing under the trees, Red stroked his beard and frowned. "Well something's not adding up here, is it boys?" he said. "So, we best go find out what the fuck's going on." He looked into the silent darkness then smiled, "It's time to go a-hunting!" With that, the group of five men and two dogs set off along the footpath heading for the landscaped gardens at the rear of the estate.

CHAPTER 32

Black Mass

Inside the chapel, apart from the nervous shuffle of feet on cold stone, it was silent. The Divinity elite stood in hushed reverence, eyes front, waiting for the proceedings to start. When a black clad Vincent Dubois emerged from the shadows and walked to the lectern, you could have heard a pin drop.

"Guardians, please be seated!" His deep baritone echoed around the walls. "This is an auspicious occasion, an occasion to savour and enjoy, and tonight, as you all know, we are especially privileged." He looked over his audience silently, then asked, "Aren't we?"

Without missing a beat, like a well drilled military unit, the entire congregation replied as one, "Yes, Monsignor, we are!"

As Dubois surveyed the faithful ranks massed before him, the sight of so many loyal and obedient disciples made the hairs on the back of his neck stand on end. Savouring the power surge far longer than he should, he raised his left hand with his palm and turned to face the audience. "Remember your pledge, brethren," he said, "and never forget your mission."

Again, the audience responded in unison, "Yes, Monsignor."

"Tonight, we will welcome new associates to the inner circle," he said. "Tonight, a select group of disciplined and committed young men will join the ranks of the Guardians." Dubois fell silent as he returned his raised hand to the side of the lectern. Then, as he placed his right hand flat down on the open book in front of him, continued,

"They have proved their worth and all are now ready to take the final step, tonight they will give their blood and accept the mark in front of and in defiance of this," he paused as he glared down, "of this... blasphemous work," and to emphasise the point he suddenly spat full force onto the opposite page.

As the crowd murmured its approval, the Monsignor stepped back from the lectern and turned to two tall dark figures standing in the half-light. He lent forward and said something to the hooded duo which was inaudible to the congregation. Seconds later, they parted and turned to show the monsignor a dark metal box on a stand. He took a long look, nodded his approval, and returned to the lectern. "Gentlemen, very soon our young men will take their pledge, one by one, with you as witness. They will honour us, but first we need to return outside, to light our celebration beacon and ask the heavens for a sign."

The Monsignor glanced toward the back of the chapel and gestured to the figure standing in front of the entrance door. Tate took the cue and immediately cracked the right-hand leaf of the ancient oak door ajar.

"Juan," he hissed through the gap into the darkness, "we are coming back out now, is everything in order?"

"Yes, Sir, Mr Tate, all clear," the chauffeur replied.

The congregation filed out as quietly and as unhurriedly as it had entered, and the junior members seated outside watched nervously as the line of dark silhouettes crossed the scrub and occupied the remaining space around the bonfire. Several members stood behind the seated area and some took up the empty seating but, standing or seated, all were focusing on the obvious centrepiece.

Dubois now stood in front of them with his back to the unlit pyre and, with his arms spread wide, his shadow was superimposed on the cross behind him.

"Tonight, we celebrate," he boomed. "Tonight, we destroy the ghosts of our enemies, we cleanse our souls... and we gain a greater strength that will prepare us for the fight ahead."

With that, he turned to face the cross, stepped close to the tinder dry bushels and looked up at the horned centre piece. He crossed himself then bowed his head.

"The heretics will burn in hell," he hissed. Then, still facing the cross, he remained bowed and silent as he retraced his steps. Eventually, he raised both arms above his head and looked to the heavens. "We are your willing servants, Lord," he screamed at the pulsating sky. "We are the Guardians of the fifth Meridian, and we await your command."

Then, perfectly on cue, a streak of light raced out of the darkness toward him. A flaming cross bow bolt missed the Monsignor's thigh by inches and struck the centre of a petrol-soaked bushel with a resounding thump. Instantly, the timber burst into flames and the audience gasped with surprise. But Dubois remained unflustered; this was his show and he was going to enjoy every perfectly choreographed minute of it. "We light our beacon in your honour," he shouted at the fire. "It burns bright for you, oh Lord," then he retreated from the intensifying inferno and added, "its flames are our weapon…and they will destroy the flesh of our enemies."

All eyes were on the black clad figure screaming into the raging fire and, with his frenzied tirade now back-dropped by the shadows dancing across the chapel, the crowd was mesmerised.

Dubois fell silent. Then, still facing the fire, he looked skyward again. This time the crowd followed his gaze and, to their utmost astonishment, a bright crimson slash appeared directly above them. But Vincent Dubois, a man seemingly possessed, was oblivious to the strange cosmic apparition and continued his demonic rant.

"It is our time," he yelled. "it is our history and our right!" As he spun to face the crowd, he didn't stop. "You are all part of this, each and every one of you is a soldier of our Lord. I tell you, it is your destiny and your duty to do his will, it is written in the stars."

Moments later, an orb of spinning white light appeared on the eastern horizon and to all present it appeared their leader had miraculously harnessed the power of Mother Nature herself. As the sky lit up, the crowd were dumb-struck.

"Behold," Dubois screamed as he pointed at the light, "our Lord shows us a sign. It is a sign we must continue our crusade, a sign we must defeat the nonbelievers and their slave army, a sign we must be willing to fight to the death."

The crowd stood staring open mouthed at the cosmos. Then, after several moments of eerie hypnotic quiet, the bright white orb raced across the sky, caught up to the crimson streak, and exploded in a spectacular rainbow cascade. Stunned by the dramatic eruptions of colour above, the mass of Divinity followers screeched and yelped in amazement; some staggered back, some cried, and some were so overawed they dropped to their knees to pray.

Now with his facial expression contorted in a combination of triumph and rage, the Monsignor hollered at the bewildered faces surrounding him, "Our Lord has spoken! His will be done!"

***

Hidden in the shadows behind the chapel, the two White Warrior bikers were leaning against the chain-link fence, staring up at the spectacle unfolding above them. As he watched, Jim Bane began to think he was tripping. "Jesus Christ, Bean, did you see that?" he exclaimed. "What the fuck is all that shit about?"

"It's that fucking comet, man," Bean answered. "You know, the one they've been banging on about for weeks." The young biker turned to look at his comrade. "That's why the highway was so crazy, bro," he said, "it's all them stargazers queuing up to get a look."

"Never heard of no fucking comet," Jim said shaking his head. "Never knew we was going to see anything like that. Tell you, man, that's the weirdest shit I ever seen,"

"Well, think of it as a bonus, Jimmy," Bean grinned. "Now, come on, let's get along this fence again, can't just stand around all night watching stars, can we? We gotta a job to do, so let's fucking move it."

As the two lean, leather-clad, outlaws started out on another sortie along the perimeter fence line, Jim sniffed the cool mountain air and grimaced, "What the fuck are those crazies burning back there?" he asked.

"Don't know and don't want to know, man. Like I said, Jimmy, let's just do our job. We ain't here to ask no questions, OK?"

"Fuckin' right, bro," came the firm reply.

***

Once the orb vanished, the rainbow tail rapidly followed suit, and so the massed ranks of The Divinity returned their attention to their firebrand leader. Dubois was now stood stock still, arms folded across his chest, flames still licking at the cross smouldering behind him. He stared blankly into the midst of his followers.

"Brethren, the signs are clear," his tone was now less energised and his demeanour less threatening. "We are on the path to life ever after," he paused momentarily as he steadied himself, "a life of peace, understanding and tranquillity…if we…if we…" he faltered again finally muttering, "stay true."

The black clad figure stopped talking. The eyes glazed over, the legs buckled and then, as if felled by a sniper's bullet, he crashed headfirst into the soft dry earth.

"Holy shit," a chiselled cheek-boned young man at the front cried. Clayton Carr, Tate's hard done-by assistant, was still reeling from the surreal experience, but was first to break ranks and arrived at the side of their fallen leader's body in a matter of seconds. Kneeling down beside Dubois's dirt splattered head, he gently shook his shoulder. "Monsignor," he said as he stared at his poleaxed leader, "Sir, are you OK, can you hear me?"

Before he could ask again, he'd been surrounded by a mass of Divinity faithful, all of whom were desperate to assist.

"Just give him some space, will you," Clayton protested. "Come on, gentlemen, back off a little, will you, please." But before he could do anything further, the black robed figure gave a loud cough, spat out a mouthful of earth and wretched. The Monsignor then struggled onto all fours and shook his head vigorously. "I am the Lord's servant," he spluttered. "I do his bidding; I do his work. It is not my place to question his will."

With that he frog-jumped into a wide-legged squat, then eased up to a full standing position and started to dust himself down. As the surrounding throng stared in bemused admiration, he spoke, "Gentlemen," he said, "we must return to the chapel…our Lord has given us his blessing. Now we must embrace new blood. It is…," he paused and pointed toward the smouldering cross, "it is… time for the ultimate step."

Unprompted, the crowd parted. Then as the robed, dirt smeared supremo set off back toward the chapel, all eyes followed him. Dubois had recovered quickly, and now, appearing revitalised, strode off toward the building. Totally confident his flock would fall in step behind him, he didn't turn back or utter a word and, despite a sense of impending dread infiltrating every one of his loyal disciples, he was right. The mass of dumbfounded Divinity faithful tagged instantly along behind their leader.

CHAPTER 33

The Invisible Man

As Red led the five man posse to the rear of the estate, he called the team at the base of the chapel stairway.

"Liam, it's Red," he said quietly into his radio, "you copy?"

"Yeah, Red, I copy" came a gruff reply. "What's up, bro?"

"Just checking in. Everything OK, any problems?"

"No, we're all good here. There's a whole bunch heading up the stairs, so it's quietened down at the moment. You OK?"

"Don't know," Red replied, "might just have a small issue. We're checking it out now, so keep your eyes skinned, will ya? You spot anything that don't look right, you get back to me ASAP, you hear?"

"Yeah, sure," Liam said. "What's your problem?"

Before he answered, the bearded biker stopped, raised his free hand above his head and clenched his fist. Instantly the group stopped. "Don't know," Red whispered into the radio. "I'll get back to you as soon as I know more. Gotta go, bro," with that he clicked off, slipped the radio back into his waistband, and stared silently into the shadows ahead.

"What you seen?" Tex asked.

"Don't know I actually seen anything," Red muttered, "but I definitely heard something."

As he pointed off into the middle distance to the left of where the group were standing, Tex aimed his torch in the same direction and squinted into the beam. "Can't see nothing but trees. What am I supposed to be looking for, bro?"

Suddenly the lead handler's leash snapped tight as his dog started with a deep guttural growl. "The dog's onto something," the handler said as he pulled back on the straining hound.

"Well, let the fuckers go, then," Red ordered. And with that the bearded biker pulled out his .45, slipped off the safety, and started walking in the direction he'd pointed out moments earlier.

The dog team didn't need telling twice and simultaneously the two guards let the snarling hounds off their leads. The five-man posse watched as the two Akitas charged headlong into the darkness. "We better get going, boys," Handler One shouted, "they move fast." As the excited canines disappeared from view, the group sprang into action and gave chase as quickly as they could.

Seconds later, the dogs started barking wildly and, although still a good distance ahead, it was apparent they'd stopped moving. "They've found something," the second handler shouted.

As they drew closer, the five men slowed to a cautious walking pace. Spread out in a tight skirmish line, Tex and Red aimed pistols in the general direction of the hounds whilst the other three raked the area with flashlights. Suddenly the criss-crossed beams illuminated a prone figure book-ended by two snarling canines.

Red raised a clenched fist. "Well, waddaya know," he said, "looks like we got ourselves an intruder." He then ventured a little closer and turned to the lead handler. "Call the dogs back – this prick ain't going nowhere."

After a command of 'Odin, heel' from the lead handler had been swiftly followed by a shout of 'Raven, heel' from his number two, the dogs fell silent. Seconds after the barking stopped, both animals returned to their owners without even so much as a backward glance. "Tell you, boys… that's fuckin' slick," Red said in admiration of the dog team's discipline. "Gotta get me a dog like that someday, just gotta …."

Still shaking his head, the burly biker now turned his attention to the figure on the ground. "Now, what we got here then?" he asked somewhat theatrically. "Obviously, a dumb son of a bitch." Then switching back into serious squad leader mode, he gestured to two of his team. "Tex, Ed, get over there and check him over," he ordered, "but be real careful, boys."

Covering the last fifteen feet, eyes focused fully on the dark crumpled form lying on the grass, the two bikers approached cautiously. As Eddie shone his torch up and down the prone figure, a famously trigger happy Tex aimed his 9mm at the bodies centre but it didn't move.

"Kick the fucker," Red barked.

Without hesitation, Ed's right leg lashed out and, as the steel toe-capped blow connected with a dull thump, the lump spasmed. "Aaah, for Christ's sake," it groaned, "that fucking hurts."

Tex stiffened and trained his pistol on the area that he now knew was the back of the head. Then the figure let out a long low moan and started to roll over. Suddenly a bloodied face was illuminated by a flashlight beam.

"It's J-Jonny," Handler Two stammered. "That's Jonny T, he's one of us, he's our supervisor."

The group stood gawping for a second as the battered form eased up onto its side. Then, propped up on one elbow, the bewildered man shaded his eyes from the glare of torch light. "Mitch, is that you?" he asked. "Help me, buddy, for Christ sakes help me, will you…."

***

Fifteen minutes later, Red and his hybrid security team had the injured supervisor back at the house. Slumped in a chair in the staff dining area, he looked a sorry state.

"What the fuck happened to you?" Mitch asked as he attempted to clean mud and blood splatters from the man's face. "You're not supposed to be here." He shook his head and frowned. "So, what the hell were you doing out there, Jon, and why were you wandering round on your own?"

The injured man looked up at the attendant guard and winced. "Be careful, Mitch," he muttered through clenched teeth. "It fucking hurts." He moved his hand to feel the gash running along his hair line and winced again. "Man, that throbs like hell," he said. "Don't know who hit me, but Lord, whatever it was they used knocked me clean out."

The lead handler moved closer to look at the oozing head wound. "It's a nasty one Jon," he said, "but you'll live. Now…," he paused briefly to glance at Red, "we really need to know why you were out there, and why the hell you were on your own?"

The forlorn figure looked around at the inquisitive stares of his colleagues and their unlikely outlaw allies but, as five sets of eyes focused on him, he didn't speak. His head throbbed, his mind was still fuzzy from the impact, and he was furious with himself for the schoolboy error. But he had to cover his tracks. He had to tell them something. The truth – definitely not. Some sort of vaguely credible explanation, yes, but what exactly?

"Err, yeah, I know it looks a bit strange," he said eventually, "but here's the deal, right." He stopped, hoping to take the sting out of the inquisition with an endearing smile. "It was a last-minute request from Clayton, you see, said he needed some extra assistance looking after tonight's fund raiser and asked would I come in and help out."

Red looked hard at the tall man in black that sat before him. He wasn't getting a good vibe. Was it the hint of arrogance, the faux tough-guy persona, or just the shitty acting? Something didn't feel right and he wanted answers. "You saying Tate's assistant asked you in for tonight, yeah?" Red spoke as matter-of-factly as he could fake. "OK, so what was your brief?"

Jonny T met the stare of the grizzly biker and held it for a second. His heart pounded, his chest tightened, and suddenly he felt a bead of sweat form on his brow. "I just told you the brief," he answered firmly. "Clay asked me to work tonight, help out with the party. That was the deal, it's dead simple." The man's mind raced as he fought for something more convincing to add. "He said he needed one extra supervisor to check on the roaming guards tonight, so that's exactly what I was doing."

Red stood silent, arms folded across his chest and continued to stare. He knew the explanation was bullshit and it was taking a big dose of self-control not to lunge forward and throttle the truth out of the obnoxious prick. "If that was the case," he hissed, "how come we weren't told about you?"

"Beats me," the man answered, "that ain't my problem."

The biker leader was now struggling to control his increasing frustration. "Well, I think it is," he said as he moved his face right up close. "See, we knew nothing about you being part of tonight's plan... and that makes no fucking sense, man, absolutely none at all. So, come on, mother-fucker, what's your story?"

Before the bloodied figure could answer, the room suddenly lit up like a Christmas tree. As white light flooded its interior, the interrogation team instantly turned to the window behind them. With the blind half down, it had only offered a basic view of a dimly lit service yard but now outside was illuminated by a dazzling light show.

"What the fuck's going on out there?" Red asked as he wrenched the blind open.

Tex and Eddie were transfixed. "Gotta be fireworks," Ed said as he gawped out of the window. "These dos always have some sort of pyro show, don't they?"

"That ain't no firework display," Tex muttered, "that's the sky, man. Check it out, it's gone fucking crazy."

All five men were now standing in front of the expanse of glass. Mesmerised by the light show exploding above their heads they stood and stared.

"It's that comet," the lead handler said, "they've been jabbering on about it on the news. But you'd never expect it to be, like, that cool, would you?"

Red was unimpressed by the distraction. "Yeah, yeah, whatever," he snarled. "Come on, back to business."

He spun round, intent on prising the truth out of the suspect supervisor, but he couldn't believe his eyes; the chair was empty and the man in black had vanished.

***

The senior Divinity members took their seats back in the chapel, while Tate ensured the junior contingent held back at the rear. Carefully, he lined them up against the back wall. One-by-one, shoulder to shoulder, they stood tall, wide eyed, and frozen with fear.

"Do not worry, gentlemen," he whispered soothingly. "Remember, you have earned the right, this is your destiny."

As Tate calmed the nerves of The Chosen at the rear, Vincent Dubois reappeared at the front. The Monsignor, still sporting unsightly smears to his black robe, had taken his place back behind the lectern and was now intent on moving to the next stage of proceedings.

"Now it is time," he boomed. "The time for us to worship our merciful Lord and to give thanks for his enduring love and protection."

All eyes again focused on their leader. The entire congregation watched him with bated breath. His every word set synapses tingling; the man was positively hypnotic, and he knew it. "Lord, you have blessed us with a sign, so now we offer you our love, our gratitude and our total dedication to the service of your divine way."

Dubois glanced over his shoulder at the two figures hovering in the wings. The taller man immediately met his gaze and simply nodded. The supremo turned back to face his audience, then pointed to the gallery of ashen faced young men lining the back wall of the chapel and shouted, "Elijah Mason, step forward."

The audience did not dare turn and look. All eyes stayed firmly fixed to the front, gazing in awe at their leader. Dubois spread his arms wide as if in welcome.

"Elijah, it is the time," he said, "the time for you to pledge your undying commitment to our Lord and prove to the Guardians that the years invested in you have been worthwhile."

As the Monsignor's voice trailed off, a slim dark-haired figure broke from the back-wall line and set off down the aisle toward the lectern. "It is a great honour for you, young man," Dubois said, directing his attention to the approaching figure, "to give your service to our Lord and be the first of your group to take the final step."

The young man stopped in front of the lectern. Then standing stock still, head bowed he quietly awaited his fate. "Look at me, boy," Dubois whispered.

Elijah hesitated momentarily as he stared at the cold stone floor, then nervously lifted his head to meet his leader's intense gaze. "Remove your shirt," the Monsignor ordered.

The nervous prospect did not protest and, undoing his two top buttons, he deftly pulled off his grey short-sleeved top and dropped it to the floor. As Dubois surveyed the slim, hairless, torso before him he felt a sudden drop in temperature. "Take my place in front of the book," he instructed, his tone now softer, "then lay your hands on it, palms down, and close your eyes."

As Dubois backed a few steps away from the lectern, the bare-chested figure tentatively edged around the imposing eagle and took the Monsignor's place. Facing the congregation with both hands flat down on the huge book, Elijah was suddenly overcome by a sense of dread. He took a deep silent breath, clenched his teeth, then - as a visible chill raced through his body - the flesh of his arms and chest broke out in a wave of goose-bumps.

"You feel His presence, Elijah, don't you?" Dubois whispered in his ear. "He now stands at your side, He is now shoulder to shoulder with you," he swallowed hard. "So, remember… from now on He will always be there for you."

The young disciple, hunched and rigid with fear, kept his eyes firmly closed, bracing himself for whatever was to come. "Do you give your undying love and devotion to our Lord and our order?" Dubois asked.

"Yes…yes, I do," the young man spluttered.

"Louder," Dubois demanded, "answer the question clearly, so we can all hear."

"Yes, sir, I do," he shouted.

"That's better, now we can hear you, now we know you mean it."

With that, the Monsignor reached out his left hand and put it on Elijah's forearm. Encircling it, he then tightened his grip and lifted the arm up off the book. As he held it firmly above the ancient script, he placed a small spiked disc onto the books right hand leaf.

"Behold, guardians," he shouted, "the mark of our Lord."

Then, without warning, the Monsignor slammed the young man's hand back down directly onto the spike. The steel barb punctured the flesh of his palm. As the searing pain shot up his arm, Elijah Mason screamed in agony. The distraught junior tried to twist away from the horror but, despite his best efforts to pull back to tend his injury, the Monsignor held firm. As blood trickled from the wound onto the ancient vellum, Dubois addressed the swaying congregation.

"The stigmata," he cried, "the stigmata is a sign…a sign of personal sacrifice." He grinned wildly then glanced behind. "Now for the fire – the ultimate proof of allegiance."

With the briefest flick of his fingers, the two figures from the wings appeared and, like gate-keepers to the afterlife, positioned themselves either side of the terrified young man. Then, with one subtle nod from Dubois, the hooded forms promptly grabbed an arm each and forced the wounded acolyte's face down into the book. As his head hit the pages with a dull thud the crowd gasped and started chanting, then Dubois spoke again.

"The brand is a symbol of your total commitment," he roared, "wear it with passion and pride." The leader bent forward to talk directly to the restrained form. "You have served us well, Elijah, you have shown real commitment, so now the time is right, the time for the final step. Are you prepared to face the fire?"

"Y…yes, sir," came the feeble reply.

With that, the black robed supremo turned full about, walked into the shadows, and disappeared from view. Seconds later, he returned to the lectern holding a glowing branding iron in a heavy leather gloved hand. As he carried it toward the lectern, the white-hot end left a faint tracer line for all to see.

"Lord, this young man pledges his life and soul to you," he said as he positioned himself directly behind the hunched figure. Then, with the first finger of his free hand he signed a cross on the man's back. "Please take care of him, Lord, as he does your bidding on earth."

With one carefully practiced movement, he brought the branding iron close to the bare left shoulder in front of him then pressed it firmly into the clear white skin. As the hiss of burning flesh echoed around the mottled stone walls, the audience knelt as one and bowed their heads.

The slim pale figure jolted screaming against the pain but, restrained by the two hulking assistants, he had nowhere to go. The body writhed for a few seconds, then the legs buckled and finally it slumped lifelessly over the wooden lectern. "It is done," Dubois announced. "Our disciple has taken the final step…he is now truly one of us."

The Monsignor gestured to the hooded figures and, as before, with the merest click of his fingers, they responded instantly. The lifeless form was lifted from the lectern and carried to the small ante room at the rear of the chapel. As the body was moved, Dubois returned to the carved eagle and stared down at the blood spotted page open before him.

"This book," he screeched as he stabbed his finger into the centre crease, "is a desecration of our belief, it is a vile slur on our faith and our way of life – it is the work of the Devil's spawn." Then, reverting to his original stance, hands clasped either side of the lectern, their leader narrowed his eyes and looked around at his congregation. "But we are stronger than they are, much stronger," he said. "As we let the blood of our devout new brothers erase its twisted message, I stand before you and promise that those who still peddle its heresy will pay a heavy price for their folly."

On cue the audience stood and clapped loudly. The Monsignor remained silent for a few seconds as he relished the adulation of his disciples, then, raising his hands to quell the enthusiasm, he continued the show.

"Guardians, please," he said loudly. "Remember, we are gathered here tonight to welcome not just one new member into our midst, but many, so please sit back down." While the audience dutifully obeyed, Dubois looked to the rear of the chapel. He scanned the line of now wide-eyed, fear-stricken faces, then pointed in their general direction and barked, "Samuel Belcher, it is your time! Please step forward."

***

FBI special agent Ken Dolan, aka security supervisor Jonny T, was furious with himself. As he scrambled full-tilt down the scree slope toward the service road, all he could think about was how close he'd come to total disaster. It literally had been a simple slip-up, but he knew whichever way you looked at it, operationally he'd fucked up big time.

Quickly dismissing his negative thoughts, he checked the road for vehicles and, happy it was clear, crossed the asphalt at a run. Not again, he cursed, as his foot caught the opposite kerb line and sent him stumbling into the undergrowth. As he flailed at the vegetation to stop himself, he realised the clump of scrub he'd blundered into offered good cover. Stopping to catch his breath, he crouched down. He took his weight on to his left knee and carefully scanned the surroundings for signs of life. Along the service road, in both directions, visibility was surprisingly good and - to his relief - it was still deserted. With only the sound of rustling trees and the faint glow of distant lights for company, he relaxed. Now confident he was out of imminent danger, he pulled out his phone, checked the time, then sent one short text: DVT mission status - code red; exit strategy 4; return ETA 02:30

Once sent, he tucked the cell phone back into his jacket, pulled his collar up tight, and headed off deeper into the scrub.

CHAPTER 34

Heaven Sent

At sun rise, the foursome broke camp, reloaded the Jeep, then joined the slow trickle of early-risers descending from the plateau. As the 4X4 bounced down the well-worn mountain track, Lucas stifled a yawn then looked across at his partner.

"Opportunities like that don't come along very often, do they, Ricky?" he said. "Something like last night, well, it's a once in a lifetime kind of experience, isn't it? You'll never see the likes of that shit again."

Rick didn't take his eyes off the road ahead. "Dead right," he replied with only the faintest turn of his head. "You won't forget that in a hurry!" He paused as he negotiated a particularly nasty looking pothole. "But now the fun really starts, eh, Sarge," he grinned, "although finding this mission thing isn't going to be easy, is it?"

"You could almost say it was mission impossible, wouldn't you, Mr Kruger?"

The South African shook his head. "Oh, very droll, Mr Roxby," he said. "You're a veritable comedy genius, you really are."

They knew the plan was far too simplistic, but it was all they had. Based on Marion's assessment of the limited information, they had decided to head back to Paradigm, pick up the old mining road heading west out of town toward Route 130, and then hang a right and follow the highway north. 130 would then take them all the way to the old pioneer town of Iron Creek. The sleepy little backwater, nestled in the foothills of the Black Mountains, was Marion's guesstimated starting point for the search. Once there the plan was to scout for a viable access onto the trail, then hike along it and search for signs of anything that resembled a chapel.

The proceedings got off to a slow start but, as soon as the snail-paced descent from the plateau was over, they joined the main road and headed for Paradigm. The route back to town was still congested although, once through the bustling centre, the traffic eased. Twenty-five minutes later Route 130 loomed into view.

"Yeah, Rick, this is the one, just up here," Lucas said as he half-heartedly indicated the slip road they wanted. "Then it's just follow your nose all the way north to Iron Creek…should be dead easy."

It was agreed that once they got to the forgotten little town, Marion would take charge of the navigational duties. She'd photo-copied map extracts from her library records and cross-referenced them with the latest large-scale maps of their target area and, whilst it was all she could do with the scant information given, she was still convinced there was a chance of success. "Finding the town's not the issue," she said as she leant through the gap between the two front seats. "Finding the location off the trail is the problem… it's a big old mountain range, so I do hope you gents are prepared for a lot of walking."

"Of course, we are," Lucas snorted, "but if we're on a wild goose chase, maybe we won't be staying that long."

"Of course, that's a possibility," Marion said, sounding confident, "but look, we know there was a church building of some description around that location, so I'm sure we can find some evidence of its existence, even if it is only a pile of moss covered rubble."

"OK, I'll think positive then," Lucas replied into the wind. "If you believe, I'll believe."

The group were making good time. State Route 130 was empty and, whilst the three passengers sat back and admired the Utah landscape, Rick grimaced through the Jeep's filthy wind shield. The sturdy 4X4 continued to roar northward while the South African's thoughts kept turning to the task ahead.

"What's the chances of finding this needle in a haystack?" he asked. "Anyone willing to quote odds?"

At first no one answered, then Marion piped up, "Even at 25 – 1," she said. "Yes, we know it's a long shot, but I think it'll pay off."

Lucas nodded his head. "I admire your positivity," he said. "Now even I'm thinking we're gonna find something."

Rick wasn't feeling it, so he kept his eyes front and didn't comment.

***

With a population of less than six hundred, the town had an eerie empty feel. It had the look of an abandoned movie set and as Rick slowed looking for somewhere to pull over. he spotted a ramshackle filling station ahead. "I'm going to stop up there," he shouted. "We could do with fuel... any one need anything?" With no audible response from his three companions, he indicated and pulled off the highway.

Seconds later, he drew smoothly to a stop in front of an antique-looking pump on the forecourt and smiled. "I feel like we've gone back in time," he said. "Look at those things!" He then turned the ignition off and asked, "D'you reckon they still work?"

Again no one answered but, as the engine note died, a welcome calm descended over the group. With only a light summers breeze and the distant jangle of a wind chime, it was suddenly very tranquil.

"How nice is that?" Marion said. "Peace and quiet."

After a few moments of acclimatisation and appreciation, they got out to stretch their legs.

"My God, that feels better," Lucas said as he shook his right leg back to life. "I tell ya, after all this I'll be stiff as board and deaf for a week."

"You English guys are so lightweight," a female voice mocked. "One night out under the stars and a little open topped Jeep ride and you're wailing like a baby."

Lucas turned in the direction of the voice to see Babb staring him down.

"What did you say?" he asked in surprise. Babb was standing hands on hips and grinning like a banshee. "You heard me, limey," she said. "You're a lightweight."

"Look, lady," he said shaking his head. "You better watch what you're saying. Any more of that slanderous talk and I might have to get nasty."

"And what do you call nasty?" she asked.

Lucas laughed. Babb's light-hearted sparring was a pleasant distraction and he was quite happy to play along.

"We English are a tough warrior nation," he said, puffing up his chest, "strong and fearless – always ready to defend our green and pleasant land." He stopped and mimicked her hands-on hip stance. "Don't forget, young lady, unlike you bloody yanks, we win our wars – so I'd say again, watch your step, understood?"

Marion and Rick watched from the side lines as their two travelling companions faced off like gunslingers at the OK corral but, just as both protagonists prepared to trade further xenophobic insults, the fun was cut short by an approaching figure.

"Howdy, folks," a plump, grey haired man shouted. "What can I get you?"

Rick glanced over at Babb. "Just regular unleaded is it?" he asked quietly.

"Sorry, Rick," she replied. "I'm afraid Ruby's very particular – she's a Premium kind of gal."

"Oh, right," he mumbled before turning to the now hovering attendant and answering, "Yeah - err, could you fill her up with Premium please?"

"You betcha," the man said. "You folks paying cash?"

Lucas cut in quickly. "Would you prefer cash?" he asked.

"Well, it sure makes life easier, mister, if you get what I'm saying."

"Yeah, no problem," Lucas said before turning to his partner and whispering, "How much you got on you, Ricky?"

As the attendant unscrewed the fuel cap and started to fill, the two HSG men emptied their pockets to check they had enough cash.

"If you've not got enough, don't worry," Marion offered. "I'll get it; I've got plenty of money on me."

Lucas shot her his best affronted look. "Thanks, but no thanks," he said, "you've done quite enough for us as it is…and if we can't sort out paying for a simple tank of petrol, then we really are a useless pair of leeches."

She smiled but said nothing. She'd have been perfectly happy to foot the bill. The sisters were thoroughly enjoying their unexpected adventure; an off-grid antiquities hunt with two intriguing strangers was not to be sniffed at.

Once fuelled, Lucas followed the attendant to his shabby wooden hut to pay the seventy-five-dollar charge. As the man handed him his change, he thought he'd try his luck.

"If you don't mind my asking, friend, how long you lived round here?"

The man looked the scruffy English tourist up and down for a second. "Suppose it depends on who's asking, really," he slurred as he closed the till, "but maybe it's simpler if you just tell me straight what you're after, then I'll see if I can help, OK, fella?"

Lucas nodded. The old soak wasn't giving much away, but something told him the conversation was worth pursuing. "Yeah, OK, I get your point," he replied. "Well, actually, we're trying to locate an old missionary chapel somewhere off the old trader's mountain trail… the Spanish historical route I think it's referred to as these days."

"Why you looking for it?"

Lucas was a little taken aback by the man's snap response. "Excuse me," he replied.

"I said, why are you looking for this chapel? What's it to you?" Again, the attendant's question was firm and direct.

Lucas thought hard as he desperately tried to come up with some innocuous believable answer. "Well, seeing as you ask," he said finally, "you see the lady in the black ski jacket?" He pointed in Marion's direction. "She has a wonderful childhood memory of a trip to a quaint old chapel with her father." He looked hard at the man, hoping for a flicker of recognition. "Apparently, it was a magical place," he said, "and it was somewhere way up in the mountains round here. Sadly, he's passed on but now she wants to find it again, for old time's sake. A sentimental journey I suppose you could call it."

As the attendant stared blankly, Lucas stood in silence trying to work out if the man was unconvinced, unmoved or just emotionally traumatised by his off the cuff explanation. Eventually the flicker of a smile crept across the man's lips.

"How very sad," he said, "but, then, how very sweet. Childhood memories are so precious, aren't they? They are the building blocks of our future, they shape our lives. It is absolutely true you know," he paused, the smile broadening before he asked, "Have you got a map?"

The exchange was getting surreal but opting for his standard 'in for a penny, in for a pound' philosophy, Lucas decided to stick with it. "Yeah, sure," he said. "It's in the car …I'll go and get it."

With that, he jogged back to the Jeep to get Marion's map. As he approached the dusty 4X4 the three occupants turned toward him.

"Roxy, what's taking you so long?" Rick asked impatiently. "We need to get going."

"Yeah, Lucas, what's the hold up?" Babb added.

"Two minutes," he grinned, "be patient…I think our friend might be able to help us."

"How?" Marion asked.

"Don't ask, I'll tell you later - just pass me that map, will you."

Marion didn't protest and handed the plastic-coated walking map over. Lucas smiled, uttered a brief Ta, then quickly made his way back to the dilapidated hut.

"Right, what can you tell me?" he asked as he spread the map out on the stained wooden countertop. "Go on, my friend, see if you can help us out."

The attendant reached into the top drawer of an adjacent bureau, pulled out an ancient looking magnifying glass and proceeded to study the map. "Let me see," he muttered under his breath. "Right, here we are. See the gas station symbol there?" he pointed at the map. "That's us, OK?"

Lucas looked on from the opposite side of the counter and, as he watched the old man's stubby finger stab the blue fuel pump symbol, he nodded. "Yeah, OK," he said. "I'm with you."

"Now, if I remember rightly that little church I'm thinking of is over here somewhere. Just a ways off to the east of the main trail," the attendant had slowly traced his finger east from the town deeper into the Black Mountains, "and if I remember correctly, it's on a tight little ridge, high up, just above the tree line, somewhere about there," he stopped and tapped the spot. "The locals used to say it was an old Navajo burial ground, but I don't recall no map maker ever putting that down in print."

"Have you personally seen the chapel?" Lucas asked tentatively.

"Yeah…but only once, mind, and it was many years ago, but I reckon it could be the one your wife's looking for. Certainly, was a real special place from what I recall."

Lucas didn't feel the urge to explain the group dynamics. "Is it still there?" he asked as he marked a small cross on the map at the point indicated by the attendant's gnarled finger.

"Your guess is as good as mine," the man replied. "Could be, I don't know. See, I'm just trying to help you out, friend, and that's the best I can do. Can't really tell ya much more, I'm afraid."

***

The white gravel car park had two other vehicles in it; both SUVs and both obviously owned by mountain biker types. The chunky all-terrain vehicles sported high tech bike racks and 'Ride High Ride Free' stickers abounded. They do love to advertise, Lucas thought as he walked back toward the Jeep.

"You worked it out yet, Marion?" he asked as he got closer.

The librarian was sat alone in the back of the Wrangler studying various maps. Both old and new variants were littered around her.

"Yes, I have, actually," she said. "From the location the old man pointed out and the historic records it looks like it could be a match, but it'll be a major hike from here."

"Is there any way we can we get closer than this by road?"

Marion consulted the map again. "Yeah, I think so. Looks to be a couple of minor roads leading up from the other side of this section of the range," she paused to do a quick mental calculation, "...maybe an hour's drive, but the walk up would definitely be shorter although a lot steeper."

"Don't care about steep," Rick said. "We can do steep... and so can this baby," he grinned as he patted the Wrangler's bonnet.

"OK, that's sorted," Lucas said. "I just need to grab a quick bite and I'm ready for action." He rubbed his hands together and grinned at his comrades. "So...are we all excited, then?"

No one spoke but everyone nodded and that was good enough for him.

***

Marion's navigational skills were good, so much so that the South African was happier with her as a co-driver than Lucas. Plus, there was an added bonus - Marion didn't get wound up at every little problem, didn't abuse other road users, and didn't shout. It was simply a much calmer experience all round.

"You're out of a job now, Roxby," Rick shouted over his shoulder. "This girl leaves you for dead, mate; much better company, way better looking, and a lot easier to understand."

Lucas looked up, locked onto the grinning face in the rear view, and mouthed, "Up yours, dickhead," then he turned back to continue the in-depth discussion he was having with Babb about out of body experiences.

Marion had picked what she thought was the most direct public road available. It was narrow, impossibly steep and, with only occasional passing places, it was not for those of a nervous disposition. "You OK up front?" Rick asked his rather worried looking navigator.

"Yeah, yeah...I'm alright," she stammered as she glanced behind her. "What happens if we meet something coming the other way?"

"Don't worry about that," he said as reassuringly as he could. "Cliff edge reversing is one of my specialities."

As they gained altitude, the occupants fell silent. It was heart-in-mouth time, but Rick was totally focused, and as he negotiated another tight hair pin bend he glanced across at his co-pilot. "How much further?" he asked.

Despite being paralysed with fear, Marion managed to look down at the map she had cradled in her lap. "Another two hundred yards or so and that'll be as far as we can get."

Sure enough, seconds later a brown 'Car park ahead' sign came into view and, as the Jeep arrived on the small but thankfully flat, parking area everyone let out a sigh of relief.

"Jesus, what a road," Lucas exclaimed. "I wouldn't want to do that every day, would you?" He gave Rick's right shoulder a playful squeeze and whispered, "Well driven, mate, steady as ever."

The rough stone plateau was deserted. Apart from one solitary information board and two heavy timber picnic tables, it was empty.

"I would've thought there'd be somebody else up here," Babb said as she wandered over to the edge. Then she looked back down the mountain and shook her head. "Although, when you look at that road, it's enough to put anybody off."

Whilst Lucas and Rick went to check the board, the sisters sat down at a picnic table. After studying the map for a few minutes, Marion looked up to see Lucas approaching. "It's all on there," he said pointing behind him. "Loads of stuff about the trail." he stopped beside the table, grinned, cleared his throat and then in true tour guide fashion started to spiel, "The Old Spanish Trail is a historic trading route that ran from Santa Fe all the way to California. It was used by early settlers and other hardy pioneering souls from as early as the sixteenth century and, at the height of its popularity in…," he stopped, looked at his staring comrades and asked, "Would you like me to continue?"

"No," Rick answered bluntly. "All we want to know about is a chapel, and that bloody board doesn't mention one so, before we run out of time and energy, I suggest you shut up and we get a move on."

Nobody disagreed with Rick's sentiment and, as the foursome stood to ready themselves for the off, it was obvious the female members of the team were better prepared for a mountain hike than the male contingent. With both sisters clad in waterproof pants plus matching jackets, wearing expensive walking boots and carrying a small rucksack containing essentials, the ever-organised Armstrong's looked the part. The HSG men, on the other hand, had the appearance of mountain men who hadn't seen a bar of soap, a razor, or comb for weeks.

"Ladies, as ever I'm impressed," Lucas sniggered. "Again, you're well prepared. Sadly, as you can see, both Rick and I aren't, but we'll manage – I hope."

"You boys will be just fine," Babb said. "You've got us to look after you." She smiled sweetly. "Now, which way we headed?"

Marion scanned the plateau, then pointed to a gap in the rock face on the far side of the car park.

"That way," she said. "The path we want is through there." Then she glanced at Lucas and smiled. "Will you take point?" she asked.

"Of course, madam," he smirked, "it's my favourite position."

Then, like a well-tuned infantry squad, the mismatched couples fell into trail line formation and headed for the gap in the rock.

CHAPTER 35

Lock Out

Once through the gap, the foursome faced several choices, but Lucas didn't break stride. He knew Marion would know which path to take and, before he'd even considered turning to her for guidance, her voice came from behind.

"Go to the right. You see the steps? Just follow them up to the top – the main trail should be up there."

Lucas obeyed and started to clamber up the rough-hewn steps on all fours. He reached the last step in a frantic flurry of dust then disappeared from view. Seconds later he re-appeared. "She's dead right," he shouted down to the rest of the group, "this is it."

At the top of the steps the rugged well-worn track stretched as far as the eye could see. It was relatively straight but in parts it looked perilously steep and, as the group stood contemplating the task ahead, Rick suddenly looked concerned.

"How far do you think we have to walk up this thing?" he asked.

Marion smiled. Rick had directed his question at her, and she liked the fact she was in charge of the finite details. "It's roughly two miles," she said. "An hour, maybe?"

Lucas wasn't convinced. "If it's all like that," he said pointing up the trail, "then two miles could take a lot longer than an hour."

Rick stepped forward. "OK," he said, "then it looks like we'll just have to suck it and see, won't we?" After a quick group conflab, they agreed they should just get on with it.

***

After twenty minutes they'd made good progress, but the wind was now noticeably cooler. Marion, thankful for her insulated ski-jacket, felt a pang of pity for the two men dressed only in t-shirts and blouson jackets.

"It's freezing up here," she shouted ahead to Lucas. "You OK?"

Lucas wasn't feeling the cold; the exertion of the climb and the hope of finding something meaningful was keeping him warm. But hearing the enquiring voice behind he felt it was only polite to stop and answer the question.

"Like I said to your crackpot sister earlier, the English are used to the cold." He grinned. "We can handle it, so yeah, I'm OK, thanks," and with that he turned back up the trail and started walking.

As the energy sapping minutes ticked by, the legs tired, the pace slowed, and as soon as they reached the hour mark, Rick piped up again.

"Well that's an hour," he puffed, "are we anywhere near?"

"I don't know, is the honest answer," Marion replied, "but if we take a break, I'll check."

The foursome stopped for a breather and a look at the map. As a pink-cheeked Babb sat down on a handy boulder, she reached into her rucksack.

"Water, anyone?" she asked holding out a blue plastic bottle. Everyone nodded then took it in turns to take a glug of the much-needed liquid refreshment.

From where they'd stopped, the view from all angles was spectacular. As the small group stood and gazed at the rugged landscape engulfing them, Lucas turned to Babb and pointed at her backpack.

"You got any binoculars in there?" he asked. "Or would that be too much even for Fully Loaded?"

Babb pulled a face. "Maybe," she said, "let me see what I can do." She reached into the bag again. As she frantically rummaged around, Rick glanced at his partner. "What've you seen, Rox?" he asked.

"I'm not sure," Lucas replied before pointing to what had caught his eye to explain further. "See that ridge line over there," he said, "looks like a roof or something, just peeking out from the far end, can you see it?"

Rick followed his colleague's outstretched arm but, before he got a chance to answer, Babb handed a small set of camouflaged field glasses to Lucas. "There you go," she grinned, "the army surplus store's finest."

Lucas shouldn't have been surprised but he was. "Jesus, woman," he said, shaking his head in disbelief. "You're bloody amazing."

Stifling a grin, he grabbed the ex-military binoculars and scanned the horizon. As he adjusted the focus control the section of mountainside he was interested in came into view. And there, to his surprise, showing just above a jagged outcrop, was the glimpse of a slated roof. "Yes," he said, "it's definitely a building. Not massive, mind, but, yeah, it could be what we're looking for. But we need to get closer, much, much closer."

"Let's have a look," Rick badgered.

"Here," Lucas said as he handed his colleague the binoculars, "see what you think."

After all, four of them had taken a good look, they turned their attentions to Marion who was now back hunched over the map spread out on the floor in front of her. "If that's our chapel," she said, "then it's a bit further west than our friend at the gas station showed us."

"Hey, come on," Lucas came to the defence of the old man, "after thirty odd years it was a pretty good guess, close enough to get us this far."

No one disagreed.

***

Clayton Carr was under no illusion his boss was on the war path. The early morning call had been brief, but long enough to know things were not all to his liking.

"Where are you?" Tate asked. "Are you out of bed?" After the assistant confirmed his status his boss replied tersely, "Well, get yourself down here fast, boy – we got a problem."

As the sun rose and warmed the farthest extremes of the Black

Mountain estate, the atmosphere in the well-manicured grounds returned to its usual tranquil state. Inside the house things were not as peaceful. As planned, the fund raiser guests had all gone before midnight and, after an early breakfast, so had most of The Divinity faithful.

So, by late morning the only personnel remaining on site were Leon Tate's entourage plus three of the biker support team. As was common with The Divinity's extravagant functions, the Security Director was tasked with the post-event clear up and the brief was always the same. Along with a select handful of the inner sanctum, Tate would stay on to ensure all areas of the venue were restored back to pristine show home conditions and that nothing incriminating or compromising was left behind.

"Clayton, come in," Tate said, "and sit down." He beckoned the younger man to join him at the table he'd commandeered as a desk, then glanced up. "What kept you?"

"Yes, sir, sorry I took so long, err…is everything OK?"

The older man fixed his underling with his usual glare, then eased back in the chrome chair and licked his lips. "No Clayton, everything is not OK," he almost whispered. "We have some issues that need resolving and we need it done before we leave, you understand?"

"Yes, sir, of course," the assistant answered, "but I am a little surprised. Everything seemed to go well last night, in fact, I'd go so far as to say, spectacularly well."

Tate raised an eyebrow. "Would you indeed? Well, I'll admit the dinner went to plan and the ceremony was sublime, but we have some loose ends and that bothers me."

"What loose ends?" Clayton asked a little too quickly.

"Well, since you ask," Tate said moving closer, "let's start with why the fuck you lied about speaking to Leonard?"

The younger man recoiled. Startled at the degree of venom in the question, he blushed, his mind raced, then he stammered, "Err, I… I don't know what you mean, Mr Tate."

"Do not fuck with me, boy," the Security Chief snapped, "you understand exactly what I'm saying. You know I miss nothing, so think twice about lying to me," he paused, "and if you know what's good for you, you won't do it again."

Clayton knew he'd been rumbled. Caught up in the whirlwind of last night's activity he'd forgotten about his simple white lie. Lenny never had rung him back and he'd not tried to call again. He now realised it was a grave error of judgement. "Yes, sir," he said. "I apologise; I don't know what I was thinking." Then, cowering like a scolded schoolboy before an aggrieved teacher, he simpered, "It won't happen again, sir, I promise it won't."

"You're fucking dead right it won't," Tate shrieked. "What the hell were you thinking? Why didn't you just tell me you couldn't get through?"

"Err, I…I don't know, Sir, I suppose I thought everything would be OK."

"Well, you supposed wrong, boy," he snarled, "and I can tell you that everything is most definitely not O-Fucking-K."

Clayton was now fearing the worse. "I'm truly sorry, Mr Tate," he mumbled. "Has something bad happened to Leonard?"

Tate stared at his whimpering gofer. "No," he snarled. "But that's not the fucking point is it….?"

***

As Lucas, Rick, and the sisters continued their slog up the trail it started to dawn on them that access from their current approach was looking less and less likely. "I don't think we're going get to it this way," Lucas announced. "It looks like it's on the other side."

Rick wasn't impressed. "You've gotta be kidding me, Sarge," he said. "All this bastard way and we can't get to it."

Babb didn't share Lucas's view. "Don't give up," she encouraged. "We'll find a way over."

Yet again the group decided to stop. Looking ahead over the rocky landscape, they could now see a good chunk of the squat stone building but, despite the last thirty minutes' hike, it still seemed well out of reach. "If it *is* the chapel," Marion said as she plonked herself down on a boulder, "and if it really *was* a place for travellers to rest up…then surely they must've been able to access it from the main trail, and that's what we're on now."

"Makes sense," Lucas agreed, "but how the hell did they do it?"

Rick stood staring across the abyss, left hand shading his eyes from the glare, methodically studying the scene ahead. "Pass me the glasses please, Babb," he said.

No one spoke as Babb passed the binoculars to Rick. Then, as the South African studied the landscape ahead, Lucas and Babb simply stood watching and Marion went back to consulting the map. "There should be a fork in the trail just up a way," she said suddenly. "Leads off to the right, looks like a secondary route, may be worth a try…"

"I can see it," Rick said still holding the field glasses to his eyes, "it's two, three hundred yards ahead, branches off sharp right…then drops down a little," he paused. "Yeah, looks to be heading in the direction we want."

Lucas pulled a face. "That's great Rick," he said, "but there's still a massive ravine between us and the building."

Rick ignored his partner's disparaging tone. "I know," he said, lowering the glasses, "but look, it's going in the right sort of direction, and who knows what's round that corner." He gesticulated into the distance. "Let's just give it a go, eh, Sarge?"

"OK, you win," Lucas smiled, "but you lead."

With that, the foursome changed their walking order and then, for the third time in the gruelling two-hour exertion, they set off along the trail.

Ten minutes later, they arrived at the junction. Although the branch trail didn't look as well-worn as the main one, it definitely got used.

"This is the one," Rick said as he reached the intersection. "We all up for giving it a go?"

Lucas shouted from the back. "Yes, yes, Ricky, of course we are, just move it, will you."

To their collective relief, the secondary trail was level. Initially it dipped a little off the main route then appeared to run flat for as far as they could see and, once heading down it, Rick picked up the pace.

"Hold on, Rick," Babb yelled, "what's with the speed walking?"

"Look, we're on the flat now, so in theory we should be able to make better progress," Rick stifled a laugh then added, "so if you would move it along without complaining, please madam, it would be appreciated."

Babb loved the banter; social interaction with fun people was something she sorely missed. Wild mountain living was a great way of life, but it could get awful lonely at times. "Yes, sir, Mr Kruger," she grinned back, "you're the boss!"

A little further down the trail, Rick's lead significantly increased, so much so that, as he rounded the next bend, he completely disappeared from view. Moments after losing visual contact, the group heard a loud wolf-whistle and, as all three raced to catch up, they again heard him before they saw him.

"Well, would you believe it?" the voice bellowed. "What a sight! Didn't show this on your bloody map, did it?"

Once round the bend, the chasing trio stopped and stared. There, clear as day, not more than a hundred yards away was a bridge. A bridge crossing the ravine they'd been cursing for the last hour.

"This has got to be a wind-up," Lucas said. "A bleeding rope bridge!" He shaded his eyes from the sun for a better look. "Which, from this distance, looks about a hundred years old."

"It could actually be older," Marion said straight faced.

Buoyed by the possibility of getting to the other side, the group upped the pace and arrived at the bridge in a matter of minutes. But, despite high hopes, their endeavours were rewarded with nothing but disappointment. In front of the final approach access was blocked by a large weather-beaten sign that read:

Bridge Closed. Do Not Use. Dangerous Structure. Access Forbidden.
By Order Of The Flint County Recreation Department.

Lucas looked at the rusty fence that barred entry, then the warning sign, then eventually focused on the gnarly old bridge itself. “Look at the state of it,” he scoffed. “You’re right, Marion, it’s gotta be well over a hundred years old.”

“Check it out, Roxy,” Rick said. “Look, from here you can see the chapel. Looks like it’s fenced in.” The South African was pointing back up the valley to a plateau sitting high up in the rock on the other side of the ravine. “See it?”

“Yeah, I can,” Lucas answered. “Could be the one, but how the hell do you get up there?”

“Bins, please, Babb,” Rick said as he held out his hand.

Once again Babb passed over her trusty field glasses. Rick then set about checking for potential ways up to the stone building. He traced the line of the rickety bridge across the sheer drop of the ravine, then along the far trail back up the valley as far as he could, and finally up and down the craggy rock faces surrounding the partially visible structure. “The only thing I can see is some sort of hollow in the rock below the plateau,” he said. “It’s at trail level, could be a doorway maybe, but it’s right on the bend so I can’t really make it out that well.”

“Let me see!” Lucas almost ripped the binoculars out of his partner’s hands.

Rick wasn’t impressed by his over eager colleague. “Take it easy, Sarge,” he snapped. “You trying to fucking strangle me?”

Lucas immediately realised he was out of order and apologised. “Sorry, Rick, sorry. I’m getting carried away again, aren’t I?”

“Too right you are,” his muscular colleague said, “but I’ll forgive you.” He unhooked the binoculars from around his neck, and handed them to Lucas, then took a deep breath and pointed across the ravine. “Now, like I said, follow the trail back up the valley, and you see where it starts to bend round out of view...got it? Can you make out the beginning of a sort of arch shape in the rock face?”

Lucas did as instructed and, as he adjusted focus on the area Rick had indicated, a figure suddenly appeared. “Ricky, there’s someone there,” he whispered. “Just stepped out of nowhere, like friggin’ magic.

Big, stocky guy with a beard. Now he's looking up and down and... shit! Now he's gone."

"Seriously?" Rick exclaimed. "Did you see where he came from?"

Lucas removed the glasses from his eyes and turned to his partner. "Out of the bloody wall! I think you're right; there's an entrance past the bend."

"Entrance to what, though?" Rick asked. "Can't be our chapel, can it? I mean, look at it, it's a good sixty feet above."

Lucas looked thoughtful. "Don't know," he said, "but I think we need to check it out." And then, turning to the surprisingly quiet pair standing behind him, asked, "What you two ladies like with heights?"

CHAPTER 36

Time For Reflection

Sarah's early morning dilemma wasn't of critical importance, but it still had to be sorted. "Come on, love, make your mind up," Margaret Stuart prompted, "how you having these eggs?"

"Fried, please," she replied, "but with hard yolks…you know what I'm like with runny eggs."

"I do, poppet – and you've always been the same," she pulled a face and looked at her husband. "Isn't that right, Raymond?"

Ray looked up. "Sure is," he said shaking his head, "always been a bit of a fussy eater, our Sarah…no idea where she gets it from."

Thoroughly enjoying putting the finishing touches to the perfect Sunday morning treat, Marg Stuart was in her element. Bespoke fried eggs were despatched, cutlery clattered, sauce bottles flew, then a big plate of hot buttered toast appeared, and a grateful family tucked in.

Fifteen minutes later, as they finished their breakfast with a second cup of tea, the doorbell rang. "I'll get it," Ray said as he started up from the table, "it'll be Gerry."

Seconds later Ray led a drawn-looking Gerry Hanlon into the country style kitchen. Ray pointed out a chair to his best friend, "Sit yourself down, Gerry. You having tea or coffee?"

"Err, I'll have coffee please," Gerry said before easing himself down onto the chair and nodding politely, "Morning, Margaret, Sarah – how are we both today?"

Mother and daughter looked at the grey-haired Irishman and smiled affectionately. Gerry really was part of the family, always had been and always would. A man so interwoven into the fabric of their lives that neither could imagine a life without him.

"Very well, thanks, Ger," Margaret answered. "Yourself?"

Gerry smiled weakly. "Yeah, I'm OK, I think, Marg," he said, "apart from this job in the States that's stressing me out, I'm fine."

"Well, go on, then," Sarah prompted, "spill the beans, Uncle Gerry, tell us the latest…anything new from Sergeant Roxby?"

"Well," he grimaced, "funny you should mention that. I actually got an email from him about twenty minutes ago, it was only brief, and I mean brief…"

Before Gerry could continue, Ray was at his side, mug of coffee in hand. "There you go, Blue, get that down your neck."

Gerry acknowledged the drink then, as Ray sat back down at the table, he winked at his daughter and turned to his friend. "So, what's this email say, then, Gerry?" he asked. "Any significant developments? Did the boys get to see the comet?"

"Yeah, they did," he answered. "Here, let me read it out to you; that's easiest."

Gerry pulled out his mobile, clicked onto emails, and scrolled down…" Right, here you go," he frowned as he focused on the screen, "this is what our man had to say."

'Gerry, all good here – comet was stunning, loads of people watching, great craic. We will start the search for the chapel in the morning. Keep you posted, regards, LR.'

"Is that it?" Ray sneered. "When you said it was brief, I didn't think it would be quite that brief."

"Some cookie, isn't he?" Gerry said with an exaggerated shake of his head. "Great craic, indeed, you'd swear the man was on a jolly boy's outing from the tone of that, wouldn't you?"

Sarah couldn't help but smile. She knew Lucas was a one-off and she knew Rick wasn't exactly the conventional type either. But they could make things happen, they got results and most importantly she smiled to herself - the fat lady hadn't even thought about singing. "Upbeat is good, Gerry," she said brightly. "Brief isn't a problem, is it? It's standard for those two…and just think, from that one liner you know they're alive and still on the case – what more could you ask?"

Now it was Gerry's turn to smile. He knew she was right. Thankfully HSG's A-team were still in the game, and if anyone could snatch victory from the jaws of defeat it was the lanky ex-squaddie and his South African side-kick.

"You know what, kid," Gerry said, "I suppose that's the way to look at it, isn't it?" As he started to feel the tension ease, he pushed back in his chair and gave a crossed finger salute. "So…here's hoping our boys do us proud."

"That's it, Gerry, that's all we can do, mate, just sit back and hope they can shake something out."

"You had breakfast?" Margaret beamed at her second favourite man in the world. "Nice fry-up set you up a treat…what d'you say?"

Gerry beamed back, "Well, if you're offering…"

***

Sat opposite his Security Chief, a pale looking Clayton didn't have a clue what was irking his boss and was now terrified about what was coming next.

Tate was in two minds about his next course of action but, after several seconds of uncharacteristic indecisiveness, looked his young charge in the eyes.

"I'm willing to overlook the Leonard incident," he drawled slowly. "I believe you know you were foolish and I'm certain it will never happen again, so let's just put it down to," he paused to think how best to put it, "youthful naivety, just simple youthful naivety, OK?"

Carr stared at his boss not quite sure he'd heard him right; why would he so easily forgive such blatant lying? Now he felt more on edge. "Thank you, Mr Tate," he grovelled. "I promise it won't happen again, truly I do."

"I don't doubt it," Tate said. "Now onto more pressing matters. Last night we had an unexpected visitor, a trespasser if you like, and it was someone known to us, someone we thought we could trust but – obviously - we were mistaken."

"Sorry, sir, I don't follow."

"I didn't think for one minute you would," Tate replied sarcastically, "so let me explain; last night a supervisor from AMS was found injured in the grounds at the back of the main house by Mr Clarke and his team."

"Oh, right, which supervisor was it?" Clayton asked quickly.

Tate didn't answer immediately; for several long silent, analytical seconds he focused on the face of his young protégé. Seeing no evidence of lying in the handsome features and, with a rather weak 'I'll give you the benefit of the doubt' rationale running through his head, the Security Chief finally answered. "It was Jon Townsend," he said. "You know, the tall one they call Jonny-T," he paused again, "who, we now find out, has only been with AMS for four months."

"Yeah, I've met him," Clayton said. "What happened to him, is he badly hurt?"

Again, Tate looked closely at his underling. The expression seemed right, the reaction genuine enough and the question rational; possibly, he was telling the truth....

"No, Clayton, what I'm saying is that this dip-shit supervisor, this Jon Townsend, was the uninvited guest, he was the snake in the grass, he was the one who shouldn't have been there but was."

"Oh, but why would he just turn up?"

"Why would he just turn up?" Tate repeated loudly. "Excellent question, young man, very astute and maybe, just maybe, you can guess the reason." He moved a little closer to his underling and leered, "Or, at the very least, offer some sort of theory."

Clayton's heart rate increased and his stomach tightened; the Director's bad mood was worsening at an alarming rate. "Err, maybe... maybe an administrative error?" he offered lamely. "Miscommunication at AMS's office?"

Tate eased back a little. "You'd like to think so, wouldn't you," he replied, "because that would make sense - but oh, no, the reason he gave so assuredly during his questioning was…," the Security Chief stopped talking then leant in close again. "The reason," he snarled, "was apparently you."

Now Tate exploded. He leapt from his chair, grabbed the younger man's hair and dragged his head hard back. Then, bringing his contorted face right up to the terrified junior's throat, his mouth caressed the exposed white flesh. "Now, why the fuck would he say that, pretty boy?" he hissed as he licked.

The young assistant was paralysed with fear. With his head held back and Tate's foul breath assaulting his every sense, he could only just manage to talk.

"Jesus Lord, save me," he spluttered. "Please, Mr Tate, please, please stop…I don't know anything about what happened, it's nothing to do with me. The man's lying, I swear to you – you've got to believe me…please, for Christ's sake."

Initially the Security Chief was unmoved, then for reasons best known to himself he began to release his grip. But as soon as the younger man's head returned to its natural upright position, Tate had a change of heart and let fly with a rocket of a cuff shot. He caught the back of Clayton's head with such force that it jolted forward and hit the polished wood table with a stomach-churning thud.

"Argaaaahh!" the young assistant wailed as the shock and pain instantly registered.

Tate now stood off to the side, staring down at the stricken aide, but held his arm aloft, poised to strike again if he felt another unstoppable surge of rage.

"You little prick tease," he snarled. "Now look at that mess! Who's going to clean it up?" Tate had completely flipped. He was screaming at the top of his voice, venting all his anger toward his faithful assistant lying crumpled over a wooden dining table in front of him. "Clayton, I don't want to find out you've let the organisation down," he yelled, "but it looks to me like you've fucked up, and fucked up big time. You must atone, you must put it right; are you listening to me, boy?"

A dazed head slowly rose from the blood smeared table, half turned to look in the direction of the demonic boss. "I, I…am Mr Tate, but you've got it all wrong," he blubbed. "I didn't say anything to AMS, not a word. What do I have to do to prove it to you?"

Tate instantly calmed. "Well, now, there's a question," he said smiling slyly. "How can you prove it to me, well, OK, we could start with something I've been thinking about for a while …"

But before Tate could finish his explanation, there was a sharp rap on the glass door followed by an anxious voice from the other side, "Mr Tate, sir, it's Juan. We're all done. Every area is clear and ready for your inspection."

Momentarily, the Chief was thrown. Jesus, he thought, I need to get a grip! But, as ever, he knew the heady cocktail of power and nubile young men would remain a chronic addiction he'd never be able to kick. For now, fulfilling his latest fantasy would have to remain on ice. "OK, OK, Juan," he replied, "just give me a moment and I'll be right with you."

Tate strode back over to the table, grabbed his still blubbing assistant by the collar, and hoisted him to his feet. "We'll finish this later, boy," he said as he cupped and squeezed the younger man's groin, "but for the time being you've been warned, OK?"

Through stinging red eyes, Clayton stared at the monster before him and, as the bitter taste of blood made him gag, a sense of hopelessness enveloped him. Suddenly he flashed back twenty years. How in God's name had he managed to replace one abusive father figure with another one just as selfish, cruel, and deviant? He'd always been a good kid, he'd done nothing wrong, and he'd only ever wanted to please. So why was he treated badly?

In an instant he snapped back to reality. As a solitary tear rolled down his throbbing cheek, he simply answered, "Yes, Mr Tate… whatever you say, sir."

***

Juan, bodyguard-cum-chauffeur, showed his boss around the entire estate. Tate was a category "A" control freak and wanted it all done his way and done right, but - worse still - he needed to see it for himself.

"Right let's move it," Tate snapped, "We'll check-up top now."

As the two men headed up the stairway to the chapel, they saw a figure standing at the top. From the silhouette both knew it was Red Clarke. The outlaw biker patiently watched the two men climb the last few flights while, subconsciously, he straightened up. "All secure here," Red said as they reached the top. "All clear and locked up as ordered."

"Thanks, Red," Juan replied. "Mr Tate is just going to undertake a final inspection." He turned to look at his frowning boss, "After you, sir."

Tate didn't care personally for the White Warrior bikers, but did appreciate they were well organised, tough, and reliable allies, allies that played a key role in protecting The Divinity's many business interests. This was a role they had successfully fulfilled on many occasions, a role for which they were always well rewarded.

"Is the well secure?" Tate asked the biker.

"Solid," Red answered, "top and bottom."

"Show me," came the unconvinced reply.

Red led the two men toward the far corner of the chapel plot. The site's 'well' was not all it seemed. At plateau level it did look very much like expected; a circular stone wall, eight feet in diameter, standing three feet proud of the surrounding flat ground. Close up, it was a whole different story.

"As instructed," Red said, grabbing the well's steel barred cover, "the hatch is chained and padlocked, and the bottom gate's double pad-locked."

The Security Chief stepped up to the wall then bent over and peered down through the grating. Once his eyes adjusted to the shaft's inherent gloom, he studied the series of vertical cat ladders and rest platforms that stretched down to the base.

"I'm going to have to take your word about the bottom gate," he said. "I have no desire to climb down there this morning."

"Feel free, I can open the hatch for you, no problem," the biker replied, "but, like I say, it's tight as a drum."

Tate didn't respond. He straightened up, stepped back, and brushed off the dust from the front of his trousers. "Juan," he ordered, now looking at his driver, "have a final check round the building, will you. I need a quiet word with Mr Clarke here, OK?"

The wiry Mexican nodded and dutifully headed off toward the other end of the plateau. Tate then turned his attention to the grizzled biker. "I checked with AMS about our friend from last night," he said, "and it seems this Townsend character hasn't been with them long. Apparently, he only started four months ago."

Red shook his head. "Doesn't surprise me," he said, "and I bet they can't get hold of the fucker this morning, can they?"

Tate grimaced. "Correct, but I'm assured they'll keep trying." He paused, "They also claim they're at a loss as to why he was at the house last night but, all that said, they're positive he's who he says he is."

"He's not, Mr Tate," the biker said. "he's a fed, simple as that. I just fucking know it."

"Look, Red," Tate said calmly. "AMS are no amateurs, they're adamant they've done all their statutory background checks. They have references and all the other bullshit they need to back up their claim." He stopped to mull over the biker's suggestion a little more. "You could be right, though," he said eventually, "and if he really is a federal agent then we've got a problem, a major fucking problem."

CHAPTER 37

A Fine Line

In the cool of a mountain shadow, the foursome stood staring at the death trap that loomed before them. Eventually, Rick broke the silence. "You want me to go first?" he asked.

The question was directed at Lucas but, before he had a chance to answer, Marion cut in, "You're not seriously going to cross it, are you?" she asked.

Lucas glanced at Rick and then at Marion. "We've got to try," he said. "And I think I should go first."

She let out a sigh of despair, then looked to her sister for support, but Babb simply shook her head and declined to comment.

"You sure, Sarge?" Rick asked. "I'm quite happy to have a go - and I'm probably heavier."

Lucas turned and smiled at his colleague. "No, it's OK, Ricky, I'll do it," he said. "Anyway, I reckon we weigh about the same now - you know, with all this rich American living." He mockingly patted his stomach for effect. "Must've put on half a stone this week."

After further discussion made it obvious they weren't going to talk the men out of a crossing attempt, the sisters were still insistent they themselves would only watch. "No way can I do that," Marion protested. "Sorry, but I'm staying here, ready to ring 911 and ask for mountain rescue if needed."

"I'm with you, sis," Babb agreed. "I love the hiking, love the mountains, love all this healthy outdoor stuff…but no way am I starting to try out high wire stunts as well."

It was agreed Lucas would cross first, Rick would follow, and the girls would stay put, primed to ring in an SOS if things went wrong.

"I know it looks dodgy," Lucas didn't sound confident, "but one at a time, dead slow, I think we should be OK. Here we go folks, it's Showtime."

No one said a word as they watched the gangly brit walk past the No Entry sign. Then he hopped the rusty barrier and edged forward to the first timber slat. As he stood on the threshold of the bridge, he reached out and grabbed the left rope rail then shook it as hard as he could. The structure gave a slight creak as it flexed under the force, but nothing more. "That doesn't seem too bad," he shouted over his shoulder, "but now for the big test."

With that, he grabbed both ropes simultaneously then stepped lightly onto the closest plank. At first, he only put his right foot down then, pushing down through his leg with increasing force, he tested the resistance. Seems OK, he thought, feels solid.

"Even better," he turned back to speak directly to the group, "first timbers look in good nick. I think the main reason it's closed is those few missing ones in the middle."

Rick was sceptical. "Let's hope it's that simple," he answered. "If its only crime is a few missing slats and looking tired, then we could be in luck."

Lucas, now buoyed by his initial structural assessment, moved his full weight onto the first board and prayed it held. Thankfully, it did. As he looked at the jagged ravine gaping below like the open mouth of a hungry great white, he set off across the slatted bridge.

The structure was no more than fifty feet in span, but at least forty of that was directly over a sheer drop, and it was old, unloved and - as he was soon to realise - off limits for a reason. At almost a third of the way across, the Englishman was getting more and more confident. Then things took an unfortunate turn for the worse. As Lucas stepped on what appeared to be another solid slat, it gave way. With a loud snap it split in two. As his right foot burst through, he yelped in surprise, giving the small audience behind a collective heart attack.

"Roxy, you OK?" Rick shouted to his stricken comrade.

The bridge swayed and creaked. Lucas closed his eyes for a second, took a deep breath and clenched his teeth. His right foot had gone right through and was now dangling in mid-air. But his left leg - although bent - was still planted and secure. With body tensed, gripping the hand rails as hard as he dared, he stayed stock still, got his breathing back under control, then - after what seemed an age - stuttered, not daring to take his eyes off the chasm below him, "Err, I...I guess so. I think it's just this one dud board."

"Can you get back?" Marion asked.

"What do you mean 'back'?" he barked sounding genuinely surprised. "Look, it's a minor issue, that's all, nothing to worry about, OK?"

He delicately extracted his foot from the snapped plank, stood up very slowly, and looked across to the other side. Once he'd steadied himself, he simply stepped over the busted slat and onto its immediate neighbour. The sisters, hearts in mouths, stared agog.

"For God's sake, Lucas, stop it!" Marion shouted. "It's too dangerous! You are going to kill yourself! Whatever's over there is not worth dying for."

Lucas could be a stubborn old dog at times and now was no exception. Without even a word in response to the librarian's heartfelt pleas, he continued across the bridge. At speed, he stepped nimbly on the planks that looked solid; Russian roulette at one hundred and twenty feet wasn't everyone's cup of tea but he'd made his mind up; as he went, he deftly leapt the missing slats dotted around the bridge's central section. A mere twenty seconds later he was safely over. Grinning like a demented fool, he turned back to look at the gobsmacked observers on the other side. A surge of relief flooded through him and he yelled over. "See, told you, piece of piss!" He cupped his ear, but no response came. "Well, Kruger, what you waiting for?" he challenged. "Are you giving it a go, or what?"

Rick, Marion and Babb looked at each other. They were all relieved Lucas had made it but a little annoyed at the arrogant gung-ho attitude.

"You're a lunatic, Roxby," Rick shouted back, "and a show boating prick if ever I saw one."

"That's a bit harsh," Lucas replied. "Look, I made it, didn't I? Now it's your turn, so just hurry it along, will you."

"OK, OK…I'm coming, Any tips?"

"Yeah, stay over to the left, it's more robust. When you hop a missing slat, take the weight off your landing with the handrails, if you get what I mean?"

"Yeah, yeah, Sarge, I get it," Rick answered. He then turned to speak to the sisters. "Bye for now, ladies," he said, looking at their worried faces, "but I promise we'll be as quick as we can."

***

Tate had seen enough; he'd toured the estate and was satisfied everything was as it should be. It was time to leave.

"Juan, that's it, let's get going," he ordered. "You too, Red, you've done your bit." Ten minutes later, the three men were back in the main house and, as the burly biker said a subdued farewell to Juan, Tate disappeared to make a call.

Back at Mesa HQ, Dan Tyler awaited another call from his boss, but it came a little sooner than he'd imagined.

"Daniel," Tate snapped as the call connected, "I want to run through a few things with you, you ready?"

"Yes, Mr Tate," came the dutiful reply.

"I need a full update," he said, then stopped to consider the priorities. "I think we'll start with AMS, any further response from them?"

"Yes, sir, AMS have confirmed they've just visited the home address given by Townsend and, bizarrely, no one at the property had ever heard of him."

"What a surprise," the Security Chief muttered. "What about the CCTV review?"

"Err, inconclusive, sir," Tyler answered. "They have footage of him snooping around the back of the house, but then he stops and turns to retreat. As he does, he drops his flashlight, then sprints off into the shadows."

"Anything after that?"

"Well, sort off…," he said but then stopped.

After several seconds of frustrating silence Tate prompted, "Well go on then, what else?"

Tyler restarted the tale. "Well, immediately after our man disappears," he said, "the big guy with the beard comes around the corner and sees the torch on the floor."

"Right," Tate said as he mentally tried to piece the jigsaw together, "so this prick is skulking round the back of the house for whatever reason. Then he hears Clarke approaching which obviously rattles him. In his panic, he accidentally drops his torch and runs to hide."

"Yes, Mr Tate, that's what it looks like."

"How long after that did they find him?"

"About fifteen minutes," Tyler said. "The CCTV clearly shows Townsend being helped back to the house," he paused, "so whatever happened to him out in the grounds happened quickly."

"Could it have been self-inflicted?" Tate asked.

Tyler was quick to answer. "Deliberately? I'd say no way, sir, but accidentally? I'd say it's a possibility."

"Interesting theory, Daniel, why'd you say that?"

"Well, the position of the wound for one and the fact there's not a shred of evidence of any other trespassers during the night's proceedings."

Tate nodded silently to himself, but had already made up his mind. He wasn't going to waste any more time dwelling on the Jon Townsend problem.

"OK, food for thought," he said before moving swiftly on. "Right, next, anything from Ings?"

"No, sir, not a word."

The Security Chief kicked out in frustration. "Shit," he said, "something's not right. No show, no call, no anything. What the hell's the man playing at? It's not like him."

"Yes, sir, it's bad news," the underling replied, "but as a precaution we've moved the woman. Keeping her here any longer was too risky."

"Good. Where've you taken her?"

"Out to the ranch," he said. "Well, for now anyway."

"Wise move," Tate said, then asked, "How did Leonard get on?"

"Err, well…he finished checking the house over but didn't find a lot, except for a folder with a whole bunch of information about the outreach projects. Real detailed stuff, you know."

"Tell me more," Tate encouraged.

With that, the flood gates opened. Tate's ever officious deputy went on to regale his boss with his colleague's feedback. Leaving nothing out, he told him how Leonard had searched the house from top to bottom, how he'd found the stash of outreach project documents, and how he'd finally locked up, cleaned up, and left the house looking undisturbed. He also explained that the two spurious construction company employees had returned an hour after their first call, but this time Leonard had not even answered the door.

"More bad news," Tate said despondently. "Whoever's on our case is getting far too close for comfort."

With his cell phone glued to his right ear, the Security Chief paced up and down the vast reception hall of the house. He looked pensive and was now genuinely concerned about the growing number of questions he couldn't answer.

"Where's Leonard now?" he asked.

"He's gone to the ranch; babysitting the package."

"OK, so where are you?"

"Still in Mesa," Tyler replied. "But I'll be heading to the ranch shortly."

"Right, let me know when you're there," he ordered. "Ask the bitch about the documents, see if you can get anything out of her but no serious damage yet, understand?"

"Of course, Mr Tate, I'll ring you as soon as I arrive."

"OK, Daniel, we'll leave it there for now," Tate hit 'call end', shook his head then, muttering quietly to himself, headed toward the stairs.

***

Much to Babb's and Marion's relief, Rick made it across the bridge without incident. He kept it steady, controlled, and calm and, as nervous observers, they couldn't have asked for more. Once safely on the other side, the South African didn't shout or yell, he simply turned, waved, then blew the sisters a kiss before striding off up the trail to find his partner.

Seconds later, he caught up with Lucas, but, as the duo drew closer to the bend, the pace slowed. Lucas flattened himself against the rock face for the final approach. Rick followed suit.

"See, Ricky, you were right," Lucas whispered as he nodded in the direction of the now obvious opening. "Neat or what?"

Rick was impressed. "Nicely done," he said as he surveyed the mysterious entrance.

Once confident no one was on the trail or lurking in the void, the two men moved out and stood in front of it. And now, from this vantage point, it was clear the opening was in fact a natural fissure in the rock face. But it was a fissure someone had taken time to frame out in brickwork, then install an iron gate and complete with an in-your-face warning sign which simply read: 'PRIVATE PROPERTY - KEEP OUT. NO PUBLIC ACCESS'.

"Well, that's telling us," Lucas muttered as he held onto the bars of the gate and squinted into the gloom behind, "and it's bloody solid."

The gate's heavy frame was set into the masonry surround and the single leaf access panel was hinged on one side but padlocked top and bottom on the other. It was a serious deterrent, designed to keep out even the most intrepid trespassers, but the HSG team weren't ready to quit yet. "Oh, for some burning gear," Rick smiled, "we'd be through that in five minutes."

"Yeah, nice thought, Ricky, but we've got nothing but our bare hands."

"Well, bare hands, rocks, and timber actually..." Rick gestured to their immediate surroundings.

The two men looked around as they mulled over their dilemma.

"The frame is built into the brick," Lucas said as he turned back to the gate. "That might be the weak spot."

"How do you mean?"

"Well, we can't get through those padlocks," Lucas said, "but what if we lever up the frame, maybe see if we can bust it out of the brickwork."

Rick looked puzzled. "How exactly are we gonna do that?" he asked.

Lucas looked behind him then back at the gate. "Well, I reckon we wedge one of those edge timbers under the gap at the bottom here," as he spoke Lucas jammed his booted foot into the small gap below the gates frame, "then get a good sized boulder under it and simply find two fat bastards to jump up and down on the other end."

Rick stared at his filthy, sweat soaked, comrade partly in admiration, partly in disbelief. "You reckon we can get through this double padlocked iron security gate with an ancient railway sleeper and a boulder?"

"Do you have a better idea?"

Five minutes later, the two men had managed to drag a large timber baulk over from the trail edge, gouge out a bit more material from underneath the bottom of the frame, jam the sleeper under, and were now manoeuvring a football sized rock under it.

"I hope no one decides to come around the corner," Lucas grimaced. "How'd we explain this little set up?"

"We haven't seen a soul all morning," Rick said. "Let's pray it stays that way."

"Right, that'll do," Lucas paused then grinned as he stood back and surveyed the makeshift lever arm. "Let's give it a go."

He ushered Rick onto the sleeper then clambered on in front of him. "You hold onto me and I'll hold the gate," he said as he edged back up the timber towards his partner. "You OK there?"

"Uh-huh," Rick grunted.

Lucas grabbed the bars. "OK. Start bouncing!"

What a strange sight they made, two sweat drenched, dust covered, unshaven men, precariously balancing on an eight-inch-wide piece of wood stuck underneath an old iron gate, halfway up a mountain.

Fortunately, no one was looking, and no one was in ear shot. As they huffed and puffed, trying their best to create maximum force without falling off, they got a steady rhythm going. After a couple of minutes of energy-sapping effort, the frame began to give a little.

"It's moving, Rick, look; the mortar's cracking."

Rick peered over Lucas's shoulder. Sure enough, the brickwork surround had started to fail, and the mortar was starting to break up.

"That's it," Lucas said. "Just keep it going, just keep fucking bouncing, baby."

Thirty seconds later, the whole frame was leaning back at an angle, bits of dislodged brick from various sections around the opening lay littered on the floor, and it looked ready to fall.

"Right, Rick, the final push. It's battering ram time. Hop off!"

Rick dutifully obliged and helped yank the sleeper out from under the frame. The two men then lifted the chunky timber and prepared for stage two of the brutal assault.

"One, two, three," Lucas counted as the pair swung the timber back and forth. BANG! It hit the iron gate squarely in the middle, As the whole frame shuddered, it lent back even further into the opening. "One more good smack should do it," Lucas shouted. "You ready?"

Rick nodded and Lucas smiled. "OK, same again. Go on 'three'!" he said. "One, two, three!" BANG! This time they drove their timber battering ram in even harder, and the gate gave completely. Like a mighty redwood at the hands of the lumberjack, it was toppled. As it fell majestically inwards, it hit the loose stone floor with a resounding thud. "How's that!" Lucas crowed triumphantly. "The things you can do with an old sleeper and a rock!"

Rick smiled at his grinning partner, then moved toward the opening for a better view inside. "Royal Engineers, eh, Sarge?" he said, patting Lucas on the back. "The most ingenious soldiers in the world," his smile widened as he gave a thumbs-up, "and some are still doing the business in retirement."

Lucas didn't answer. He was now focused on what lay behind the flattened gate. As the dust settled, he stepped cautiously through the opening into the gloom.

"Well, fuck me, Kruger, look at this," he said, beckoning Rick to follow him. "Now that's what I call clever."

Standing hands on hips in the centre of the cavern, the ex-sapper was now staring upwards, admiring an array of ladders and platforms that stretched away above his head.

"Come on, Kruger," he said pointing at the first ladder, "race you to the top."

CHAPTER 38

A Leap of Faith

As the sisters watched their companions disappear from view, Babb couldn't disguise her frustration. "Don't know about you, sis," she said, "but I can't just sit here and do nothing, can you?"

Marion wasn't listening, she was staring intently across the ravine. Sat out of the glare of the sun, field glasses in hand, she was totally absorbed as she scanned the trail on the other side of the bridge.

"Err, hello!" Babb said sarcastically.

Slowly her sister unglued the binoculars from her eyes. "Sorry B, I missed that, what did you say?"

"I said: I can't just sit here and wait, I've got to do something."

As Marion turned to her sibling, a look of bemusement appeared on her face. "Are you serious?" she asked. "I'm not moving, I've told you. I'm staying put." She pointed at the dilapidated bridge. "Crossing that thing, well, it's plain crazy."

"I know it is," Babb agreed, "but it doesn't change the fact that I'm not just sitting here and waiting for ever and a day, OK?" She now sounded genuinely peeved. "So, whether you like it or not, I'm off down the trail a bit, see what I can find."

Marion finally snapped from her trance and realised what her sister was saying. "Oh, sorry, yeah, yeah, that's fine," she said. "For a minute there I thought you'd changed your mind about crossing the bridge."

Babb's eyes widened. "Come on, sis!" she said. "Yes, I'm into a more adventurous way of life these days but, as I said, there's no way I'm going that far for thrills - not a hope."

Marion smiled, stood up, rubbed her legs back to life, then grabbed her sister's hand. "OK, B," she said enthusiastically, "let's give it a whirl. Let's venture a little further down and see what we can find."

***

Lucas reached the shaft's top platform seconds ahead of Rick. Both men, out of breath from their rapid ascent, stood and looked up through the rusted iron grillage now inches above their heads.

"Another padlock," Lucas panted as he grabbed the offending lock and gave it a yank, "and, again, chained solid."

"Aww, come on, Rox, Engineers don't give up"

"For fuck's sake, Kruger, as if anyone's giving up. I just need a minute to think, OK?"

Lucas took hold of the heavy padlock again and shook it from side to side. The attached steel chain rattled against the iron of the grill. As the metallic jangling echoed down the shaft, he listened to it for a few seconds.

"Right, I've got it," he said smiling, "this time we need to go for a twist..."

Rick shot his partner a puzzled look. "A twist? How'd you mean?"

Lucas pointed to the chain that secured the hatch to the grillage. "Watch this," he said as he stuck his finger into one of the middle links and wiggled it. "See that little bit of play – there! That's the Achilles heel."

"OK, if you say so. So, what next?"

"Pass me that bit of old handrail and I'll show you."

Rick followed the line of Lucas's outstretched finger along the open mesh floor below. At the leading edge of the platform, lying tight up to the kick plate upstand, was a single length of metal tubing. On closer examination, Rick saw it matched the profile of the handrails.

"Yeah, OK, Rox, I got it," he picked up the tube and handed it to his colleague, "So where's that going?"

“Right in there,” Lucas said before sliding the yard-long steel tube through the chain. “Now get hold of that end…and let’s go anti-clockwise.”

Rick nodded his understanding. Then they stood facing each other with a firm grip on opposite ends of the tubing.

“One, two three,” Lucas counted then they started to push. The tube moved half an inch as they took up the slack, then the chain tightened but held fast.

“That’ll never go,” Rick growled as he stared at the solid knot of links above him.

“Who’s giving up now, eh?” Lucas gave a resigned shake of the head. “OK, right, let’s try back and forth. That might work better.”

“Alright, but you count it and I’ll follow.”

The two men looked each other up and down for a second and registered what a vision they were. Both filthy, dishevelled, stinking, sweat drenched, and out of breath. They couldn’t have looked any worse but, still, they had to smile.

“You and me get all the good jobs, don’t we?” Lucas laughed.

Rick pulled a face. “Every time, Sarge,” he grinned. “And would we want it any other way? Would we, bollocks!”

Lucas didn’t comment, he just nodded then gave the count. Again, on three the pair started to work the tube, but this time from side to side. It was a frenzied effort with both men growling their exertion as they went, but the approach got results. After sixty seconds of carefully choreographed back and forth power strokes, the chain snapped. Once the weakest link gave, the resistance disappeared and both men lunged forward in opposite directions. Lucas shot toward the platform edge. He struggled to regain his footing and hit the steel handrail hard. It hurt, but it did the job. On impact, he let out a yowl of pain then grabbed the top rail with both hands to steady himself.

“Thank fuck for that,” he spluttered as he peered down the shaft, “for a moment there, I thought I was going over.”

Rick, on the opposite side of the platform, had collided with the shaft side and, now desperate to recover from his exertion, slumped to the floor to catch his breath. Sitting propped up against the hewn stone wall, the South African shifted his weight forward and looked up at the broken chain swaying in the still air of the well.

"Jesus, that was hard work," he said between gulps for air, "but we cracked it. Another good call, Rox, bloody good call." He sat back for a few seconds trying to get his breathing under control, then finally asked, "Now, we ready to get out of this bastard thing?"

Before Lucas could answer, Rick stood up, straightened, then deftly unwrapped the broken chain from around the grillage. He held the lashing aloft for a second as he inspected it, then dropped it down the shaft. As the chain hit the bottom with a resounding whump, Lucas took the cue. Positioning himself directly below the hatch, he grabbed the bars with both hands and pushed up hard. The hinged steel lifted a few inches then stopped. Quickly, he realised he needed to be four foot taller to get it upright. "Shoulders please, Ricky," he ordered.

"Here you go, Sarge," Rick knelt on one knee and helped his partner clamber on board.

Seconds later, after a brief struggle, the hatch snapped back and slammed down onto the main grillage. "There she blows," Lucas crowed as a loud clang reverberated down the shaft. Now, with head and shoulders poking above ground he shaded his eyes from the bright sunlight and had a good look round. The plateau was deserted. "Looks OK up here, Rick," he whispered down to his partner, "not a soul in sight and guess what, we've found our chapel."

***

The sisters still hadn't seen anyone else all morning but, as they continued to wonder why, they suddenly spotted a group of hikers.

"My goodness, Marion, look," Babb said in mock surprise. "Other people!"

Seconds later the sisters stopped and stood off to the side as the all-male group got close. On a tight trail, giving the bigger group right of way was good hiker etiquette, something Babb was a stickler for.

"Thanks, ladies," the leader of the group acknowledged. "Beautiful day for it."

Marion and Babb both nodded and smiled politely back and then did the same to each subsequent member of the group. In turn as they went by, each man duly reciprocated. Once they'd passed, Marion looked up the trail and watched the group stride off. As soon as she was sure the men were out of earshot she turned to Babb.

"They looked an odd group, didn't they?" she said quietly. "Not your usual Sunday walker types, would you say?"

Babb raised an eyebrow. "I wouldn't like to speculate," she replied. "Hikers come in all shapes and sizes you know. I mean, just look at me."

Marion pulled a face. "They all looked alike," she said, "all dressed the same, same backpacks and all a similar age. Strange, don't you think?"

"Yeah, suppose it's a bit weird, but, look, it's not our problem, sis, nothing to do with us, so..." she suddenly looked worried, "or is it?"

Marion rolled her eyes as the question bounced round her head. "Hopefully not," she replied. "They just seemed right out of place to me, that's all." She stopped, mind still whirring, then finally added, "Ah, never mind, let's just forget it, eh? We'll just keep walking." Babb, happy to oblige, turned smartly down the trail and strode off, now determined more than ever to find something meaningful.

Five hundred yards further down the trail, the ravine began to narrow and, as the rate of shrinkage increased, it now seemed possible the gap between opposing faces could go down to touching distance.

"This is so weird," Babb said as she lengthened her lead, "and very claustrophobic."

The trail itself was still very narrow but, with the tightening gap, the valley sides above now seemed almost past vertical. As she approached an obvious pinch point, Babb slowed up. "What's up, B?" Marion shouted ahead to her now stationary sister. "Can't you get through?"

Marion's trail blazing sibling had stopped mid-stride and was now stood stock still, open mouthed staring at the sight before her.

"Get up here," she yelled back down the trail. "Come and look at this, it's amazing." Marion picked up the pace and within seconds was stood behind her. Grabbing her sister's shoulders, she stood on tip toes and peeked over for a look at what lay ahead.

There not more than twenty feet in front of them, was a miracle of erosion; a near perfect arch of weathered Navajo sandstone. The arch linked one side of the ravine to the other and below it was a natural jump off from the trail that aimed into the narrow gap between faces.

"Look, Marion," Babb whispered excitedly, "see on the other side? See the ledge and the ladder? It could be our emergency exit."

"Oh, my Lord," she exclaimed, "what's that all about?"

"Well, looking at that, I'd say you were supposed to jump the gap, wouldn't you?"

As they got closer, it looked likely that was exactly what used to happen. Their trail snaked so close to the other side of the ravine that, at a point directly under the stone arch, it was close enough to leap across. In the half mile trek down from the rope bridge to the arch, the sisters had been conscious there was no footpath on the other side, until now. Opposite the jump-off, set back into the side of the ravine, was a ledge no more than six feet wide. It was hewn out of the near sheer sandstone cliff face and, at its far end, a hooped cat ladder was embedded into the rock. The ancient steel rungs stretched up ten feet and lead directly to the start of a steep path which then meandered its way back up the mountain in roughly the direction they'd come from.

"Bet that leads to the chapel," Babb said as she stared across at the mountain track. "Check the map see what it shows."

Marion took Babb's backpack off her, rummaged through it, then pulled out her trusty walker's map. She spread it as best she could across her sister's shoulder blades and studied it closely for a few minutes.

"Well, what can you see?" Babb asked impatiently. "Anything obvious?"

"If I'm reading this right, then, yes," Marion replied. "This footpath is shown and we're currently at the stone arch and it says here that it's called..." she paused, "'Gunner's Leap'. This has got to be it, then, hasn't it? I mean the leap bit makes sense when you look at it, doesn't it?"

"A fair assumption, but what about the other side? Is that trail, the one back up the ravine, marked?"

Marion murmured thoughtfully before answering, "Well, yes, it is, and you're right, it does seem to go back toward the chapel."

"I thought you said the chapel wasn't shown."

"No, no it's not," Marion answered quickly, "but if we are where I think we are, and have come from where I think we were, then that path over there should loop back in that general direction, follow me?"

"Yeah, sort of," Babb said. "Basically, what you're saying is that, if you've read the map right, you know where we are. If not, then we're lost - it's dead simple to understand that!" She straightened up. "So, we finished with map reading for now?"

Marion stowed the map back in the backpack, then the two women moved closer to the arch and stood staring. The sandstone had been eroded almost symmetrically across the mid-point of the ravine. Its perfect form, vermilion colour, and setting were simply breath-taking.

"It's beautiful," the admiring sisters said in unison.

In bygone times the Leap would have been a risky proposition for anyone desperate enough to use it. Now – in a modern, risk averse world - things had changed. As befalls many of today's high-risk activities, some anally retentive government body had taken draconian steps to neutralise the hazard. Marion thought maybe the fun police from Flint County's recreation department were to blame. Whoever it was hadn't taken any chances. The Health and Safety quango that decided to install steel mesh side protectors across the ravine and patterned metal plates just below the stone level had now made it impossible for the modern-day leaper to fall into the gaping abyss below.

"You first," Marion gestured.

"Ok, sis, here goes..."

Babb stood at the edge of the take-off stone and tossed her backpack across. Then she about turned and moved back several feet.

"What the hell are you doing?" Marion asked.

"Look, you know what they say, sis," she said, "when in Rome..." Then, without another word, Babb took a short run up and launched herself across the gap, landing sweetly on the other side. Might only have been five feet or so, she thought to herself, but she'd done it, and done it perfectly. Now, she had turned a chuffed pink. "Yessss," she yelped. "See that, Marion, that's how to do it - just like that!"

Big sister was impressed. And, whilst it was all a bit unnecessary when you considered the killjoy brigade's safety features, Babb could now claim hand on heart she'd done it the good, old fashioned way. "Nicely done," Marion clapped, "like a true pioneer."

Quickly, she followed her sister across the gap. But the cautious librarian did it the easy way; she simply held the steel guiderails and two-stepped carefully on the fixed metal plating that spanned the void. Once Marion was safely across, the sisters made their way to the base of the ladder. "Over the years," Babb said, "I wonder how many didn't make it." She was talking over her shoulder as she led the way up. "How many intrepid souls do you think have plummeted to their deaths down that chasm?"

"I have absolutely no idea, B," Marion replied, but I'm sure there's been a few."

***

Whilst Lucas was satisfied the place was deserted, there were no guarantees; as the ex-sapper made his way across the rough ground toward the chapel, he remained in a running crouch. Five seconds later, Rick did exactly the same and caught up with his comrade at the near front corner of the building.

"What's been going on there?" Lucas said as he looked back at the patch of charred debris off to the side of the chapel. "Something got torched."

Rick knelt down and touched the blackened ground. "It's still warm," he said. "Must've been last night."

After a few seconds of quiet contemplation, the two men peeked round the corner. They assessed their surroundings for any signs of CCTV, trip wires, infra-red monitors, or other clues that might indicate remote surveillance, and they were thorough. As Rick looked over every inch of the rock face at the back of the plateau, something caught his eye.

"Roxy, check it out," he said quietly. He pointed towards a large boulder to the left of an opening in the cliff face. "Looks like a beam trip across there."

Lucas looked in the direction indicated, smiled, but said nothing. He then put his finger to the tip of his nose, tapped it twice - the sign for Rick to stay put - and scuttled off. Rick ducked back behind the corner, waited a few seconds, then popped his head round to check his colleague's progress. But Lucas was nowhere to be seen. "Where the fuck's he gone?" he muttered.

It was a strange place they'd discovered: an ancient little chapel perched on a plateau high on a barren mountain ridge, protected by high tech security fences on one side and sheer rock faces on the other, all seemingly accessed by a secret ladder system in a fake well. Who in their right mind would set this kind of weird shit up? Suddenly, his wandering mind snapped back to reality.

"Over here," a voice hissed.

Rick looked in the direction it came from; he could just make out his dishevelled colleague trying to attract his attention, calmly waving from a thicket of brush just to the left of the large boulder. "Get over here," he said as loudly as he dared, "check this out."

Rick didn't hang around. In true Looney-tunes road runner fashion he set off across the sixty foot of open ground at the speed of light. As he ran, the South African left a tell-tale vapour trail of rising dust in his wake. He joined his partner in a tight huddle behind the scraggly thatch of tinder dry brush then spluttered, "What you got?"

"Look at that," Lucas said pointing to the top flight of the stone stairway, "obviously that's the usual way up here."

"Now, that is pretty cool," Rick said in sweat drenched admiration. "But where the fuck does it go?"

Lucas raised an eyebrow, "No idea, but I reckon it's time to find out."

CHAPTER 39

The Final Straw

Heading back to the airport, Clayton sat alone in the rear of the luxurious SUV staring out of the window. Lost in a dark abyss of depression, the handsome young Georgian was trying to make sense of his tormented life. But it was to no avail: after thirty tortuous soul-searching minutes, he had failed to generate anything positive and resigned himself to the fact he had reached rock bottom.

Tate's whipping boy had orchestrated separate travel arrangements with a little creative last-minute thinking. As a result, he had ended up in the last vehicle of the three-car convoy. But now, as he pushed back into the plush leather and dabbed a despondent tear from his eye, he was hit hard by the realisation that the only highlight of his miserable existence was finding himself in a different vehicle from his demonic boss. As a host of depressing thoughts swirled in his mind, he took a deep breath and closed his eyes. Suddenly, a sharp pulse of vibration caused him to exhale. Seconds later, after some indiscriminate pocket searching, he located the source. Through a fog of tears, he checked the screen. The text read: 'Sorry Clay - didn't mean to ignore you - Len'.

He stared at the message for a few seconds: 'Didn't mean to ignore you' he repeated to himself quietly. 'Didn't mean to ignore you'. If only the old goat knew the grief his lack of communication had caused, he'd surely have sent a different message. But now, at least, this 'better late than never' apology explained one issue away, albeit not the big one. As the near suicidal assistant sat cradling his smart phone, he thought about the AMS man using his name. Why Townsend had said he was there at his request was a mystery and why would he, a junior, be giving orders in the first place?

It made no sense. He touched his bruised cheek and was instantly reminded that the uninvited guest was a major worry for his boss. The fact that the dubious supervisor was able to get onto the property undetected was baffling. Then to be found inexplicably injured in the grounds only added to the intrigue. But, more alarmingly, the fact he'd lied through his teeth then managed to disappear without a trace couldn't and wouldn't be viewed as anything other than a serious breach of security.

Now Tate wanted to believe a theory that the rogue supervisor was simply a well prepared and patient thief. His preferred scenario was that Townsend deliberately sought employment with AMS to allow him to gain knowledge of and access to high value properties with a view to ultimately stealing from them. The Security Chief even suggested the fund raiser was his target – and why not? The money on the night from the auction alone was $125,000, with nearly fifty of that being in cash. It would've been a fine haul by anyone's standards. But if the so-called Jonny T was, as the ebullient Red Clarke had suggested, an undercover agent, then the shit would soon start to fly.

"Clayton, you're awful quiet back there," a voice piped up, "everything OK?"

The young man snapped back to reality and looked up to answer. "Err, yeah, yeah, I think so," he lied. "Just got a lot on my mind at the moment, you know how it is?"

"What the fuck you got to worry about, boy," the voice came back. "All you gotta do is keep blowing the boss and you got it made."

Clayton didn't respond; what was the point of rising to it? It was the usual abuse he got. He'd crossed a line a long time back and he understood it came at a price.

***

Tate's vehicle was ahead of the others and, as Juan checked the rear view for signs of those following, he eased off the gas. In the back, his frustrated boss was preoccupied so failed to comment on the deceleration. On the phone to Dan Tyler the furrow-browed Security Chief was listening intently to his underling.

"I've just arrived, sir," Tyler reported calmly. "Everything's quiet and looks as it should, nothing to worry about at the moment."

"Good," Tate said, "exactly what I needed to hear. Now, did you question the woman further? Did she offer any explanation for the files?"

"Yes, sir, I have briefly," he replied, "but she won't admit a thing, she's still playing the wide eyed innocent. All we're getting at the moment is 'I've done nothing wrong so why the hell am I here?'"

"Bitch," Tate snapped. "Does she not realise we know what she's been up to?" he took a long, exasperated breath. "Does the stuck-up Baptist do-gooder think we're just a bunch of braindeads that couldn't spot a non-believer?"

In case Tate wanted to spew any more vitriolic abuse down the line, Tyler didn't respond immediately but, after several seconds of silence had confirmed his boss was done, the younger man finally answered. "I don't know, Mr Tate. All I can tell you, sir, is she's denying any involvement in an investigation and is adamant she's only ever had our interests at heart."

Tate sighed with frustration. "If she doesn't start talking," he said, "I'll kill the meddling old hag myself." He fell silent as he thought for moment. "Right…just keep her locked up. I'll get to you as quickly as I can and we'll put the problem to bed then, OK?"

"Yes, sir, Mr Tate."

But Tate wasn't quite finished. "Oh, Daniel, one last thing," he added, "was there any more news on our overseas visitors? The collection bozos? Do we know if they went home?"

Again, Tyler paused, but this time only to ensure his recollection of the facts was correct. "They accepted our offer to meet," he said, "and promised to come back with a location and time…but we've heard nothing yet," he stopped and cleared his throat. "It would've helped if Ings had stayed on the surveillance, but he seems to have disappeared without a trace."

"I know, I know," Tate replied. "Another shit storm to face but we'll leave that for now, so…," he paused as he looked out of the window, before asking, "do we actually know where those two pricks are?"

Tyler didn't have good news. "Well, unfortunately, sir," he said, "the reality is we have no idea where they are." He went quiet for a second. "Although I personally believe they've left the country. I'm sure the carjack news did exactly what we hoped it would."

"I hope to Christ you're right," Tate said. "We've got enough shit to deal with without worrying about those two," and, with that, the Chief bid his deputy a curt goodbye.

After finishing the call, Tate shifted round in his seat, stared at his phone screen for a few seconds longer, then leant toward the driver and asked, "How much further, Juan?"

***

Waiting in the sparsely furnished office, the two smartly dressed Spaniards couldn't help but notice the hive of activity whirling round them. They watched an army of diligent, determined professionals go about their duties. Pedro Grillo was as impressed as ever. "Always a busy place," he said to his companion, "and always they look like they know their business, eh, Miguel?"

Miguel Lerado looked at his colleague and forced a faint nod. "Si, Pedro," he said quietly, "always, always so busy."

Dedicated to tackling organised crime affecting Europe, Europol was an organisation not to be underestimated. From its iconic headquarters in the Netherlands, the re-branded European crime agency linked up with likeminded forces across the globe to fight underworld adversaries from everywhere and anywhere. One on-going high-profile operation, code named 'Stormbringer', was being run by the drug distribution division and involved working hand-in-glove with US, Spanish, and Honduran authorities plus some surprisingly brave civilian allies. The multi-agency operation had been live for nearly eighteen months and had been overseen from conception to present day by a senior Europol supervisor named Virgil Koeman. Koeman was a bespectacled forty-two-year-old ECA whizz-kid whose only aim in life was to stop bad guys. He was a no-nonsense straight talker who loved his work, made no apologies for his crime-fighting obsession, and currently he was happy.

Stormbringer was making better progress on all fronts of than expected. The wily Dutchman was keen to press the advantage and had asked to meet the Ebro executives one last time to discuss the operation's closing stages. Walking into his office, Virgil greeted the two men warmly.

"Ah, Pedro, Miguel how are you?" His smile was a dazzling white. "So good of you to come at such short notice."

"Always a pleasure," Pedro replied, "we are used to our little last-minute trips now, aren't we, Miguel?"

His still unsmiling companion didn't respond immediately but, as they were ushered toward a small circular table, he spoke.

"It is not a problem to me," he said quietly, "not a problem at all."

The three men settled down around the corner table. As coffees were dished out, they chatted innocuously. After a few minutes, when all were happily ensconced and properly catered for, Koeman got down to the business in hand.

"As you know, gentlemen, the final play of the operation is imminent," he said, "and, whilst I appreciate you're fully conversant with your specific brief, I still wanted this final session to be in person…just to be sure, if that's OK?"

Both Spaniards smiled and this time it was Miguel who answered, "We are fine with this, Señor Koeman. We think it is right; for us, it is better to run through face to face, so yes…it is OK."

Koeman sat back and relaxed. As he flicked through the papers in front of him, he thought again about the godsend Ebro had been to the investigation. The Europol team would be forever indebted to the

Spaniards; without their co-operation and assistance, progress to date would have been woefully short of the mark.

"Again, thank you, gents," the Dutchman said. "And I mean thank you for everything you have done over the last fifteen months: the commitment, the courage, all of it – everyone appreciates the effort, and everyone realises there would have been no operation without your help."

"As we have said all along," Pedro replied, "this is a subject close to our hearts, and we are able to help, we want to help, so we do - and it is good."

It was by innocent association that Ebro had been identified as a perfect cover for Europol's investigation. As a bona fide support organisation to The Divinity's Central American outreach programme, Koeman realised the Spanish logistics company offered a potential way in. From the moment his team made its first, tentative approach, Pedro, Miguel, and the entire Ebro organisation had been nothing other than enthusiastic about buying into the Europol proposal and making it work.

From mechanics to riggers, from roustabouts to plant operators, the opportunities for getting undercover agents close to the heart of The Divinity business across Central America had ended up being numerous. And eventually, as the cautious, painstakingly slow infiltration developed, it started to pay off. The intelligence gathered by a cadre of covert operatives identified an intricate cocaine distribution operation that was ruthlessly run and highly efficient. It stretched from the jungles of Columbia, through Honduras, then across the Pacific to Western Europe. From source to final shipment, the evidence supplied by the agents of five international federal agencies would play a significant part in ending The Divinity's stake in the narcotics trade.

Koeman beamed a trademark grin. "It is much, much more than that," he said loudly. "It is truly astonishing," then he deftly slid his glasses onto the bridge of his nose and handed out a two-page document to each of his guests. "Now, before we start, if you guys would check through the itinerary in front of you and tell me if I've missed anything, it would be appreciated."

The Ebro executives exchanged glances, then without another word looked down and started to read.

CHAPTER 40

The Dogs of War

"What first?" Rick asked in a stage whisper. "We checking the building or heading down the steps?"

Lucas was in two minds. The chapel had been the target from the outset and its untold secrets could be key to their current predicament, but the lure of the stone staircase was too strong. "Bollocks to it, Ricky," he said. "Let's go down it, see where it leads, eh?"

"Your call, Sarge," the grinning South African replied before gesturing toward the steps, "but you first."

Lucas moved out from behind the scrub and headed toward the top of the staircase. Cautiously, he stepped over the trip beam and edged onto the first step, then stopped. Peering around the curve as best he could without losing his balance, he looked down the first section then turned back to his colleague. "Looks clear from here," he said. "Follow me down, but don't get too close, OK?"

Rick didn't say a word; he just gave a thumbs up and smiled. The plan formally agreed, Lucas started down the staircase. Tentatively creeping forward, focused on getting the best view, he kept close to the inside wall and craned his neck outwards for maximum effect. Rick matched his partners cautious pace, ensuring he only ever got close enough to maintain visual contact. Neither man made a sound.

As the steps disappeared in a never-ending sweep around the escarpment, the duo kept up their patient descent. At times, eager to see where they were heading, Lucas was tempted to speed up the pace but each time he thought better of it. After what felt like an age, the curve of the stairway lessened and then, as it finally began to straighten, the end came into view. Lucas stopped a few steps up from the bottom and promptly sat down. Rick followed suit. "What the hell is this place?" he asked.

The two men stared silently at the expanse of beautiful landscaped gardens that stretched before them. After a while, Lucas smiled.

"Shangri-La," he said quietly. "Well, that's what it looks like to me."

As soon as the words left Lucas's mouth, a deep guttural growl made the HSG men freeze. Rick spotted the dog first. "Oh, shit!" he said pointing wildly into the garden. "Over there Rox, look at the size of that fucker!"

Lucas turned to follow Rick's gesture and immediately his stomach knotted. The snarling beast was no more than twenty yards away. The muscular Akita had emerged from a copse of closely planted pine trees but had stopped to appraise its target.

"Jesus, Ricky," Lucas whispered, "that thing's a monster!" He quickly checked the immediate area. "Is there anyone with it?"

"At this moment I can't..."

It didn't matter. Before Rick could finish his answer, the dog broke cover and charged headlong toward them. The dishevelled figures sitting frozen at the bottom of the staircase didn't stay frozen for long; the fear-induced thaw was instantaneous.

"Run!" Lucas yelled. They both leapt to their feet and started scrambling back up the steps as fast as their dehydrated legs could carry them.

They were never going to outrun a hundred and twenty pounds of lean, mean, killing machine - and they knew it. The dog caught them in a matter of seconds. Leaping onto Lucas's back, the beast knocked the Englishman flat to the steps, then started to bite down on his shoulder. The poleaxed brit screamed out in pain. "Jesus, Ricky," he squealed, "get it off me!"

Rick knew he had one shot, a split second to save his comrade from the vicious jaws.

"Stay down," he ordered as he spun round and readied himself to kick the marauding animal. His balance wasn't perfect, but in the circumstances it was as powerful a blow as he could muster. As his right boot connected with the dog's head, the beast released its grip and reeled back, yelping. Rick knew one blow wasn't enough; the hound would only be briefly distracted before coming back for round two in a matter of seconds.

"Come on," Rick grunted as he hauled his dazed colleague to his feet. "Get up, and get climbing."

Despite the pain of his savaged shoulder, Lucas was quick to understand the instruction. The long staircase was cut into the mountain side, the outside slope battering down to ground level and the inside being the near vertical weathered rock face.

"We can get a good way up there," Rick said as he pointed to the gnarled fissured rock above them. "Get us away from this bastard thing for a start."

Before Lucas could comment, round two began. It started sooner than the adrenalin-pumped duo had hoped. This time, the dog came at them slow. With its head low, eyes up, and emitting the unmistakable growl of an animal intent on blood, it inched forward with purpose. "I'll take him," Rick said as he turned to face the hound. "You start fuckin' climbing."

Lucas didn't argue. Big Rick was as tough as they come. If anyone was going to stand up to the monstrous dog, it was HSG's own street fighting ridgeback. As the wounded Englishman got a leg up onto the first accessible ledge, he watched his colleague whip off his belt and wrap it tightly round his right fist. Then the dogs of war clashed, head-on.

The Akita lunged low, but Rick second-guessed the move. Again, the right boot did the trick; not a clean contact but enough to give him breathing space. The dog quickly came again and, as it bounded forward, Rick wrestled the brute, desperately trying to avoid the glistening canines getting ever closer. But very quickly, as the sweat drenched South African ran out of steam, he knew it was do or die time.

With the huge drooling jaws relentlessly snapping at his chest, the animal eventually got a mouthful of jacket and started to rag it violently from side to side. As the cotton ripped apart, Rick battled hard to remain upright. He stumbled back a couple of steps but miraculously managed to stay on his feet. His body pushed hard against the frenzied attack as he slipped the heavy leather belt around the dog's neck and threaded it deftly back through the buckle. Grabbing the free end with both hands, he flung himself backwards. The rapid movement caused the belt to tighten. The dog was dragged on top of him. It released its grip and squirmed wildly. Rick closed his eyes as the huge bulk suffocated him. Under the crushing weight, flying drool, and flailing claws, he pulled down on the belt like his life depended on it - which he knew full well it did.

Lucas stopped his climb the second he was safely above head height and now looked down from his perch. Transfixed by the gladiatorial man versus beast struggle playing out on the stone steps below, he roared his champion on.

"Go on, Ricky, kill the fucker," he screamed at the top of his voice. "Come on, come on, you can do it."

Rick, oblivious to his partner's vitriolic encouragement, was thrashing round on the hard stone steps, fighting for his life. Close to passing out, he was focused on only one thing – survival. Now summoning every last bit of fight he had left, he gave one final desperate tug on the belt. Seconds later, the massive lump of killer canine rolled back its eyes, gasped, and went limp. With that as his cue, Lucas dropped back down from his perch and rushed to help his flattened colleague.

"Fuck me, Kruger, that was insane," he said as he started to drag the unconscious beast off his friend. "Where the hell did you learn that shit?"

Rick didn't respond. Stunned, bleeding, and gasping for breath, all he wanted was out from under the stinking body. Lucas finally got the animal off him. Rick tried to sit up and speak. "That fuckin' thing's not dead," he spluttered. "You need to finish it."

Lucas didn't need telling twice. In a flash, he did just that. With a vicious neck stamp and an extra-long twist of the belt, the beast finally expired.

"Fuck!" Rick exclaimed as he watched the dog's brutal end. "That was fucking nasty. Kill or be killed; what a choice, eh?" He sat up and wiped his face with his hands. "Now pass my belt back, will you," he said.

Lucas had started to disentangle the belt from around the dog's neck when the sound of raised voices could be heard in the distance.

"Oh, bollocks," he muttered. "Time to skedaddle, Rick. You good to go?"

"Surprisingly…" Rick winced as he struggled to get up. "No, I'm not, but what choice have I got?"

"None," came the terse reply. "We gotta move it."

***

Finding the dog's lifeless form laying across the steps, the AMS team went straight for the radio.

"Control, this is Charlie One," the guard snapped into his handset. "We've got intruders in the West Gardens." He glanced up the steps, then added, "Don't know how many but looks like they're headed up to the chapel."

"Roger that, Charlie One," came the curt reply. "Checking cameras now."

"They killed Odin," the guard continued. "They killed the fucking dog."

The radio was silent for a few seconds before the controller came back, "Say again, Charlie One."

"I said the mother fuckers killed one of our dogs," the guard snarled.

"Son of a bitch! How?"

"Don't know, but he's dead," he answered. "Don't know how they did it."

"Are they armed? Did you hear gunshots? Did they shoot it?"

"No, we heard nothing and there's no sign of bullet wounds."

"Why weren't you with the dog?" the controller asked.

"You know how it works," the guard answered defensively, "they go roaming - it's the best way to cover the ground."

"OK, Charlie One, I guess that's the norm," came a sympathetic reply. Then after a short crackle of static the voice continued, "We're not picking anything up on camera at the moment, OK, but we'll keep checking. Back-up's on its way."

"Thanks, Control, but be quick, will you? We're starting up the steps now."

"Roger that, Charlie One."

The two guards drew their weapons, simultaneously clicked off the safety, and started the long climb up toward the chapel plateau.

***

Lucas and Rick made it back to the upper level in record time. They rounded the big boulder at the top of the steps and tucked in tight behind it. Out of sight, desperate for a chance to catch their breath, Lucas turned to his blood splattered colleague.

"Ricky, this is killing me," he said. "I haven't felt this bolloxed in a long time."

"Well it ain't over yet, Sarge," Rick spluttered, "not by a long chalk."

Standing next to his equally exhausted partner, Lucas stared down into the baked dust, hands on hips, and gasped for air.

"Chapel or back down the shaft?" he asked.

"Your call," Rick replied, "But you know we'll have company any minute, don't you?"

"Of course," the ex-sapper said attempting a smile, "but we've come a long way, gone through a lot of shit, not to..."

Lucas didn't need to finish the argument. Despite his injuries, Rick set off like a jack rabbit across an open prairie. Heading for the back of the building, with his shredded jacket wrapped around his waist, his blood-stained t-shirt flapping in the breeze, and his blond head streaked with grimy sweat, he looked like a crazed brave on the war path. Lucas, who didn't look any more presentable, shook his head in disbelief then stumbled after him.

"Well, that's the decision made," he said when he caught him up.

"Gotta take the chance," Rick answered. "Just a quick peek; like you said, we've been through a lot of shit…"

Praying it opened inward and not out, the South African shoulder charged the rear door of the chapel. Fortunately, his guess was right, and the door gave on the second hit.

"Jesus Christ," Lucas said, yet again impressed by his partner's physical prowess. "Rick Kruger, folks, the human battering ram."

"If the cap fits…" Rick smiled as he shoved the ancient door open and peeked inside.

The Chapel's annex was dark and dingy, but as his eyes acclimatised to the gloom, Rick checked out the layout. There was only one room, about twenty feet long. Despite the blazing heat outside, the bare stone walls and hard granite floor kept it cool. Once he was happy no one was home, he stepped across the threshold and started across the floor. After only half a dozen steps he noticed an old-style hospital bed set up to his left and a stack of foldaway chairs piled up against the wall to his right. "Look at this, Sarge," he shouted back toward the door. "More weird shit."

Lucas heard the shout but didn't respond immediately. He was keeping watch, staring across the plateau with eyes fixed on the top of the staircase, praying no one appeared.

"Yeah, OK, Ricky, I'm coming," he finally replied, "but we gotta be quick."

***

The radio crackled into life.

"Come in, Charlie One," the voice said. The lead guard, two steps up from his partner, stopped and turned to look back as his colleague now took the call.

"Charlie One receiving," the second man answered in hushed tones. "Go ahead."

"We've got an alarm on the back door of the chapel," the controller said. "Looks like your dog lovers have broken in."

"Roger that," he paused as he glanced up the steps. "You got eyes on them?"

"No," came the flat reply. "The cameras up there are out."

"Pity," the guard tried to hide his disappointment, "but we're near the top, so what's the latest on back-up?"

"The chopper team are seconds away, heading straight for you, OK?"

"Roger that, Control, let's see those fuckers get out of this one."

***

"Oh, shit!" Lucas exclaimed. "Do you hear that?"

In the ghostly half-light of the annexe, Rick stood dead still and cocked his ear. The unmistakable sound of helicopter rotor blades started to get louder. He looked at his bedraggled partner and shrugged.

"What the fuck?" he growled. "Can't be coming here, can it?"

"Ricky, I hope not," Lucas replied, "but looking at those grounds, someone's got a lot of money, and big money needs - and pays for - big security. Maybe it is."

Rick looked worried. "Yeah, maybe it is," he repeated.

After the brief exchange, both men raced back to the busted door and peeked out. "No one at the steps yet," Lucas said, "but they're coming. Our only way back is down the shaft, OK?"

Rick nodded then scanned the expanse of blue above, desperate to locate the approaching helicopter. "Where the fuck is it?" he asked. Lucas didn't answer. He just ran.

The two men were halfway across the open ground when the chopper appeared.

"Stop now!" the on-board PA boomed. "You are trespassing on private property."

The Bell 320 had come in low down the valley then popped up above the plateau from below. This stealth mode approach had caught the HSG team off guard. No wonder we could hear but not see, Lucas thought to himself as he reluctantly slowed. Now, caught out in the open, unarmed, and with no realistic escape route to consider, they had a serious problem.

The pilot, well aware of the significance of the shaft, set the four-seater down directly in front of it. Then, in a perfect show of strength, two smartly uniformed guards appeared at the top of the staircase with guns drawn. Instantly both aimed in their direction.

"Freeze, motherfuckers!" Guard One shouted. "On the ground now!"

Guard Two, not wanting to be outdone, yelled even louder, "You heard the man! Hit the dirt or you're history!"

Paralysed by a whirlwind of dust, pinned down front and back by armed security, the HSG duo had no other choice but to obey. As both men stopped and put their arms up in surrender, Lucas shouted over the roar of the chopper to his partner. "Don't you just hate it when we get rumbled?"

Rick forced a wry smile then knelt down. As he started the whole humiliating lie-down-flat-on-your-front-arms-behind-your-back routine, he muttered, "Shit happens, Sarge, but we've seen worse."

CHAPTER 41

The Book of Revelation

Once the intruders were back at the house and safely locked down, AMS Control contacted The Divinity.

"OK, OK," Dan Tyler said. "Just run through those details again, will you."

For a second time the AMS duty supervisor went over the descriptions of the two trespassers they'd just apprehended on the Black Mountain estate. "The obnoxious pair are refusing to confirm their names, Mr Tyler," the supervisor said, "But according to IDs we've recovered, it looks like we got ourselves one Lucas Roxby and one Richard Kruger." He took a breath, paused, then asked, "Are either of these two known to you or your organisation, sir?"

Although the security deputy recognised the names, he didn't answer immediately. After a few seconds, he decided it was best to simply ignore the question completely. "Where are they now?" he asked.

"We're holding them at the site at the moment, sir," came the reply. "Is there anything specific you want us to do with them?"

"Have you called the police?" Tyler asked, a little too eagerly.

"No, sir, obviously we need to check in with you first."

"Good, right, OK… for the time being just keep them there!" Tyler ordered. "I need to speak with a colleague and then come back to you, OK?"

"Yes, sir, that's fine – but come back to me as soon as possible, please."

"No problem. I'll ring you back in the next ten minutes."

***

Rick and Lucas were both suffering. To add insult to injury, in retribution for killing the dog they'd been given a swift kicking by the AMS team before being frog marched back to the house. They were now awaiting their fate, shackled to a steel bench seat in the back of a security patrol van. The makeshift cell was cramped, foul smelling, and uncomfortable, and - to make matters worse - both men were sporting a variety of wounds which were still bleeding.

"Well, Sarge, what we going to do about this, then?" Rick asked as he tried to stem the blood oozing through a rip in his jeans.

"Fuck knows," Lucas replied. "At the moment, mate, I'd say we're screwed."

Rick watched as his partner took a long slow glug of water then grinned. "At least the fuckers gave us water," he said pointing at the water bottle Lucas was holding. "I mean, they didn't have to, did they? Suppose you gotta be thankful for small mercies, eh?"

Lucas looked at his battered and bleeding wing man. Sat handcuffed to a steel bench in the back of a baking hot van covered from head to toe in dust, grime and blood, Lucas was amazed his partner could still find a positive to focus on.

"You're unreal, Kruger," he snorted. "Just look at the fuckin' state we're in, and yet you still sit there smiling and thinking happy thoughts."

Rick's pained grin broadened. "Well, you know, I'm a half-full type of guy, don't you, Sarge?" he replied. "It's gonna take a lot more than a little setback like this to piss on my parade."

Lucas stared in disbelieving admiration at his South African colleague then asked, "OK, then, Mr Half-full, what do you suggest we do next?"

***

When Tate received the news from Dan Tyler, he couldn't believe what he was hearing. Unable to quell his anger he had to shoot the messenger.

"How in God's name did that pair end up there?" he bellowed down the phone. "Are we actually sure it's the same two fucking guys?"

"Absolutely, Mr Tate, absolutely," Tyler responded as calmly as he could. "Both men were carrying passports and AMS have checked them. One's from the UK and the other's South African. It's definitely the two collection agents."

The silence from Tate was deafening. "Jesus Christ, Daniel, that's not possible," he said eventually. "They couldn't have known about the estate or the chapel." He went quiet again as he thought about the situation. "And even if they did," he continued, "how the hell did they get in?"

"I don't know, sir, but we're due a full report from AMS shortly, although at this moment in time they say it's still too soon to comment formally."

"So, where are our visitors now?"

"Locked up in one of their vehicles," Tyler replied, "and I'm sure you'll be glad to hear, sir, they haven't called in the local PD yet." He paused. "Wisely, they felt it was best to check with us first."

"Thank God," Tate said, sounding genuinely relieved. "OK, Daniel, call them back, tell them to keep hold of the problem and I'll go back to the house now and sort it out personally."

The Security Chief was close to boiling point. With every passing hour, another headache reared its ugly head and it was starting to get to him.

"Are you sure that's wise, Mr Tate?" Tyler asked. "I mean wouldn't it be better to get AMS to bring them to us…or even better send someone else to collect them on our behalf?"

"Probably," Tate snapped, "but whoever we send will likely only fuck it up." Tyler didn't respond to the outburst and Tate quickly calmed. "Maybe you're right, Daniel," he said. "It does make sense. Let me think on this for a while. Give me twenty minutes and I'll call you back."

With that the Chief promptly ended the call and slumped back into his seat to think. As he sat in seething silence, head down, gently massaging his temples, Juan slid back the privacy screen. "Is everything OK, Mr Tate?" he asked.

Tate lifted his head and focused on the dark Latin eyes in the rear-view mirror. "No, Juan," he said, "unfortunately it's not. Right now, the sad truth is we have more questions than we have answers …"

***

Despite the ever-challenging gradient, the Armstrong sisters had made good progress on their trek back. With Babb leading and Marion following, both had kept up a decent pace. Whilst the little used path was steep, it was thankfully even under foot. With the wind at their backs and the only interruptions being occasional water breaks, the ladies were in good spirits.

"You're just like Mr Roxby keeps saying," Marion teased. "You really are prepared for everything, aren't you, B?"

Babb looked at her sibling as she handed back the water bottle. "Like I told you, sis, your first priority is to stay well hydrated in these conditions, especially now as it's warmed up," She wagged her finger theatrically and smiled, "And if you don't, you'll be sorry, lady, real sorry."

"I know, I know," Marion said, holding her hands up in mock surrender, "but it's not me I'm worried about." She smiled at her little sister. "Fortunately, I've got you to look after me, haven't I? It's those two gung-ho fools I'm worried about. They went off with no plan and no water and that was well over two hours ago."

"They'll be OK," Babb said in her most reassuring tone. "You do know good men triumph in the end, don't you?"

Marion didn't look convinced. As she sat down to retie her laces, she eased her neck round in a slow looping circle. "Is it really like that, B?" she asked. "I mean; can you really say that? Isn't that just a myth? Isn't it the bad guys that usually come up trumps?"

Before she answered, Babb studied her sister's gracefully ageing face, a face she thought still looked sweet and innocent. "No, sis," she smiled, “you really have to believe that good will win out. Even with my divorce, and everything else that has happened to me, I certainly do. I tell you, I will never think otherwise, not in a million years. Maybe you should try it.”

Marion looked thoughtful. “Excellent advice,” she said. “And you never know, at some point I might just take it,” then she stood up and gestured up the trail. “Pep talk over - shall we get back to it?”

***

Fifteen minutes later, the sisters had stopped again, but this time it wasn’t for any kind of comfort break, this time it was the view.

“Oh my God,” Babb shouted. “Quick, come look at this.”

Marion raced up the trail, stood next to her then followed her gaze. There in front of them was a perfect panoramic view across the valley, and picture framed just left of centre was the chapel.

“Well whaddaya know,” she said in genuine surprise, “it’s beautiful…although it looks nothing like I thought it would.”

Babb smiled. “We only glimpsed a few roof tiles from the other side; you couldn’t tell too much about it from there, could you?”

“Yes, I know, but still it does look rather lovely, doesn’t it? Like I say, it’s not what I expected at all. Truth to tell, I expected a ruin at best.”

As the sisters stood gazing over the valley, Babb slipped of her rucksack and set it down at her feet. After a few seconds of rummaging, she pulled out her trusty field glasses, focused them on the chapel and started to sweep its surroundings.

“That’s odd,” she muttered, “looks like a path leading from the door to the cliff at the back there. Wonder where it goes?”

Marion wasn’t paying too much attention to her sister’s ramblings. She had more important matters on her mind. “Any sign of the boys?” she asked.

Babb was still using the field glasses. “No, nothing, not a soul,” she replied, eyes still glued to the lenses. “I wonder where they’ve gone? Do you think they actually got up there?”

"Who knows, maybe they didn't, maybe they're back at the bridge looking for us."

"Check your phone," Babb ordered. "See if you've got a signal, or if you've got any messages."

Marion immediately unzipped her jacket and reached inside. "No, nothing," she said as she checked the screen. "I don't think any network has a signal up here, it's a waste of time even trying."

Babb shrugged her shoulders. "Never mind, let's keep going and see how close we can get, OK?"

"Fine by me," Marion said. "Let's go find them!" With that, the Armstrong sisters started back along the trail with renewed vigour.

***

As a wisp of high-altitude cloud drifted past the afternoon sun, Juan parked the SUV outside hangar B6 and turned to the open privacy screen. "Shall I load the bags, Mr Tate?" he asked.

The Security Chief, still stewing over the catalogue of problems he was simultaneously trying to resolve, was slow to answer. "Yes, Juan," he said eventually. "Get them on board and hurry the others up, will you. We need to get going."

Juan nodded. "Yes, sir, Mr Tate," he replied.

Tate had made his decision within five minutes of the call from Tyler. Although the thought of dealing with the HSG intruders personally was genuinely very tempting, he'd quickly realised Dan Tyler was right; it really was too risky. He had also considered the option of AMS turning the two collection agents in to the local police, but almost immediately dismissed it as a non-starter. But the idea of sending someone to collect them on his behalf was definitely viable and very quickly he realised who best to send.

With no Mordecai to call on, the devious Security Chief contacted the White Warriors direct. When Mike Connolly realised that the duo to be collected were the men responsible for seriously injuring two of his Phoenix Chapter, he was eager to help.

So, with the deal done, and an uncharacteristically courteous goodbye still ringing in his ears, the Ironman got on the phone.

"Red, it's Mike," he said. "Listen carefully, man, I've just had a call from Leon Tate himself. You ain't gonna to believe what the motherfucker wants us to do..."

Connolly quickly explained the request; he made it clear to his squad leader what The Divinity supremo expected. As he'd hoped, Red was keen to take it on. After the call, and with the sweet taste of revenge already tingling on his tongue, the burly biker swung the grey Chevy battle wagon round in a squeal of rubber and pulled over. Fifteen minutes later, after several calls and a bit of rapid reorganisation, Red Clarke had his team ready for action. He'd got Tex Arden, Eddie Croker, and Remy Hilton on board for back up and the four strong White Warrior lynch mob was now blazing a trail back to the Black Mountain estate.

CHAPTER 42

Homeward Bound?

During the Mountain House incarceration, Lucas had decided to take Mr Half-full's advice and keep his volatile nature in check. Despite the fact they'd been left stewing in the back of the stinking van for over an hour, he was still relatively calm. As they awaited their fate, the duo used the time wisely; wounds were cleaned and patched, of a fashion, thirsts quenched and their predicament - including the delicate issue of abandoning the Armstrong sisters at the bridge - was discussed several times over.

"If only the bastard phones worked," Rick said, shaking his head, "it might not be as bad."

"I know, it's a complete ball-ache," Lucas replied. "T-Mobile's signal's non-existent out here. Bloody useless, might as well not have a phone at all." He shook his head as he thought about their present situation then pulled a face. "Exactly as we are now, in fact!"

Rick didn't comment. He sat in silence studying the grain of the van's plywood lining. "What do you reckon these pricks have in store for us, then?" he asked as he stared down at the swirling patterns.

"Don't know, but they look totally legit, don't they?" The Englishman was squinting out the back window of the van as he spoke. "I'd say they've called the boys in blue and are just waiting for them to show."

"See anything?" Rick asked hopefully.

"Next to fuck all, mate," came a blunt reply, "just paving and blue sky."

The relative quiet was suddenly disturbed by the arrival of a vehicle and was quickly followed by the sound of slamming doors and muffled voices. Again, Lucas tried his best to get sight of what was happening outside but with filthy glass, sun glare, and limited mobility to contend with, it was still useless.

"That the police?" Rick asked.

"Can't tell, can't get a decent look."

The voices grew louder so the duo eased back from the doors. As heart rates increased and adrenalin started pumping, they prepared themselves for the worst.

"Fuck knows what's gonna happen now," Lucas whispered. "If it's the real law then we've got a chance, but if it's not," he pushed himself as tight up against the back wall as he could, "then we got to take the first opportunity to make a break for it, OK?"

Rick agreed. "Too right," he said. "I'm not hanging round for another beating or - worse - the Reverend Coleman treatment."

Suddenly, the rear doors swung open. The sun's laser-like rays blinded the two men. A deep southern voice boomed. "Well if it ain't our favourite tough guys from England!"

It took a few seconds for their eyes to adjust, but when they did the sight that greeted them filled both men with dread. Standing at the back of the vehicle, flanked by two of the AMS day shift, was the heavy-set figure Lucas had seen earlier on. It was the bearded biker who had magically appeared out of the rock face in the canyon. Behind him were three of the meanest looking Neanderthals the HSG team had ever laid eyes on.

"We've come to take you fellas home," Red said. "Relax, no heroics, do as you're told and then…" he forced a half-smile, "then you should have nothing to worry about, OK?" He turned to the trio of sneering muscle surrounding him, "That's a fact, ain't it, boys?"

Tex was the only one to speak. "Sure is," he drawled as the others looked on and merely grunted their acknowledgement. As the group stood quietly sizing up the HSG duo, Red's phone rang. Whilst the two uniforms removed the leg irons and pulled their captives into the daylight, the biker leader moved off to take the call. No sooner had Lucas and Rick been stood up and patted down again, then Red finished his conversation and headed back to the group.

"Tex, get them two pricks in the van," he ordered. "Hook 'em to the cargo lugs at the back, and make it quick, will ya? We gotta go."

Seconds later, Lucas and Rick were bundled into the back of the Warrior's crew bus, handcuffed to the steel floor loops, and knuckle wrapped for good measure. Whilst the three charmless nomads stood guard over their prisoners and unleashed a torrent of abuse, Red ambled back to the AMS van to talk to the lead guard.

"Mr Tate wants you to destroy all records of this incident," he said. "He wants no further mention of it, and he doesn't want any written communication on the subject. You got that?"

"Yes, sir," the supervisor replied. "We got it, there will be no argument from us. Whatever Mr Tate wants, Mr Tate gets – period."

"And don't forget that means CCTV footage as well."

"Yes, sir, we understand. Everything will disappear, you don't have to worry. It will all be erased."

"Good," Red said firmly. "Now we gotta get going but I need the passports, phones, and anything else you took off them."

"Yes, sir," the man said again. "Let me make a call." With that, the security supervisor reached for his radio and spoke quickly to a colleague. Within minutes of the call, a short, stout, but again smartly uniformed man arrived carrying a brown envelope.

"As requested," the man said as he passed over the package. "Two passports, two cell phones, one set of keys, and a watch. That's the lot."

"Thanks, Casey. That's all we need for now; you head back."

As the diminutive guard about faced and headed back toward the house, the supervisor turned to Red and handed over the sealed envelope. "I take it from all this that those two crazies," he pointed over at the grey Chevy van, "are well known to Mr Tate's organisation?"

Red moved a step closer to the man and then, as the faintest of smiles played across his lips, he answered, "Absolutely right, my friend, those two fuckers have been a thorn in the organisation's side for long enough." He stopped to study the guard's expression closely, then decided to toss him a well-chosen bone. "And now their…err… campaign of hate is over… and that's all thanks to you and your team." He smiled at the supervisor as he patted him reassuringly on the shoulder, "You've done a great job, and for that Mr Tate will be ever grateful."

"Glad to be of service," the supervisor beamed. "That's what we're here for. AMS pride themselves on ensuring the client's needs are always met and, if possible, exceeded."

"Well, you sure exceeded today, my friend," the biker said as convincingly as he could. "I know Mr Tate and his colleagues will be very happy."

Red was keen to leave; he knew if he had to keep this sycophantic pretence up for much longer he was likely to throw up. "Again, well done," he said as he started to back away toward the Chevy. "We gotta go now, buddy, need to get these two nut-jobs back to Mesa as soon as possible."

"Yes, I understand Mr Clarke," the guard said. "You get on your way." Then, as the biker got in and turned on the ignition, the man smiled, "You drive safe, now, you hear."

"Will do," Red replied. He slipped the Chevy into drive then, with a feigned half salute, he eased off the hard standing and put his foot down. Seconds later, as the van wound its way around the first of a series of twisting bends, the bearded biker had to say what was on his mind. "Those fucking puffed-up lame brains," he snarled. "Give 'em a uniform and they think they're God's gift! Dumbass phoney motherfuckers, every last one!"

"That's bullshit, bro," Tex snapped. "Those dumbasses' just earned you your pay-check and a big chunk of payback, so I'd stop bitchin', man, know what I'm saying?"

"Yeah, yeah," Red grinned, "maybe you're right."

***

At the bottom of the service road, the Chevy slowed. It made its final approach to the security gate and finally drew to a stop. Sat impatiently in the driver's seat, Red drummed his fingers hard on the steering wheel and glared at the steel monstrosity blocking the road in front of him. Unimpressed by the fact it was still closed, he gestured toward the gate's CCTV camera cluster and flashed his lights.

"Come on, you pricks," he muttered. "You know who we are so just let us out."

For several seconds, the gate remained closed then, just as he'd decided to get out to approach the intercom, the gate buzzed, then made a metallic clunk.

"About fucking time," the biker snarled. "Now let's get down to some real business."

As the four men watched the gate slide back, Red glanced over his right shoulder. "You sure them two fuckers are OK in the back, Bean?"

"Trussed up good style," the young biker replied, "on the deck, cuffed to the cargo loops like you told us."

"That'll do, bro," Red sounded satisfied. "Right, now it's time to get outta here."

As soon as the gap got wide enough to allow the van to squeeze through, Red hit the accelerator. "Jesus, where's the fire?" Tex grabbed the dash as the Chevy shot through the gap with only inches to spare. "We got some major deadline to meet?"

"Look, Tex," Red said calmly, "you just let me worry about all that shit, OK?"

***

A couple of miles out from the estate, Red indicated right. He swung the big Chevy round in a tight ninety and glanced in his wing mirror.

"What the fuck!" he yelled. "The back door's swinging open."

Skidding to a stop in a plume of grey dust, the burly biker was out of the door in seconds flat. He raced to the back of the vehicle, shouting. "No way, man, no fuckin' way!"

Red's three-man support team, taken aback by their leader's wild antics, got out quickly and followed him to the rear of the van.

"You have got to be shittin' me," the wild-eyed biker screamed as he looked into the back, "it's not possible, not fucking possible. Those Goddam limey motherfuckers!"

The four bikers stood huddled at the back of the Chevy and stared incredulously at the open toolbox now in the spot where their captive duo should have been.

"Shit, Red," Tex said, "how the fuck did that happen?"

Red didn't answer. He just slammed the doors shut, clicked the handle and headed back toward the driver's seat.

***

'Less haste, more speed' is a wise old saying, but Red Clarke would never get to figure out that, in his desperation to get away from the mountain estate, he'd given his captives the lucky break they'd prayed for.

Despite the rough handling and his beleaguered state when Rick Kruger had been bundled into the Warrior's vehicle, years of training meant he instinctively checked out its interior. To say he was impressed would be an understatement. The set-up, the order, the range of tools and equipment on display, was enough to send any self-confessed DIY mechanic into paroxysms of ecstasy. When the van suddenly screeched off through the estate gates, Rick couldn't believe his luck as a small, unsecured toolbox slid along the floor toward him. "What's this?" he said as he grabbed the metal box with his free hand. "Could be interesting."

"Well held, Ricky," Lucas said. "What's in it?"

Rick had the box open in seconds. He pulled out a small hacksaw and couldn't help but smile.

"Thank you, Lord," he said quietly, "just what we needed. Me first, then you, OK?"

Lucas was in no position to argue, so just nodded and watched as the ex-shipyard fabricator made short work of his hand-cuff chain.

"OK, Sarge, you're next," Rick said, "but keep it tight." The ex-sapper did as instructed, pulling the cuffs as tight as he could. Then Rick teed up the blade and started cutting. As the hacksaw blade whipped back and forth, the South African glanced up. "Another couple of minutes," he grunted, "then we're out this door, OK?"

Lucas didn't have to answer; it wasn't a question; it was simply the only option. But it was an option he was happy to pursue and, although the thought of another hard landing wasn't that appealing, he was in no doubt it was the lesser of two evils.

***

The Armstrong sisters were still maintaining a good pace, especially now they were on a steady downward gradient, but morale had dipped. The chapel hadn't come any nearer and now it had disappeared completely from view, Babb grew concerned. "Have we missed a turning," she wondered. "Are we lost?"

Marion didn't know how to answer. Yes, she had the same worries as her sister, and yes, it did look very much like they were wandering aimlessly with no idea of where they were going. But, despite that, she felt an overwhelming urge to keep going.

"No, not really," she replied, "Although I suppose technically, on paper, we are."

A bemused Babb stood and stared at her sister. "More riddles," she said, "are you saying we're actually going in the right direction?"

Marion thought for a few seconds before answering. "Yes," she said with confidence, "that's exactly what I think, so yes, we just... keep going."

"But it'll start getting dark soon," Babb protested. "We've walked for miles with nothing more than aching legs and blisters to show for it... plus we've no idea where Lucas and Rick are," she stopped, hung her head and muttered, "and we'll never get back to the Jeep."

"As you told me earlier," Marion said sternly, "good men triumph in the end...so if you truly believe that then, equally, you should believe good women do too," she paused and put a comforting arm around her sister. "I reckon you and I are going to be OK."

Babb stood silently staring at the ground; after several seconds with still no answer Marion tried again. "Don't you agree, Barbara?" She asked with a gentle squeeze.

Babb needed a few more moments to gather her thoughts. After several seconds of further silence, she finally lifted her head, smiled, and pointed down the trail. "Sisters keep doing it," she said. "Pep-talk received and understood. Let's get going again."

***

Much to their relief, thirty minutes later the sisters came across civilisation and with it salvation. From the point of Babb's mini melt-down, the trail had continued to descend but in places the gradient had become extreme. Just as the pair were helping each other negotiate a particularly treacherous section, a line of tents came into view.

"My God, look, you were right," Babb said in genuine appreciation of Marion's decision to keep going, "you're a goddam genius."

The camp site was neatly laid out. It consisted of two lines of multi-coloured bivouacs interspersed with a variety of parked vehicles. The sisters wandered in along the stone track running through the middle. Several expensively attired outdoor types were quick to nod hello.

"Excuse me," Babb said, waving at a tall athletic looking man wheeling a mountain bike, "are there any rest rooms on the site?"

"Yeah, sure, ma'am," he replied, "just keep following this path down that way and you'll see them on your left."

The camp was getting busy. It was late afternoon and groups of hikers and mountain bikers were heading in. After a hard day pounding the rugged trails, many were ready for home, but plenty more were looking forward to chilling out round a campfire before a cosy night under canvas.

Marion, enamoured by the site's facilities, spent a good fifteen minutes making full use of the rest rooms. Then, feeling decidedly more human, the much-relieved librarian went out to join her sister in the site's picnic area. They sat at a wooden table, sipping on freshly brewed coffees bought from the refreshment stand, while Marion spread her map out. The pair started to discuss the day's adventure.

"I can't believe we found this place," Babb said. "It's an absolute godsend, in fact it's a miracle; all mod cons, friendly people and," she held her cup aloft, "we've even got decent coffee."

"Sure is wonderful," Marion replied. "The weird thing is, looking at this," she squinted into the glare, "if this is that campsite," she tapped a little tent sign on the map, "then I'm completely baffled as to how we've ended up here."

But before Babb could comment they were interrupted by a deep male voice.

"Howdy, ladies," it said, "did y'all get to see the comet last night?"

The sisters turned simultaneously to see where the voice was coming from. When they saw a smiling silver haired man standing only yards in front of them, they just stared.

"We met yesterday in Paradigm," the man prompted. "JB Collins from Colorado…remember I spoke to you and your friends on Main Street yesterday?"

Babb looked at Marion and then back at the man. "Oh, yes, Mr Collins," she said. "I'm so sorry for a moment there I -" she paused to correct herself. "I mean, we didn't recognise you immediately, did we, sis?"

Marion couldn't believe it; there before them was the guy Lucas had befriended in the centre of Paradigm. He was the man with the silver hair that matched his pick-up perfectly, the man who was good with accents and the man who'd kindly given them a map.

"Well, hello again, Mr JB Collins," she said warmly "What a very small world we inhabit – what on earth are you doing here?"

The man laughed. "This is where me and my old lady are camped," he said. "After we saw you guys, we had a quick mooch round the town then came straight here," He pointed over to the furthest line of tents and added, "Watched the big show from right over there, we did."

"Oh, very nice," Marion said. "Amazing, wasn't it?"

"Sure as hell was," he replied. "Couldn't believe it, worth all the hassle – something you'll never forget, even better than all the hype, I reckon." JB stood smiling expectantly in front of the sisters but didn't quite get the response he'd expected.

"Where's your pick-up parked?" Babb asked bluntly.

The man paused for a second, then moved a little closer. "Why do you ask," he said with a quizzical frown. "You ladies aren't in any kind of trouble, are you?"

"Strange you should ask that, Mr Collins," Marion replied sweetly, "very strange indeed..."

CHAPTER 43

The Silver Saviour

It didn't take long for the sisters to explain their predicament. As the amiable silver fox stood and listened, it was obvious he couldn't wait to help.

"OK, OK, ladies," he said. "First things first. Let's have a look at the map of yours and you show me where you think you've been."

"Oh, yes, of course, Mr Collins," Marion smiled, "please come sit down."

With that JB pulled up a chair, sat down, and looked at the walker's map Marion had open on the table in front of her. As she took a deep breath and prepared to try and talk him through the day's events, JB tutted loudly. "This is a bit basic, give us a sec - I'll be right back."

A couple of minutes later, the ubiquitous Mr Collins was back, this time with a detailed map covering the entire South West region of the Black Mountains. "That's more like it," he said as he spread his monster map out over the picnic table. "Now let's see if we can't work out where you left that little Jeep of yours."

***

Marion and Babb described the small remote car park surprisingly well. So well, in fact, the Coloradoan stargazer was sure he recognised it from one of his many previous trips. "If it's this one here," he said, tapping a stubby finger on the map, "which it sounds like it could be, then we're only a half hour away by road."

Before turning to face their new friend, the sisters glanced at each other, then - as if on some magical telepathic cue – they put on their best damsel in distress faces.

JB couldn't miss the hint and his reaction was instant. "I'll go get the truck," he said quickly. "Take you over right now." He paused. "All I gotta do is tell Cindy and we're gone, OK?" Then he glanced between the bereft looking sisters but suddenly stopped dead. "I take it that is what you ladies actually want, isn't it?" he asked, double checking he'd got it right.

Babb broke into a smile. "Mr Collins," she purred, "you're an angel, an absolute angel."

"Yes, thank you, Mr Collins," Marion added quickly, "that would be wonderful." She looked back down at the map and shook her head. "Looks like we've spent the whole day walking round in a giant circle, doesn't it?" She stopped as if waiting for an answer, then changed her mind. "Thank the Lord we found this place," she said, then, sighing, added, "I really don't think I could have managed another step."

"More like a giant U," JB grinned. "Cos you never quite made it back to the start, did you?"

Marion smiled sweetly. "Yes, of course, you're right Mr Collins," she said, "but you're about to change that for us, aren't you?"

"Yes, ma'am," he beamed. "I sure am."

***

Forty minutes later, JB's pick-up pulled onto the small mountain plateau and there, much to the sister's relief, in the spot Rick had parked in nearly nine hours earlier, was Babb's Jeep. "That's us, Mr Collins," Babb said, pointing over to the far side of the nearly empty car park. "The blue Wrangler in the corner."

"Yeah, I remember it," he said. "Didn't catch that it was actually yours, though," he smiled and winked. "You got a good eye for a vehicle, lady, gotta give you that."

Insisting on staying to help check the vehicle over, their knight in shining armour was chivalrous to the end. He even waited for Babb to find the spare keys in her backpack.

"You OK for gas?" he enquired after Babb turned the ignition and revved the engine. "I got a spare jerry can if you need."

"You are too kind, Mr Collins, too kind," she replied. "But the tank's nearly full, so we're fine for the time being. Thank you all the same."

"Right then," he clapped his hands together, "you ladies ready to follow me down?" The sisters nodded less than enthusiastically so the Coloradan offered a little advice. "Just keep it nice and steady, OK," he said, "low gear all the way and don't worry, I'll go real easy."

As the sisters buckled up, they glanced at each other and smiled. They couldn't believe their luck; their silver haired Samaritan was the type that just kept giving and, at that moment in time, they were more than happy to take every morsel of help offered.

"Lead on, Mr C," Babb shouted. "We'll be right behind you."

***

The Divinity's flight back to Phoenix was bumpy. The jet was constantly buffeted by high altitude turbulence but, undeterred, Tate spent most of the journey at the front, glued to his phone. Whilst the domineering boss continued as normal, an unhappy Clayton sat on his own as far back as he possibly could. Although the young man's desire for isolation was blatant, no one except the immaculately dressed stewardess took any notice.

"Are you OK, sir?" she enquired politely. "Can I get you anything?"

The Security Chief's dejected assistant lifted his head to look at the source of the soothing voice with red rimmed eyes. He shook his head gently. "No, it's OK, thank you," he said. "I think I'll be alright as I am."

The stewardess smiled at the sad looking young man slumped down in his seat and wondered why he'd chosen to sit so far away from his colleagues. She tried again. "Are you sure I can't get you a nice cup of coffee," she asked, "or maybe something stronger if you like?"

Clayton focused on the hostess's gleaming white teeth and somehow managed to produce the faintest of smiles. He decided to change his mind. "Yes, maybe that would be good," he shifted up in his seat. "A black coffee with a heap of sugar might help."

As the kindly woman disappeared into the galley, at the front of the plane Leon Tate became embroiled in a heated discussion. The angry exchange with a member of his entourage sat behind him could be heard by all.

"I will simply not accept that idea," Tate said loudly. "It is pure speculation, nothing more."

"But, Leon, we've seen the email," said a bald man in an expensive, ill-fitting suit, "so now you've been copied in, I suggest you read it."

"I assure you I will," Tate snapped, "but just remember, Michael, right now we need actual proof, not more conjecture." The Chief stopped and glared at the haranguing suit. "As you're well aware," he snarled, "at present we've got enough problems to deal with and we don't need another quite yet, do we?"

"OK, Leon, I understand what you're saying," the man answered, "but this issue needs to be investigated – and fast."

The Security Chief shot his balding associate a look that stopped the discussion dead in its tracks then, without another word, he stood up and made his way calmly back along the aisle to talk to other members of the party.

Tate was well aware of the email in question. He'd read it, but not taken it too seriously. He had enough on his plate without more headaches to contend with and his argument had been valid; it really was all pure speculation. The brief communiqué in question was from a mid-ranking member of an outreach project management team and hinted at suspicious behaviour, but only vaguely at that. The email didn't offer any clear evidence or proof of wrongdoing and Tate had heard it all before. Random theories about federal agency moles were ten-a-penny; paranoia running wild was his usual assessment and, for now, that's exactly how it would stay.

***

Lucas and Rick's escape plan now required one key ingredient - a tight left-hand bend. Where they'd land was purely down to chance, but they could live with that. All that mattered now was freedom. When Red slowed to swing the grey Chevy round the hairpin, Rick prised open one leaf of the rear door and the duo bailed out like paratroopers from a plane. The impact was sudden and painful. Both men bounced down the asphalt for twenty yards and ended up lying out of sight, face down in the bottom of a roadside gulley.

"That hurts," Lucas groaned as he tucked his head down to escape the enveloping dust cloud.

They lay there motionless, but the bikers' battle wagon didn't slow. It continued rattling down the mountain road and quickly disappeared from view. The second it vanished, the dishevelled duo took their chance. Scuttling like demented crabs, they made their way across the rugged hillside and, in a matter of seconds, reached the cover of the first clump of vegetation they could see. The thicket targeted was less than a hundred yards from the road, but they were happy with it. Even if the bikers came back, they knew their chosen patch of scrub was sufficient to keep them out of sight.

Five minutes later in the quiet sanctuary of their hideaway, Lucas was sat holding his breath and looking upward. The thought of watching a sweating, cursing Rick wield a hacksaw so close to his wrist was a definite no-no. In the back of the van, the South African only had to cut through the chain to allow the break for freedom. But now, out on the run, they wanted rid of the cumbersome wrist bracelets and that was a far trickier proposition.

"Stay still, will ya," Rick ordered. "If you're not careful, I'll end up sawing your fucking hand off."

"OK, OK," Lucas whimpered. "I just can't watch…"

"I don't care if you watch or you don't, just bloody stay still."

Seconds later, Rick made another strong, controlled pass with the saw and the metal cuff started to separate. But, as the blade finally broke through, it caught the skin. The contact was only slight, but it drew blood.

"Owww," the Englishman squawked as he pulled his hand back to inspect the damage.

Rick shook his head. "It's just a scratch," he said in a mocking female voice, adding sarcastically, "You are such a good boy, Lucas! Haven't you been a brave little soldier for Mummy?"

"Very funny, dickhead," Lucas rubbed his freshly un-shackled wrist, "but nice job, mate, not easy, that. Nice to see you've still got it with the old blade."

"Like riding a bike, Sarge," Rick said, "some skills you just never lose."

After he gathered up the fall-out from his hacksaw surgery, Rick scooped out a hollow in the dry stony earth and deposited the dismembered hand-cuffs into it. Then he covered them over with a handful of small boulders, looked over at his partner, and asked, "What's next, then?"

Lucas had moved a few feet away and was now sitting cross legged in the dust, running both hands through his straw-like hair in a vain attempt to remove the general detritus engrained in it.

"A shower would be nice," he replied as he repeatedly tugged on a congealed lump of Utah grime on the top of his head, "but I've got a weird feeling that's gonna have to wait. In the meantime, Ricky, well, we just keep heading down this mountain."

Looking at his dishevelled partner, Rick was unable to disguise his amusement. "You know who you look like when you do that?" he chortled.

"You what?" came a bemused reply

"I said, do you know who you look like when you do that?"

"What the fuck are you on about now?"

"You're a dead ringer for Stan Laurel," Rick giggled. "Tell you, absolute spit."

Lucas stared in disbelief at his sniggering comrade. "Fucking hell, Kruger, you South African freak, you're at it again, aren't you? "

"What do you mean?"

"I mean this, well…this 'don't give a fuck can't get me down' attitude is unreal, and I mean absolutely un-fucking-real."

"What you trying to say, Bru?" Rick asked. "You saying I've got a shitty way of thinking or is that some sort of compliment?"

"To be honest," Lucas replied thoughtfully, "I'd have to say it's a compliment. I mean, it's like when the chips are down you get a hard-on… and I just don't understand it."

Rick pulled a face. "Practice," he said, "years of practice."

Lucas shook his head in disbelief. "If you say so, Kruger," he grinned before taking a brief look outside. "Right, now let's focus. We need to get going. We gotta find those girls.

Before moving, Lucas needed to check the contents of the envelope he'd retrieved from the van before they'd jumped.

"Thank God for that," he smiled as he examined the items inside. "Everything's here." He moved toward Rick to hand him his effects. "Here you go," he said, "wallet, mobile, passport and a set of keys."

Rick nodded. "Thanks, Sarge, you're a gent."

As Lucas checked his watch, Rick turned on his phone. "It's working," the South African said after a few seconds, "but there's no signal."

Lucas wasn't surprised but tried to remain positive. "Should get better the lower we go," he said as convincingly as he could muster.

Rick didn't agree. "Doubt it," he muttered, "this whole bastard mountain's a dead zone," then he took one last look around and nodded. "Right then," he said, "let's get going. You lead, I'll follow." The HSG duo peeked out from their scrubland hideaway, double checked it was all clear, then headed down the scree slope toward what they hoped would be civilisation.

CHAPTER 44

A Bit Steep

The journey down the mountain proved anything but easy. Zigzagging across the steep slopes trying to stay upright and out of view, the two HSG men moved like pantomime skiers. With both desperate not to take a tumble, start a rockslide, or hit an obstruction, concentration levels were high.

"This is bloody hard work," Rick shouted across to Lucas as they waded through an ever shifting layer of scree, "might've been better using a snow board."

Lucas managed a smile. "Yeah, could be right," he said, then yelped, "Jesus H. Christ, this is steep," as he jammed an arm hard down to steady himself. With one eye on their footing and one on their surroundings, the hike down was taking its toll on the embattled Brit. "Ricky, you wanna take a break for a minute?"

"Not bothered," the South African replied. "Do you?"

"Yeah, I need a breather," Lucas said pointing across the slope. "Head over there, by that little ridge."

As the two men sat down, Lucas's mobile buzzed. "Looks like we've got a signal," he said as he pulled the phone from his inside pocket. He looked at the screen; for the first time since Iron Creek it was showing three bars of signal strength. Immediately he clicked on messages and looked at a text from Marion. It read simply: Where are you?

"What's it say?" Rick asked.

"It's from Marion," he smiled. "Funnily enough, she wants to know where we are."

"When did she send it?"

"Now," he replied, "just this second."

"That means she's somewhere they can get a signal. Ring her."

"Yet another brilliant suggestion," Lucas said sarcastically. "You're a genius, Kruger, an absolute genius. That would never have crossed my mind."

Rick laughed; stating the obvious was not something he was usually guilty of but at that particular moment he just couldn't help himself.

***

"You ladies OK from here?" JB asked.

"Wonderful, Mr Collins," Babb smiled, "just wonderful, you're an absolute godsend...we really can't thank you enough."

"My pleasure," he beamed. "Now you sure you two are gonna be OK finding them young fellas of yours?" he asked.

"I hope so," Marion said. "we'll give it a good go...and if we're struggling we've got your number," she paused, smiled coyly, then in her sweetest voice added, "So you never know, Mr Collins, you might just have to save us again."

"No problem," JB laughed. "Anytime you need saving, you just give me a call, you hear."

"Thanks again," Babb said. "We owe you one."

"You be good now, girls," he said. "See you next time!" With an enthusiastic wave from the window, the silver pick-up pulled onto the highway and headed back in the direction of the camp site.

The sisters returned JB's wave for several seconds. When his taillights had faded into the distance, they turned back to the Jeep. Walking side by side they chatted about their good fortune and how unbelievable it was that in such a desolate expanse of country they should have met the same kindly stranger twice in twenty-four hours.

"Real nice guy," Babb said, "a genuine good Samaritan. How lucky are we?"

Marion reached the Jeep and opened the door. "I would say we were very lucky," she replied, "and that the world needs a few more JB's in it." Then she got in and shut the door. "He's like a guardian angel, isn't he, sent to watch over us?"

Babb didn't answer; she just smiled to herself as the hairs on the back of her neck started to prickle.

Once settled in her seat Marion opened the glove compartment and checked her phone. "You're not going to believe this, B," she said. "but we've actually got a signal." Without waiting for any kind of response from her sister, she sent a short text to Lucas. Then, desperately hoping a response would instantly ping back, she stared expectantly at the phone. "I hope they're OK," she said. "It's been over seven hours… and who knows what's happened in that time."

Babb patted her sister's knee affectionately. "Like we've already discussed," she said, "I think they'll be OK so let's hope we get a call back. In the meantime, though, I think we head back to town, maybe see if we can find a hotel. It'll be pitch black soon."

Marion couldn't argue with her sibling's logic and grabbed for the map. After a quick orientation check, she looked up and pointed in what she hoped was the direction back to Iron Creek. "Looks like a straight run from here," she said. "Just follow this road that way and then I'll tell you where to turn."

"OK, sis," Babb said as she checked her mirrors, "here we go!" With a swirl of dust, they pulled away and headed north. After less than half a mile Marion's phone rang. "It's Lucas," she said excitedly.

"Answer it," Babb ordered, "before the signal goes again."

"Hello," Marion answered. "Lucas, hello…Lucas are you there?"

Initially there was no response, just white noise, then suddenly a voice came, "Hello, Marion, yes, I'm here. Can you hear me, are you OK?"

"Yes, yes, I can hear you," she said, "and, yes, we're OK. But, more importantly, where've you two been? Are you alright, where are you now?

Lucas quickly ran through the events of the past few hours, explaining all bar the finer details, of their injuries. As Marion listened open mouthed, Babb kept her eyes on the road but lent toward her sister trying to listen in. "Are they OK?" she whispered from the side of her mouth. "Both alive?"

"Yes," Marion mouthed back simultaneously giving a thumbs up.

"Sorry, Lucas," she said turning the phone back to her ear, "Babb's just asking if you're both still alive, so sorry, yes, you were saying."

Lucas went on to explain they didn't know their exact location but were currently mid-descent and hoped to hit some sort of public road soon. "Are you driving?" he asked.

"Yes, err, well, B is," she replied. "It's a long story and I'll tell you later, but let's just say that with a little help from a friend we got back to the Jeep," she paused for breath. "Now we're heading back to Iron Creek."

Lucas was genuinely impressed. "Well done you. How'd you manage that? I thought Rick had the keys."

"He has," she replied, "but Babb, God bless her cotton socks, had a spare set in the backpack."

"I tell you," Lucas laughed, "you and Fully Loaded are a pair of superstars, aren't you?"

"We do our best," she said modestly.

Lucas moved the phone away from his ear and glanced over at a quizzical looking Rick. "Good news," he whispered as he pointed at the phone, "the girls have got the Jeep and are on their way back to Iron Creek."

Rick didn't say a word. He didn't have to; his startled expression said it all.

***

Thirty minutes later, after a series of phone calls, the Armstrong sisters finally located the HSG team. Stood at the side of I-14 staring into the fading light, the exhausted duo had been scanning the road ahead. As yet another set of headlights approached, their hopes rose again.

"Looks good," Rick said, "yes, this could be them. I can see the four spotlights on the roll bar."

The Jeep drew closer and the two men let out a joint 'yee-haw' of appreciation.

"Looks like our ride's finally here, brother," Lucas said, stepping out from the roadside brush to flag the 4X4 down. Marion was not prepared for the sight that greeted her. She stared in disbelief at Lucas's battered and bruised form.

"Oh my God," she gasped. "What the hell happened to you?"

Before he could answer, the equally dishevelled figure of Rick Kruger stumbled into view. This immediately prompted a second round of 'OMGs' from the sisters. Marion, mortified by the sorry sight, jumped out of the passenger seat and started to inspect the damage. "We need to get you two to hospital," she said, running her hand gently over Rick's heavily bloodied jeans. "Anyone know where the nearest one is? Any ideas, B?"

Babb started to open her mouth to answer but Rick cut in. "Ladies, please," he said, holding up his hands. "Don't worry, honestly, it's nowhere near as bad as it looks," he then turned to his partner for back up and asked, "Is it, Sarge?"

Lucas was dead on his feet but tried to hide it. "The man's right," he said, "it's nothing a hot shower, six pints and a good night's sleep won't cure."

***

With the walking wounded shoe-horned into the rear seat, the drive back to Iron Creek was a non-stop barrage of questions about the day's dramatic events. "So, did you get inside the chapel?" Marion asked.

"Only the back bit," Lucas explained. "Ricky bust open a door at the rear, but it was just a storeroom, nothing like a church."

Rick grinned. "We got disturbed before we could check out the main building," he said, "and it was bloody obvious the security boys weren't happy with us, especially after the dog thing."

"The dog thing?" Babb asked. "What's the dog thing?"

Lucas looked at Rick and subtly shook his head, but Rick didn't need advice on how to handle this most delicate of subjects. "It's just I kicked one of their dogs, see," he lied. "the thing took a bite out of my leg, so I took a swing at it and I think they took that personally."

"You'll need a tetanus shot if you've been bitten," Marion said. "I've already told you, we should take you to hospital, you should see a medic."

"Look, ladies, I don't want to repeat myself," Lucas said, "but really, we'll be fine... so let's just find a hotel and get cleaned up, OK?" Despite their fatigue, the dark and the roar of the cool evening wind, the group's animated banter carried on all the way back to Iron Creek....

***

Daisy Edgerton's boarding house on the outskirts of the sleepy little town was the only accommodation they could find. But it was late, everyone was tired, so beggars could not be choosers and two twin rooms with en-suites in a shabby little B&B would do just fine.

"You boys take the bigger room," Marion said as she handed Lucas the key. "You need more space than us," she stifled a giggle as she looked the two men up and down, then shook her head. "Go on, I'd get up those stairs quick if I were you, before someone starts asking questions."

Lucas and Rick didn't argue and, despite their exhausted state, turned smartly on their heels and headed up the small flight of stairs desperate to find the sanctuary of Room Seven.

***

An hour later, in what had been described by Daisy herself as the resident's lounge, the foursome regrouped round a small table for a night cap. The room was cramped, dark, and musty and, with its peeling wallpaper and threadbare carpet, it was well past its sell by date. But an ever-positive Richard Kruger was not easily deterred.

"Great shower though," he said as he surveyed the dismal surroundings, then, raising his freshly filled glass, added, "And you can't fault the whiskey either. Cheers, gang! Here's to surviving one hell of a day!"

Lucas, Marion, and Babb smiled approvingly and immediately held their drinks aloft. "Cheers!" they chorused before enthusiastically clinking each other's glasses. By now all four members of the Wrangler crew were feeling better. Although still worn out, the temporary recuperative powers of a decent shower, a change of clothes, and a stiff drink could never be underestimated.

"You two look so much better," Marion said. "I can't believe the difference."

Rick couldn't stop smiling; he sat chest out, shoulders back, proudly wearing his best 'made it out alive' face for all to see.

"See that look, ladies," Lucas said, gesturing toward his grinning colleague, "that look means old King Richard of Stellenbosch here is happy, happy his wounds have been cleaned and patched, happy he's washed his ridiculous bleached blond hair, and happy he's put fresh underwear on," he stopped and smiled. "And now, to top it all, the man has a large whiskey in his hand and is acting like he hasn't a care in the world."

Both sisters laughed; despite their chronic exhaustion they were enjoying themselves. With their entertaining travelling companions rejuvenated and back in the land of the living, things felt good. And, if the truth be known, they'd be more than happy if their adventure was to continue a little while longer.

***

The HSG duo were conscious they should ring Gerry. He'd left several voicemails earlier asking for an update, but they agreed he wouldn't appreciate the timing so didn't even try.

“No one wants to be woken up at that hour,” Lucas said before downing the remnants of his bourbon. “It’s half five in the morning back home so we’ll leave it ‘til tomorrow, eh?”

Rick didn’t argue. Reporting in to the boss was the last thing on his mind. Even the thought of ringing home didn’t appeal; all the South African wanted now was his bed. It had been a long gruelling day, he was dead on his feet and struggling to keep his eyes open. But he wasn’t alone; everyone felt the same. After a brief round of ‘sleep well see you in the morning’ the quartet broke for the night and headed off to their respective rooms, all desperate for a good night’s sleep.

***

When the phone rang, Gerry Hanlon was sitting at his desk. He had his reading glasses perched precariously on the end of his nose and was looking intently at his laptop. He let the phone ring out a few times before glancing away from the screen. The LED display above the keypad flashed ‘Ray’. Happy to take the call, he reached for the receiver. “Morning, Raymond,” he answered. “How are we today?”

“Average for a Monday morning, I suppose,” came the reply. “How are you?”

“About the same really,” Gerry said. “I’m just sat here checking out the news reports about that comet. Seems like Lucas was right. By all accounts it was some show.”

“Oh, right, might have a look myself later,” Ray said, “but, more importantly, though, any more news from the boys?”

“I’m afraid not,” came the apologetic reply. “Nothing since yesterday.”

“Have you tried ringing?”

“What do you think?”

“Sorry,” Ray said. “Just going to voicemail, is it?”

“Every single bastard time.”

Since Lucas’s brief email was tabled at the Stuart family breakfast, nothing further had been heard from Arizona, and now the ongoing lack of communication was a problem both Directors were anxious about.

"This little job," Ray said. "It really is a pain in the arse, isn't it?"

"You're not bloody joking," Gerry snapped. "From day one it's gone awry, nothing's gone to plan, the whole things been a cock-up from start to finish. It's a complete disaster that's made us look like a right bunch of incompetents."

"Hold on a sec," Ray protested. "Agreed, it's not gone well, but why so bitter all of a sudden?"

"I just am," Gerry said. "Takes a lot to piss me off but that's how I'm feeling this morning."

"Look... we've said it before, those two may be a law unto themselves but if anyone can salvage something from this mess, it's them. So, like we said yesterday, it's just a waiting game, nothing more we can do, OK?"

"Yeah, yeah, I know you're right, it's just...," Gerry paused as he looked back at his laptop screen. "Well, it's just I keep getting the feeling we're missing something."

"Like what?" Ray asked.

"I don't know...it's probably nothing, just me getting frustrated by lack of progress I suppose."

"Well, we're all feeling a bit like that, but there's not a lot we can do about it, so I wouldn't let it get you down."

"Yeah, maybe I should take a leaf out of your book," Gerry replied. "Maybe I should just relax about the whole bleedin' thing."

"It's a better philosophy," his partner replied cheerfully. "Let's just sit it out and see what oddball shit happens next!"

CHAPTER 45

Change of Heart

At 9:05 am, Ronnie Stafford's XJ pulled up outside the HSG compound. At the wheel was Excel's Chief Accountant Maurice Brown, in the passenger seat Ron Stafford.

The ever-dependable finance executive edged the black Jaguar toward the security barrier, his face a picture of concentration. Eventually drawing level with the gate's intercom box, the grey-haired accountant leant out of the window and pressed the button marked: Push to speak.

"Good morning, can I help you?" a clipped accent asked.

"Yes, good morning," Maurice answered. "It's…err, it's Ron Stafford and Maurice Brown to see Mr Stuart. We have an appointment."

After a brief silence the intercom crackled back to life. "OK, that's fine," the voice said, "after you come through the gate drive straight up to the top car-park and park on the left in the section marked for visitors and wait there. Someone will be down to you shortly and they'll escort you to Mr Stuart."

"OK, thank you," Maurice replied.

Seconds later the steel gate behind the barrier emitted a loud metallic click then, accompanied by a droning whirr, started to slide open. When the panel juddered to a halt, completely open, the barrier lifted. Once it was fully upright, the Jag drove through the entrance and made its way past the portakabin security lodge before heading up the sloping blacktop to the car park area. At the top of the road, as instructed, it turned left and pulled up in the well signed visitors section. It was empty. Spoilt for choice, Maurice chose the centre bay of the five highlighted with a bright yellow "V".

At the other side of the car park, Steve Harrison deftly negotiated the steep reception steps then strode across the plain asphalt yard towards the Jaguar. Ray had deliberately designated the R & I chief as official meeter and greeter for the morning's visit and his motive was simple: he wanted Steve to meet Ronnie first, on his own, to glean a feel for the man.

Over the years, Ray and Gerry had come to value the ex-DI's people reading skills; even from the briefest of meetings, he'd proved to have a sixth sense for judging an individual's core persona. Maybe it was old school copper's intuition - who knows - but he'd got it dead right too many times for them to ignore.

As Steve reached the car, Maurice was already out and was standing at the driver's door whilst Ronnie was in the process of easing his sizeable frame out of the passenger door.

"Good morning, gents," Steve said. "How are we? All OK, I hope. I'm Steve, Steve Harrison, nice to meet you," he held out his hand to Maurice first who shook it firmly and smiled.

"Yeah, hi, Steve – nice to meet you...I'm Maurice Brown, Mr Stafford's colleague – he's asked me to come along with him to this morning's meeting."

Steve smiled back at the smartly attired accountant. "Smashing," he said, "welcome to the HSG, Maurice." He then turned his attentions to the man himself. Big Ron was now stood about ten feet away, ferociously hitching up his trousers before smoothing down his jacket. Looking at the man mountain before him, the R&I chief couldn't help but hear Ray's description echoing round his head; the man truly *was* a monstrous gargoyle.

Steve wasn't fazed. He walked over to Ronnie, arm outstretched, and greeted him like a long-lost friend. "Mr Stafford," he said warmly, "welcome to the HSG. Like I said to your colleague, I'm Steve Harrison, it's a pleasure to meet you."

Ronnie returned the smile and the handshake, but both were deliberately restrained. Somewhere deep in the murky swirl of his subconscious a spark of recognition fired and now he was trawling the memory banks, asking himself, where've I seen this face before?

"Hello, Steve, yes… I'm Ronnie, how are you, my friend?" The big man took a long slow deliberate look at the still grinning ex-cop. "I've got to say, Steve," he said slowly, "you look remarkably familiar. Have we met before?"

"Not to my knowledge, Mr Stafford, I'm pretty positive…" Steve almost laughed as he spoke but managed to keep a lid on it. "I think I'd definitely remember you if we had," he added with a practiced straight face.

"Ah, well, never mind, you must just look like someone else, that's all it can be. Anyway, less of the formalities, it's Ronnie, OK?"

"Yeah, no problem, Ronnie it is," Steve said, then continued with his welcome patter. "So, gents, if you would follow me up to the main board room, Mr Stuart's in there with his co-Director Gerry Hanlon and there's coffee and a light breakfast to keep everyone going."

The R&I chief led the two guests along the flagged footway, into the building through the spartan reception area and up the stairs to the first floor. The door to the board room was closed but Steve knocked gently on the frosted glass panel and instantly Gerry's dulcet tones emanated from within. "Yeah, come in – it's open," he said.

The introductions were courteous and friendly and once all five men were armed with a coffee and a Danish pastry they settled down around the top end of the table.

"I've got to say Ray, and Gerry of course, you really have a fine set up here, and this boardroom, well - I am impressed. It looks good, doesn't it, Maurice?" Ronnie directed his compliment at the two HSG Directors before turning to his chief accountant for a response.

"Yes, absolutely," Maurice said, "it looks a very professional operation, well-ordered and - one would assume - well managed. What sort of turn-over do you do?"

The Excel money man was genuinely interested in the HSG set-up. The compound, out buildings and office arrangement was extensive and looked well maintained and, from experience, Maurice was well aware it would need a serious level of business to sustain it.

"Anywhere between ten and fifteen," Gerry replied. "Anything less than ten would usually be classed as a bum year – but you know how it is, it's not always about turnover, is it? It's about margin, and I mean *real* margin."

"Very impressive," the accountant replied, "and yes, I know exactly what you mean, Gerry," he stopped and smiled. "It is all about that true bottom line, always has been and always will be…but some people just don't get it, do they?" As Maurice spoke Gerry was gently nodding his approval. Dead right, he thought, nice to meet a man who understood the base principles of business as clearly as he did.

Ray, on the other hand, was getting impatient with the small talk. Keen to focus everyone's attention on the reason for their get-together, he brought the table to order. "Right, gents, time is of the essence….so please, let's get this show on the road, eh?"

As all eyes focused on Ray, he started, "So, Ronnie, as I see it you're here to put us in the picture about some new information you have about your…. Well, your problems, so why don't you just tell us what's changed?"

The big man didn't need asking twice. "Well, Raymond," he said, "it's kind of like this…."

***

The force with which Ronnie Stafford let loose was as unexpected as it was intense, and while the HSG men sat back in amazement he didn't let up. The pace and eloquence were impressive; no one wanted to stop the flow, and no one felt a burning urge to butt in - not even Gerry Hanlon.

"So, gents, in a nutshell," Ronnie wound to a finish after his fifteen-minute oratory, "it's a strange one, quite a revelation really…. but you can see how it looked at first, can't you?" Stafford wasn't quite finished yet but was now ready to get some feedback from HSG's top-brass.

Ray responded first. "You've got to be making this shit up, Ronnie," he said. "Never mind quite a revelation, it just doesn't sound possible."

"Totally stunned when I found out," Ronnie said, before looking over at Maurice. "Couldn't believe it, could we, Mo? It just came out the blue, didn't it?"

Maurice glanced round at the three staring faces. "It was unbelievable, gents," he said. "We had absolutely no idea until that first phone call on Saturday afternoon."

As Ray sat shaking his head it was Gerry's turn to have a go. "Why didn't you tell Ray this on Saturday when he rang you?" he asked Ronnie.

"Because I hadn't got the full story then," Stafford replied, "and, as you well know, I was fuckin' pissed."

"That's true, you did sound half-cut," Ray said, "and to be honest by then I wasn't in the mood for listening anyway."

So far Steve hadn't said much, but he couldn't hold his tongue any longer. "Gentlemen, I'm sorry for sounding thick," he said looking between Ronnie and Maurice, "but you're going to have to explain that again. This radical change of circumstance has left my head spinning. I'm lost."

Ronnie smiled. "OK, Steve," he said. "What bit don't you get?"

"All of it," came the blunt reply. "All of it sounds ludicrous."

Maurice could sense Steve's frustrations bubbling and stepped in. "Look, Steve," he said, "it does sound farfetched and I know it's bloody hard to believe, but over the course of yesterday we got additional information, cross checked it, and it all stacks up."

"How?" Steve asked. "How does it all stack up? How can it suddenly go from Ebro being a bunch of criminals that have ripped you off to them being a key ally of Federal agencies in an undercover sting on The Divinity?"

"Yeah," Gerry said backing his colleague up, "how does a little thing like that happen?"

Ronnie raised his hand and looked over at Maurice. "Show them the letter," he said. "Let them read it for themselves."

Ten minutes later Ray, Gerry, and Steve had each read a copy of the Ebro letter and sat in silence; it made interesting reading....

***

Unbeknownst to the Excel organisation, Ronnie Stafford's insignificant Import and Export Company had got itself caught up in the tail end of an elaborate international investigation. The Europol-led multi-agency plan was far from simple, extremely ambitious, and relied heavily on several legitimate companies to assist, but Excel's unwanted involvement was pure fluke.

"Like I said when we met Ray," Ronnie explained, "at the beginning of the week it still looked like we were the victims. To me it was a case of being ripped off by the Spanish and I wanted to do something about it."

"Yeah, I got that," Ray replied. "You wanted us to help you recover goods you'd not been paid for and we agreed to give it a go," he glanced at Gerry and shook his head, "but this is some turnaround."

Ronnie was sat directly across from Ray with his huge hands clasped in front of him. "I know it is," he said. "That little Irish prick dropped us right in the shit and now we – Excel, that is - look like a right bunch of wankers."

Steve Harrison still looked puzzled. "So, this junior accountant," he said, "this Owen Carroll fella managed to hoodwink you both, took the balance payment from Ebro, and got the money paid into his own bank account?"

"Well, yes," Maurice replied, "although technically it was a dummy business account he'd set up with him as the sole signatory."

"Conniving little shit managed to siphon off a hundred grand," Ronnie added. "We didn't realise they'd paid, so I went after them. Like I told you we thought they'd just tried to stitch us up."

"But now you've found out your problem was internal," Steve said, "and have had to apologise to Ebro for the aggressive behaviour. Is that what you're saying?"

Ronnie could see Steve was going to take some convincing. "That's certainly part of it," he answered. "I'd gone legal with the winding up order and had you guys lined up to fly under the radar and go try get my goods back."

"So, this letter," Gerry said, picking the piece of paper up off the table, "is Ebro's official statement refuting the non-payment allegation and requesting you drop your legal challenge with immediate effect, yes?"

"Again, that's correct," Ronnie said, then turned and smiled at Steve Harrison. "See, Steven, someone gets it."

Steve didn't appreciate the barbed comment. "Look, Mr Stafford," he said. "I get the gist of that bit, no problem, but what I'm struggling with is the link to this alleged investigation into The Divinity. That letter says fuck all about any of that."

"It's dead simple," Ronnie said with a slow shake of his head, "Ebro are working for the investigation team, they're providing a cover for federal infiltration out in Central America."

"And they told you this?" Gerry asked.

"They certainly did," Ronnie sat back in his chair. "They told us because our legal challenge was causing them problems and they needed it to disappear."

"Sounds like bollocks to me," Steve said. "I can't see it personally."

"Well its fucking true, OK," the big man snapped. "I've explained it to you twice now and everything I've said is fact. There's fuck all I can do about it." He paused and glared at the ex-DI. "Anyway, it's us who've fucked up and have the problem, not you, so other than wasting your time, HSG won't suffer."

"Alright, gents," Ray said firmly, "let's keep it civilised. Ronnie's right: it's no skin off our nose, is it? Some wasted time, as you say, but no damage done."

"Exactly, Raymond," Ronnie said. "I'm glad you see it that way... and to be honest I want to make it up to you, you know, for fucking you around so much. It's the least I can do."

"There's no need," Ray smiled, "it's just one of those shitty situations. Happens to the best of us and in truth we haven't really done anything meaningful for you yet."

"Well, I appreciate your understanding, I really do, but now we know a little more about the overall situation we think we can help you," he stopped and looked sideways at Maurice. "It's only a starter for ten, mind," he grinned, "but go on, Mo, show them what else we got."

The accountant appeared hesitant, but then started gently nodding. "Yeah, yeah, OK," he said, "if that's what you want." The HSG men looked quickly at each other then all stared at Maurice.

"Well, come on, then, Mr Brown," Gerry prompted. "What else do you know?"

Maurice shifted awkwardly in his chair, then reached for his inside pocket. "This mustn't go any further," he said quietly, "it really mustn't, OK?"

The three men nodded as the accountant opened a small manila envelope and pulled out a silver USB stick. "Am I OK to use the laptop, Gerry?" he asked, pointing to the silver Dell in the centre of the table. "Is it hooked up to the overhead?"

"Why, what you going to show us?" he asked.

"Sit back and watch," Maurice said. "This makes interesting viewing…."

CHAPTER 46

The Devil's in the Detail

Ray and Gerry sat alone in the board room.

Ron Stafford and his likeable finance chief had left ten minutes earlier, Steve Harrison had just been ushered out and, as Gerry looked over at the blank projector screen, he sat back and folded his arms.

"That was unexpected. Who would have thought you could get so unlucky?" He turned to face his partner. "Good old Ronnie's not shy about telling it as it is, is he?"

"No, very candid," Ray replied, "and you know what… I believe every bloody word." He took a sip of lukewarm coffee, then winced. "Anyway, you can't argue with that kind of proof, can you?"

Both men knew the likelihood of it being a pack of lies was slim. Truth could often be stranger than fiction and this was one of those times; it was a hell of a story. At first, they'd been sceptical but, as the tale unfolded, Ronnie and Maurice's explanation, supported by documentary evidence, had soon had the HSG trio convinced. And now, as the pair sat brainstorming in the aftermath, Ray was hoping what they'd just heard could somehow ease their troubles in Arizona.

Like Ray, Gerry was keen to use what they'd been told to their best advantage but wasn't hopeful of an easy fix. "We need to talk to Lucas first, then we can decide." He stopped to think about it for a moment. "Unless you have a better idea, that is."

As he mulled over possibilities, HSG's CEO looked round the room. Finally, he found himself focussing on a coaster on the table in front of him. "I know it's a long shot," he said, staring at the patterned silver disc, "but maybe trying to find this…this so-called Education Centre is an option."

"Why do you say that?"

"Well, you think about it. If Ronnie's inside information is right then, it's the only other high-profile place we know about. If the boys can find it, we might be a step closer to the book," he stopped and reached for a blank sheet of paper and a pen then started to draw on it. "If this is them," he said placing a little x in the top left hand corner of the page, "somewhere north of Cedar City, then they're probably five hours away by road to this brainwashing centre, which, according to this new intelligence, is here," he drew a small circle just up from the bottom right hand corner, "just west of the Devil's Canyon on the Utah/Colorado state boundary."

Gerry grinned. "Why am I not surprised about the name?"

Ray looked up from his simplistic scrawl and shook his head. "More to the point, why am I wasting my time trying to draw this? Just go on Google Maps, will you, get the mid-west United States up on the screen, and we'll do this properly."

Gerry grabbed the laptop and dutifully obliged. "How much easier is that?" he said as seconds later he was staring up at the huge map on the screen. "Now we're cooking."

Ray stood up, grabbed the extending pointer of a side table and walked in front of the giant map. "Right. Like I said, hopefully our boys are around here, and this education place is somewhere…," he peered closely at the screen then slapped the pointer down, "yeah… somewhere about here," he hesitated for a second then added, "and look, wouldn't you know it - it's off Highway 666 – how apt is that?"

Gerry was sat to the right of the screen watching his friend closely. "Worryingly so," he said loudly, "but let's not get too hung up about names at this stage eh - just crack on will you."

"Yes, O Great One," came the sarcastic reply.

Ray then went on to explain his thoughts about this latest twist. Using the map as his sounding board, he summarised the comings and goings of Lucas and Rick so far on the trip and then ran through possible scenarios for the book's whereabouts. As he spoke, HSG's CEO was his usual animated self and, as Gerry sat back and enjoyed the show, he couldn't help but think that a Ray Stuart presentation, even to an audience of one, was always entertaining.

After a few minutes, Gerry interrupted. "Hold on a minute," he said, jokingly holding his hand up, "can I just ask a quick question, please?"

"Fire away."

"This mind-blowing revelation by *your* Mr Stafford," he said, "which we both agree is probably true, only affects us directly because we are now aware of another operating base, for want of a better description, for these Divinity charlatans, yes?"

"Well, yeah…I suppose so."

"When you cut through all this fancy spiel of yours, this big plan is simply to contact Lucas and tell him and Rick to go find this education centre, yeah?" Gerry stopped as he watched. Ray slowly nod his head then he continued, "With the outside hope being that (a) it exists and they can find it, (b) they can get in and (c) the book is there and they can snaffle it away without anyone noticing. Am I getting this right?"

Ray turned the pointer toward his partner and scowled. "Have you got a better idea?" he asked.

***

Man Mountain Stafford, ably assisted by his accountant Maurice Brown, had enthralled the three-man audience. Listening to the elaborate tale of commercial wrangling and industrial espionage, the HSG trio had heard it all before but this particular tale had a nice additional twist. Ultimately, Ray and Gerry were happy to learn the Ebro team were aligned with the good guys. It backed up everything the old sea dogs had said about the Spanish from the start, but the fact the Ebro organisation had been so heavily involved with an international drug trafficking investigation was still pretty impressive.

“Some balls, eh?” Ray said several times during the session. “Don't know how they did it, but good on them...bloody good on them.”

However, the biggest revelation from the meeting was the level of confidential information Excel had been party to during the last couple of days. Ronnie's aggressive stance over a late payment issue had rattled so many cages that their *'back-off'* deal had included several snippets of classified intelligence, one being the existence of a little-known Divinity training facility in Colorado.

Ronnie again explained that his late payment claim related to the ten Land Rovers he'd supplied Ebro. Whilst that small fleet of highly prized vehicles had been hard at work in the jungles of Central America - engaged in what The Divinity would call its great humanitarian calling, but Europol and their many investigation allies would call narcotics distribution – he'd been none the wiser.

During the discussions it was obvious both Excel men were relieved to find out the truth. Although a little late in the day, and ultimately very embarrassing to have doubted Ebro's business practices so openly, the issue had now been resolved with no permanent damage done. Ronnie got his money back, Owen Carroll got his come-uppance, and Maurice Brown learnt a major lesson in the pitfalls of modern-day recruitment. More importantly, the HSG gleaned a little more information about an organisation that continued to frustrate them.

***

Gerry thought about the question for a second. “No not really,” he said as he faced the blunt tip of the metal pointer. “It's just that your *big* plan does seem a little weak and a little vague and maybe a little optimistic,” he shook his head then smiled. “That's only in my eyes, obviously.”

“You're right,” Ray said, “but we've got to do something, I mean, especially now we know what we know.”

Gerry pulled a face. "Look, at this moment we don't have a clue where our boys are… do we?"

"That's par for the course, though, isn't it?" Ray said answering a question with a question.

Gerry didn't bite. "Look, since we last heard from them anything could have happened, couldn't it?" he said, "So who knows what kind of state they're in."

"So, what you saying, then?"

"I'm simply suggesting we speak to Lucas first before we decide the next move, OK?"

"Fine by me," Ray answered sharply.

"But if pushed," Gerry said, "I'll go for them heading back to Mesa for a final crack at the HQ as a better option than another potential wild goose chase."

"OK, fair enough," Ray replied, "but like you say, let's see what the boys have to say first."

***

When Rick woke he felt like he'd been hit by a freight train. His head throbbed, his throat was dry, his legs were leaden and, whilst he was grateful for a good night's sleep, it was obvious he was still suffering from the previous day's exertions. His left leg was the worst: the ache was savage and the bruising around the gash on his thigh was the most colourful he'd ever seen. As he sat for a moment, perched on the edge of his bunk he looked from his leg to the sprawled form in the next bed.

"Roxby, you old goat" he whispered. "You awake yet?"

Lucas grunted, rolled over and rubbed his eyes. "What you saying?" he muttered.

"I asked if you were you awake."

"No, of course I'm not," came a disgruntled reply. "It's way too early."

Rick looked hard at his bleary-eyed colleague and laughed. "Sarge, you don't look good," he said. "Haven't seen you this rough for ages." But the ex-sapper was in no mood for abuse, however well-intentioned it was.

"Just piss off, you South African gob shite," he said, pulling the covers tight up, "and leave me alone."

Rick ignored the attitude; he wasn't fazed, Lucas had never been a morning person. Opting to leave his grouchy colleague a little longer, the aching South African decided to get washed and dressed. As he stood up, the after-effects of his injuries suddenly became even more apparent. He stood still for a few seconds to get his balance then gently rolled his shoulders and stretched. It did the trick. The stiffness started to ease as he limped across the bedroom to the sorry looking dresser by the window. On top of the sagging antique were his phone, keys, wallet and passport. The phone showed two missed calls and a message. He checked the voicemail, it was from Gerry: "Rick, it's Gerry - ring me as soon as you get this message. It's urgent."

Rick knew the same message would have been left on Lucas's phone. Gerry Hanlon was a persistent old bastard when he needed to be and wouldn't rest until he had the latest update from at least one of them. The South African shook his aching head – it was time to give Sleeping Beauty a proper wake up call.

***

Twenty minutes later, Lucas and Rick were sat downstairs in the lounge sipping on freshly brewed coffee. In the cold light of day, the room looked even more down at heel than it had the night before. The dust danced in every streak of sunlight and it suddenly felt like a throwback to the old west. "You two fellas look a bit worse for wear," the gnarled old waitress said as she took their breakfast order. "Y'all been in an accident?"

Lucas looked up and smiled. "Well, yes, we did take a bit of a tumble yesterday," he said matter of factly, "but we'll live." The wizened waitress looked them up and down for a second and slowly nodded, then turned on her heels and doddered back to the kitchen. Once she was out of ear shot, Lucas looked at Rick. "Jesus," he said, "they've even matched the staff to the décor."

The two men continued to chat amongst themselves for a few minutes more but stopped abruptly when Marion and Babb appeared at the lounge entrance. Lucas commented first. "Well, look at these two," he said pointing across the room. "It's the one and only Arizona Armstrong's."

As Rick beckoned them over the sisters waved and headed toward them. "So how are the wounded today?" Marion asked as she reached the table.

"Battling on," Lucas said as he pulled out two chairs. "Sit yourselves down, girls."

The sisters sat down, ordered breakfast and then awaited a full report; but there wasn't one.

"Just a bit of bruising, really," Rick gently patted his thigh, "but I'm feeling alright for a Monday morning, all considered – ready for a new day."

Lucas grinned. "Like I said when you picked us up, it was nothing a shower, a stiff drink and a good night's sleep wouldn't cure."

The girls rolled their eyes at each other across the table, but they knew there was no point in fussing, these two were never going to complain.

Before they could say anything, both men's phones began to vibrate.

"Looks like we're popular," Lucas said picking his phone up off the table. "Which one you got? "

"Ha! I've got Gerry," Rick grimaced. "You've drawn the short straw!"

Lucas replied as he squinted at the screen, "Ricky, don't tell them everything," he said, "just the basics, leave the girls and the dog out of it, OK?"

As Rick nodded his understanding, Lucas stood up and turned to the sisters. "Ladies, our leaders are calling. Back in a few minutes!" With that Lucas hit the green button and headed for the street, Rick followed a few steps behind, off to seek the privacy of Room Seven.

"Yeah, OK, boys," Marion said as she watched the two men leave, "y'all have fun."

***

The simultaneous calls had been Ray's idea. "You ring Kruger and I'll ring Roxby, "he'd said. "Pair of bastards can't ignore both of us at the same time, can they?"

"They better hadn't," Gerry snapped, "because if they do, I'll sack the pair of them. The free styling is all well and good, but sometimes I tell you, they take the fucking piss."

The HSG Director's tactic worked. Lucas and Rick both knew that when the Top Dogs rang at exactly the same time it was serious.

"Gerry… thank God," Rick answered as sincerely as he could. "You won't believe the shit we've been through…."

Out in the sunshine of the quiet side street, Lucas was equally as deferential. "Mr Stuart, what a nice surprise," he faked. "Can't believe you've actually got through. Haven't spoken to you in ages. How's it going?"

"You know bloody well that I have absolutely no idea how it's going. Don't get smart with me!" the CEO replied. "I'll ask you a very simple question, Mr Roxby: what the hell is happening?"

"Err…well, it's, it's all happening, boss," came Lucas's hesitant reply, "I mean since my last update just after the comet showed, we've had a crazy old time really – and to say it's been full-on would be a bit of an understatement."

"I'd hardly call your last contact an update."

Lucas was again slow to answer. "Well, I suppose that's because there wasn't much to tell," he eventually replied, "but a lot's happened since."

"I'm in no rush," came the now calm reply, "so go on… fire away, Lucas - tell Uncle Raymond all the juicy details."

CHAPTER 47

The Wind of Change

As the HSG field team regaled the bosses with an edited version of the search for the chapel, the Directors listened open mouthed.

"Are you shitting me, Ricky?" Gerry asked incredulously. "You telling me you went in there without a backup plan or telling us?"

"That's exactly what I'm saying," Rick replied. "We've established that this chapel actually exists and it's in a private estate patrolled by security guards. We got in the building, you know, but only as far as a store at the back."

"Did you find much?"

"Not really – a load of foldaway chairs and a hospital bed was about it."

"So, the place isn't derelict?"

"No – it's in good nick and looks well used – in fact we reckon something had just been going on."

"Like what?"

"No idea, but the chairs looked new and we found a big patch of warm, freshly scorched earth… so your guess is as good as mine."

"OK, so these security guards," Gerry questioned, "what were they like? Did they seem legit? Did they give anything away?"

Again, Rick answered quickly. "They looked the part," he said. "Smart logoed uniforms and all top kit," he stopped as something struck him. "But, here's a thing, considering they had us bang to rights, they were remarkably tight-lipped."

"Did they say anything of interest at all?" Gerry asked hopefully. "Like who owned the property."

"Yea, they gave us their full names and addresses while they were flattening us on the floor, reading us our rights and throwing the cuffs on," came Rick's retort.

"Less of the lip, Kruger!" Gerry barked back.

Rick silently shook his head, then continued, "After a few sly digs, they marched us off to this big flashy house, locked us in a van for an hour then handed us over to a gang of ugly looking bikers."

Gerry was puzzled. "Bikers," he repeated, "Why the hell would they do that?"

"Don't know," Rick said slowly. "It was bizarre, really, and not what we'd expected at all. We were all geared up for the local law and having to contact you with our tails between our legs…but, no, instead we got Redbeard and three heavies."

"That's your second run-in with two wheeled types this week, isn't it?"

"Yeah, but this lot were in a van. There wasn't a motorcycle in sight."

"Could it be the same crowd; could they be working for The Divinity?"

"With what's gone on over this last week, Gerry, nothing would surprise me."

"Yeah, tell me about it," came the weary reply.

***

Lucas finished his call with Ray then headed back into the guest house. As he came through the front door, Rick was walking toward him.

"Where you going?" he asked.

"The Jeep," Rick grunted. "Gerry wants me to ring him back with a grid reference for this place."

"Oh, right," came the bemused reply. "I just told Ray it should be easy to find on any decent small-scale map and he seemed happy with that."

Rick muttered as he limped past his partner, "I'm just following orders, Sarge. I'll be as quick as I can…I'll be back in five, OK?"

Exactly five minutes later Rick re-joined the others in the lounge, but now the breakfast settings had all been cleared away and the foursome were the only guests in the room.

"Did you sort it for him?" Lucas poured Rick the dregs from the cold coffee pot.

"Yup, he's happy now," he replied. "Well maybe 'happy' is not the right word, but he's got what he wanted."

To the group's surprise, the humble backwater of Iron Creek had turned out to be a communication hotspot. It was rumoured a geological quirk ensured all cell phone network reception was good, and now, as the sisters listened to Lucas and Rick discussing that very fact, Marion's mind wandered to Meredith. She thought about the strange out of character message she'd left and ultimately the loss of contact. Almost immediately her mood darkened. But aware that her cell now had coverage she reached for her inside pocket. She checked for missed calls, texts and voicemails. There was nothing new from anyone. Her stomach tightened as she began to fear the worst.

"I think she's dead," she suddenly blurted out. "I think she's been murdered."

The others stopped talking and turned to look at her. "Who's been murdered?" Babb asked.

"Meredith," she said. "That's why she hasn't called back."

Lucas looked at the glum faced librarian. "Listen," he said, "it could easily be something innocent, something totally innocuous, so don't you worry about it, OK?" But he caught Rick's eye in silent agreement that now they both feared the worst.

"Well, maybe…yes," Marion nodded, "but we've even been to her house and look what happened there."

Babb suddenly looked accusingly at Lucas. "Anyway," she snapped, "you're the one who said she's working undercover, you're the one who said she was likely some sort of federal stooge."

“I was joking at the time, but now I’m not so sure,” he replied reluctantly.

Rick started to rise from the table, “We need to go find the truth out then, don’t we? As our leaders have just so politely pointed out, they’re sat in a plush office five thousand miles away, paying us to find out the truth, and currently they have sweet Fanny Adams to show for it. And the clients aren’t happy.”

“So, what next?” Marion asked.

Lucas lent on the table, looked across at Rick then back to the sisters. “We are going to Colorado!” he announced. “We’re heading for a place called Cortez in the south west of the state. The gang back home will get an exact location over to us while we are en route.”

“Colorado?” the girls chorused in surprise. “What’s in Colorado?”

***

The Directors’ indecision had been brought to a head with a little help from Steve Harrison. During the parallel calls both field ops had confirmed the search for the chapel, albeit successful in one way, had turned up no concrete leads in the hunt for the book. In simple terms they’d expended a lot of effort and taken a beating for nothing. But Steve knew they weren’t going to take being recalled well, so the ex-DI cut to the chase, “If they’ve found nothing major by now,” he’d said, “allow them one last scout then bring them back.”

Despite Gerry’s reservations, the R&I Chief’s casting vote tipped the balance and collectively they agreed to send HSG’s A-team East to Colorado.

***

The sisters were still more than happy to continue their impromptu adventure so, after indulging in one last cup of coffee, the foursome packed their bags, paid their bill and said goodbye to Daisy Edgerton and her ramshackle guest house. Ten minutes later, under a cloudless

Utah sky, the 4X4 turned north onto I-70 heading for what Gerry had sarcastically referred to as The House of Spiritual Enlightenment.

Resuming her role as co-pilot, Marion now sat in the passenger seat with Lucas's dog-eared road atlas spread across her lap and, after several minutes of scrutiny, lifted her head and frowned.

"This is going be a long one," she said as she turned to Rick. "It's about three hundred and fifty miles as the crow flies," she stopped and pulled a sad face, "but as we're not remotely crow-like, we'll have to go the long way round."

"Doesn't bother me," the South African replied. "Point me in any direction and I'll just keep driving until you say Stop."

In the back, Lucas had nested in his chosen corner and was almost asleep. Snuggled next to him, Babb was happily leafing through a guidebook she'd picked up at the guest house. With her sunglasses on and the wind now whipping through her hair, she was focused on an article that caught her eye. It was a piece on the history of a legendary Black Mountain landmark and as she studied the old sepia photograph of a small, but perfectly formed stone arch she checked the title block below. It read: Gunner's Leap, circa 1905

"You've got to be kidding me!" she exclaimed. "How weird is this?"

***

It had been several days since they'd removed Coleman, and Dubois was still unhappy about it.

The leader of The Divinity was meticulous; he didn't leave loose ends.

What infuriated the Monsignor the most was it should never have happened in the first place.

The Reverend's tenure with the organisation had been short, but in that time he'd reportedly carried out his duties well and with great enthusiasm. Coleman was not inner sanctum; he was simply part of the front, part of the polished public face of the organisation. Employed as a member of the team that promoted the organisations humanitarian works in Central America, he knew nothing about the dark side of the operation. He came across as an innocent man, almost naïve, a man who simply wanted to help others. He appeared to relish his role in the missionary project programme; he had worked hard, travelled extensively and seemed to be fulfilling lifelong philanthropic dreams.

And then a small package addressed to him was inadvertently opened by an admin assistant at the Mesa Office. The envelope in question contained a passport bearing the Reverend's photograph but carrying a different name. Instantly subtle alterations to Coleman's supervision were made. His duties were revised, he was kept closer to home and, unbeknownst to him, he was closely watched by several sets of eyes wherever he went. Dubois was furious with Tate for not having picked up on it sooner.

Assigning him the role of custodian of The Book of Martyrs had been Dubois's own idea. Coleman had broken trust and become expendable, and this arrangement was one the Monsignor could easily manipulate, especially if the pressure to return the book got out of hand.

Tate's men, detailed to find out who Coleman was, and what his game was, observed the Reverend twice meeting two unknown males. On both occasions Coleman had said he would be somewhere else at the time but had been followed and photographed with the same two mystery suits in the same out of town restaurant. When the men he met were subsequently identified as police officers, his fate was sealed.

Dubois's first reaction was to remove Coleman from the organisation with immediate effect, but - after consideration - he decided on a different course of action. Under the guise of needing a short-term decoy to protect the book, he sent its official custodian into hiding. But then the Reverend got twitchy, Tate got impatient and the whole thing started to unravel…

Tate had had no business taking matters into his own hands. "Goddam freaking imbecile," Dubois muttered to himself every time he thought about it.

After the event, in spite of his vehement defence of his choice of hired help, the Monsignor had remained far from convinced about the arrangements. It didn't matter how well it had been explained or how well it had been executed. By despatching Reverend Coleman so publicly, Ings and his two young enforcers had reached the end of their useful life. Dubois knew the authorities would assume their disappearance was gang related. He personally made sure the three low-life red necks disappeared without a trace.

Dubois had had a far neater solution up his sleeve. The UK collection agents would have been the perfect foils; who better to set up and frame for the Reverend's death? Three birds with one stone; what a result that would've been! A result like that would've generated so much negative publicity, the book's return agreement would have paled into insignificance. In fact, so much so, it would probably never have raised its ugly head again. But, no, Tate had had to jump the gun. He had enticed Coleman out of hiding, then had him driven to the desert and executed. True, the car-jack charade had rid them of a suspected infiltrator and offered a viable cover for the books non-return, but it had also brought a boat load of trouble: the police were asking more questions about the organisation and Coleman's role in it, and the annoying UK collection agents were still making their presence felt.

Dubois did not take well to having his hand forced but, when it was, he always dug in and fought dirty.

***

In the aftermath of the car-jack furore, Dubois had undertaken a damage limitation exercise, but it hadn't been his main focus. The Monsignor had needed to concentrate on more critical matters and now, having successfully master-minded the weekend's spectacular events at the Mountain House, he could sit back and take a brief well-earned break.

***

After spending most of Sunday travelling, the Chief crossed the Colorado state line and reached his destination late afternoon. Debating how to prioritise his requirements, he parked the black Mercedes in the hotel's valet zone then made his way to reception. As he was a regular visitor to the exclusive five-star facility, check-in was a mere formality, and nothing was too much trouble for the sycophantic staff. So now, with sixteen hours of luxurious self-indulgence to look forward to, the supremo quickly made up his mind about what he'd like to do first. After he pocketed his key card, he slipped the concierge an order for the company of two of the finest girls on the hotel's 'Secret VIP' menu, then headed for Suite 302 with only one thing on his mind.

***

As the dawn broke, Dubois awoke feeling rejuvenated; the recharge was a complete success. So, after showering, he got dressed and headed downstairs to the foyer. As arranged, he met Dominic Williams by the reception desk and from there the two men were led to the private dining suite for breakfast. Once settled into a luxurious two-tone leather booth they were served coffee, toast, eggs benedict, and a bottle of the Monsignor's favourite French mineral water. After the waiter asked if they needed anything else, Dubois shook his head once then dismissed the man with a flick of the hand. The young man knew his place and instantly backed off. The two men were now left to discuss the weekend's fundraiser in private.

"Dominic, that was the best yet," Dubois crowed. "A triumph on every level."

Father Williams was in awe. "Incredible result, Monsignor," he gushed. "One hundred and twenty-five thousand in cash on the night and a further hundred and fifty pledged – it's un-believable."

"Worth all the hard work," Dubois said with a sly smile, "and our ceremony was a masterpiece, an affirmation of our crusade." He placed a clenched fist to his chest. "I truly felt the presence of our

Lord," he said, shaking his head. "I really did; it nearly killed me, but it was worth it. Everyone felt it, I know everyone felt the power."

"Absolutely," the Father agreed. "We all did, it was mind blowing, an incredible revelation...I have never witnessed anything like that in my life."

Dubois smiled again. "The perfect conditions for a long-awaited celebration," he said, "but way, way too long to wait..."

CHAPTER 48

A Downward Spiral

By the time Tate's entourage arrived at the ranch, the widow Higham's state of health had seriously deteriorated. Albeit usually a fit sprightly sixty-four-year-old, the effects of the harsh treatment had taken its toll. Her wrists were raw, she was short of breath, the ache in her head was unbearable. As her condition steadily worsened, she lost the will to protest.

"Looks like she's going to die," Tyler remarked as he stuck his head round the door.

"If she does," the man by the bed replied, "it'll save me a job."

The ranch was another of The Divinity's property gems. Located in Arizona's sparsely populated western desert, it was straight out of a Hollywood movie set. The main house, set in an ornately landscaped oasis, was reached by a never-ending drive that wended its way from the desolate highway across acres of arid farmland. And, like all real estate owned and used by the organisation, it was well secured.

Moments after the lead vehicle drew up outside the ranch-house, Tate was storming up the front steps. He double-stepped the entire flight, barged through the doors and accosted the first person he encountered.

"Where's Tyler?" he roared at a smartly attired man in the hallway. "I need to see him now."

"Yes, sir, Mr Tate," came the instant reply.

As the man raced off, the Security Chief turned back to face a large bay window and stood studying the figures milling around the line of dust covered cars in the parking area. Finally focusing on the last vehicle in the line, he saw the forlorn figure of his assistant emerge and suddenly felt a faint twinge of pity.

"Oh, sweet little Clayton," he muttered to himself. "You poor boy…if only you weren't so goddam edible."

Suddenly his depraved thoughts were interrupted by another handsome male; a flustered Dan Tyler was scurrying toward him. Tate turned from the window.

"Mr Tate," Tyler said loudly. "You've made excellent time."

The Security Chief grimaced. "Time is precious," he said. "So, we need to be quick."

"Absolutely, sir," the underling replied. "Please follow me."

With that, Tyler turned smartly on his heels and led his boss down the hallway toward the rear of the building. Tate was keen for an update. "Has the woman said anything new?" he asked. "Any sign of a confession?"

"Nothing, sir. In fact, she's stopped talking completely."

"Meddling bitch! Why the hell did she have to get involved in the first place?"

"No idea, sir," Tyler replied. "But she did."

"I still can't believe it," the Security Chief said in obvious annoyance. "I should've realised early on she was too good to be true."

"Fooled us all," Tyler said. "Everyone fell for it. I mean, who in their right mind would have suspected she wasn't genuine? Who'd have believed one of our own generous supporters, a sweet old lady to boot, would spy on us?"

"Fucking unreal," Tate said. "Never saw it coming in a million years."

Tyler frowned. "And we thought it was Coleman," he said. "All that shit about late night meetings and not being where he said he'd be…he was his own worst enemy, the self-righteous asshole."

"We should have waited," Tate said slowly. "Dubois was right."

"Well, it's too late now, it's water under the bridge… Now we got this one to sort and this time there's no misunderstandings."

Tyler stopped at a small door in the back wing of the house and knocked gently. Tate stood next to his deputy as they awaited a response.

"Yeah," came a voice from within. "Who is it?"

"Leonard, it's me and I have Mr Tate with me."

The door opened and a tall grey-haired man ushered them into the room. "Good afternoon, Mr Tate," the man said. "We didn't expect to see you so soon."

The Security Chief could not hide his frustration. "Leonard," he snapped, "as I have already explained, we cannot waste time. If the noose is tightening, we need to be quick."

"Of course, sir, I understand," came the man's sombre reply.

Tate remained expressionless, then looked across the room to a bed in the corner. "So, she's finally shut up, has she?" he said with a sneer. "Nothing more to ball about, no more lies."

"Not a word," Leonard replied. "Not a single word for hours now."

"Are you sure she's alive?" Tate asked.

"Only just, I checked ten minutes ago…she looks like shit but she's still breathing."

"Not for much longer," Tate said as he picked up a pillow and headed for the bed.

***

The Security Chief wasn't wrong; the noose was tightening. But it was happening much faster than he could ever have imagined…

The ranch had been on the FBI's radar for months and, when satellite surveillance confirmed the arrival of a high-level delegation at the desert hideaway of The Divinity, an army of federal personnel were immediately mobilised. The take-down raid was authorised good to go and one of the many operational personnel ready to be deployed was special agent Kenneth Dolan.

Dolan had endured months of painstaking undercover work and was now itching to exact revenge on an organisation he knew was evil to its core. The long-serving forty something had put a serious amount of time into his AMS cover and all that patient effort had just started to pay off. After four months on the job as Supervisor Jonny-T, he'd gained unrestricted access to the Mountain House estate and was starting to get an insight into the strange practices of The Divinity organisation.

But then the operation had faltered. Two days before the high-profile fund raiser, the security rota was changed. At first Dolan thought he'd been rumbled, but he hadn't. It was a simple administrative choice by AMS's management that scuppered the plan. He couldn't protest; it would look suspicious. So, when informed by his line manager he was not part of the overnight team he stayed calm, nonchalantly shrugged his shoulders and smiled.

"Whatever you want, boss," he'd said. "So what shift am I on?"

"You're doing Sunday," came the reply. "Day shift, eight to eight, OK?"

Again, Dolan had remained seemingly unfazed. "No problem," he'd said. "Gives me a Saturday night to myself. Reckon I'll go play poker and sink a few beers."

"Yeah, Jonny, you enjoy," the manager had replied, "but don't lose too much and remember to take it easy on the booze."

The rota change was a huge disappointment. The Divinity fund raiser was the event of the year and an inside view could've been a major boost to the investigation, but it wasn't to be. Or was it? The collective thought of the investigation team was it was too good an opportunity to miss. The idea of an unofficial snoop round during the event was put forward by Dolan's support team and it didn't take long for the top brass to make a decision. It was quickly deemed worth the risk and, once approved by the investigation team's Deputy Assistant Director, the one-man covert insertion went ahead.

Agent Dolan knew the lay of the land like the back of his hand; getting in wouldn't be an issue but staying undetected throughout the whole event could present a challenge. What the FBI hadn't bargained for was the involvement of a tenacious hired hand, an outlaw biker no less, who took his role as Event Security Coordinator extremely seriously. By Dolan's own admission, dropping the flashlight was a schoolboy error, but hitting the low hanging tree branch at a full-on run was not only excruciatingly painful but also inexcusable. There was no way back after that. From the point the miss-matched security team found him lying injured in the grounds, the ill-fated sortie was a write-off. When it became obvious the canny biker was far from convinced by his feeble excuses for being there, it was time to leave.

The appearance of the comet was a stroke of luck. That moment of divine intervention, coupled with an intimate knowledge of the estate's layout, gave him the chance for a surprisingly successful escape. His five interrogators were momentarily distracted by the heavenly pyrotechnics. Dolan hadn't hesitated. In the blink of an eye, he'd left the room, turned an immediate right, and shot through the kitchens unnoticed. After a quick glance confirmed the coast was clear, he'd left the temporary respite of the timber clad bin store and high-tailed it across a poorly lit courtyard. Once cloaked in the shadows of the gardens on the west of the estate, he stopped to catch his breath. Peering out from the undergrowth, he again checked for pursuers and - to his relief - still hadn't been followed. He took a deep breath then exhaled slowly. Feeling somewhat calmer, he wiped the blood from his eye and headed for a spot on the service road he was beginning to get to know well.

Apart from a throbbing head and a stumble over the kerb, his fifteen-minute retreat through the grounds to the perimeter fence went better than he could've ever expected. Once back at the well-researched CCTV blind spot, he squeezed through the gap cut in the wire and began the long trek back to the highway and his waiting colleagues.

***

But now, less than 48 hours later, Ken Dolan was in the front seat of a camouflaged Hummer that smashed through the gates of The Divinity's Arizona ranch. His was the lead vehicle in a convoy of two other Bureau hummers that was followed a 100 yards back by a cavalcade of squad. cars. And, as it headed full tilt for the front door of the desert stronghold, the authority's late afternoon charge created a humdinger of a dust storm. But it didn't matter – it only added to the effect. The full-on frontal assault was a deliberate tactic; the investigation's hierarchy had decided enough was enough, the evidence was damming, and the time was right for this so-called religious order to be destroyed.

"Jesus Christ, buddy," Dolan shouted over the roar of engine, "this fucker can move!"

Before the driver could answer, there was a blinding flash to the right of the vehicle and a split second later the behemoth shuddered under the force of an explosion. The blast sent the huge 4X4 veering of the driveway into an adjacent field.

"Mother of God," the driver screamed as he fought to control the wheel, "what the hell was that?"

Agent Dolan didn't answer; he was out cold. With a face full of glass shards, his blood splattered head was now bobbing up and down like a rag doll. As the Hummer ploughed on through the rough ground, the driver shouted into the rear-view mirror, "You guys OK back there. Anyone hurt?"

The five-man team in the rear were shaken but uninjured and quickly acknowledged. "Yeah, man, we're OK," came a gruff voice, "few bumps and grazes but nothing serious."

"Looks like Dolan's hit bad," the driver said. "I'm gonna have to get him back."

As he glanced again at his wounded passenger, the driver shook Dolan's shoulder. "Kenny, can you hear me?" he said. "Just hold on, we'll get you outta here, man; it'll be OK." The slumped figure didn't stir. Quickly returning his right hand to the wheel, the driver steered the mighty Jeep back toward the access road. The wounded Hummer bounced over a small drainage ditch and re-joined the main convoy. But now it was behind the others and, as the roaring 4X4 played catch up, the radio jumped to life. "Romeo Three: what's your status?"

The driver grabbed the mike. "One casualty," he answered quickly. "Dolan's hit…and it doesn't look good."

"Understood, Three, drop your team and head back."

"Affirmative," came the brief reply.

The sound of semi-automatic weapons was now impossible to ignore. The damaged Hummer pulled up behind several small trees when suddenly the area in front of it was raked with gun fire.

"Shit," the driver muttered. "Bad spot for a drop-off."

"Don't sweat it, bro," came a controlled voice from behind. "It's hot, but we got it. OK, boys, on three: one, two, three – go, go, go!" The Hummer's rear door flew open and the five-man weapons team exited in a blur of Kevlar-clad determination and scrambled for the nearest cover.

Although Tate did everything in his powers to ensure The Divinity were cautious and vigilant, today the ranch securities had been breached at such pace and with such ferocity that his ever-secretive organisation was caught cold. By the time CCTV operators could comprehend what was happening, only one of the strategically placed anti-personnel mines was detonated with meaningful effect. With the big deterrents by-passed so easily, the defence of the facility was down to small arms. The ranch weapons cache was significant, but it would rely on the guile and skill of those pulling the triggers to turn the tide, and that was a tall order for even the most ardent of believers.

During a forty-five-minute firefight, sixteen hard-core Divinity faithful and seven Honduran illegals put up the best defence they could. Raining gunfire on the approaching federal forces from every available vantage point took its toll on the FBI onslaught but only slowed the inevitable outcome. The swarming siege army was relentless; it would never be ordered to back off. When the holed-up fanatics were outflanked by two camouflaged SWAT teams moving in cross-country from the east, resistance finally crumbled.

***

In the immediate aftermath of the shoot-out, the bureau's Deputy Assistant Director appeared on scene. As he took a situation report from his senior operator, he couldn't help but be staggered by the facilities.

"Talk me through the set-up here," he said. "I want to know what kind of devious shit these bastards were up to."

"Well, they got it all here, sir," the agent replied. "High tech surveillance across the whole site. We've found a major weapons stash, thousands in cash, and a drug processing plant in an outbuilding that would put the top Mexican cartels to shame."

The Director shook his head. "How the fuck did these religious crazies get so organised?" he asked in genuine amazement.

"Not a clue," came the reply, "but they are." The agent hesitated as he looked at the chaos surrounding them. "This is some set-up, sir, no wonder they didn't want to give it up."

"It's just greed, pure evil greed," the Director said. "Now come on, Ben, show me round, let me see this place for myself."

The DAD and his underling left the throng outside and headed up the front steps. On the veranda they were met by two uniformed officers.

"Sir," the first officer said to the supervisor, "you're needed upstairs. They've just found another body."

But before the supervisor could comment, the Director raised his eyebrows, glanced quickly at his colleague and then back at the officer. "Male or female?" he asked.

"Male, I think," the man replied, "in one of the bedrooms at the back."

As the two FBI men hurried into the house and headed for the stairs, the Director's phone rang. He stopped on the bottom stair to answer. "Go on, what's the latest?" he asked.

"We got an update on Dolan," a voice said. "He's banged up bad, broken ribs, major facial lacerations. Probably gonna lose an eye, but he's going to make it."

"OK. Anything changes let me know."

"Yes, sir."

The Director turned to his expectant colleague. "Dolan's gonna live," he said as he put his phone back in his pocket. "But he won't look pretty."

The lead agent shook his head. "That's one shit deal," he said. "If it wasn't for bad luck that guy would have no luck at all," and with that the two men set off up the stairs.

At the top they came onto a large rectangular landing and started to look for the room they'd been told about. "This way, sir," a squat jeans-clad man beckoned. "It's this one."

They followed the man's direction and entered a large, heavily carpeted bedroom. Once through the door, the men stopped in their tracks. In front of them in the centre of a king size bed lay the prone semi naked figure of a male. The body was stripped from the waist down and was lying on its side, soaking in a glistening crimson wet patch.

"Jesus," the Deputy Director said loudly, "what a fucking mess." He moved two steps forward then crouched down to take a closer look at the body. "If I'm not mistaken," he said, studying the contorted face, "that's Leon Tate." He paused. "What the hell's happened here?"

"Single stab wound to the neck," a voice from behind said. "Eight-inch stiletto letter opener right through the jugular."

The two men spun round to face a plump black man in a white paper coverall. "So, where's the blade?" the lead agent asked quickly

The man frowned and cocked his head toward the bathroom door. "In there with the other one," he said.

The FBI men looked bemused. "What do you mean the other one?" the Director replied.

CHAPTER 49

A Time for Reflection

After breakfast, Williams waited patiently for Monsignor Dubois to check out. He then sat twiddling his thumbs in the lobby for a further twenty-five minutes as The Divinity supremo got side-tracked by phone calls.

It had been agreed that Father Dominic would join his leader on the onward journey to the teaching centre and, as ever, he was keen to make himself useful. "Would you like me to drive?" Williams asked the Monsignor as they finally prepared to leave.

Unlike the organisation's other senior figures, Dubois didn't use a chauffeur or bodyguard. Adamant he didn't need one, he insisted on driving himself wherever it was he was going and, when colleagues questioned him about personal protection, he simply smiled and flashed his omni-present Glock.

"No, Dominic I don't," came his stern reply. "You're too goddam slow. It would be quicker to walk than let you behind the wheel."

***

The Garden of Prayer, at the rear of the Colorado facility, snaked along a small valley as far as the eye could see. With its many criss-crossed trails, the woodland paradise gave its visitors choices galore. The walking routes, as if representing the paths of life itself, had no indicators as to their final destination and were neither waymarked nor straight. Along each one sculptures and water features abounded. Dotted amongst the myriad of trails, nestled in shady enclaves, these thought-provoking artworks were designed to both calm and inspire in equal measure. And, whilst the layout of the lush green utopia appeared unstructured, it was simply an illusion. It had always been Dubois's vision to provide The Divinity faithful with a safe haven, a private sanctuary for devotees to contemplate the meaning and purpose of their lives and it never failed to impress.

Although the well-groomed Divinity leader had never felt the need to question his own purpose, the desire to educate others about theirs was unstoppable. He thrived on imposing his view of the world on everyone and anyone he met. Throughout his life he'd been able to manipulate and indoctrinate at will. It was a talent he'd never been shy of exploiting and, whilst he truly believed his crusade was righteous, the fact he'd built a profitable organisation promoting those beliefs was doubly satisfying. It was wealth and power that made Dubois tick and when the money had started rolling in, so had the opportunities for making more.

He moved into the major leagues after sanctioning the use of a fledgling missionary project as a conduit for a cartel drug shipment. It was a big risk and he knew it. But, despite his apprehension about the 'one-off' deal, Dubois remained calm and it paid off. The drug Lords were impressed; the cover was convincing, the arrangements had gone like clock-work, and from that point on there would be no going back. And, as an unlikely alliance blossomed between the Columbian gangsters and the religious order from Arizona, Dubois's personal standing steadily went stratospheric. Now, ten years on, the extent of The Divinity's humanitarian programme had grown ten-fold and Vincent Dubois found himself head of an organisation that was rich beyond his wildest expectations. With a US property portfolio now running into hundreds of millions of dollars, a lucrative side-line in narcotics, and thousands of generous well-heeled supporters, the franchise was nothing short of a licence to print money.

But Dubois had not come from money. His formative years were spent immersed in a world of deprivation and religious extremism, a world that had warped his young, impressionable mind forever. The descendant of a long line of French Catholic zealots, he'd been brought up in a melting pot of bitter and violent agitation and the damage done was irreparable. Indoctrinated with radicalised ideals, he grew to believe his life's singular calling was to impose the doctrine of the Church of Rome on all he encountered.

As the years passed, the twisted yet erudite young man began to see opportunities in the blinkered world around him. The idea he could promote his own unique brand of sanitised extremism intrigued him. Quickly he grew to believe he could create his own code, his own philosophy of belief, his own movement. He would attract a following, a following he would lead, a flock he could control and guide all the way to his own skewed version of the Promised Land.

And he wasn't wrong. As the flame of determination burned bright, he worked non-stop, honed his ideas, and slowly the seed began to grow. His unending drive never diminished. It only got fiercer and stronger and, as it did, the crusade to establish his own Order became his primary objective. The founding of 'The Divinity of Christ the Redeemer' and its elite leadership cadre, 'The Guardians', was his calling and his destiny, and it was a mission he undertook with such verve and passion that at times those of a certain mind-set found him utterly intoxicating.

Dubois lost no sleep over those that fell by the wayside. Those that didn't fit the profile came and went with regular monotony. It was those he exploited and humiliated yet still stayed the course who intrigued him the most. Why so many weak, pathetic souls allowed themselves to be enslaved and manipulated never ceased to amaze him. To some degree he empathised with those that genuinely came looking for spiritual guidance, but those who were openly seeking total domination he found distasteful. Whilst at times he couldn't hide his contempt towards these people, he was thankful for their existence as it was on the back of these sad, lost individuals that he'd built a business, a successful business, a business that never took a backward step, a business that had gone from strength to strength, year in year out.

But behind the charismatic façade, the man was a controlling psychotic who loathed with fierce intensity. Jews, Blacks and Muslims all came close to the top of his kill list, but they were not his most hated. Surprisingly, the ultimate target of his vitriol was the privileged white Protestant ruling classes. The rich, stuck up, democrats that disrespected and despised those of his beloved Catholic faith, the 'holier than Thou' Presbyterians who thought they knew best, and the vicious Klansmen whose atrocities against his denomination he could never forgive: they were his true enemies.

From a very young age, Dubois had never doubted his destiny. In his eyes, the historical evidence of expectation could not be disputed. His validation was his lineage; the proud military history of his family and its ever-present connection with the Church of Rome were indelibly engrained in his DNA.

At the Colorado teaching centre, the self-proclaimed Monsignor had built a memorial to honour a beloved ancestor. He never failed to pay his respects there whenever he visited. The object of his honour was a soldier, in his eyes both a gladiator and saint. Ravel Dubois, a sergeant in the French army, was the true embodiment of a Warrior of God, a paragon of the Catholic faith, and a man destined to fight the good fight to the end. History recorded that when the tough Parisian was sent with the rest of his unit to join Bonnie Prince Charlie's forces in Scotland, he went with his head held high, and that - during the ensuing Jacobite crusade - the mighty French sergeant and his fellow regulars proved their worth. Standing shoulder to shoulder with the young prince's Highland brigades, the Frenchmen's skill and courage in battle impressed. At Prestonpans, Falkirk, and Sterling, the Prince's Catholic forces showed steely determination as they outthought and outfought the English aggressors.

But, despite the young prince's early successes, his bold rebellion was destined to end in abject failure. On the morning of April 16th, 1746, on a dark grey, sleet streaked moor, east of Inverness, the end came quickly and mercilessly. The historical significance of that day would never be forgotten; the battle of Drumossie Moor, more famously known as Culloden, saw the humiliation of Prince Charlie and the end of the House of Stuart's claim to the throne. It also spelt the end of the Highland Clan system and a way of life that had existed for three hundred years, but for many it was the barbaric slaughter of innocents in the immediate aftermath - the shockwaves of which are still felt today – that would forever haunt.

For those who bore the Dubois name, that final battle on British soil was regarded as a family tragedy. As Charles Edward Stuart's army hastily retreated, Ravel was wounded by musket fire and, like many injured on that fateful day, the Frenchman was left bleeding and alone out on the boggy moor. But as he lay silently praying for his comrades to return and save him, time ran out. He was discovered by a scout from a party of Clansmen loyal to the English and was quickly surrounded by a horde of Argyle militia cut-throats. Sadly, there would be no escape; in a frenzied attack, the Duke's loyal Highlanders stripped the French sergeant, beat him, then hacked him to death. That dark day saw the loss of a much-admired patriarch. As a mark of respect, the Dubois family had acknowledged the significance of the battle ever since.

Young Vincent was fascinated by his famous ancestor whose remarkable, well-documented, military career and macabre end became an obsession he would never be able to shake. Ravel's legendary prowess in battle, his numerous citations for bravery, and his unquestioning faith never failed to impress and astound. The power of the obsession was so strong it prompted the adolescent Dubois to swear he would always honour the spirit of this awe-inspiring crusader. He vowed to continue his fight, a fight against Protestant oppressors, which he felt was as valid today as it had ever been.

***

After dinner, Dominic Williams headed upstairs to his office. As a high-ranking member of the organisation, the much-travelled cleric was a regular visitor to the Colorado facility and enjoyed the privileges of rank whenever he was there. But today he had been especially honoured; today he'd shared not only breakfast with the great man but also an evening meal. Before leaving the table, he'd watched in silent awe as his revered leader strode out of the dining room, crossed the sun deck and disappeared, ghost-like into the gardens.

It was a rare privilege, this chance for a one-on-one. To listen to the Monsignor talk in-depth about the importance of their calling was an experience he would never grow tired of. As a true disciple of the order, Williams knew his place and his role and would be committed to the man and the cause until his dying day. The illegal exploits of the organisation had never fazed him; in his book it was a necessary evil to facilitate the good works they genuinely did undertake, and he'd played a significant part from the very beginning to make that complex contradiction work. Having proved his worth to Dubois over many years, the ever-faithful Father was without doubt the epitome of Divinity allegiance.

During the meal, Dubois had been in good spirits and had again talked about the events of the weekend. He was adamant that for those present it was something they would never forget, a happening that defied the imagination of even the most fertile minds, and it was a view Williams was completely in agreement with. Nine proven disciples had entered the ranks of The Divinity inner circle; nine more young men had made the ultimate commitment to the 'Guardians' cause. They had felt the undeniable power of their leader and witnessed an astonishing sign of approval from the heavens. Then, in front of the assembled brotherhood, they'd spilt their blood and surrendered their flesh to the fire. To all involved they were truly now Inner Sanctum, nine new 'Guardians of the Fifth Meridian', and blessed for all eternity.

As Dominic sat down at his desk he gently shook his head and sighed. To have been an integral part of such an incredible occasion was surely the pinnacle of his ten-year Divinity association. Could it actually get any better? he asked himself as a smug smile of satisfaction spread across his well-fed face, but before he got time to contemplate the answer, the phone rang.

"It's who, sorry?" he asked to the switchboard operator in puzzled tones. "Juan Rodrigo, oh yeah, yeah, that's fine. Put him through."

"Juan, this is a surprise. How can I help you?"

"Señor Williams, I have terrible news," came a distant agitated voice. "The ranch has been shut down."

"Say again, Juan," Williams said quickly. "This is not a good line."

"The ranch, Señor, it has been raided. The Federales, they know everything."

Williams didn't respond; his mind froze. A direct call from Leon Tate's bodyguard was an unusual occurrence. In fact, he couldn't recall it had ever happened before. "Don't fuck around, Juan," he said eventually. "Surely you're mistaken."

"I'm not fucking around, Señor, they are here. A whole army. The compound has been taken, everyone is being held."

"Where the hell are you, then?" the dazed cleric asked.

"I managed to escape, I've made it to the fence…but they're everywhere. There are swat teams, suits, and state troopers all over the place."

Williams felt sick. "Jesus Christ," he said. "Where's Tate?"

"No idea. Last I saw of him he was in the main house. It was chaos."

"Are you on your own?"

"Yes, Father, it's just me. But I'm hurt, I won't get far."

"Dear God…. what the fuck do we do now?"

Juan didn't answer; the sight of two red dots dancing across his chest had suddenly rendered him mute.

***

As the spruce trees swayed in the evening breeze, Vincent Dubois measured his stride to their gentle rhythm. Tonight, alone in the tranquil surroundings of one of his favourite places on earth, he walked and contemplated the future. After a while the trail he'd chosen lead toward a small pond. He felt compelled to stop and look across its gently rippling surface, admiring how the path kissed the water's edge.

"Paved with gold," he said quietly to himself. "For some, the road to salvation is always paved with gold."

Standing motionless at the water's edge The Divinity leader suddenly became aware of an approaching figure. The figure was doing its best to run toward him. It was Dominic Williams. As the chubby cleric got closer, Dubois grew concerned.

"What's the matter?" he shouted. "Why the hurry?"

"Monsignor, you need to come with me," he replied. "We have a major problem."

"What major problem?"

"It's the ranch, sir," the panting cleric blurted. "It's been raided."

***

After twenty-five minutes hammering down Highway 666, the dust-caked Wrangler crossed the Colorado state line. As the 'Welcome' signs disappeared in the haze of the late afternoon sun, Marion felt a twinge of excitement.

"Hey, Rick," she smiled as she pointed to a passing road sign. "We're getting close."

The location details they'd received were difficult to understand but Marion had read the email on Rick's phone several times over and was adamant she could decipher them. The Divinity facility was remote and the publicly available information about its whereabouts was deliberately vague, but Ray had done his best. He'd pieced together Ronnie's inside information and Sarah's last-minute research, then sent over his assumptions, praying it was detailed enough for them to use. It wasn't, but it didn't matter: The Wrangler crew had Marion Armstrong as Chief Navigator and that was their trump card.

"Probably another ten minutes or so on the interstate," she said, with her head in the map, "then it's a left onto this canyon road and follow your nose into the wilderness. After that, well, it's anyone's guess."

"Marion," Babb said, leaning into the gap between the two front seats, "are you sure you know what you're doing?"

"Not one hundred per cent," she replied hesitantly, "but I'll give it a go."

Babb sat back and smiled. "God loves a trier," she said, "and, boy, is my big sister a trier." Suddenly, she leant forward again. "Hey, you know that arch we found yesterday, the one I jumped across? Apparently, it's famous – I read an article on it."

Marion looked up from the road atlas but didn't appear to acknowledge her sister's comment. "Right, Rick," she said, looking at the road ahead, "two miles and we should find an exit...should be signposted Papa Cub Lee National Park – OK?" Rick didn't speak, he simply acknowledged his navigator with a series of faint nods as he stared through the bug splattered windshield, focused on the road ahead.

"Sorry, B," Marion said as she spun back round to look at her sister, "what were you saying?"

Babb, relieved she hadn't been ignored, inched forward. "It's in this little booklet," she said, tapping the tourist guide in her hand, "about that quaint arch we found...according to this it's a landmark of some significance."

"Sounds interesting," Marion replied. "Tell me more."

"Well, apparently it was used by early travellers and missionaries as a short cut to the main trail...but back in those days it was obviously a risky proposition."

"Obviously," Marion said. "Even today with metal plates and safety barriers it's still terrifying," she paused, "and to think you actually did jump it!"

Babb laughed, "Yeah, I did, and guess what it says in here about people who've made the leap?"

"No idea," Marion said. "Go on, so what does it say?"

"Well, there's quite a bit of detail about origins of the trade route, the missionary work and the pioneers who built the chapel, but the bit I liked was that, according to legend, those who crossed the Leap and lived were protected from evil." Babb smiled. "So apparently I'm now immune from the dark side!"

Rick suddenly interrupted. "Is this the one we want?" he asked.

Marion swivelled back to face the road ahead and focused quickly on a looming exit sign. "Yes, Rick, this should be it," she paused as she dropped her gaze and scrutinised the map again. "Yes, take it," she said as she looked back up, "and just follow the National Park signs for now, OK?"

Rick nodded his acknowledgement then started to slow down and indicate. Just as he pulled onto the exit slip, he heard Lucas pipe up from behind him. "How long have I been asleep for?"

Babb turned to face her fellow back seat passenger and smiled. "You've been out for at least three hours," she said, "curled up like a hibernating bear."

Lucas looked sheepish. "Have I been snoring?" he asked.

"A little," she giggled, "but over the road noise you could hardly hear a thing."

As the Jeep slowed to a stop at the bottom of the slip-road Rick looked at his partner via the rear-view mirror. "Welcome back to the land of the living, Sarge. Feeling any better?"

Lucas sat up and rubbed his eyes. "Yeah, actually, I do, thanks… Just can't believe I conked out for so long."

"Yeah, it's been great," Rick said with a mischievous grin, "really nice and peaceful, hasn't it, girls?

Marion and Babb both guffawed at the South African's comment but Lucas wasn't amused. "You're one cheeky bastard, Kruger," he retorted loudly, "but at least you're consistent."

"You know me, Sarge," Rick replied, "always dependable."

The dishevelled Englishman shook his head and tutted. "But moving on to more important matters," he said, "are we anywhere near?"

"I reckon thirty minutes should do it," Marion answered, "depending on whether we can find the right road."

"So, what we gonna do if we actually find this place?" Rick asked.

"Yeah," Babb said. "Do we have a plan?"

Lucas stifled a yawn. "We could do like the man suggested," he replied glibly. "Maybe we simply turn up and book in for some spiritual enlightenment."

CHAPER 50

Freak Show

The CSI spoke animatedly as he led the Director and his underling to the door of the bathroom. "This one," he said, "hanged himself. Looks like he stabbed the older guy then came in here to check out."

The FBI chief peered into the marble tiled en-suite and stared at the lithe form hanging from a belt looped round the shower rail. "This gets weirder and weirder," he said as he looked the pale body up and down. "Any idea who this guy is?"

"Not yet," the CSI replied, "but come take a closer look." He stepped into the room and beckoned the two bureau men to follow him. "We can't touch anything yet," he apologised, "we're still waiting for the full team to arrive…but you're OK to look." The CSI moved cautiously along the side wall then stopped by a double hand basin and turned back to face his visitors. "The blade's in there," he said pointing into the bathtub, "but check out the guy's right shoulder."

The body was naked except for a pair of blood splattered ankle socks and matching white briefs. It was suspended with one foot in the bath and one out and was angled toward the door. Viewing the scene from the far side of the room, the two FBI men looked up at the right shoulder blade. "See it?" the CSI asked. "See the mark? Looks like it's burnt on," he shook his head lightly. "I'd say this poor sonofabitch's been branded."

The Director turned to his colleague, "You ever seen anything like that before, Ben?"

"No. I mean I've seen a lot of ink work, gang tats, piercings and all that shit, but nothing like that, Chief. That looks savage."

In the eerie silence of the bathroom, the three officials stood and studied the strange symbol seared into the porcelain flesh of the young man's back. As they continued to stare at the gruesome apparition dangling before them, the CSI spoke again. "It's some kind of cross," he said. "Wonder what the hell it means?"

"Couldn't begin to guess," the Director replied. "But it's obvious we are dealing with a group of seriously deranged individuals who needed to be brought to account."

Suddenly a voice came from the bedroom, "Chief Sterling… where are you?"

"In here, in the bathroom," the CSI shouted back, then turned to the two FBI men. "Right, gentlemen," he said earnestly, "my team's here and we got work to do. So, if you guys don't mind, can you give us a bit of space."

"Yeah, no problem," the Director said. "I've seen plenty enough."

The CSI led them out of the bathroom and into the bedroom. The large square room was now filled with white suited forensic investigators. The two FBI men made their way through the throng. CSI Chief Cole Sterling had wasted no time in putting his underlings to work.

"Jackson," they heard him bark at a young man with a large camera, "you know the drill: get everything in close-up and then wide, OK?"

Once out on the landing, the assistant Director walked over to a balcony door overlooking the rear of the ranch and gazed out. "You see this, Ben," he said pointing out of the window, "this is what we're up against, all this shit."

"How do you mean, Chief?" the agent asked.

"This sweet, innocent looking landscape, this beautiful ranch hidden away in a remote desert location looking all picture book perfect," he shook his head, "but it's all make-believe, isn't it? It's all just a front. In reality, the place is a drug distribution centre run by psychos masquerading as God-fearing do-gooders. It's fucking madness, it really is. It defies belief."

The Field Supervisor stood shoulder to shoulder with his boss and looked out of the window. "Yeah, it's frightening," he said. "Just think, that bunk house out there was home to a horde of Honduran illegals double shifting a production line that cut enough coke to keep half of Arizona's dealers going."

The Director frowned, rested his head against the glass, and gently sighed. He cleared his throat to reply but was suddenly distracted by the sound of footsteps pounding up the stairs behind him. As the two men spun to see who it was, an out of breath figure appeared at the top stair.

"Sir," the man gasped as he looked straight at the Director. "You need to come with me. They've just found another body."

***

After the untimely death of her husband, Meredith Higham had felt a fresh start in a new State might be a good idea. She had convinced herself that looking for an outlet for her compassionate nature in an unknown environment would be cathartic. But even in her wildest dreams, the kindly widow could never have imagined she would end up working for the Federal Bureau of Investigation.

Three months after her Arizona move, lunch with an old friend led Meredith to a chance meeting with Vincent Dubois. She fell instantly for the piercing blue eyes and magnetic rhetoric and was easily seduced into thinking The Divinity were exactly the kind of organisation that needed her help. She had the money, the time, and the inclination; the causes were worthwhile, he was a dreamboat, and the few supporters she'd met so far appeared divine. It seemed the perfect fit.

But all was not as it appeared. When Senator John Davis, a very dear friend of her late husband's, contacted her to see how she was, Meredith had no inkling there was an ulterior motive. It had been weeks since his last call, so it was wonderful to hear from him and they chatted warmly for what seemed like an age. Towards the end of the call - as she had done on previous occasions - she suggested he should come visit.

"That's one of the reasons I've rung, Meredith," he replied cheerfully. "I'll be in Flag day after tomorrow."

The widow was both pleased and surprised in equal measure. "What wonderful news, John," she purred. "It'll be great to see you. Is Celia coming with you?"

"No, sadly, it's just me," he replied. "Flying visit. You know me, all work and no play, but we will grab a quick get together, I promise." So, with that it was promptly agreed he would finally get to visit her new home for the full tour and a proper catch-up.

Meredith, excited at the prospect of the visit, was eager to impress and, as usual made sure everything was in perfect order for her visitor. The senator was punctual. He was looking a little drawn but was obviously pleased to see her. After a guided tour of the house, they sat in the rear parlour looking out across the perfectly tended garden. She served iced tea and blueberry shortbread while they discussed life in Arizona. "You sure have a beautiful house, Meredith," he'd said, "and what a climate! But don't you miss Oklahoma?"

She eased back in her chair, wrinkled her nose then smiled. "Of course I do, John," she replied. "I'm a Sooner born and will be a Sooner dead, but I still feel it's the right thing to do." She went on to explain that she did hanker after her old home and friends but the new life in Arizona kept her from dwelling too much on Barry's death. "It's not like I've lost contact with anyone," she said. "I mean, people come visit all the time and I talk to Mary Beth and Becca almost every week."

As the conversation ebbed and flowed, she talked about the people she'd met and new projects she was getting involved with. She mentioned The Divinity, how she had come to get to know them and why she felt they were worth supporting. As she further expounded the virtues of their extensive humanitarian work and her ever growing role in the organisation, the Senator held his hand up and smiled.

"Meredith," he leant towards her and his smile subsided, "it's funny you should mention that particular group because there's something I really need to explain to you."

She looked at him quizzically. "You know them?" she asked.

He shook his head. "I don't know them personally...but I know *of* them."

"Sorry, John, I don't follow," she frowned.

"Well, you know my eldest, Ethan, is with the National Security Agency? He's currently part of a taskforce that works alongside the FBI."

"Yes, of course I know Ethan," she smiled. "A lovely young man. But I thought he was an accountant."

"He is, but not quite as you'd imagine," he paused for a sip of iced tea. "Ethan's what's known as a forensic account analyst. It's specialist work, highly classified, and he loves it. But, boy, does he work hard to earn his corn!"

Meredith looked blankly at her visitor. "So, what's the relevance, John?" she asked.

The senator edged a little closer. "Well, a couple of nights ago he came over for dinner. Said he'd been working down in Tucson and wanted to tell me about an on-going investigation he'd got involved with," the senator moved even further forward in his seat and looked Meredith in the eye. "He wanted to warn me that one of the names thrown up by the investigation was a personal friend of mine, the wife of one of my closest friends, a friend who before he passed away asked me to keep a watchful eye on her...and the name Ethan said was mentioned was yours Meredith, your name was included on a long list of others, down in black and white on an official FBI suspect list - Meredith Higham: female/widow/ resident of Flagstaff."

"John, that can't be possible," she said, now totally confused. "There better be a dam good explanation for this because you're starting to scare the hell out of me."

The tale was convoluted but Senator Davis was a master of detail and half an hour later widow Higham was sat shell-shocked in her favourite armchair trying to contemplate what she'd just been told.

"I can't believe it," she'd said repeatedly. "I mean they all seemed so genuine."

But it was all true, every last word, and from that point on Meredith's relationship with Vincent Dubois and his 'The Divinity of Christ the Redeemer' would never be the same again. In reality, the transformation from loyal Divinity supporter to FBI stooge had been a subtle one. It had evolved at a snail's pace over many months, but in the end it became a portal for the investigation team to use in their never-ending quest to glean every scrap of information about their target.

***

It looked like the raid had disturbed a burial team.

The body was face down, half covered in a shallow hollow, and two shovels lay abandoned in the dust at its side.

"Oh, for Christ's sake," the Director winced, "don't tell me it's the Higham woman."

"We think so, sir," a man in a grey flak jacket said, "but we can't be certain yet…we got another forensic squad on its way."

"This shit just gets worse," the FBI chief sneered in obvious disgust. "What's the next surprise going to be?"

The field supervisor didn't answer immediately. He knelt down at the side of the body and stared at the pale, stocking clad legs protruding from the mound of earth. "Wouldn't like to say, sir," he said, "but on this one… I don't think there's any doubt this is gonna be Mrs Higham."

"These motherfuckers don't give a rat's ass about anyone, do they?"

"No, sir," the agent said as he stood up. "When even sweet old ladies get murdered for getting in the way then things don't really get much sicker."

"Jesus, Ben, I wish to God we'd never got her involved," the Director said. "She had friends in high places. She'd been warned off. She didn't have to help, did she?"

"No, sir, she didn't," he answered, "but she made it very clear she wanted to."

"I know she did...and without her intel all this probably wouldn't have happened as quickly as it has, would it?"

"Absolutely right, sir," came the reply he wanted to hear. "She did a great job."

The Director looked down at his dust covered shoes. "Tate getting knifed by some toy boy bitch is a bonus in my book," he said, "and taking this place down is nothing short of a triumph." He surveyed the ranch, which was now host to dozens of scurrying groups of flak-jacketed officers. "Banging up twenty plus gun toting religious lunatics is also a great result...but this," he turned back and pointed at the grave, "the murder of a kindly old lady, is a tragedy, an absolute fucking tragedy."

***

Standing in the arid swirling dust of the Arizonan desert, the FBI men felt sick about the collateral damage from their ranch raid. But they were only two of hundreds of personnel involved in the operation imaginatively code named 'Stormbringer'. The multi-agency co-ordinated strike was the culmination of eighteen months' worth of extraordinarily complex investigation work and was now playing out in several locations around the world.

Holed up back at Stormbringer Command in the Netherlands, Virgil Koeman and his team were quietly confident the operation was progressing as hoped. In their expansive fifth floor office, the Europol agents were in a frenzy of activity. Functioning on little more than coffee and adrenalin, every individual was focused on playing their part in the operation. Its ultimate aim was to dismantle an intricate drug supply network that stretched from the jungles of Columbia via Honduras to the streets of the US and Western Europe. So far, progress was good.

As he stood staring at a bank of monitors above his head, the investigation's bespectacled leader studied the satellite images on each screen in turn. They showed individual strike areas: Arizona, Utah, Colorado, the Honduran port of 'La Ceiba', and Southern Spain.

A dark-haired female agent, sat with two colleagues to his right, looked up. "The Cadiz Team have just left the Port Authority building, sir," she said quickly. "Two containers impounded, and eight employees taken into custody for questioning."

"Link up with Spanish police, OK?" he asked, not looking at her, his eyes glued to the screen above him.

"Slight issue with the level of resources," she replied, "but it hasn't caused a problem."

"OK, fine," he quickly turned to look behind him. "Rolf, get me an update on the Mesa progress will you, please, then patch me into FBI Control." He removed his glasses and cleaned the lens with a tissue. As he held them up to the light to check they were clear, he asked, "Any sign of Dubois?"

The tall, broad-shouldered man he was talking to remained expressionless. "Nothing at the moment, boss," he said. "But we're not finished yet, are we?"

Koeman carefully put his glasses back on. "You are absolutely right, Rolf," he said smiling, "we are most definitely not finished yet."

***

Since pulling off the interstate, the sound of the wind rush had decreased and now, as Rick eased the gutsy 4X4 along a winding stretch of tree lined black top, the sound of bird chatter could be heard.

"Dear Lord, do you hear that," Babb said. "Isn't that just wonderful"

"It sure is," Marion replied. "I love Colorado; it's such a beautiful state...but I don't think people appreciate it the way they should."

Rick turned quickly to look at his navigator. "I think it's gorgeous," he said before asking, "am I just sticking on this road for the time being?"

"Yes, Rick, we're fine for a while," she replied with a confident smile, "and don't worry, I'll give you plenty of notice when I think we need to turn."

The South African smiled back. "You listening back there, Roxy?" he shouted over his shoulder. "This is how a proper navigator behaves."

Lucas didn't answer. He just pulled a face at the rear-view mirror then went back to admiring the lush green scenery passing by. Moments later, as the Jeep passed a National Park information sign, Lucas's phone started to vibrate. As he attempted to retrieve it from his inside jacket pocket, the zip jammed. "Oh, for Christ's sake," he cursed, "of all the bastard times for that to happen."

Babb looked at him and frowned. "What's the matter," she said. "Why all the cussing?"

"Sorry for the language," he replied tugging at his jacket. "It's just that the zip's stuck and I can't get my phone out."

Just as he finished his explanation, the phone stopped vibrating. "Now it's gone off. Wouldn't you bloody know it."

"Come here," she said leaning over to him. "Let me help you." Babb slid her sunglasses onto her head, inched up the seat then hooked her finger into the pocket, and, with one deft tug, the zip gave. "There you go," she said grinning. "Easy as pie."

"I'm saying nothing," Lucas laughed, "except thank you." Yet again impressed by Babb's never-ending skill set, he retrieved the phone from his pocket and checked the screen. In the late afternoon sunshine, the display was hard to see, so on went his battered reading glasses, then he held the phone down in the shade between his legs. "It was Gerry," he said. "Probably looking for another update."

"Mine'll go in a second," Rick said as he handed his mobile over his shoulder to Lucas. "You answer it; I'm driving."

No sooner had Rick passed the phone back than it started to ring. "You guessed right," Lucas said, squinting at the screen, "Grumpy's trying again."

CHAPTER 51

A Long Time Coming

As they raced back toward the building, the men of The Divinity knew the clock was against them. How the situation had reached critical without anyone realising was a mystery and now, as their world went into meltdown, they had to act fast.

"Jesus Christ, Dominic," Dubois shouted over his shoulder at the lumbering figure behind, "get a move on, will you."

But the sweat drenched Father couldn't keep up. Whilst Dubois's obsessive vanity kept him in shape, Dominic Williams had let the excesses of success take its toll. At five eleven and two hundred plus pounds, the cleric looked far from the athletic figure his leader cut, and now the difference couldn't be more obvious.

"I can't," he panted. "I'll have to stop…I'm going to have a heart attack."

"I wouldn't if I were you," the Monsignor snarled. "If they've hit the ranch, then this place will be next."

"I know, I know," the cleric said as he slumped down on a bench. "You go. I'll stay and tidy up."

The Divinity as an organisation had always been careful. Dubois and Co. went to extreme lengths to maintain privacy and utilised every trick in the book to keep the Order's caring, humanitarian image as authentic as possible. But even the best in the business could attract unwanted attention. There had been occasional rumours from the outreach projects about individuals who were under suspicion of being informers, but nothing was ever proven and, as a precaution, the suspects had always been swiftly relieved of their duties. Also, over the years there'd been probes by government agencies, particularly from the Treasury. Whilst investigations into the organisation's financial standing had become a regular occurrence, they'd never actually come to anything. Their army of lawyers and accountants were good at their jobs and always earned their fat retainers by proving time and time again that 'The Divinity of Christ the Redeemer' was simply a compassionate, well-supported charity with only the interests of those less fortunate at its heart.

But more recently the van stop in Tucson had caused increased interest from the authorities. Then the circumstances surrounding Coleman's death had been a PR disaster. Finally, hot on the heels of those two debacles, to discover the Higham woman was actually the problem had been nothing short of humiliating. But still, despite this catalogue of incidents, a full-blown raid by federal agencies had never been on the cards. It was a bolt out of the blue that prompted one solitary question: 'How the hell had it so suddenly come to this?

For now, Dubois wouldn't dwell on the answer, neither would he waste time waiting for the pot-bellied cleric. Without a second thought, he left his underling on the bench to get his breath back and continued on alone.

Five minutes later he reached the steps leading back to the sundeck and stopped. What if they're already here? he asked himself as he gazed up the flight of wooden steps. What if the building's surrounded by the feds right now?"

After a few seconds of deliberation, the cult supremo decided to abandon the stairs and opted to stay low level and head for the centre's basement. Time was precious, so after a glance behind confirmed he was still alone, he turned sharp right and sprinted off along the timber edged pathway.

The single steel door was hardly visible through the tangle of vines, but Dubois knew it was there. It had been designed originally as a fire exit, but plans had changed during the build. As he fought through the vegetation to the right of the door, he was glad it had. Within seconds the Monsignor found what he was looking for. The keypad was small and well camouflaged. He flicked the protective cover open deftly and punched in a five-digit code. After a faint mechanical whir, the door started to open. As it slowly slid to the left he peered inside. Calming his breathing to listen for signs of intruders, he let his eyes adjust to the dimly lit interior. The corridor leading away from the door was illuminated by a long series of strip lights fixed to the ceiling. The lights' lack-lustre glow reflected in patches along bare concrete walls and was mirrored in the shine of the vinyl floor, but inside nothing moved. Dubois stayed motionless as he stared down the narrow passageway then smiled - apart from the faint hum of a ventilation system, it was empty and quiet.

Relieved, he stepped inside and closed the door. Once the heavy door clunked shut, he started to follow the strip lights toward the basements core. The air moved slowly but was refreshingly cool and by the time Dubois reached the end of the corridor the sweat had run cold on his back. He stopped in the shadow cast by the last column and peered ahead. Thankfully the car park was as deserted as it had sounded - and there, taking pride of place in a line of gleaming vehicles, was his black Mercedes.

As he made his way toward the coupe, he noticed a faint red glow in the distance and in the half-light it was hard to decipher where it was coming from. As he got closer, he could make out a small circular light on the far wall which, as he peered at it, began to flash for a few seconds before it changed to green. The penny dropped: this was the main door control system to the basement. Red indicated the roller shutter was closed. When it flashed, it was about to open. Solid green signalled it was opening.

As soon as Dubois saw daylight creeping in at the far end, he ducked behind his car. With no idea if it was friend or foe he stayed hidden. Quickly he discovered it was neither. A small blue van drove into view. He shook his head. "Just when you want an H-VAC engineer," he said under his breath, "as if by magic, one arrives."

The compact VW eased up in an empty space and cut its engine. The driver remained inside for several seconds then got out and slowly walked to the rear of the vehicle. The man placed the clipboard he'd been studying on the roof, then stood and stretched his back. After a pensive look around, he opened the back doors and leant inside. As the man started to rummage around, Dubois checked to make sure he was on his own. There was no obvious sign of a colleague in tow. The Monsignor made his move. "You OK there?" he asked as he approached the van. "You here to fix the fans?"

The slim, boiler-suited engineer jumped at Dubois's unexpected appearance. "Jesus, buddy," he said. "Where the hell were you hiding?"

"Sorry," the monsignor feigned. "I was just fetching something from my car...didn't mean to spook you."

The man relaxed a little and tried to smile. "Like a ghost from the shadows," he said, "you came out of nowhere," the man paused for a moment. He took a deep breath, then exhaled sharply as he looked over at the plant room. "Yeah, emergency call out. I'm here to fix one of the AC units."

"Good," Dubois said. "Any problems getting in?"

"A little," the man answered. "but I suppose it's always like that, isn't it?"

Dubois nodded but said nothing. He then stepped forward, took a quick glance behind and, without warning, swung a ferocious punch at the HV engineer. The rapier-like upper cut caught the unsuspecting technician square under the chin and the force of the blow knocked him clean off his feet. As he went sprawling across the concrete floor, Dubois followed in for the kill, but he had nothing more to do; the poor unfortunate would be out for a lot longer than your average ten count.

***

Lucas was right: Gerry simply wanted an update. Another five hours had gone by and that was as long as the impatient Irish grouch was willing to wait.

"You're where?" he asked after Lucas confirmed their location. "Is that close?"

"Yeah, it is," Lucas replied as politely as he could. "By our reckoning we're half an hour away at the most."

"I take it Rick's driving," the Director barked, "so why didn't you answer your phone when I rang?"

"Mine's dead," Lucas lied. "Flat as a witch's tit, needs charging."

"Well, I don't care how you do it," he said, "but make sure you ring me the second you've found this place, OK?"

"Yes, boss, we get the message

"And if the book's there, take it. Don't hesitate. Remember the law's on your side."

"Yebo," Lucas replied, mimicking Kruger's accent perfectly.

"Hurt a third party, mind, and it will be a whole different ball game. You be discreet, you understand me?"

"Yebo."

"Don't get cute, Roxby!" Then the line went dead.

During the call Babb had watched Lucas closely and, as she listened, she couldn't help but feel his frustration. But in the front seats Marion and Rick were none the wiser. All they could hear were brief garbled snippets of a one-sided conversation and, as soon as he'd rung off, they wanted feedback.

"Well, Sarge," Rick said loudly, "what'd he say?"

Lucas leant back in his seat and shook his head. "I tell you, at times that man drives me crazy. It's always push, push, push. And he's such a grumpy bastard. No wonder I never want to ring him, it's just too much like hard work."

Rick looked at his partner in the rear-view mirror. "Never happy, is he?" he said. "But don't worry, he's five thousand miles away. Next time, just don't answer."

Lucas grinned, leant forward and patted the South African's shoulder. "OK, big man," he said, "that's exactly what I'll do."

Babb smiled sympathetically at the grizzled Englishman. "Your boss sounds like a proper ogre," she said. "Is he really that bad?"

"Well, in reality we've got two bosses," Lucas explained. "We've got our Operations Director Gerry, that's the growly bastard who's just been on the phone, the one that barks at you during every conversation you have with him," he stopped as he thought about his next statement, "and then we've got our Chief Exec, Ray," he said, "and Ray, well, he's almost the opposite, he sort of tries to charm you."

Marion turned round and stuck her head between the seats. "You mean like a good cop/bad cop kind of set up?"

Lucas laughed. "Well, yeah, I suppose so," he said. "But whatever it is, it works. They're a pretty formidable double act."

"Like us, eh, Sarge?" Rick piped up from the front. "Another dynamic duo."

Lucas started to really laugh. "Yeah, Ricky, just like us," he said. "Just a lot better paid."

As Marion turned back to check on progress, something on the roadside caught her attention. "Hold on, Rick," she said quickly, "we just passed a marker."

Rick slowed up. "What marker? I didn't see a thing. You want me to go back?"

"Yes," she said. "I think we need to."

Rick dutifully slowed the Wrangler to a stop, checked his mirrors, and executed a perfect tyre squealing 'U' turn.

"Whoa, Ricky," Lucas shouted. "Where the hell we going?"

Marion stuck her head through the seats again to explain the change of direction to the backseat occupants. "We're just going back a couple hundred yards," she said. "I'm sure I just saw some sort of signpost. We need to take a look."

Lucas and Babb nodded their understanding, then started to scour the roadside. "There it is," Marion said, almost taking Rick's eye out as she pointed across to the opposite verge. "The timber post by the rocks, see it?"

"Yeah, got it. Hold on." With that, he executed an even more tyre shredding manoeuvre and seconds later, as the Jeep pulled up in a dust cloud at the side of the road, he turned to Marion. "Close enough?" he asked.

She smiled sweetly. "Perfect, Rick," she said. "Very nicely done."

They were now only feet from the wooden marker and, as she was closest, Marion was out of the passenger door in a flash. "Check this out," she shouted as she stood next to the innocuous looking post. "It's got a Chi-Rho cross carved in it with an arrow and 2M underneath it."

"What the hell does that mean?" Lucas said. "Does it help us?"

Before Marion could answer, Rick joined her for a closer look. "Let's have a look," he said as he knelt down by the post. After running his finger over the carving, he looked back at the Jeep. "Hey, Rox," he said. "It's like the one we saw in Mesa."

Lucas raised an eyebrow. "Like what one we saw in Mesa?"

"We saw this symbol," Rick said, "on the door intercom in Mesa, looks like a P stuck over an X?"

Marion smiled. "Like I just said, it's a Chi-Rho cross. It's an early Christian symbol, been popular since the time of Constantine."

"Are we talking Roman emperors?" Rick enquired.

"Absolutely right, Mr Kruger. We're talking 310 A.D, so this is real ancient symbolism, and it's the stuff of legend. Constantine might have made it mainstream, but it had existed secretly for hundreds of years before he championed it."

"Championed it," he said. "In what way?"

"Well, the story – and of course, there are various versions - goes that the symbol came to him via prayer. Apparently he'd asked for a sign of divine protection to put on his soldiers' shields. Then he saw this cross appear in the sky," she stopped and looked round at the three faces staring at her. It was obvious they were intrigued so she continued, "He took it as a direct message from God and from that point on adopted it as his universal emblem." She paused and pulled a face. "It worked. Only days later he fought the Battle of Milvain Bridge while flying the Chi-Rho and was victorious."

"And now? Why a symbol for The Divinity?" Rick asked.

"Well, over time it became regarded as a Catholic emblem. But nowadays there are those who feel it has gone further than that. Some think it is linked with extremist views, a badge for modern Catholic elitism."

"That makes sense," Lucas grinned. "The Divinity adopting a symbol of religious extremism is a perfect fit!"

"It is," she said. "So, let's get going," she pointed at the sign. "As it says, Rick, straight ahead for two miles then we'll come to another marker – OK?"

Rick looked at her in puzzlement. "It's that simple, is it?" he asked. "You're saying that post gives directions to this teaching facility?"

"That's what I'm saying," she answered. Then she hopped into the passenger seat and smiled. "In fact, I'm one hundred per cent positive it does, so let's get a move on."

Lucas didn't attempt to question her, he simply beckoned Rick to get back in the Jeep and drive. "Come on, Ricky," he said. "Don't argue… just do as the lady says, will you." With that, the South African jumped back behind the wheel, turned the ignition, checked his mirrors then with a squeal of rubber launched the Wrangler up the road on a quest to find the next odd-ball marker post.

After three hundred yards of deserted Colorado black top, Lucas suddenly sat bolt upright. "I know where else I've seen it," he announced, "that bloody cross thing! He ran a hand through his hair and moved forward in his seat. "There was a small one by the chapel. It was etched in the side of that massive boulder at the top of those steps."

"You sure?" Rick asked. "I didn't see anything."

"Listen, Kruger," Lucas grinned, "at times you're so wrapped up in your own little world that you wouldn't notice a fifty rand note stuffed up your left nostril, so I wouldn't worry about it."

CHAPTER 52

Another Hidden Gem

The two miles went by in a flash. No sooner had Rick hit his cruising speed than Marion was giving orders for him to slow down.

"Whoa, Rick," she shouted. "Can we ease off the gas a little, please. I'm sure we're close."

"OK, OK," he said. "I just don't want to waste time that's all."

"There's no chance of your wasting time," she laughed. "but there's a good chance you'll overshoot the mark." Rick knew she was right and, as he slowed on the approach to a sweeping right hand bend, Babb leant out to scour the roadside. "Look, Marion," she shouted, "over there…looks like another one."

Sure enough, up ahead nestled into the overgrown foliage at the side of the road was another small circular post. "Well spotted, B," Marion said. "Another pit-stop, please, driver."

Rick checked his mirrors and dutifully obliged. Again, Marion exited the Jeep like a whirlwind and headed for the timber post. The marker was exactly the same as the previous one except for the inscription below the cross. "Right," she said after a quick inspection, "according to this we're turning left in half a mile, OK?"

"Whatever you say," Rick grinned. "You're the navigator."

This time Rick took it slow from the off. The Jeep rumbled along with all four occupants looking eagerly ahead for an approaching turn. As they scanned the left-hand side of the road they spotted a break in the trees.

"Is that it?" The South African asked as he peered through the bug splattered wind shield. "Doesn't look like much."

Marion put her hand lightly on his right arm. "I don't think this is what we're looking for," she replied, "but we better check it out just in case."

Rick parked the Jeep up on the verge opposite what looked like a forest track. This time everyone decided to get out. Marion and Rick exited first and crossed quickly to the other side. For Lucas and Babb getting out of the rear of the two-door 4X4 was not an easy task. But with a little help from each other and some assistance from the Wrangler's roll bar both eventually stood up and stretched. "My God, that's a tight fit," Lucas said, "my legs have bloody seized up."

"Cosier than a goffer's nest in winter," Babb grinned. "Good job we're both skinny."

Lucas wasn't convinced by her analogy but nodded anyway, then clambered over the side. Once on terra firma, he turned to offer his back seat companion some assistance. "Grab my hand," he said, "And jump down."

Babb didn't hesitate; she took hold of his out-stretched hand and, with one deft leap, landed softly on the dry gravel next to him. "Thanks," she said. "You're a gent."

As Lucas tried to shake his legs back to life he looked across the road at the non-descript entrance. It was deserted. Marion and Rick had disappeared from view. "You'd think they'd bloody wait for us, wouldn't you?" he said. "I mean it's not as if we're not interested, is it?"

Babb laughed. "They're obviously keen," she said. "Or maybe we're just slow."

As Lucas checked for signs of traffic, something caught his eye. "Babb," he whispered, "look up to your right, in the trees at the side of the track…"

Babb lifted her head and, as directed, started to scan the foliage. "What am I looking for?" she asked.

"Cameras," Lucas said. "CCTV cameras."

Just as he finished speaking, Rick appeared by the entrance. "Come and look at this," he shouted across the road. "It's weird." Lucas and Babb glanced briefly at each other then raced across the road toward the beckoning South African.

"Keep it down, will you Ricky," Lucas said as he got closer to his colleague. "We're being watched; they've got cameras in the trees."

Rick glanced up. "I'm not surprised," he said, "and when you see what's up here you'll understand why."

Quickly, the South African led the way back up the access track and, as they ventured along it, things began to change. From the roadside the innocuous entrance looked little used and simply appeared to be a woodland access. But all wasn't as it seemed. After 75 yards the stone track abruptly widened and turned to blacktop, and from that point on there was a smart single lane carriageway. The private road was edged with granite kerbs, the vegetation was neatly trimmed back along both sides and ornate streetlights were positioned at regular intervals along its full length.

As Rick, Lucas and Babb stood in the middle of the road inspecting the junction of the gravel and the asphalt, Marion came walking towards them. "This has got to be the place," she said, gesticulating over her shoulder. "From up there by the bend you can just make out a building, but it seems quiet."

"So, what we doing, then?" Babb asked. "Can't just stand here, can we?" Lucas looked between Rick and Marion but, before any of them answered, the group was distracted by an approaching vehicle. "Oh, shit," he said under his breath. "We've been rumbled."

"What do you expect?" Rick snarled. "They've probably been watching us on CCTV for ten minutes."

As the vehicle got closer it showed no signs of slowing.

"What the hell's he doing?" Rick yelled. Very quickly it became obvious the van was not intending to stop.

"Run," Lucas shouted, grabbing Marion's arm and dragging her to the side of the road. At the same time as Lucas and Marion dove for cover, Babb ran headlong into a bush and Rick flattened himself against a tree. They got out of the way just in time; the small blue VW wasn't stopping for anybody. And as it flashed past like a bullet train, it passed from blacktop to gravel and threw up a dust cloud that swirled in its wake all the way down to the main road.

"Jesus Christ," Lucas exclaimed as he stepped back onto the roadway. "What's his bastard problem?"

"I thought we were about to get pulled," Rick said. "I wasn't expecting to get flattened."

As the four stood and watched the speeding van disappear from view, Babb spoke up. "If I didn't know better," she said, "I'd guess that guy was in a hurry to get home."

"Did you get a look at the driver?" Marion asked. "Anyone we know?"

Lucas laughed. "Anyone we know?" he repeated with an obvious sarcastic overtone. "It said Cool Flow Engineering on the side, so I doubt it."

"Oh, sorry," she replied in similar tones. "I didn't read the livery. I was too busy trying not to get killed."

"Look, gang," Rick interrupted their little spat. "Whoever it was wasn't interested in us, so let's get the Jeep and pay this place a proper visit. And I'd quite like to get there before dark."

"OK by me," Marion replied, "but what's our story?"

Lucas gazed thoughtfully down the track, watching the dust settle in the fading light of evening. He scratched his head. "You girls take the lead," he said. "Say a friend told you about the organisation and you were passing by, so you thought you'd drop in and collect a leaflet."

There was silence for a few seconds, then Rick spoke. "That sounds lame, Sarge," he said. "Who says they'll have information leaflets to hand?"

"OK, then," Lucas replied. "Give us an alternative."

No one commented. The eclectic foursome just stood rocking on their heels, contemplating their predicament. After several seconds of silence, Rick shuffled over to Lucas and grabbed his shoulder. "You know what, Sarge," he said. "Maybe it's time for us to play the wild card."

Lucas turned and looked at his partner with a quizzical scowl. "And what exactly is the wild card, Ricky?" he asked. "Is there something you're not telling me?"

"No…what I'm saying is Babb is our wild card," he grinned. "She's the only one unknown to them, so maybe we try it - let her go in on her own, ask for some general information and see how it pans out."

"Alright," Lucas said relaxing his scowl. "In lieu of anything better I suppose that'll have to do!"

***

As the Jeep edged along the blacktop, the streetlights came to life. Gradually the illumination increased and thirty seconds later the full length of the road was bathed in an eerie amber glow.

"Very classy," Lucas said admiringly. "These characters don't spare any expense do they?"

Rick drove cautiously. As their eyes acclimatised to the lights, all four stared expectantly ahead, then, as the rumbling 4X4 rounded a bend, the building came into view.

"Another fine example of classic religious architecture," Lucas mocked.

Rick was quick to understand. "I know," he said quietly. "They're not exactly into the churchy look are they?"

As with all Divinity properties, the teaching facility was luxurious. It was tall, sleek, and, like the Mesa HQ, smacked of money. The building was set back from a large parking area. The front facade was a mix of intricate timber mosaic and black glass and a large sign on the car park approach left the foursome in no doubt they'd found what they were looking for. It read: The Divinity of Christ the Redeemer Welcomes You. Our Lord and His Teachings Are a Gift and This Sanctuary Is Dedicated to The Education of Our Fellowship in His Holy Name.

"What a load of shit," Rick said as he pointed to the sign, "but at least we know we're in the right place."

The parking area was virtually empty but, despite the deserted appearance, the cautious South African chose to park up in the shadows as far from the building as possible. "Don't want to make our arrival too obvious," he said with an apprehensive smile.

Marion was first to comment. "Doesn't look like there's too many people home. Maybe it's closed."

"Could be," Lucas replied, "but that might suit, if you get what I'm thinking."

In preparation for the task ahead, Babb reached for her rucksack and rummaged around inside. Seconds later she pulled out a small mirror and checked her appearance. "Can't say I look my best," she grimaced, "but it'll have to do." She tapped Marion on the shoulder, "Come on, sis, let me outta this thing, will you - I've got work to do."

Marion got out of the Jeep, took a moment to straighten her clothing, then pulled the seat forward for her sister. "Stay safe, B," she whispered as she gave her a hug. "Don't do anything foolish."

Babb smiled but said nothing, then hitched on her backpack and set off across the car park towards the entrance. As Marion stood and watched her stride away she looked pensive. "Suppose all we can do now is sit and wait," she said. "She'll be OK, won't she?"

"She'll be fine, and anyway, she's got us three for back up, hasn't she?"

Lucas was already out of the Jeep, stretching his arms above his head. "I don't know how long this is going to take, but I'm going for a quick scout round while we're waiting."

"Want me to come along?" Rick asked.

"No, you stay here with Marion and watch the front," he said. "I won't be long," and with that he slipped silently into the surrounding darkness.

***

As Babb closed on the building, she peered eagerly through the glass frontage. Inside lights were blazing brightly, doors were open, but there was no obvious sign of life. Thankfully, as the light outside had faded, the illumination inside ensured a perfect view of the lobby layout. Babb identified a large reception desk. Like everything else inside, it was unattended, but she decided it was a good starting point. Mind made up, she took a deep breath and pushed firmly on the entrance door. Despite its heavy appearance, it opened easily. Fooled by this misleading impression, she had pushed it too hard and stumbled in. Embarrassed by her undignified entrance, she looked round nervously to see if she'd been seen. She hadn't. The lobby was large, with high vaulted ceilings and an array of neatly clustered seating areas, but it was deserted. Relieved, she made a bee line for the reception desk, stopped in front of it then turned back to face the door. She was impressed. It was a remarkable space and, as she stood admiring the intricate timber panelling overhead, she heard a muffled female voice behind her.

"If you could just be patient," it said. "I'll be with you in just a minute."

Babb turned back round and realised the voice was emanating from a door she guessed lead to some type of office. "Yeah, that's fine," she replied. "No rush."

As she stood nervously waiting for the owner of the voice to appear, she had a sudden sense of déja vu. Looking across the reception area to a side annexe she noticed what looked like a museum display. Along the length of its back wall were glass cabinets that bore an uncanny resemblance to the public exhibition area Marion had once proudly shown her in Phoenix's city library. Unable to contain her curiosity and with still no sign of the woman, she walked across to take a look. As she stood in front of the wall, she knew she was right. It was a display and, whilst it didn't contain anything she was familiar with, she thought it an exquisitely laid out presentation.

"Hello," a voice suddenly trilled from behind, "apologies for your wait, but I'm done now...so how can I help you?"

Surprised, Babb spun away from the cabinets and looked toward the desk. The woman, pallid, thin and sunken eyed, was not a pretty sight, but still Babb managed a smile. "Oh, hi, yes," she said as she made her way back toward the reception area, "I'm here to find out about the possibility of joining the organisation." She stopped several feet short of the counter and tried desperately to maintain her jaunty pretence. "Is there anyone here I can talk to?"

The woman didn't acknowledge the question at all, she simply picked up the cordless phone in front of her and started to dial. "Can someone see me now?" Babb asked hopefully. "That would be wonderful."

The walking cadaver glanced up briefly, held the phone to her ear, then turned and walked calmly back into the office and shut the door. Babb was aghast. What kind of reception school did she go to? she asked herself. Who in their right mind treats visitors like that?

"Excuse me," she called loudly toward the door. "Do you mind not being so rude."

But the door remained shut and the lobby deathly silent. Suddenly, there was a voice over the tannoy. "Maybe I can help," it said. "Please clarify who you are why you are here?"

Babb was baffled. Had she heard right? Had she just been asked a direct question by a tannoy system? Unnerved, she looked around for signs of the source, but nothing was obvious. The place was empty.

"I need an answer," the voice snarled impatiently. "What is your business here?" Realising they'd make a huge tactical mistake, Babb was halfway to the exit when a series of metallic sounds startled her. Thud, thud, thud. The unmistakeable sound of locking doors echoed round the spacious lobby. Her heart sank. Undeterred she grabbed the push bar handle and yanked on it as hard as possible. But the door wouldn't budge. Now in panic mode, she banged on the glass and screamed, "Let me out of here!"

But the only response was an ominous whirring noise from above. Looking up at the ceiling, she felt her stomach tighten. "Oh God, no," she whimpered as the steel security shutter started to descend. "Please, please don't do that."

Realising it was too late for escape she stepped away from the door and reached for her phone.

"I wouldn't," the voice said, "Or that will be the last call you ever make."

***

Out front, settled in the Wrangler, Rick and Marion waited patiently in the shadows. Both were focused nervously on the main entrance and both were on the lookout for signs of trouble. "Oh, shit," Rick said as he saw a silhouette banging on the glass. "Looks like we've gotta problem."

Marion sat bolt upright. "That's Babb," she said. "Why can't she just open the door?"

Rick reached for his phone. "Shit - she's been rumbled. Better let Roxy know," he said as he began to text his partner. "Then we move, OK?"

Marion felt sick. "What do we do?" she asked. "Why's this happening?"

"Don't panic," he replied as he attempted a reassuring smile that didn't come off. "It might not be as bad as it looks." He shoved open his door and clambered out. "Come on," he said, pointing toward the building, "we better go save your sister."

CHAPTER 53

A Word to the Wise

If Roxby and Kruger could have heard Gerry's honeyed tones, they'd have been lost for words. The straight-talking Irishman loved his God-daughter like she was his own and had always believed she was capable of anything.

"Think of it as a challenge," he said, "nothing more, nothing less."

Sarah looked at her family's closest friend with a mixture of wonderment and dread. "I don't think I can do it," she said. "I mean where the hell would I start?"

Gerry smiled. "This is for your benefit as much as the company's. We all need to know, so let's take it one step at a time. We'll just start at the beginning and build from there, OK?"

"OK, then," Sarah said with a shrug, "you tell me what the beginning is, and I'll see what I can do."

A grin spread across his face. "That's more like it, chicken. Now, pull a chair up and I'll show you where I think we should start."

***

The HSG Directors were on a roll: hot on the heels of Ron Stafford's Colorado tip off, Gerry had received a call from Wiseman & Scott and was now adamant the ensuing conversation had unearthed a gem of information.

"Finally," he said, "something about this bloody book that sounds interesting, a reason that makes it different."

The fact the PCOS had loaned out their book to the American Literary Society was old news to many. Most knew the Illinois Expo was the starting point of the saga. But knowing the real reason why it was deemed such an important exhibit, sharing centre stage no less, was apparently not something they wanted to shout about.

Straight after Calvin's call, Gerry rang Ray. He caught HSG's CEO still mulling over the earlier meeting with Excel. Despite his obvious preoccupation, Ray was still keen to hear yet another revelation. "Bloody amazing," he said several times during Gerry's explanation, "it just gets better and better. It's almost by the hour now, isn't it?"

"Non-stop barrage of intrigue," his partner replied.

Ray didn't comment immediately. After several seconds of thoughtful silence, he asked, "But why didn't Dr Reid or any of his cronies tell you this when you met them…is it something they're ashamed of?"

"Unlikely," Gerry answered. "As our man said, they wouldn't have let it be exhibited with that as its claim to fame if that was the case would they?"

"Yeah, suppose he's right - but it's all a bit cloak and dagger, isn't it?"

"Very," Gerry said. "I mean – think about it from Calvin's point of view…they're employed by the PCOS, yet they didn't even make it clear to them – so why hold back?"

"Very odd," Ray answered. "So how did Calvin find out?"

"Read an article on a website apparently, some art history site he regularly visits."

"I take it he's into all that stuff then… a bit of an anorak, is he?"

"Just like your Sarah," Gerry replied. "Mad on it…sounds like the two of them regularly talk art news - you know, mysterious disappearances, thefts, frauds all that kind of dodgy shit."

Ray laughed. "Pair of weirdos," he said, then asked, "So what's our next move?"

"I've told Calvin to ring Sarah and compare notes," Gerry answered, "then we'll take it from there."

***

It had come out of nowhere. Calvin had phoned Gerry in a purely professional capacity to enquire about the recovery mission progress. But, after getting a summary of the as yet unresolved search, the amiable Scot hadn't been in a hurry to hang up. With nothing pressing, he'd asked after Sarah and inadvertently ended up babbling on about their joint obsession. "Yeah, Sarah loves all that kind of stuff," Gerry said after listening patiently to several of Calvin's favourite anecdotes. "All that history mystery malarkey really does seem to float her boat."

"I'm exactly the same," Calvin replied enthusiastically. "We compare notes regularly." He stopped as a thought popped into his head. "In fact, that reminds me," he said. "I need to ring her, I need to let her into a secret about our Book…I have a little tale to tell."

"What tale?" Gerry asked suspiciously. "Is it something I should know about?"

"Probably, although I doubt you'll be interested. It won't help you find it - but I'll tell you anyway…."

***

Calvin's tale was far from little and his comment about Gerry's interest couldn't have been further from the truth. Yes, it was common knowledge the PCOS's Book of Martyrs was a genuine first edition and, on that basis alone, a rare and valuable piece. But seemingly it was its place in Scottish folklore that made it unique. The amiable Scot explained the book had a back story, a story so beguiling that it had led the American exhibition organisers and their army of researchers to hound Doctor Reid's synod for weeks. The expo's main gallery, entitled 'The Gods of War', was to be dedicated to displaying classic works of literature that had a warfare-related history. It was thought by many in the business that to have the PCOS's famed copy of Foxe's classic tome as a centre piece would be a major coup.

In pursuit of their dream, the American Literary Society representatives were relentless. They bombarded the PCOS with requests to exhibit the sacred first edition and they were very persuasive. The Society's big-wigs went to great lengths to explain to the Elders how their ancient tome would draw in many hundreds of literary aficionados and that the exposure generated by the exhibition, plus a fat display fee, would help improve the church's financial position. The literary obsessives were right - it was a tempting offer that simply couldn't be ignored. Bowing to this relentless pressure, the Synod sat down to give the proposition due consideration. Ultimately Dr Reid and the elders let financial necessity influence their judgement. As they couldn't afford not to, the proposal was approved. And, after a formal eight-week loan deal was sanctioned, the American Literary Society had got its prize exhibit.

In certain elite academic circles, the book was big news. With provenance that established the old Presbyterian's copy had been involved in a notorious eighteenth-century ceremony, it was considered nothing short of iconic. Historic records showed that on the evening of April 15th, 1746 a blessing service took place in a run-down church outside the town of Nairn. On that wild, rain lashed night in Scotland, the old chapel was bursting at the seams. Inside, a seething mass of the Campbell Clan's hardiest members had rallied to a call for civil war and, as they were called to order by a young cleric, the fearsome highlanders had no inkling the sermon they were about to receive would be forever embedded in Celtic folklore.

At the time, English forces, led by the Duke of Cumberland, were in dogged pursuit of Bonnie Prince Charlie's rampaging army. In an attempt to source additional manpower for a major engagement, the English generals had turned to sympathetic clan chiefs for support. The Campbell clan, ardent Protestants, didn't hesitate in joining the Duke's crusade and were quick to bolster the ranks of his faithful Argyle Militia. During their private preparations for the long-awaited battle, the Campbell's had a brilliant young local preacher preside over a service that saw an old country church packed to its rafters. Legend has it that in a vitriolic address the young firebrand read extracts from the Book of Martyrs and whipped the Campbell faithful into a bloodthirsty frenzy, swearing to inflict the same punishments on their enemies as had been inflicted on the martyrs. It was reportedly John Foxe's accounts of the barbaric treatment of Protestants by Catholic persecutors that helped incense the Clansmen to fever pitch and as they left that ramshackle Church - to a man - they swore an oath to put all Jacobite invaders to the sword.

But when Calvin revealed the name of the young preacher, the hairs on the back of Gerry's neck stood on end. "You gotta be kidding me," he spluttered down the phone. "This is so bloody weird; Cal. Jeremiah Gunn is one of the names mentioned in the journal you gave Sarah. With a name like that it's gotta be the same guy, hasn't it?"

Calvin didn't reply; he was stunned into silence. He'd never been told about the outcome of Sarah's ledger analysis and had yet to ask if she'd done anything with them. "More like you kidding me," he finally gasped, "but how does that come about and - more to the point - does it mean anything?"

Gerry thought for a second. "Not a clue. You need to speak to Sarah, let her explain the journals, then we can try to make sense of all this mind-boggling info together, OK?"

***

Sarah had nearly dropped the phone as she leapt for joy. "I bloody knew there was something about that book," she said triumphantly, "and what a belter of a story…it's amazing, but what's the bigger picture then, Cal? I don't see it, do you?" she paused in anticipation of a response but couldn't wait. "How does any of this relate to The Divinity?" she asked. "Why would the book's dubious Highland history mean anything to them?"

Calvin didn't have a clue. "That's your department," he said. "You'll have to figure it out."

***

Now, ten minutes after saying goodbye to her fellow geek, Sarah was sat with Gerry trying to decide exactly how they would go about figuring it out. "OK, here we go," Gerry said. "This is how I see it, you listening?"

"I'm all ears," she said as she settled in the chair next to him. "Fire away."

Gerry did the best he could, but whichever way they looked at it, it was a tall order. Trying to conjure up a meaningful research strategy that would help them understand why a little known religious order from the USA, a missionary chapel in the mountains of Utah, and the Jacobite rebellion of 1745 might be linked was nigh-on impossible. "OK, you're right," he said. "Maybe it can't be done, maybe as you say there is no starting point - or maybe there's no link at all – think, we might actually be getting our knickers in a twist over nothing."

"Yeah – we might be," she said quietly, "but I doubt it…there's definitely a link, but we aren't going to find it with just the info we have."

"Pity," he said. "I'd love to know what all the fuss was about, especially now we know more about its past." Sarah sat back in the chair and frowned. "Although that makes it even more intriguing doesn't it?" she said.

"How d'you mean?"

"Well think about it, we know The Divinity are a Franciscan missionary movement," she paused for a moment as she thought about what she'd just said. "Let me rephrase that somewhat. We know that's what they *claim* to be, yeah?

Gerry simply nodded. "Yeah, OK, I'm with you so far."

"If they are what they say, then they're a Catholic organisation, which probably goes a long way to explaining why all their humanitarian projects are in Central America."

Gerry looked puzzled. "Come again," he said.

She rolled her eyes. "Uncle Gerry, have I lost you already?"

He smiled awkwardly. "A little," he said. "Just run that second bit by me again, will you?

Sarah took a deep breath. "OK, it's like this," she said. "The Divinity only seem to work in countries where Catholicism is the dominant religious belief, places like Honduras, Guatemala and El

Salvador are renown Catholic strong holds and these are exactly the places they establish their aid projects," she paused and looked at Gerry for signs of understanding. "My point is, if The Divinity are so obviously Catholic biased, why would they be interested in a book famed as Protestant propaganda, a book so blatant in its hatred of papal beliefs that it has helped fuel centuries of religious divide?"

"OK," he said. "I'm with you now, I get what you're saying, but I'm getting the feeling there's more."

"Of course, there's more," she said as she shifted in her seat. "Now think what we've just found out," she smiled wickedly. "We've been told this particular book was used as a tool to incite loyalist clansmen before the battle of Culloden. It was wielded by a radical cleric who motivated Protestant highlanders to help destroy an invading army, a primarily Catholic army, an army led by a monarch intent on imposing the beliefs of the Church of Rome on all he conquered." As she spoke Sarah looked across the desk at Gerry but now dropped her head. "It makes no bloody sense, does it?" she mumbled at the floor. "It's the polarised view. I can't understand their interest."

"It's obvious," Gerry yelped in a sudden moment of inspiration. "They hate the book! These bastards stole it with the sole intention of destroying it!"

***

In Ray Stuart's world, listening was everything. It was a skill he'd honed over the years, a skill that at times he'd taken to another level. The day's revelations had come thick and fast and, although hard to believe, his instincts told him not to doubt any of what he'd heard. The trick now was to analyse the questions thrown up and make sense of them. In his mind there were many, but the most niggling was the question he'd immediately asked Gerry. "Why hadn't the PCOS revealed the book's significance to us at the meeting in Glasgow and why had it never been properly explained to anyone involved from the start?"

He was sure solving this frustrating conundrum was important.... but that wouldn't last for long.

CHAPTER 54

Behind Closed Doors

Lucas looked at the screen and his heart sank. Rick's text simply read: Babb in trouble.

It had been ten minutes since he'd left the Jeep. Although he hadn't got far, from where he was, he couldn't see the car park. To get back quickly in the pitch dark wouldn't be easy. Two steps in and a flash of movement to the right caught his attention. Instinctively he killed his torch, ducked low, and stared into the shadows within the shadows. Nothing moved and nothing made a sound. Apart from the gentle rustle of leaves in the breeze there was only silence. He stayed crouched for a few seconds, waiting patiently for signs of danger. But when nothing stirred, he exhaled slowly then stood up. As he reached his full height he sensed the movement again but this time he didn't duck, this time he knew it wasn't human.

He turned on the torch again and pointed it into the void ahead. Instead of the solid façade of the main building, he was confronted by the outline of a long, domed tent. As the ex-sapper inched closer it became apparent it was big. The moonlight shimmering across its upper surfaces gave it an eerie glow. He realised the faint movement he'd sensed had been a loose flap ruffling in the wind. "What the hell!" he said to himself. "Of all the things to get jumpy about."

The moment of relief was short-lived; the torch suddenly dimmed to an amber pulse and died.

"Dammit, dammit, dammit!" he muttered, feeling his way forward by the moonlight reflected on the canvas. He reached the flap, pulled it back gingerly, and looked into the inky black interior. Inside, the darkness was impenetrable and there was not a sound to be heard.

Even after several seconds of optimistic blinking he still couldn't make anything out, so with Rick's worrying text praying on his mind, he let the flap drop and turned his attention back to more pressing matters. Spinning smartly on his heels he made his way across the grass. He passed a shadowy line of ornate benches, then homed in on a streetlight in the corner of the car park and, as he drew closer to the solitary column, he upped his pace.

Descending a low rise at a gallop, Lucas could now make out two figures silhouetted outside the entrance. Seconds later he arrived at the Wrangler to find it empty. He was about to head off to the front door when a voice whispered from the shadows, "Roxy, wait up, will you! We're over here!"

Lucas caught a glimpse of a beckoning hand and headed for the mass of well-tended shrubs five yards to the left of the Jeep.

"What's going on?" he asked as he found Rick and Marion skulking in the shrubbery. "What's happened to Babb?"

"Keep your voice down, will you!" Rick said. "She's stuck inside and now we've got visitors." As he spoke Rick pointed over to the front of the building at the two figures that were pacing up down outside.

"When did they get here?" Lucas asked.

"About two minutes ago," Marion whispered. "Just as we got out, a car appeared out of the blue and two guys jumped out."

"Who are they?" Lucas asked.

Rick pulled a face; "How the hell am I supposed to know?" he said. "Could be bloody anybody."

"Alright, Kruger, I just thought you might have an idea. I mean are they Divinity security or the law, were they in a marked car…any signs, sirens or blue lights?"

"Did you hear anything?" he snapped back. "Plain black sedan, lights off, super quiet approach. It was pure fluke they didn't see us – OK?"

Lucas flashed a smile. "Yeah, OK, I get your point," he said. "Just checking."

Suddenly the hush of the night was disturbed by the distinctive 'crack' of gun fire.

"Jesus!" Rick exclaimed as he watched the two prowling figures run for cover. "Where's that coming from?"

"Up there," Lucas said pointing to trees on the far side of the building. "See it, see the muzzle flashes?"

"Got it," Rick said as he caught sight of small intermittent explosions of white light winking through the trees. "How many shooters?"

"Just one," Lucas said confidently, "but it's an assault rifle."

Marion was now utterly terrified. "What about Babb?" she whimpered.

Lucas turned to Rick. "We've got to get inside that building."

***

Inside the building Babb was still being stalked by the all-seeing PA system and was now hiding in a far-flung corner of the lobby. Still clutching her phone, hoping against all odds she was out of view from the tyrannical voice, she looked at the screen and scrolled down to Marion's number.

"Do not use your cell," the voice ordered. "You have been warned."

Babb dropped the mobile in defeat then slumped to the floor asking herself, Why the hell have I got involved in this nightmare?

As her frustration grew, she wrapped her arms round her knees, hung her head in despair and felt like screaming. But then the sound of banging on glass lifted her head and her spirits. She struggled to her feet to look across the lobby. As she focused on the door, expecting to see Lucas and Rick arriving like knights in shining armour, she was surprised to see two men she didn't recognise. Through the small squares of mesh security shutter, she could make out the heavy-set duo glaring in.

"Hey, lady," the man closest shouted through the locked doors. "You gonna let us in or not?"

Babb was now even more confused. "Who are you?" she yelled at the menacing looking figure.

"FBI!" the man shouted. "Get this door open now!"

At the mention of the word 'FBI' her heart soared. But almost immediately the euphoria vanished as the sound of shots ricocheting off the pavement outside sent her scuttling back to the sanctuary of her darkened corner. After several seconds and several rounds had flashed by, she peeked round the protective barrier to take a look. The lobby's bright lights made it difficult to see outside. She'd only been able to see the two men banging on the glass because they were so close but now, staring out into the gloom, she could see nothing.

With only the sound of sporadic gun fire coming from outside, Babb decided staying put was fruitless. Suddenly, moving felt very right. Darting forward, she turned a sharp left and made a beeline for the door behind the reception desk. It was still closed. She twisted the handle and simultaneously shoulder charged it with all her might. The door gave under the force. She cannoned into the room, coming to an abrupt, thigh banging halt in front of a small, tidy desk. The room was empty. There was no sign of the sunken-eyed witch who had so rudely ignored her earlier, and the room - like the lobby - was deserted. As she looked around Babb marvelled at what was not quite the back-office affair she'd imagined.

The desk she'd clattered into was close to the entrance and was the only one like it in the room. The rest of the immaculately clean space was taken up by what looked like rows of high-tech filing cabinets each sporting a small LED display unit on top. Babb made her way along the narrow aisle that ran down the left wall, trailing her fingers along the line of glowing red read-outs as she went. At the end of the room, there was a small recess with double glass doors.

"An elevator," she muttered as she looked at the end wall. "How very handy."

Suddenly, with a loud 'ping', the neon display above the doors sprang to life. L3, L2...Babb realised L1 was next. She only had seconds. The cabinets were the closest and most obvious place to hide. Crossing the room like a sprinter out of the blocks Babb squeezed herself into the narrow space behind the units lining the opposing wall. Then through the tiny gap between the two cabinets shielding her she watched the doors slide open. "But I've told you, Dominic," the sunken eyed woman said as she stepped out. "It's not that simple."

The bearded overweight male accompanying her looked pensive. "It fucking is that simple," he snapped, "and it has to be done." Fat man didn't say another word; he stood still, produced a handkerchief, dragged it across his brow then continued on toward the front desk. At the desk he stopped and picked up a piece of paper. "So just get on with it," he turned back to face the woman, "and you better be quick about it."

Babb could no longer see either of them.

"I'll try," the woman whined, "but I'm telling you it's a tall order."

"Just do it," the man screamed as he kicked the desk. "You've got twenty minutes while I stall them, then we're gone, OK?"

"Yes, Father," she mumbled to his retreating back as he stormed out of the room and slammed the door behind him. Babb waited patiently, trying to establish if the door slam meant she was now alone. A rasping cough confirmed she wasn't. Then, just as the numbness in her legs started to tell her it was time to move, the door opened again.

"The woman's not there," she heard Fat Man say. "Where the hell did she go?"

Sunken Eyes looked at the questioning cleric and shrugged. "Beats me," she said. "Last time I looked she was waiting out there."

"Well she ain't there now," he said. "Come see."

As the woman followed the man out into the lobby, Babb took her chance. She scooted backwards out of her hidey-hole, got to her feet, then headed for the lift. Thankfully the doors were still open, so she hopped inside. She checked the operator's panel and without thinking hit the button marked 'Basement'. The elevator gave its cursory "Ping," the doors slid shut and instantly she was being whisked down into the bowels of the building.

***

Whilst Babb continued her game of hide and seek inside the building, her travelling companions were busy outside playing catch up. Lucas led his comrades away from the gunfire as he retraced his steps from his earlier sortie. But this time, knowing the layout and with Rick's flashlight still working, progress was much better. After a couple of minutes, they came to the first of the ornate benches on the side lawn and, as the trio passed the third one, Lucas gestured into the darkness with the torch. "The big tent's up here," he said. "We've gotta have a look inside…I'm sure it'll link to the building."

"Yeah, whatever you say, Sarge," Rick answered. "We're just following you."

Seconds later they reached the marquee. As earlier, it was hidden in the shadows and apart from the familiar ruffle of a loose side flap, it was still deathly silent.

"What the hell's this," Rick whispered as he got close. "Someone getting married?"

"I doubt it," Lucas replied. "More like brainwashed."

Wasting no time, the eager Englishman pulled back the flap and shone the flashlight into the pitch-black interior. Inside, exactly as he'd envisaged, the place was set out like a lecture theatre. Rows of wooden chairs were lined up facing a fancy stainless-steel lectern and behind it was a large white projector screen.

"Like I thought," Lucas said as he turned to his team, "a portable indoctrination centre."

As he played the beam around the interior, he spotted what he wanted. The large marquee had been erected up against the side of the facility and there, illuminated by the torch, was a door into the building.

"Bingo," Lucas triumphed, "that's exactly what we need."

As the trio peered at the door in the spotlight, the silence was punctuated by a faint cowbell chime.

"B!" Marion gasped, pulling her phone from an inside pocket. "She's OK," she whispered. "She's hiding in the basement. Oh, thank God!"

"Good news," Rick said patting the much-relieved librarian on the back.

But before Marion could respond Lucas cut in. "Yeah, it is good news," he said. "But how d'you find the bleeding basement?"

***

Outside the main entrance, pinned down behind their car, the two federal agents were running out of options. The holy sniper was not wasting ammunition or effort but every time the men looked to make an escape or had the audacity to return fire, bursts of 5.56mm rounds rained down on them. But with the black sedan parked centre stage, a dash for freedom was a seriously high-risk proposition, so for the time being the FBI team opted to stay behind their armour-plated vehicle and make another call for back up.

CHAPTER 55

Going Underground

Back at Stormbringer Command, the intensity of activity had now lessened. But there was still work to be done. Although Chief Koeman was satisfied with the progress thus far, he was expecting more to come from the big finale of the international operation.

In the three key target areas, eighteen months of intense effort was coming to a head.

In Arizona, despite some federal casualties, the Phoenix ranch raid had exceeded all expectation. In Spain, the Cadiz dockyard infiltration had uncovered a 200kg cocaine shipment, seen the arrest of six corrupt port officials, and closed the cartel's European point of entry hopefully for a long time to come. On top of that, the initial reports from the Honduran authorities were positive and, although the swoop on 'La Ceiba' had been chaotic, violent, and had resulted in fatalities on both sides, it could still only be viewed as a success. The remaining locations identified as being of strategic importance were believed to play a lesser role in the illicit trade, and so far the evidence uncovered had backed up the expectation.

The Utah house search had revealed little. A mini bureau invasion of the luxury estate hidden in the Black Mountains had been meticulous in its execution. But, other than surprised protests from the incumbent security company, it had met with zero resistance and as yet had produced little evidence of organised criminality.

The Mesa HQ had been successfully shut down; the raid had encountered mainly admin staff going about their daily duties. But it had gone down without incident or casualty and now the building and its contents were subject to an in-depth forensic analysis that would take days to complete. The only significant target untouched was The Divinity's Colorado teaching centre. The religious sect's isolated retreat thirty miles west of the city of Cortez was the least high profile of the investigation's target locations, but FBI sources hinted it could be important, so the innocuous seeming facility made number six on Operation Stormbringer's Top Ten Hot Properties list.

"Virgil," a bald man in a t-shirt shouted as he waved a handset in the air, "FBI Tucson again, line 2."

The bleary-eyed Dutchman put his umpteenth cup of coffee aside and headed toward his beckoning colleague. "Thanks, Frank," he said to the man as he passed him the receiver. Then cupping the mouthpiece, he forced a weary smile. "More good news, I hope."

As the team's bespectacled leader sat down to take the call, those closest turned to eavesdrop on the update. After a few seconds of pensive nodding Koeman frowned. "OK, OK I get it," he said. "I understand the potential…it doesn't sound good." He then leant back in the chair and started to tug his hair with his free hand. After several minutes of intermittent hair smoothing and face pulling the Dutchman spoke again. "Are you sure?" he asked. "Can we really assume that?"

Koeman continued to gently massage his head as he listened to the FBI commander relay the latest progress from the US but as the call drew to an end he stopped and moved his hand to the desk in front of him. "We will," he said slowly as he drummed his fingers on the desktop, "and let's hope it works like that. Only time will tell. OK thanks for the update. Mr Wells, and goodbye for now."

As he put the receiver back into its cradle Koeman sat back. "Well, guys," he announced, "it looks like our main man may have slipped the net."

***

The latest news from Tucson Control was positive but it still appeared The Divinity's top dog was unaccounted for. The FBI update confirmed the latest findings from the ranch raid and the on-going search of the Mesa HQ were proving better than expected, but the report also included news of the team deployed to monitor the Colorado retreat, and none of that news was good.

***

The teaching facility deployment had been planned initially as a surveillance operation and had never been envisaged as a full-blown raid. Whilst bureau intelligence, corroborated by Meredith Higham, confirmed it was regularly visited by high level Divinity personnel, in reality the FBI believed it genuinely was the sanctuary for reflection, teaching and prayer it was promoted as and from the very outset it had been viewed by the authorities as yet another part of The Divinity's polished front, designed to convince a legion of wealthy benefactors they were doing the right thing.

But as no one knew for sure, the building had remained under federal scrutiny and, utilising the guise of janitorial staff and air conditioning engineers, FBI agents had periodically infiltrated the complex to snoop. But today they'd come unstuck, today the plan had unravelled.

"Plus, they've lost an agent," the Europol chief said as he stood up from the desk. "They're a man down and they don't know why."

No one spoke. The weary staff - now twelve hours plus in the darkened room - looked expectantly toward their leader.

"He was using an AC engineer cover. Tracked as far as the premises. They say he definitely entered the building, but fifteen minutes after that his vehicle was monitored leaving the facility at speed and subsequently found abandoned at a gas station five miles away. Radio comms with the agent were down, so standby units were despatched. Now one unit has approached the teaching centre and come under fire. Gentlemen, we are going to have to give the FBI a little more time on this one." Koeman scanned their faces. "Under the circumstances I think it's the least we can do!"

***

Lucas had led his team through the marquee to the door. Marion was in second spot and Rick brought up the rear. Lucas twisted the handle and tugged. As expected, the panelled door was locked. Undeterred, he squatted down in front of the handle and shone the torch into the keyhole. "Key's in the lock," he grunted, scanning the ground with the beam of light. "What have we got to…"

Before he could complete the thought, Kruger had wrenched the torch from his hand and with a sharp *'crunch'* punched the shaft through the glass panel closest to the handle. "This, Bru," he said, "is how we do it."

He didn't withdraw the torch immediately but stayed stock still. As they listened for sounds of an alarm, nothing came, so he deftly knocked out the remaining shards from the frame and reached inside. The key was easy to locate. With one swift revolution, the door swung open into the darkened corridor beyond. As they filed through, movement sensor night lights came on around them.

"Which way?" Rick asked as Lucas emerged through the doorway. "Left or right?"

Lucas rubbed his eyes, looked both ways, but didn't answer.

"Right," Marion said quickly. "I've got a feeling we need to go right."

Lucas glanced at Rick and shrugged. "The navigator has spoken," he said. "Best not argue," He turned to his right and led the team along the corridor further into the unknown.

***

Dominic Williams couldn't understand where the female visitor had vanished to.

"She was right here," he said to his zombie-eyed colleague. "I was watching her on the monitor," he paused as he pointed to the corner where Babb had tried to hide. "Last time I saw her; she was right here."

"Well she ain't now," the witch said, "but she's nothing, she's the least of our worries, it's out there we need to concentrate on."

As soon as the words left her mouth, another volley of assault rifle rounds echoed from outside.

"It's too much of a coincidence. She's gotta be a goddam fed," the cleric said as he ducked out of view. "Sent in first to scout around."

"Nah," the woman replied. "She's no G-man."

Father Williams narrowed his eyes. "That's what they said about Meredith Higham and look how that turned out."

"Point taken," she nodded, "but I'm still not convinced; she looked harmless, too sweet and innocent if you ask me."

"Exactly," Williams snapped, "the perfect fucking cover."

The two glared briefly at each other before the Father spoke again. "No other choice then," he said. "We'll forget her for now and carry on as planned, OK?"

The woman nodded. "Only thing we can do," she said. "You keep 'em busy and I'll pull the files."

***

As the lift doors parted on the basement, Babb's heart pounded like a steam hammer. After several nervous glances confirmed she was definitely alone, she stepped out and headed for a line of parked cars. She crouched down behind them, slipped her backpack off her shoulder, leant back against the cold concrete wall and pulled out her phone. Two bars. She texted Marion: 'In the basement. Looking for an exit.'

She continued her stealthy walk around the walls, half crouching behind the cars. Every couple of yards she stopped and checked for signs of company. And each time she did the shadows cast by a mass of grey concrete columns played tricks on her imagination. Suddenly she stopped again. This time it wasn't something she'd seen that halted progress, this time it was a noise. Or was it? As her pulse quickened, she listened to the background hum of the cavernous void and waited. There it was again, a low moaning sound, and it was definitely real. Babb thought it sounded human and she knew it was close.

Conscious of her panicked breathing, she tried to calm herself. Eventually she got her respiration under control and strained to listen. Seconds later the sound came again. This time it was protracted and now she could gauge it was coming from a recess signed 'Emergency Stairwell 2'

She reached the door and squinted through its glass panel into the murky shadows. A man lay on the floor by the base of the staircase. It looked like he'd come down from the floor above and collapsed at the bottom of the stairs. He wasn't moving. She had to help; it was who she was. Friend or foe – if they needed help – she'd do it. The heavy emergency exit door gave with one firm shove.

The man was tall, of medium build, and dressed in dark blue overalls. He was lying on his side facing her and his hair was matted with blood.

"Oh, dear Lord," she said as she knelt down next to him. "What happened to you?"

The head wound looked bad. Whilst his face was bloodied and bruised, the major injury was obviously to the side of his skull. She thought the gash was the result of blunt instrument trauma or maybe hitting the concrete floor, but there was no point in guessing. Whatever the reason, the man needed help. Again, she slipped off her trusty back-pack and rummaged around inside. Seconds later she pulled out a green plastic box. As she set the first aid kit on the ground next to her, she heard several pairs of footsteps approaching down the stairs. She froze.

"I'm guessing this is it," came a familiar English accent, "given that I'm nearly at the bottom and the wall's got a bloody great B on it."

"Lucas Roxby!" she called out. "I'm here."

The dishevelled Brit appeared around the return in the staircase above. "Jesus Christ, Babb," he exclaimed. "Are you OK? What did you do to your friend here?"

Babb couldn't contain her relief; she jumped up, leapt over her casualty, and enthusiastically wrapped her arms around the ex-sapper.

"Yeah, I'm alright," she mumbled into his shoulder, "but he's not. I found him like this. He's been here for a while, judging by the amount of dried blood."

"How'd it happen?" Kruger asked as he and Marion came down the stairs to join them.

"No idea," Babb shrugged, as the two sisters embraced. "Like I said, I've literally just stumbled across him this minute."

"Check him for ID," Lucas nodded to Marion. "His overalls may say 'Cool Flow - Ventilating the Nation' but if someone took the trouble to give him what I'm beginning to think of as an Arizona kiss, then something's definitely amiss."

Marion pulled back the heavy cotton material of the unconscious man's overalls. Underneath, he only wore a grey t-shirt, but she felt around and found an inside pocket. "Got something," she said as she carefully extracted a brown leather wallet. "Here you go."

Marion passed the fold-over wallet to Rick for examination. The big South African flipped it open and started to analyse the contents.

"Yup, he's no ventilation engineer" Rick answered. "I think what we've got here, Sarge," he said slowly, "is one FBI special agent Wade Dooley based out of Tucson, Arizona."

Lucas shook his head. "Well, would you believe it?" he said with a wry smile. "Looks like those bloody rumours were true after all."

CHAPTER 56

Karma

His world had crashed.

Dominic Williams's beloved organisation was at the brink of extinction and now, with only the aid of two die-hard associates, he was undertaking a last-ditch damage limitation exercise.

After ten rewarding years, the end had come. Like an arrow to the heart, the news from Arizona had been a devastating blow, but The Divinity's ever faithful servant wasn't going down without a fight. In an attempt to destroy evidence before the authorities burst through the door, he activated the protocol every member of The Divinity's inner sanctum had practised but hoped never to initiate for real: files, accounts, hard drives, and general correspondence were now being readied for destruction. But time was running out.

As the Father rifled through another cabinet in Dubois's own version of the Oval Office, he was muttering to himself, "Oh for fuck's sake, come on," as another overflowing file jammed on its runner.

Williams's sunken eyed assistant had been right; with the feds scouting party already banging on the front door, they had a lot to do in a short space of time but so far, with limited resources, they were managing to stall the invaders. The building had been secured, the CCTV was being used to good effect, and the destruction of evidence had started. For a three-man team it was a stretch and, as it became obvious a full-blown raid was imminent, they'd resorted to desperate measures. Deciding to open up with an automatic weapon to buy time was a serious gamble, but it was working. Although one man with an assault rifle could only buy so much time, Williams knew every little helped. Then, as the heavily breathing cleric dragged out the contents of another drawer and stuffed it into a refuse sack, his phone rang. He jumped at the interruption then checked the caller ID.

"Monsignor," he answered breathlessly. "Where are you?"

"Safe, Dominic," came a muted reply. "I'm safe…but I assume you're not?"

"We've got visitors," Williams answered, "and we're expecting more."

"What's happened?"

The bearded cleric hung his head. "First some random female appeared asking about joining us, then two guys turned up and tried to force their way in."

"Feds?" Dubois asked quickly. "Are they inside?"

Williams was keen to spare his leader the true nature of the situation. "Could be FBI," he said as calmly as possible, "but they're outside and that's how it'll stay for a while."

"Good," Dubois replied. "Keep it like that and burn everything. Don't leave a shred of paperwork behind, you hear me?"

"Yes, sir," the cleric replied. "We'll do our best."

The line went silent for a second. Then Dubois hissed, "If they don't get the records, we will be OK. The authorities will struggle, and we'll recover, and we'll rebuild."

"As you say, Monsignor," Williams replied. "I understand."

Dubois knew his man would do what he could. Both loyalty and fear would play their part. "Think positive, Dominic," he added. "You can make this happen, you really can. Letting me down is not an option, remember." He hung up.

Williams shuddered, threw his phone back on the desk, then continued to ram files and folders into the refuse sack.

Five minutes later he appeared down in the lobby carrying four bulging sacks. He set them down on the reception counter and looked to the open door. "Erica," he called out. "You done in there?"

“You kidding me? “squealed a pained voice from within. “Like I keep tellin’ you…this ain’t an easy task.”

The previously pristine records office was now a mass of strewn paper and discarded drawers. Long lengths of computer print-outs spewed from the front of every cabinet and the floor was littered with opened files.

“Come on, woman,” Williams shouted. “We’ve got to get this stuff cleared.”

She glared at him. “Well fucking help me, then,” she snarled. “Start filling bags. Go down the other end and start following me round.” The Father didn’t say a word; he grabbed a handful of refuse sacks off the floor and started to do exactly as he’d been ordered. The trick was to gather up all the discharged paper ready for burning, then reset the electronic display units to ‘Clear’.

After he’d torn off the first unruly roll and put it in a sack, he looked to the side of the cabinet. He tapped in a four-digit code on the square keypad and stood back. Once the code registered, the digital display on top of the unit started to flash. He hit the reset and clear button. After several seconds the display changed to ‘Clear’.

“One down,” the cleric muttered, “fifty-one to go.”

As Williams frantically worked his way down the first line of cabinets, he looked up to check on his co-conspirator. The wild-eyed records’ clerk had now completed printing out from the last few cabinets and was heading back towards him, bagging reams of dangling paper as she went.

“I’m taking the first load to the basement,” he said as she got close, “then I’ll come back for the rest.”

Miss Crazy Witch looked up from her paper ripping frenzy and shook her head. “No fuckin’ way,” she hissed, “you gonna wait ‘til I’m finished, then we take it down together.”

Williams bit his tongue. Even by The Divinity’s warped standards, Erica Gomez was a strange fish, but he knew that whatever she said usually made sense. “OK,” he replied begrudgingly, “we’ll do it together.”

Minutes later, the duo were loading the glass-fronted lift with a mass of bursting plastic sacks, piling them ceiling high. The cleric stood with his back to the bags to stop them spilling out. "Put the last ones there," he said nodding to the small area of floor in front of him. "Then you get in."

Once the final bags were loaded, she squeezed in and hit the Basement button. "That furnace better be roaring," she said. "Coz this is a lot of shit to burn."

***

As the lift descended, the mismatched pair were none the wiser about developments outside. Unbeknownst to them, whilst they'd been clearing confidential files from the records room, at the front of the building the besieged FBI agents had made a break for freedom. Having finally abandoned the shield of their vehicle, the two men had managed to sprint across the car park, skirt round the building, and get out of the sniper's line of fire. The duo were now hunkered down behind a large bronze sculpture waiting for reinforcements to arrive.

***

At basement level, the elevator arrived with a gentle bump. The doors slid open. Williams, assisted by his demonic colleague, began to throw out the bulging sacks. "Grab one of those carts," the Father said, pointing through the doors, "it'll be quicker."

This time it was Miss Gomez receiving the orders and she jumped to it. The two linen carts had been left abandoned opposite the lift and they couldn't have been more suitable if they'd been ordered specifically for the task.

"Divine intervention," she muttered as she retrieved the closest one. She positioned the cart directly in front of the mound they'd created and they both started to hoof the bags into it, unaware they were being watched.

"Check this out," Lucas whispered as he peered through the side of the glass window. "What are those two up to?"

Babb tapped him on the shoulder. "Is one a skinny woman in a black smock?"

"Yes, a tall, pencil slim female wearing black."

"She's the receptionist. When I asked for information about joining, the miserable bitch just picked up a phone, turned her back on me, then walked out of the room."

The man at her feet gave a low moan. For a few seconds, the group stared thoughtfully at their casualty.

"Are we sure he's going to make it?" Rick asked. "Looks like he's got worse."

The South African wasn't wrong; the injured man had visibly paled. "Dear Lord," Babb said as she felt his wrist, "there's no pulse." She put her ear to his chest. "He's not breathing either. I think he could be dead."

"Shit," Lucas said. "Mouth to mouth or chest compressions?"

Rick eased the man's head up. "Mouth to mouth," he said. "It's a lot quieter." He pinched the casualty's nose, planted his lips over the mouth and started to blow. As the chest rose Rick pulled back, took another lungful and then blew again.

"Keep it going, Rick," Marion encouraged, "just keep it going."

Lucas looked out again but the figures by the lift had disappeared. "The weirdos have scarpered."

"You go after them," Rick panted between blows. "I'll stay here with the girls."

Babb looked up at Lucas. "I'm coming too."

***

Williams pushed the linen basket up a narrow corridor. He was huffing and puffing like an old steam train.

"You're outta shape, Father," Gomez sniped from behind. "You need a hand pushing that thing?"

She was a blunt bitch and he knew she was right, but the sweat drenched cleric wasn't going to give her the satisfaction. "No, I don't," he snapped. "I can manage just fine on my own." He paused to glance behind. "In fact, now we got this thing you might as well go back; you can clear the safe while I get rid of this shit."

She stopped dead. "You sure now? You sure you can cope without me?"

"Yes, I can sort this," he replied. "You go."

She wasn't arguing. "OK," she said. "I'll meet you back in the lobby when you're done," and with that turned smartly on her heels and headed back down the corridor.

***

As Lucas and Babb approached the lift, there was still no sign of the mismatched pair or their over-flowing linen cart.

"Which way did they go?" Lucas asked quietly. "There's nowhere *to* go, is there?"

Babb didn't respond. She was too intent on assessing options. From their position in front of the lift they had a good view of the main parking area which included several stairwell enclosures and a much-signed plant room. But as everywhere was quiet and there was no obvious sign of a quick escape route, they were stumped. As Babb stared harder into the gloom, her eyes continued to acclimatise. "Over there," she eventually said pointing to a darkened corner. "Is that a doorway?"

Lucas followed her outstretched arm and frowned. After a few seconds of pained squinting he too saw the outline of an opening. "Yeah, I've got it," he said, "and I think it is."

But the sudden sound of footsteps was followed almost immediately by the appearance of a tall, willowy figure.

"Oh no," Babb muttered as it got closer. "It's the woman from reception."

At the sight of two people approaching, Erica Gomez slowed her pace then stopped. "You!" she said glaring at Babb. "I wondered where you disappeared to." She curled her lip a little further and shifted her gaze to Lucas. "And who's your scruffy friend?" she drawled.

Babb found the woman's steely confidence totally unnerving. "Err…this is Meredith Higham's lawyer," she blurted without thinking. "He's here to help me find her."

"Well, sweetie, that's a new one on me," she mocked. "So, I'm afraid you're barking up the wrong tree – I have absolutely no idea who you are talking about."

Lucas shook his head, he'd heard enough and the strange stand-off was bizarrely surreal. "Look, lady," he said in his most authoritarian tone. "We need to see Mrs Higham - we need to speak to her urgently."

"Lawyer, huh?" the witch snapped, looking him up and down. "Are you shittin' me. Are you for real?"

Lucas did all he could to restrain himself. "I'm very real," he hissed. "So, I would respectfully suggest you help us with our request."

The woman stared for a second. "OK, then, just give me a minute," she said with an unconvincing shrug. "Wait for me by the elevator, I just need to get something from my car."

The pair of them stopped in front of the glass lift and watched the woman walk on towards the line of parked cars. "I don't trust her for a second," Lucas whispered in Babb's ear. "Get ready to run if she tries anything funny, OK?"

Babb nodded. "Sure," she said, "but what can she do?"

Seconds later the retort of an automatic weapon answered the question. "Oh shit," Lucas yelled as he dragged Babb toward the safety of the nearest lump of concrete. "She's got a gun."

The first volley of shots was well off the mark, but the intention was clear. The sunken eyed witch was out for blood and, as she headed back to the lift with an Uzi machine pistol in hand, she wanted everyone to know about it. "You can't run," she shouted, "and you can't hide, but you can come out nice and slow with your arms up."

As she reached the screen by Stairwell 2, Rick suddenly appeared. And before the ghoul even had a chance to register his presence, he'd blasted her full in the face with a fire extinguisher. The freezing cold cloud of CO_2 took The Divinity's resident harpy completely by surprise. She dropped the Uzi, screamed loudly, and started to claw at her eyes. As she recoiled in squealing rage, Rick followed up with a swift kick to the back of her legs which dumped her straight on her scrawny backside.

"Now you fucking behave yourself," the South African shouted. "You know that's no way to treat visitors."

***

Dominic Williams heard the echoing clatter of gunfire as he frantically shovelled papers through the small aperture of the furnace. With the small observation door open fully, the heat in the boiler room had passed the point of merely being oppressive and was now bordering on unbearable. With only two bags left to empty, the panting cleric was convinced he could finish the task before he fainted. Choosing to ignore the shots, the sweat drenched Father mopped his brow, summoned up a final reserve of energy, and continued with his vital mission.

Back in the underground car park, Lucas, Babb and Rick had surrounded Erica Gomez. The incapacitated woman was still wailing. Her hair and face were caked with white CO_2 residue which gave her the appearance of an ancient, withered clown.

"I told you," Lucas said to Babb. "I knew we couldn't trust her."

Babb was ashen faced. "She fired at us with a machine gun," she said. "That's just plain crazy. I've had enough…this whole situation has got completely out of hand."

"And it could easily get worse," Rick said. "We need to get out of here."

"What about the book?" Lucas asked. "We're here for the book; no other reason."

Babb and Rick looked at the now wild-eyed Englishman. "But Roxy, it was a long shot," Rick said. "One that we didn't really believe, so maybe we just forget it for the time being, eh?"

"No way," Lucas said glancing at the groaning woman on the floor. "I think we ask Ugly here what she knows."

As Rick locked eyes with his colleague, he knew his mind was made up. "OK, Sarge," he said, "give it a whirl; it's your call."

For a moment Lucas remained expressionless, then he bent over and grabbed the snivelling woman by the ear. "I need your help," he snarled as he twisted her pierced lobe, "and if you don't cooperate, my dear, I'm going to hurt you really badly."

As the receptionist from hell squealed in pain, Babb turned away. "Is this really necessary, Mr Roxby?" she asked.

"Yes," Lucas snapped, "it is, and if you're squeamish then I suggest you go back and help your sister with the patient."

Babb didn't need any further encouragement and scampered off back to the stairwell as fast as her aching legs could carry her.

CHAPTER 57

The Last Stand

Federal reinforcements took their time arriving, but when they did, they weren't subtle. The first units through the tree-shrouded entrance raced down the access road and arrived in the car park with a squeal of rubber and a wail of sirens. The three armoured vehicles fanned out in front of the building and, as a swarm of Kevlar clad storm troopers emerged from the hulking machines, the lone Armalite opened up. Within a matter of seconds, fifteen highly trained special weapons officers had established the shooter's position. A wall of return fire erupted from the car park and the dense vegetation on the steep embankment imploded. No match for the backup forces and with no choice but to abandon his position, the sniper headed for cover. The authorities kept up the incessant volley of rounds for several seconds before the lead officer called time. Then, after five tense seconds of silence confirmed no incoming rounds, two forced entry teams targeted the front door and a second wave of armed units hot-footed it down the side of the building.

The sudden cacophony of sound could be heard for miles. In the basement, the noise reverberated so loudly through the bare concrete it could have registered a 7.5 on the Richter scale.

Rick shouted, "What the hell's going on out there?"

In surprise, Lucas let go of the woman's ear and she slumped to the floor. "Shit, that's a lot of shooting," he said as he listened to the volley of gunfire. "I hope it's friendly."

As the two men stood transfixed by the noise, Marion appeared. “What the hell’s going on?” she shouted over the noise. “Is it the cavalry?”

“Better had be,” Lucas answered. “Because if it isn’t, then we’ve got some serious problems.”

Suddenly the noise ceased, and the basement fell silent. Marion looked at Lucas then pointed at his feet. “Has she said anything?” she asked looking at the wild-haired mess on the floor. “Any info on the book?”

Lucas pulled a face. “I haven’t asked yet,” he said. “If you hadn’t noticed, we just got rudely interrupted.”

Before Marion could respond, the woman looked up and spat at Lucas. “I wouldn’t tell you shit,” she snarled. “You can go fuck yourself.”

Instantly Lucas reached down, grabbed her ear again and yanked her back to her feet. “I’d watch your mouth, freak,” he said as he pulled her upward, “or it’ll only get worse.”

The woman howled in protest. “You will die for this, heathen,” she hissed through gritted teeth. “You will all burn in hell.”

The threesome looked incredulously at the crazed woman now dangling ranting from Lucas’s outstretched arm.

“Who the fuck do you think you are?” Rick jammed his face up to hers. “The wicked witch of the west?”

The woman rolled her red streaming eyes and smiled. “Ye of little faith,” she said coldly, “you’re always the easiest to fool.”

Lucas had had enough; the woman was clearly deranged and appeared close to losing it completely. “Ricky, you take her,” he ordered. “I can’t be doing with the bitch.”

The South African dutifully grabbed hold of the woman by the neck of her dress. Just then, Babb appeared.

“Patient update: he’s breathing on his own now,” she said, “but it’s still touch and go.”

Lucas tried to smile but it was a struggle. “OK, nurse,” he said with a simple nod, “we won’t try to move him. But we need to find out what’s going on. The glass lift, where does it go?”

"I only went two floors," Babb replied. "I got in at L1 and came down here – that's it."

"What's on L1?"

"The main lobby, a reception area and some weird storage room," she shrugged, "that's all I saw."

"Nothing else?"

She thought hard about the question. "Well there's restrooms," she said with an unconscious rub of the dimple on her chin, "and in the lobby there's all kinds of fancy seating. And some sort of exhibition."

Lucas furrowed his brow, "Exhibition? An exhibition of what?"

"Military History I guess," she replied. "There were old manuscripts, flags, swords and other weird stuff all on show in a line of glass cabinets."

"OK, thanks," he muttered. He turned to his partner who still had tight hold of the demonic female, keeping her at arm's length, facing away from him. "She still causing grief?" he asked.

"She's vile," Rick answered. "Keeps spitting and foaming at the mouth – it's disgusting."

Lucas grimaced. "You'll have to put up with it for a little longer," he said. "You, me, and witchypoo are going upstairs for a nose about."

Rick shrugged. "Whatever you say, Sarge," he replied, but Marion didn't look taken by the idea.

"What about me and B?" she asked. "What are we supposed to do while you disappear?"

"You look after Dooley," he said, "and wait for the cavalry."

***

The lift flew past L-2 and reached L1 in a matter of seconds. Thankfully the room was clear and, as the doors slid open, Rick pushed the woman out first and looked over her shoulder. "Which way's the lobby?" Lucas asked her.

"Go fuck yourself, dickhead," she spat. "I ain't telling you shit."

Lucas could contain his rage no more. He strode out of the lift, moved a step to the side, then turned and smacked the woman hard across the back of the head. It was only a glancing blow with an open palm, but it made him feel a whole lot better. "I told you to watch your mouth, bitch," he said as her head snapped forward, "but would you listen?"

She was now muttering a stream of profanities. Death threats, curses, and obscene slurs on his character were coming thick and fast. "Jesus, Ricky," Lucas said as she continued her depraved jabbering, "this woman's a friggin' nightmare…we need to ditch her."

"Where exactly?"

"Don't know," Lucas replied. "But we need to find somewhere quick before I kill her."

Rick nodded, then pushed the woman forward. Lucas instinctively moved past to take point, then stopped to peer round the corner of the room's short side. As he checked the lay of the land, the banks of steel security cabinets that ran up and down the main floor area intrigued him. "Some set-up, this," he said as he looked them over. "I'd love to know what it's all for."

Before Rick could comment, the witch spoke. "Bet you would," she said. "You want me to explain it to you?"

Lucas turned to face the wild-eyed harpy. "I don't doubt for one minute you want to," he said, "but we're really pushed for time, so save it for later, eh."

Her eyes widened in anger. "Funny fucker, aren't you, white boy?" she snarled, "That'll soon change."

Lucas shook his head in despair. "Come on, Rick, let's keep going, let's see what's through here."

The strange trio negotiated the small front desk, went through the doorway into the reception area and filed past the long counter. Then, just as they turned, they caught a glimpse of activity outside. On the other side of the lobby, through the tight squares of the metal shutters, the two men could see swathes of sparks illuminating the darkness. The fiery orange arcs shooting upward were generated by power-saws cutting through the frame of the external doors. They were mesmerising. As the duo stood and watched the action, the noise increased. "We should let them in," Rick said. "It's crazy not to."

"I agree," Lucas replied. "But how do you open up? Where's the control box, where the fuck d'you start? It's gonna be a remote high-tech system, it'll be in a master control room but that could be anywhere in the building!"

"Oh, clever boy," the witch cackled. "Not just a pretty face, are we?"

Rick looked at his partner and shook his head. "Maybe I'll kill her first," he said. "Save you the trouble."

Lucas nearly laughed but thought better of it. "They'll be through those doors in minutes," he said, "and I want to find this exhibition thing before they do."

"Well, I'm putting her in the bog first," Rick said.

"You mean in there?" Lucas asked pointing at the restroom.

"Yebo, that's the plan, and I'm gonna jam the door shut with one of those chairs."

Lucas watched as Rick bundled the Wicked Witch of the West into the Ladies, then slammed the door and wedged a chair tightly under the handle. "Nice one," he said over the furious banging coming from the other side, "you've done us all a favour."

As the noise of power tools mingled with the harpy's continued protests, the HSG team set off to explore the lobby. Desperate to find the glass cabinets Babb said she'd seen, they crossed to the far side of the enormous room. It was Rick who found it. "Over here, Sarge," he shouted from behind a timber archway. "It's just like she said."

As the two men leant over the first unit, Lucas pulled out the twisted remains of his reading glasses and balanced them on his nose. "This is amazing," he said after a few seconds of scrutiny, "but what's the relevance to this place?"

"Couldn't tell you," the South African answered. "Doesn't make any sense to me."

The display was much like Babb had explained. It was indeed military themed and consisted of an array of paraphernalia including medals, weapons and portraits. On closer inspection it became apparent it charted the exploits of a French infantry regiment over a period of nearly a hundred years. Cabinet one was dated around 1652 and the display ended in late 1746.

"Use your phone," Lucas ordered, "take photos of everything."

As Rick did as he was told, Lucas continued reading some of the ancient manuscripts on display. "Fuck me," he said as he studied the copper plate script on a tatty yellowed parchment, "this is a commendation dated 1742." He took a deep breath. "Here's your connection, Ricky! Get this: it's for '*des actes de bravoure*' and is awarded to a Sergeant-at-arms called Dubois, one Ravel Claude Dubois."

"Dubois?" Rick said loudly. "As in the guy we were told about in Mesa?"

"Got to be," Lucas replied. "The name here is Dubois and Coleman's boss was called Dubois; a little too coincidental, don't you think?"

Rick didn't get a chance to answer; suddenly the heavy clatter of booted feet distracted them from their studies and in an instant they were surrounded by a group of black clad armed men.

"You two on the floor," the lead figure screamed. "Both of you now."

Lucas and Rick knew the drill. Instantly they clasped their hands at the back of their heads and knelt down.

"We're not armed," Lucas said nervously. "We're friendlies."

"I'll be the judge of that, motherfucker," came a gruff response, "but for now, if you two boys stay nice and calm we just might not have to shoot you."

Rick looked at Lucas and nodded then turned back to face the array of pointing weapons. "Whatever you say, officer," he said politely. "We won't budge an inch."

***

After Marion watched Lucas and Rick leave the basement, she re-joined her sister who'd stayed tending their casualty. Special agent Wade Dooley had rallied a little since his near passing and now Babb was trying to encourage him to talk.

"Mr Dooley," she cooed. "You feeling any better? Are you warm enough? Would you like a sip of water?"

The man's eyes were open, he was conscious, but still - other than groans - he didn't speak.

"I think we just keep him warm and comfortable," Marion said. "He's not up to talking."

Babb smiled and started to plump up the ski jacket they'd placed under the agent's blood smeared head. "I know, sis," she said. "I just want him to be OK."

At the sound of approaching footsteps, the sisters froze. Marion looked wide eyed at her sister and in hushed tones asked, "Is that the boys coming back?"

"It might be," Babb whispered, "but it only sounds like one person."

Babb was right, it was the sound of lone footsteps. But the size 10's making them belonged to Dominic Williams. As the rotund, sweat drenched father appeared around the doorway of Stairwell 2, the sisters were as shocked as he was.

"Who are you?" Babb blurted at the surprised man. "Are you with the FBI?"

The cleric stopped dead at the apparition before him and his mind went blank. A vision of two middle aged women tending a prone, bloodied body in blue overalls was not a sight he was expecting. Seemingly, it was a sight he also couldn't process.

"Hey, mister," Babb came again, "are you here to help agent Dooley?"

This time, Williams recognised the woman asking the questions. It was the visitor he'd tracked earlier on the CCTV, the woman he'd interrogated over the PA and who'd ultimately vanished from the lobby.

"No, I'm not," he said, looking straight at Babb. "Are you with the government?"

There was an awkward silence. The cleric and the sisters stared at each other for a second.

"Sorry," Babb eventually said. "Did you just ask me if I'm with the FBI?"

As the question hung in the air like a bad smell, Williams now rued his decision to take Stair 2 to the strong room. It was a bad one and it was time to leave. Without a word of explanation, he about faced and walked away.

"Hey, where you going?" Marion shouted. "Come back here and help us."

The sisters looked fleetingly at each other, then Babb got to her feet. "I'm going after him," she said. "Whoever he is, surely he can do something."

As she charged out of the stairwell enclosure she yelled after the lumbering figure, "Hey, wait up, will you, we need some help here."

The barrel shaped Father stopped and turned. "Back off, lady," he warned, "just fucking back off."

Babb was astounded at the man's attitude but ignored the threats and continued toward him. The exasperated cleric stood his ground, shook his head, then reached under his shirt. "I'm warning you," he said, now waving a gun in her direction, "stay the fuck away from me."

As she stopped and spun away in horror, the revolver fired. It was meant as a warning shot but the .38 calibre round hit a concrete pillar and ricocheted across the basement. The shot slammed into Babb and sent her sprawling across the tyre blackened concrete like a ten-pin skittle in full flight. The Father didn't hang round to find out what the damage was; he simply slotted the snub-nosed Colt back into its belt pouch, wiped his ever-sodden brow, and shuffled off.

Marion, startled by the shot, immediately raced to check on her sibling. At the sight of her sweet baby sister lying face down on the floor, her heart sank. "Oh, Lord Jesus," she screamed as she sprinted to her aid. "Please, please don't let it be."

Babb was out for the count; her knees were skinned and her face was grazed, but she was breathing. Marion frantically patted her down looking for evidence of a bullet wound but found nothing. "It's my back, sis," she eventually moaned, "it's stinging like crazy."

Marion was relieved to hear her talk and now focused on the small nylon back-pack her sister had carried religiously all trip. It was nestled in its usual place in the middle of her back but now it had a fresh tear right across the front.

"Let me get this off," she said as she flicked her finger back and forth through the hole. "Can you roll to one side?"

With a pained groan, Babb part rolled on her left side allowing Marion to feel underneath and pop the chest clasp open. "Good girl," she whispered, "now the other side." Seconds later, Marion had whipped off the backpack and was cautiously examining her sister. With no obvious signs of blood, she peeled up Babb's shirt. "Jeepers creepers," she said as she exposed two angry red welts centred just below her bra strap, "that's gonna bruise like hell."

Now assured Babb wasn't dying, Marion grabbed the backpack to look for answers. "I need to check your bag," she said as her sister started to ease up onto all fours. "Don't know what happened but something sure did."

She tipped the contents onto the floor, then let out a gasp of disbelief. "Oh, my sweet Lord," she said as she picked something out of the pile. "This is unreal!" Her eyes widened as she examined the deformed .38 slug embedded in the focus mechanism of Babb's field glasses. "You're not going to believe this, B," she said shaking her head, "but you just got saved by the army surplus store!"

As the exhausted sisters sat on the concrete floor trying to come to terms with Babb's death-defying experience, Marion hugged her trembling sibling. "That was close," she whispered. "You're a very lucky girl, Barbara. Someone's sure looking out for you."

Lost in their world of utter relief, the sisters were oblivious to the SWAT team that had crept up behind them.

"Ladies," a deep voice echoed from the gloom. "Nice and slow if you don't mind, hands behind your heads and don't move a muscle...."

CHAPTER 58

A Sigh of Relief

After the raid, Lucas, Rick, and the sisters were taken into custody by the FBI. Quickly, the shell-shocked foursome were split up and interviewed separately. Unsurprisingly, their accounts of who they were and how they'd come to be snarled up in the chaotic Colorado siege all matched. But despite this indisputable corroboration, it still took the federal investigators some time to verify the details and, although ultimately their explanation was accepted, it had been an uphill battle.

"You sure you're OK, ma'am?" the agent with the square jaw asked. "That's a hell of a whack you've taken there."

As Babb hobbled out of the holding cell, she looked up and managed a smile. "I'll be fine, thanks," she said. "I'm all strapped up and dosed with pain killers…so I reckon I'll live."

The man laughed. "OK, Mrs Teller," he said, "you just follow me down the corridor. You can go sit with your sister while we finish up the paperwork."

"What about Mr Roxby and Mr Kruger?" she asked. "Are they here?"

"No, ma'am, they're at another facility, but they'll be fine."

Babb looked relieved. "That's good," she said softly, "but it's such a pity they didn't find what they were looking for."

The agent smiled. "Well, don't you fret about it, ma'am." he said reassuringly. "The important thing is you all got out in one piece."

She shook her head gently. "You're telling me," she replied. "I still can't believe I got shot in the back by a man of the cloth. How'd you explain that at the Golf Club?"

***

Ray Stuart did not expect a call at 7.30am on a Wednesday morning from the FBI in Cortez, Colorado, but he got one. "Yes, yes, I know Lucas Roxby," he said indignantly. "The infuriating man works for me."

Twenty-five minutes later, he said goodbye to the agent with the cool mid-western twang and slumped down at his kitchen table with a resounding bump. As soon as the scrape of the chair had finished echoing round the room, a voice drifted down the stairs.

"Ray, is everything OK?" it asked. "What was that all about?"

"I've been better," he shouted back, "and if you want more than that, then come down here."

Margaret Stuart could tell by her husband's abrupt tone he wasn't happy. During thirty-five years of wedded bliss some things never changed. "OK, love," she said. "I'll be right down."

Ray pushed back his chair, stood up, and went to the sink. He filled the kettle then set it down on its black plastic base and flicked the switch.

"What a pain in the arse," he muttered to himself. "Two weeks' work and sweet FA to show for it. Now this."

The crafty old dog wasn't prone to exaggeration but now and again, when he needed to make a point, he wasn't averse to manipulating the truth and using it to his advantage. And whilst it hadn't been two weeks since Lucas and Rick flew out to Phoenix - more like ten days - the crux of his gripe was justified.

But Ray could still not believe one of HSG's senior field teams had gone to the USA on a straightforward collection assignment and failed. Not only had the job run overtime but the whereabouts of the client's cherished asset was still unknown and now he had the unenviable task of passing on the bad news. But that wasn't the CEO's biggest problem. What annoyed him the most were the commercial implications of failure. Recovery contracts were notoriously one sided and always results based. No find, no fee could hurt sometimes, and Ray knew that on this one the HSG would only feel pain.

"Now, Raymond," Margaret said as she walked into her well-ordered kitchen. "Who's stressing you out so early this morning?"

Ray chose not to answer the question straight off. "I'm having a coffee first," he grunted. "Do you want one?"

She smiled at the disheartened figure standing by the kettle. "The usual, please," she said, "and don't skimp on the cream." Although Ray was less than impressed with the latest developments from the US he was still intent on starting the day with his favourite brew.

"Yes, dear," he replied. "It will be perfect."

Coffees made, husband and wife settled opposite each other at the kitchen table. Margaret knew it would be easier if she made the first move. "Come on then, grumpy," she coaxed softly. "What's happened now?"

This time Ray responded immediately. "You know this job we've got in the US," he said. "the one that's not been going quite to plan?"

She pulled a face. "Of course I do," she said. "If you think back to Saturday, it even kept me up late, so, yes, I'm well aware of it."

Ray gestured toward the phone on the work top by the window. "Well, that call was from the FBI in Colorado," he said. "Our two superstars have been caught up in some major federal investigation and are now in custody giving statements."

Margaret's eyes widened in amazement. "You're joking! Lucas and Rick have been arrested?"

"No, no, it's not quite that bad," he assured her, "but they've got a hell of a lot of explaining to do."

She sat back in obvious relief. "Will you call them home now?"

"Of course I will," he said. "We'll have them back before you know it." He stopped to smell his coffee, "but it's a pitiful result and we're at least ten grand out of pocket, but I suppose I'll have to shoulder some of the blame."

Margaret gently shook her head. "Will you, love? Why's that?"

Ray stroked his stubble and frowned. "Well, it was me who bloody convinced them to carry on and go to Colorado," he said. "That was a bad move. I should've aborted the job way before that came up. I mean, it was obvious by day three we were never going to get the book but oh, no, we knew best: we soldiered on, and where did it get us?"

She smiled and put her hand over his. "Look, Ray, no one's died," she said, "no one's been injured, and it sounds like your two boys will have some good tales to tell, so I'd just chalk it up to experience, love. You can't always get it right, can you?" she shrugged. "As the old saying goes…you win some you lose some."

Ray sat back in his chair and looked thoughtful for a few seconds. "Maybe a touch simplistic, Marg," he said eventually, "but you know what - on this one you could be right."

***

Forty minutes later, Ray arrived at the office, headed straight to the first floor and, as hoped, found Gerry at his desk. But very quickly it became obvious his co-Director wasn't going to take the breaking news quite as philosophically as his wife had.

"How the fuck did that happen?" Gerry squawked as the early morning call from Colorado was explained.

The Ops Director remained behind his desk as Ray slumped in the leather armchair opposite him then hung his head in despair.

"Beats me," he said. "It's an even bigger fuck up than I imagined."

Gerry grimaced. "Have we heard from the boys themselves?" he asked.

"Not a dickie bird," Ray said with a shake of the head. "But the guy from the FBI said it could be hours before they're released, so it's just a matter of waiting for them to call us."

"And in the meantime, what we supposed to do?"

"Well, for starters we should brief Sarah and Steve," Ray said. "Then I reckon we ring Calvin and explain the whole thing's finally gone tits up."

Staring glumly at his equally miserable partner, Gerry picked up the phone. "OK, Raymond," he said as he punched in Steve Harrison's extension number, "let's get them up here."

***

The coffee looked like dishwater and the biscuits were as hard as bricks, but Lucas and Rick had taken the late gesture of hospitality as a positive sign. And, whilst the tale of how they'd been snared in a federal operation and why they had two middle aged sisters from Arizona in tow, was more than a little convoluted it was something the investigators were slowly beginning to believe.

After the initial round of interviews, the HSG duo had spent a further two hours mapping out every single stage of their ten-day stay on US soil. But eventually - with the help of several phone calls, their own company paperwork and various internet searches - the authorities realised that everything the pair were claiming was actually true.

"Mr Roxby," the FBI captain finally said. "I'm sure you realise we can't divulge any more investigation details to you. It's all confidential, sir, classified information."

"Yeah, yeah," Lucas said quickly. "Of course, we understand all that. It's just that at the end of the day we're not your average Joe Public, are we?" He raised his eyebrows as he awaited some sort of acknowledgement but got nothing back so just carried on. "You see, we came to the US purely to collect a book," he said, "an important book, a book we've gone on and on about for the last five hours, so I don't think it's unreasonable for us to ask if it's been recovered, do you?"

The Captain nearly smiled but thought better of it. "Like I say, Mr Roxby," he said calmly, "I am not at liberty to tell you what, if anything, has been recovered from any of the buildings currently under investigation. You should remember that anything we do find may form part of our evidence portfolio and as such will be deemed government property, at least as long as the investigation is still live."

"But this is just an old book," Lucas protested, "I can't see how it will have any relevance to your investigation."

"Mr Roxby," the captain snapped, "you have absolutely no idea about what's relevant and what's not, so if I were you I'd quit while you're ahead and prepare to leave while I deem you are still free to do so," he paused and turned to a dark suited colleague. "Dobson, take these two gentlemen to the ground floor, will you. I'll follow you down in a minute."

"Is that it?" Lucas asked. "We get tipped out on the street with nothing but a 'get lost and good riddance' ringing in our ears?"

The captain's bull neck started to flush with frustration. "This is the United States of America, Mr Roxby," he said, "and you will be treated with the respect we accord all our visitors, but if you continue to be obstructive I will have no choice but to arrest you. And that is no idle threat."

Lucas stared at the man for a moment, "On what charge?"

But before the FBI chief could answer, Rick was swift to diffuse the situation. "We're going, sir," he said as he grabbed Lucas by the arm. "My colleague and I fully understand the position and we thank you for your help."

"Do we?" Lucas snapped as he pulled away from his partner. "Do we really?"

The South African wasn't being swayed. "Roxy, just move it, will you," he said with a firm shove. "It is time to leave."

"Very sensible, Mr Kruger," the Captain said. "Now, if that's all, will you gentlemen please follow agent Dobson down to the desk where he will ensure all your personal effects are returned to you," he gestured toward the door, "and I will be down shortly to formally sign you out of the building, OK?"

Lucas glared at the FBI Captain but now, much to Rick's relief, he remained silent and this time, when shoved lightly towards the door, he didn't resist.

"That's it, Sarge," Rick whispered. "Let's just get out of here… it's time to go home."

True to his word, ten minutes later the FBI captain appeared in the main reception to bid farewell to the HSG team. "Well, gentlemen," he said. "I trust you have had everything you came with returned to you."

Rick held out his battered old travel bag. "Yes, sir," he smiled as he shook it, "all present and correct."

"Mr Roxby?" The Captain asked. "Have you got everything?"

Lucas was now calmer but still unhappy and was reluctant to answer. "Yeah, it's all here," he said eventually; but then - after a furtive glance round - asked, "So what happens now?"

The Captain locked eyes with the disconsolate Brit. "Firstly, we'll sign off the official release forms." As he spoke, Lucas thought he saw the first sign of a smile appear on the bureau stalwart's face. "Then Dobson here is going to drive you two boys downtown to reunite you with your travelling buddies and that fancy 4X4 of theirs. Then, hopefully, you can all head home."

Lucas and Rick glanced at each other, then Lucas turned back to the Captain. "Well, that's a bit better than I was expecting," he said, "but one last question if you don't mind, chief?"

The Captain shook his head and sighed. "Yeah, sure, Mr Roxby," he said. "Shoot!"

"Our Book of Martyrs, if you do actually find it and it's not used as evidence, can we get it back for our clients?"

The FBI chief remained silent for a moment then finally broke into a grin. "Mr Roxby, if that's how it pans out," he said, "then rest assured, sir, we'll be in touch."

***

Agent Dobson dropped the duo outside the FBI's Colorado headquarters on Central Boulevard and told them to wait. "This is your stop, guys," he said as he pulled up outside the impressive stone facade. "That's our building and your lady friends will be out in a minute, OK?"

"Yeah, that's great, Mr Dobson," Lucas replied. "Thanks for the ride. But what about the Jeep?"

"Don't worry about that, sir," the agent replied. "As soon as the ladies have been discharged, it'll be brought round to you," he paused. "You're best waiting over there," he said, pointing to a drop-off lay-by just up from the entrance steps. "The vehicle will pull in there."

***

When Marion glimpsed Lucas and Rick standing outside, she couldn't contain her relief. "Look, B," she said excitedly. "Looks who's here." Minutes later, as big sister helped little sister down the steep stone steps, Marion was desperate to attract the attention of the waiting duo. "Yoo-hoo!" she shouted. "Over here!"

"Finally," Lucas said as he spotted the sisters descending the steps, "the Armstrong's make an appearance."

The foursome greeted each other like long lost family and, despite their overnight stay in federal custody and very little sleep, all four were remarkably chirpy.

"How's the injury, Babb?" Rick asked. "What did the medics say?"

Babb pulled a glum face. "Well," she said, "they were amazed at what had happened. Apparently, I've got an imprint of a pair of field glasses in the middle of my back, surrounded by a massive bruise. One doctor reckoned it looks like a deformed butterfly."

"Sounds nasty," he said. "How bad does it hurt?"

"Not too bad now," she grinned. "Co-codamol washed down with strong coffee seems to have done the trick… All I need now is a good night's sleep."

"Sleep on the way home," Lucas said. "Best way to pass five hours."

As the four of them stood outside on the pavement recounting the events of the last twelve hours, the blue Wrangler pulled up in the lay-by.

"Here she is," Babb grinned as the obviously road worn Jeep arrived. "My precious Ruby come to whisk us home."

Lucas grinned. "Could have bloody washed it," he muttered to Rick. "It's the least they owe us."

Rick chuckled, then a tall man in overalls jumped out of the driver's seat. "Mrs Teller?" he enquired as he looked at the group huddled on the pavement.

"Right over here," Babb waved. "That's me."

The man smiled and nodded. "All I need is one signature, ma'am," he said, raising a clip board, "then you're good to go."

CHAPTER 59

Going Home

The answer was still No, and Europol's investigation chief was not happy about it. Whilst Operation Stormbringer would be hailed by all as a massive success and lauded for years as a shining example of the power of unified co-operation between law enforcement agencies across the globe, in Koeman's personal book of achievement it was not enough.

"Are we sure there is no sign?" he asked for the third time. "Are we one hundred per cent positive he's escaped?"

From the FBI's base in Tucson, the special agent in charge had already explained the situation several times. He'd gone over and over the latest feedback from the Colorado raid more times than he would've liked. And each time he made it crystal clear that the closest they'd come to Vincent Dubois was an agent with a fractured skull and an abandoned blue Volkswagen van.

"But why didn't you hold him?" Koeman asked. "Why did your guys let him slip away?"

The FBI lead had the greatest respect for his Europol counterpart, but from five and a half thousand miles away he wasn't easy to convince. "Virgil," he said firmly. "It wasn't quite like that…like I have said, initially we had one agent infiltrate the building, that's all." He cleared his throat. "And, yes, that operative should have recognised Dubois, but he didn't. He appeared out of the dark of the basement and caught him off guard, OK?"

"But to be that close," the Dutchman groaned, "to be that close, then blow the chance, and now know the psycho's slithered back under a rock. It's…it's too painful."

"We will get him," the SAC said reassuringly. "He'll get sloppy. It's just going to take time."

"But have we got time?"

"Look, Virgil," came the frustrated reply, "you've got to remember the man has nothing now. His organisation is in tatters, his support network's all but gone, and The Divinity's bank accounts have been frozen. He's on his own."

The Europol boss remained silent for a few seconds as he digested his distant allies' words. "But you must find him," he said. "The man is pure evil; he is a cancer that must never be allowed to grow again."

"We know how dangerous he is," the SAC said. "His capture is a top priority and will remain so until we have him in custody." He took a deep breath. "We have a nationwide APB out to all federal agencies, all state police and all transport networks. The airports and ports are on stand-by. Currently, Vincent Dubois is in America's Top Five Most Wanted. If he makes a move, we'll know about it."

Again, Koeman was slow to answer. "OK, OK," he said finally. "All I can say, then, is best of luck and thank you again to you and the bureau for its supreme effort over the last eighteen months…you have been incredible."

"Well, thank you too, sir," the FBI man replied. "It's been a pleasure and an honour to have been of service…and Virgil," he paused, "rest assured we will get him, I promise. We just need a little more time so please, please, be patient!"

***

The journey from Cortez, Colorado back to Arizona's North Peak National Park would be another long one. Rick took his usual place behind the wheel while Lucas informed Marion he was taking back his role as navigator.

"Don't argue with me, lady," he'd said in a mock John Wayne voice. "I'm back in the front seat for this one. You've done your share, so you get your head down, snuggle up, and get some rest."

Marion had been relieved at the Englishman's insistence. Whilst she'd enjoyed the challenge and the adventure of the last few days, now, after the events of the last eighteen hours - particularly the awful news concerning Meredith Higham - she was ready for home. "Thank you, Lucas," she said sweetly. "I really do need to get some sleep."

With his trusty road atlas back on his knee, the ex-Staff Sergeant was ready to guide the weary squad back to the mountain cabin. "OK, Rick," he said. "It's back to the old days, but this time I'll try and be a bit more Marion-like in my navigation style, OK?"

Rick nodded then looked in his rear view. "Ladies, you ready for home?" he asked.

"We sure are," Marion mumbled, "so much so that Barbara can't keep her eyes open."

Lucas turned to check on their passengers and smiled at the sight of Babb with her head on a blanket, out like a light. "Ahhh," he said as he looked at the comatose form in the corner, "now that's the way to travel."

As the Jeep pulled out into the steady traffic of the main thoroughfare, Rick retrieved his sunglasses from a side pocket and slipped them on.

"Don't leave it too long, Sarge," he said. "You've got to do it sooner or later, so I'd get it out of the way now."

Lucas new exactly what he was referring too and simply pulled a face. "I'm going to leave it awhile," he said. "I'll need to psych myself up for this one." He scraped his fingers through his matted hair. "Ringing Gerry is hard enough at the best of times. Lord knows what he'll say about this one."

***

When Jo Knox put Lucas's call through to Gerry's office, she hadn't expected such a fierce reaction.

"Of course I want to take it," the Operations Director snapped. "That man has some serious bloody explaining to do."

Without a moment's hesitation, Jo put Lucas through to his boss. "Transferring you now, Lucas," she said. "Enjoy."

"Thanks, Jo," he replied, but she'd already gone.

"Lucas Roxby," Gerry said loudly. "Finally, we get a call. We are honoured."

The ex-sapper was prepared for the attitude and the tirade that would inevitably follow. "Yes, Gerry, it is I," he said hoping humour would ease the tension. "And do I have a tale to tell."

Gerry was oblivious to the tactic. "I'm sure you have," he replied fiercely. "Raymond's told everyone about his conversation with the FBI and now we're all desperate to hear your side of the story."

Lucas decided to change tack. As the ever-present wind rush made conversation a little difficult, he used it to his advantage and feigned difficulty in hearing his boss when he tried to butt in.

"So that's it in a nutshell, really, Gerry," he said toward the end of his long tale. "Then the place was crawling with SWAT teams and FBI guys shouting at us. We all got arrested and that was that. It was game over."

Gerry had given up interrupting but now there was silence. "Any trace of the book?" he asked hopefully. "Anything positive we can report back to the client? Any news at all?"

Lucas's response was instant. "The FBI wouldn't tell us a thing," he said, "but they did confirm that if the book turned up during the remainder of their investigation and wasn't deemed to be evidence then they would let us know."

"Do the authorities understand it's not Divinity property?"

"It took a little time, but eventually they accepted the book belongs to others and that we were entitled to be looking to recover it on their behalf."

"Well, that's good to hear," Gerry said. "At least that's one thing cleared up." The line crackled briefly, then he asked, "Where are you now?"

Lucas answered without thinking. "Heading back to Flagstaff," he said.

"Why?" Gerry asked. "What's in Flagstaff? Why don't you off-hire the car at the nearest airport and get back home?"

For the first time during the call, Lucas was stuck for words. "Err…well it's a long story," he stammered. "One I'd rather explain to you face to face if that's alright."

This time it was Gerry's turn for silence. "You do worry me at times, Roxby, you really do," he said after the pregnant pause, "but you know what, kid, I think we'll leave it there for now…We just want you two home safe and sound, so hurry up. Pick your flights, then ring it in and we'll sort it, OK?"

Lucas was taken aback by Gerry's sudden considerate tone. "OK, boss. We'll call you later."

"Good," came a gentle reply, "safe journey, bye for now."

Gerry still pulled his usual instant hang-up routine and didn't get to hear the reciprocated good bye, but Lucas wasn't fazed.

"Did you get that?" he said turning to Rick. "At the end there, our super chief sounded almost kind and caring, even said he's desperate to get us back safe and sound."

Rick laughed. "Are you sure you were speaking to the right Gerry Hanlon?"

Now Lucas laughed. "Yeah, I think so," he said, "but maybe he's had a personality transplant."

***

Two hours into the journey and progress was good. They were now deep in Arizona, but the team needed a break. The sisters were asleep so couldn't have a say in the matter, but Lucas was busting for a piss, Rick was starving, and the Jeep was down to a quarter tank of fuel.

At the next exit showing a filling station sign they pulled off the highway to search for the much-needed services. Thankfully they didn't have to go far; no sooner had they come off the slip road than a gleaming new Exxon station appeared in view.

"That was too easy," Lucas said. "But that's not a complaint, mind." Rick didn't comment, his stomach was growling loudly and all he wanted to do was silence it.

Ten minutes later, the Jeep had been fuelled and, as the two men returned to the vehicle bearing gifts, they announced their return. "Wakey, wakey, ladies," Lucas said to the dazed looking occupants of the rear seat. "Any one for coffee and nibbles?"

Despite their catatonic state, both women accepted the offer eagerly and then, after Rick had driven the Jeep to an adjacent parking area, the foursome settled down to enjoy their roadside picnic. As they tucked in, Marion was keen to work out how far they'd travelled. "Two hours twenty" she said, checking her watch. "We must be over halfway."

"Close," Rick said. "So, yeah… I reckon maybe another two and half hours should do it."

As they finished off their ad hoc lunch, Babb gathered up the empty cups and wrappers. "I'm going to get rid of these," she said addressing the group. "Then powder my nose. Anyone need anything else while I'm at it?"

Her companions said they were fine, so Babb headed off, and as she disappeared into the rest room Lucas turned to Rick. "We haven't shown Marion the photos, have we?" he had a sudden thought. "Maybe she can shed some light on the display."

Before Rick could answer, a now curious Marion cut in. "Photos of what?" she asked.

Lucas quickly brought her up to speed. He explained how during the sortie to the lobby he and Rick had discovered ancient military paraphernalia displayed in the line of glass cabinets Babb had mentioned. "Sounds odd," she said, "but intriguing. I'll take a look while we're driving."

***

Back on the highway, Marion hunkered down and started to study the photographs. To see the screen of Rick's phone clearly, she'd put on her reading glasses then draped the picnic blanket over her head to block out the sun's glare. Five minutes later, as the Jeep sped west on Route 160, she pulled the blanket off her head for a gulp of fresh air.

"It's hard to see the detail," she said, now looking like a Celtic royal with the tartan blanket draped round her shoulders, "but to me it looks like it's simply a tribute to several generations of a family with the surname Dubois that served in the French military from the 17th to the 18th century."

Lucas swivelled round in his seat to talk to the librarian. "One of the things I read was a commendation for bravery. Have you seen that one yet?"

Marion nodded. "Yeah, that's the one I'm trying to read now, I think," she said. "Was it for a Sergeant Ravel Dubois?"

"That's the one," Lucas replied. "From the bit I read, I'd say he was one tough hombre."

"Let me keep reading," she said, "then I'll be able to tell you more." She whipped the blanket back over her head to continue with her studies.

"What's she saying?" Rick asked as Lucas turned back to face forward. "Has she got any ideas?"

Lucas shook his head. "Not yet," he replied, then gave a thumbs up and smiled, "but she will."

***

News of The Divinity's federal mauling spread like wildfire. The implications for its many underworld partners and associates were significant. They varied dramatically in severity; some were more fortunate than others.

In Arizona, The White Warriors Motorcycle Club was one of the lucky ones. Surprisingly, the outlaw bikers escaped the annihilation of Dubois's cult completely unscathed. Only ever employed as hired guns and muscle, at the time of the raids not a single member of the club was on Divinity duty and for that Ironman Connolly was thankful.

"Bastard feds," he'd said when first told. "How the fuck did they know?" Then seconds later, after realising how close the MC had come to being snared, he shook his head in amazement. "Boy, did we pick the right day to stay away," he muttered as he looked up and crossed himself.

Now, sat in a Phoenix safe house talking through the news with Red Clarke, Mike Connolly couldn't stop thinking about the timing. "Forty-eight hours earlier and we'd have been right up shit creek without a paddle," he said. "Talk about touching lucky."

"The sun shines on the righteous, bro," Red grinned, "and we're as righteous as they fuckin' come."

As the discussions continued, the biker boss conceded that even losing the two collection agents from the back of their van was a blessing in disguise.

"Think on, Red," he said. "Imagine if we'd got hooked in 'coz of them two dickheads. Fuck, that would've been a disaster!" He stopped and grinned. "Now there's no ties, no trail back to us, and no need to worry about the feds."

But the club's burly Quartermaster didn't see it quite the way his President did. Red was still smarting from the brazen escape the two UK visitors had pulled off on the mountain road. He couldn't believe they'd had the balls and the nous to do it, but they had, and he'd still like nothing more than to find the pair of them and slit their throats. "We gotta hunt those motherfuckers down," he said to his leader, "and dish out some major payback."

The Ironman smiled. "Listen, Red," he said calmly. "We've had a close call, bro, so let's not push it, let's leave it for a while. We'll let the dust settle, see what crawls out of the rubble, then decide, OK?"

Whilst Red respected his leader, he didn't always agree with him. "Whatever you think's best Mike," he said begrudgingly. "But if it was my call, I wouldn't be so cautious…."

Mike Connolly nodded slowly but didn't speak; he'd made his point, there was nothing more to say.

CHAPTER 60

Swan Song

By the time Rick had the Wrangler rumbling through the outskirts of North Peak National Park, Marion had studied the photos and pieced together her theory about the military display. Despite the mild-mannered librarian being tired, hungry, and desperate for a shower, it hadn't been enough to dampen her enthusiasm for unravelling the mystery.

"Listen up, gentlemen," she said as she folded the tartan blanket away, "I have a cast iron connection and a believable backstory, but I think you're going to find the whole thing a little hard to digest."

"We're all ears," Lucas said as he twisted in his seat to look at her, "so just give us your take on it and let us decide if we think it's believable or not."

"Yes, yes, OK, Lucas," Marion said. "Here goes," she paused, let out a faint cough then continued, "I think we'll start in Scotland in 1746 and work from there, OK?"

***

Half an hour later, as Rick pulled the Jeep up the cabin's steep drive, the tale of Vincent Dubois's formidable French ancestors, particularly the exploits of Master Sergeant Ravel Dubois, had been re-run several times.

"But why would France send soldiers to fight in Scotland for Bonnie Prince Charlie?" Rick asked as he got out for a much-needed stretch. "I thought it was just an English versus Scots thing."

Marion shook her head, then in a tone that suggested she knew her subject well, started to explain. "That's a common misconception, Rick," she said, wagging a cautionary finger at him, "But you can rest assured it was far more involved than that. It ran a lot, lot deeper than just warring neighbours."

***

Once the road weary comrades had finished unpacking, they sat in the lounge for a much-needed breather. And as they savoured fresh, strong coffees they continued discussing Marion's theory.

"I'm still not following all this," Rick said. "What's the connection with our book?"

The link between Vincent Dubois, his French ancestors, and the 1746 battle of Culloden had been clearly established by the exquisite display in the lobby of the teaching facility, but how that ultimately linked to the PCOS's Book of Martyrs would now require a massive leap of faith.

"Look," Marion said as she swung the laptop screen to face the two men, "this is a photo we got sent after the Illinois exhibition."

Lucas and Rick looked at the image of a printed information card on screen. It was the card that had accompanied the PCOS's book in its display case during the event. "That's some claim to fame," Rick said after reading the description, "but how do you prove something like that?"

"It's like all these things," she answered. "Historians spend thousands of hours meticulously recording how they see the world around them, then researchers like me spend an equal amount of time trawling every ancient written word to try and separate the facts from the myths, legends and folklore."

"But surely that's what this is," Lucas said as he touched the computers screen. "A myth, a myth that gives the book its own USP, a USP that ultimately adds to its value and status. Am I right?"

Marion looked deadly serious for a moment but chose not to answer the question directly. "When I got involved in the initial investigation," she said, "I had to undertake some heavy research and I mean heavy," she stopped, eased back in her chair but held the furrowed brow. "I've read a copy of the original Book of Martyrs and I can tell you it's not a pleasant task, in fact I'd go as far to say it was traumatic, but," she paused again although now looked less angst ridden, "…but it made me realise that the claims about this work being used to incite religious hatred were undoubtedly true."

"Do you mean generally or just in relation to this event?" Lucas asked.

"Both," she replied.

"OK," he said nodding slowly. "But can you be more specific for our particular book."

"Well, for one, the timescales match perfectly," she replied. "Secondly, the locations all tie with the PCOS's records and, most importantly from a non-ecumenical point of view, if ever there was a book that could fan the flames of Catholic hatred then this is it."

Lucas smiled. "So, what you're saying is that even if it was just a fanciful notion used to spice up highland folklore, the physical circumstances surrounding the claim do all stack up to a formal audit."

"Yes, in a way," Marion replied, "although I think what I'm really trying to explain is that historically the facts align. The dates, the location, the political backdrop, and, of course the religious turmoil of the period is right, so we know ninety-five per cent of the story is accurate. But that final five per cent… The packed church, the young preacher, a near two-hundred-year-old copy of the book of Martyrs being used to enrage an entire highland clan…well, it might just as well be make-believe."

As Marion talked the two men had perched on the edge of their seats listening avidly to her every word. Lucas had asked several probing questions, which she'd answered. They were both now sat back in thoughtful silence. Eventually Lucas spoke again. "Do you believe the five per cent is spin, then, Marion?" he asked, "Or do you think what's claimed about this book actually happened?"

Marion shrugged her shoulders and fixed him with a blank stare. "What *I* believe is immaterial," she said. "The story is out there, and that book went into an international exhibition with that claim as its reason for taking centre stage. Some will have believed it and some will have dismissed it as pure fantasy," she stopped and smiled. "but now I'm sure I know of one person who went to that exhibition and believed."

"Who?" Rick piped up.

Marion wrinkled her nose. "Well, I'd say that was obvious by now, wouldn't you?" she said. The small but attentive audience glanced between themselves then back to her. "Go on," Rick said. "Tell us."

But before she could answer Lucas cut in. "Vincent Dubois," he said. "Your guess is this Divinity top man saw it at the exhibition, then spirited it away after the event," he stopped and looked to the demure librarian for acknowledgement. Marion didn't comment but nodded her agreement, so Lucas continued. "OK," he said, "but why go to all that trouble, what exactly would he do with it? Yes, the book's supposedly connected to a famous battle one of his ancestors died in, but is that it, is that the sole reason? If it is, then, more importantly, what the hell has he done with it?"

"We don't know the answer to that," Marion sighed, "and you know what, I don't think we ever will."

***

It was now twelve hours since the foursome had been released by the FBI, but it felt like a lifetime. In the short period since arriving back at the cabin they'd unpacked, showered, laundered clothes, eaten, and phoned home. In the clamour for the bathroom, Lucas had valiantly volunteered to be last to use the facilities but when he finally appeared scrubbed clean in fresh clothes, his smile said it all. "Thank you, Barbara, I haven't enjoyed a shower so much in a long time."

Babb was tending a pan on the stove. "Feels good, doesn't it?" she said as she glanced to look at the appreciative Englishman. "Now go sit yourself down; it's time to eat."

It wasn't just the shower that had been hammered; the washing machine was put through its paces, the tumble drier worked overtime and everything still vaguely edible in the cabin had been thrown together for the eagerly anticipated meal. The landline had also been utilised to full effect: Rick rang home, Lucas rang Gerry, and Marion rang her boss. As a bonus, the eight-hour time difference worked in the visitors' favour; it gave their team back in the UK a whole working day to sort out flights, something Lucas knew the ever-efficient Ms Knox would appreciate.

During the eclectic supper, the itinerary for the following day was discussed. As Babb dished out piles of mashed potato and green beans, Lucas read out his thoughts from a scrap of paper. "Marion drops her car off at home, then Babb brings Marion to Glendale. We meet you two at the Hertz rental place, we'll give the Mustang back, then we all head to the airport in the Jeep, OK?"

Everyone nodded. "I think it's great that you want to see us off," he said after running through the details for a second time. "It's a long way to go just to say goodbye, but if you're sure that's what you want, then it helps us out and it's appreciated."

"We wouldn't have it any other way," Marion said, then looking to her sister asked, "Would we, B?"

Babb placed the serving spoon back in the empty bowl and smiled at the two men. "Absolutely not," she said. "After what we've been through these past couple of days, well…" she chuckled. "Well, I'd say you two boys were practically family now."

***

Despite the cabin only having two bedrooms, Babb was still the perfect host: she made the beds up in the spare room for Lucas and Rick and let Marion bunk in with her. It was a cosy arrangement, but the weary foursome slept the sleep of the dead. When the piercing rays of early morning sunshine started to make their presence known, Lucas was first to stir. As he rubbed his eyes and yawned he looked across at his still slumbering colleague.

"Hey, Ricky," he said quietly. "It's time to get up, mate…we got a big day today." He leant over and gently shook the South African's shoulder. "Happy days, Kruger, we're going home."

***

CHAPTER 61

Adios Amigo

As the Armstrong sisters waited patiently under the shade of a bright logoed awning, Marion took a peek through the glass into the reception area.

"Seems to be taking a long time to sort out," she said as she watched Lucas gesticulating wildly at the rental counter. "A lot of hassle by the looks of it."

"I'm not surprised," Babb said. "I mean; did you see the man's face when he saw the car?"

Marion and Babb had watched from a distance as the HSG men led the Duty Manager out to the Ford. But even from their remote vantage point, it was obvious the man had been appalled by the state in which the car had been returned. As he stormed back into the building, Lucas and Rick followed close behind.

"But surely we're covered on our insurance, err, Marcus, is that right?" they heard Lucas say as he read the Manager's name badge, but Marcus was far from sympathetic.

"Yes, it's Marcus, sir. And you're Mr Roxby, sir. Mr Roxby who has no record of an accident, no proof of police involvement, no accident record... It's classed as malicious damage. I'm sorry to say it's a serious issue that I will have to report up the line." Marcus' voice rose in exasperation.

Twenty minutes later and, despite Lucas appearing briefly to assure the sisters it wouldn't take long, there still seemed to be no end to the negotiations.

"You OK, Marion?" Babb asked as she looked closely at her sibling. "You look a little peaky."

It was true. The dazed librarian wasn't feeling one hundred per cent. Marion was struggling to come to terms with the events of the last couple of days, particularly the news about Meredith Higham. Whilst the FBI had been keen to eliminate the sisters from their investigation, when Marion asked about Meredith the interview had gone in a whole new direction. Eventually, after a long-winded question and answer session finally established her connection, the agents confirmed that the socialite had been a casualty of the operation. But the bureau men would tell her little else. Nothing further was explained about the circumstances of the tragedy; there was no how, why or where given. On all counts they remained resolutely tight lipped.

"I don't feel great," Marion replied, "but I think I'll live..." She rubbed her forehead. "I'm just thinking about Meredith, that's all. It's such a terrible ending."

"But you don't know the facts, do you?"

"No, but that's irrelevant," she said. "It's still very sad she's gone, however it happened."

"Obviously," Babb said, "but how'd she get caught up in the mess in the first place? I mean, why would her involvement with those screwballs get her killed?"

Marion looked despondent. "They wouldn't tell me anything more. I can only guess she was simply an innocent in the wrong place at the wrong time."

Babb looked at the floor. "Do you think Lucas was right?" she asked. "Was his theory about her being some sort of stooge correct?"

Marion shrugged. "I don't know, but it might help explain things... and it would mean she was on the right side of the law." She looked her sister in the eye. "But it's a bit far-fetched, isn't it?"

"I don't know," came the answer. "Given the week we've had, is it really *that* difficult to believe?"

Marion didn't reply. She'd been distracted by someone getting out of a beige sedan in the drop-off at the front of the building. A smartly dressed man, probably in his fifties, was looking intently at the vehicles parked in the Returns Zone. He shut the car door gently, then started to walk towards the reception. As he drew closer, Marion couldn't take her eyes off him.

"Would you take a look at this guy, B," she whispered as she nudged her sister. "He looks rather… suave."

"Good morning, ladies," the man said as he suddenly veered toward them. "I wonder if you can help me?"

Marion glanced at her sister then to the man. "If we can, we will," she said, instantly drawn to his piercing blue eyes. "What's the question?"

Blue Eyes smiled. "The white Mustang over there," he said with a subtle flick of his hand. "Is that yours?"

Marion automatically looked in the direction he'd indicated. "No, it's not," she said. "It's…" she stopped to think about her answer. "It's nothing to do with us," she mumbled, realising giving away personal information to random strangers - however good looking - was a bad idea. But from his expression she knew she hadn't sounded convincing.

"OK, then," he drawled. "Any idea whose it is?"

Babb stepped forward. "Who's asking?" she said, now feeling a little uneasy. "And why ask us?"

He turned his mesmeric gaze on Babb. "I'm with The Bureau, ma'am," he said politely. "FBI special Agent Dooley at your service."

The sisters exchanged surprised glances before Babb held out her hand. The feds? Again? This was getting ridiculous.

"Let's see some ID, mister," Babb snapped. "You could be anyone."

Blue Eyes continued talking as he reached into his jacket. "You're right there," he said with a knowing smile. "You just can't trust anyone these days, can you?"

As he placed the heavy shield in Babb's outstretched palm, she suddenly flashed back to the gloom of the Colorado basement. The injured FBI man on the floor, the man in the blue overalls, was called Dooley.

Her hand trembled faintly as she looked closely at the badge. She was no expert, but to her the shield looked authentic. When she turned it over to check the back she saw an inscription that read: *FBI Special Agent Wade Dooley.* Instantly her stomach lurched, and her blood ran cold. Oh, dear Lord, she thought, as she recalled Rick Kruger reading out that exact name, what are the chances of meeting two FBI agents called Wade Dooley in the space of just three days?

"You alright, ma'am? Something wrong?"

Standing frozen, silently staring at the badge, it was obvious from her pallid complexion there was a problem.

"What's the matter, B?" Marion asked. "Are you ill?"

Ill? Yeah, that's it, Babb thought, I'm ill.

"Oh, my God," she gushed suddenly appearing unsteady on her feet. "I'm so sorry… I've just come over all faint." As Babb feigned the collie-wobbles, Marion instinctively grabbed her round the waist to steady her.

"Dear Lord, Barbara," she said. "What on earth's wrong with you, you look awful? Let's get you inside for a sit down and some water."

Blue Eyes knew something was wrong but couldn't quite figure out if the reason given was genuine. "Lady," he said. "You better go do as your friend says… and I'll take my badge back."

Babb handed the shield back and then, holding onto her sister for support, limped off toward the reception. He watched the two women for a few seconds then turned back towards his car.

As soon as the sisters were out of earshot Babb whispered, "He's no FBI agent and that's not his ID."

Marion was confused. "I don't understand. How can you tell?"

But before Babb could start explaining, Lucas emerged from the building looking flustered.

"Look, Marcus, mate, I can show you," he was saying in a loud voice. "It's simple to prove. Come on, follow me and I'll show you." From his demeanour it was obvious his negotiations were still not going well. "Girls, I apologise for the wait," he said as he flashed past the staring sisters. "This dick is annoying the shit out of me."

Babb tried to grab him as he went. "Lucas, just wait a minute, will you? I think we've got a bigger problem," but the Englishman was striding ahead, only focused on one thing.

"Yeah, yeah, in a sec," he said brusquely. "I just need to show this obnoxious moron our company insurance then I'll be with you."

A now frustrated Marcus was hot on the heels of the irate ex-sapper and could clearly hear his comments. "That's slander, man," he protested loudly. "I'll sue your ass off, *Mister* Roxby, if you carry on like this."

Lucas didn't respond; he just carried on toward the battered Mustang. But, before he could get to it, he was confronted by the sister's sinister stranger.

"Is this your car?" Blue Eyes asked, as he looked the Englishman straight in the eye. Lucas froze; something definitely didn't feel right. Then, as the flustered Hertz rep caught up with them, the stranger pulled a gun.

"Jesus Christ!" Lucas yelped as he stared at the pistol in disbelief. "What the fuck you doing?"

"I asked if this is your car," Blue Eyes snarled as he pointed the weapon at him. "All I want is an answer!"

Before Lucas could respond, the rental manager started to protest. "Are you insane, man?" he shouted. "This place is covered by CCTV and we're linked direct to the Sheriff's office." He stepped forward fearlessly, before adding firmly, "So, if I were you buddy, I'd put the gun down."

The pistol wielding blue-eyed suit didn't say a word. He shook his head, calmly aimed the gun at Marcus and pulled the trigger twice. The 9mm rounds slapped into his chest with sickening force and he crumpled to the baking hot concrete like a rag doll. Lucas was rooted to the spot, trying to process what he'd just witnessed and with his life flashing before him.

"Now I'll ask again," Blue Eyes said far too calmly. "Is this your car?"

"Sweet Jesus, Marion - he's shot the rental guy!" Babb shrieked across the car park. Marion didn't answer. She was now suffering the same temporary paralysis as Lucas. "For God's sake, sis, come on!" Babb shouted. "We've got to get help."

"But we can't leave Lucas!" the shell-shocked librarian muttered.

"All we can do is pray," Babb said as she grabbed her sister's hand and started to drag her away to safety. "We've got to get the cops here - now!"

As Lucas stood silently in the return zone, the stranger stared at him and smiled. "Cat got your tongue?" he hissed.

"I'm just trying to work out who you are," the ex-sapper had found his tongue. His every instinct screamed to insult the stranger, but his military training kicked in: keep it on an even keel, Roxby, he told himself, and play for time.

The stranger kept the gun trained on the Englishman but with his free hand reached into his inside pocket. "I'll give you clue," he said as he walked closer to the Mustang. Then, with a deft flick of the wrist, he threw something onto the bonnet and grinned. "You left that for me last time you came calling."

Lucas looked at what was now lying in the centre of the Ford's dinted, dirty hood. From what he could make out, it looked much like a business card and, as he stepped closer to get a better look, the bright yellow logo seemed familiar. "Go on, pick it up," the suit said. "Check it out."

"Can't see a thing without my gigs," Lucas said with fake bravado, buying every moment he could for his team. "Are you OK with me getting them out?"

"You limeys make me laugh," Blue Eyes replied in a mocking tone. "Yeah, go on, you get your 'gigs' out, whatever the fuck they are."

Lucas wanted to laugh at the American's lack of understanding, but the grip of fear was far too tight. The sneering figure before him was a contradiction. He was trim, handsome, well dressed, and obviously educated, but his ability to kill indiscriminately without a moment's hesitation made him terrifying; he was truly beauty and beast in one.

"Thank you," Lucas said as he rummaged around for as long as he could before pulling out his decrepit glasses and waved them in the air, "and I assure you these will help."

The handsome stranger didn't comment; he just kept the pistol trained on the lanky Brit and watched him pick the business card up and study it. Lucas was right, as soon as the card came into focus he confirmed it bore the HSG logo and, what's more, it was his own personalised business card.

"Where did you get this?" Lucas asked.

"From you, Mr Roxby, albeit indirectly."

"I don't follow." Lucas was wracking his brains for a connection. "I have never set eyes on you before, yet you know my name and have turned up out of the blue to find me. Why?"

"Why, Mr Roxby," he grimaced and stepped a little closer. "Because I never forget a threat, that's why. You see, I take it very personally. Any man that threatens me or causes me harm will always pay a price for his lack of respect."

"But I don't know you," Lucas tried to sound casually puzzled. "So how have I caused you a problem?"

Those blue eyes narrowed. "You do disappoint me," he hissed, "but for simplicity's sake let's just say I see you as a harbinger of doom. For the misery caused since your arrival, you must be punished."

The sudden roar of an approaching engine drowned out Lucas' reply. A huge recovery truck was barrelling straight for them. Blue Eyes whipped around to see what was happening, but in an instant had spun back again and pulled the trigger. Lucas had started to move too but the stranger was faster. The round clipped him in the right shoulder, sending him spinning over the battered bonnet of the Mustang. As Lucas flew through the air, the gun man turned back to face the onrushing vehicle and took aim. He fired several times. The wind shield disintegrated in a glittering eruption of glass to reveal the contorted face of Rick Kruger behind the wheel.

"Die, motherfucker," the incensed South African screamed as he aimed the monster truck at the gun man. "Die, die, die."

Blue Eyes was fast on his feet. He dodged contact with the front of the thundering beast with a single daring matador sidestep. Rick was furious he'd missed his target, and slammed on the brakes, desperate to try again. The vehicle screeched to a halt, leaving solid black streaks smoking on the concrete before coming to rest with an earth-shattering crunch in a line of parked cars.

The South African was running on pure adrenalin. He looked round frantically for signs of the attacker but couldn't see him. Shards of glass cascading from his hair, he sat for a moment breathing heavily as the sound of wailing sirens started up somewhere not too far away. They got closer and louder. Then three gun shots rang out, a woman screamed, and his heart hit his boots.

***

The emergency services response to the 911 call was rapid. At first glance, it was hard for the state troopers to tell what had happened, but it looked like the threat had been neutralised. Several marked cars had surrounded the car rental area, lights flashing.

"Put the gun down, lady," a tall, black officer's commanding voice came through the loudhailer. "Place it on the floor and get your hands on your head."

Rick jumped down from the truck's cab and sprinted towards the Mustang, his heart thumping. He'd heard the officer's order but couldn't see who it was directed at.

He'd almost reached the vehicle when a voice boomed from behind him, "Hold it right there, big boy! Let's take it easy, shall we?"

He stopped dead and placed his hands on his head. From this new vantage point he could now see a pair of jean-clad legs sticking out from behind the Mustang's front wheel. Immediately he knew it was Lucas.

"I gotta help my friend," he shouted back to anyone who'd listen, but before any of the officers could respond, a distraught looking Marion popped up from behind the Ford.

"Rick, he's alive," she screamed, "but he's been hit in the shoulder."

Rick looked relieved – two comrades safe, one to go. "Where's your sister?" he screamed back. "Is she hurt?"

She's over there," she pointed across the parking lot. "She's unhurt, but she's in shock."

Rick stepped forward for a better look.

"Don't do it, blondie," the voice boomed out. "One more step and I will shoot you dead."

"OK, OK," the sweat drenched South African yelled. "I won't move a muscle."

Rick didn't need to; with that one extra step he could now view the main attraction.

There, in a narrow gap between two red Hyundai SUVs, stood Babb. On the floor in front of her was a small black pistol, and behind her - face down in a crumpled pile - lay the blue-eyed stranger sporting a cluster of three neat holes in the centre of his back.

CHAPTER 62

It's a Wrap

Virgil Koeman took the call as he got off a busy city centre tram, but still he couldn't contain his joy. "Fantastic news," he shouted punching the air and surprising the hell out of his fellow commuters. "It is just what we needed to hear," he said. "It is the icing for our cake."

The Dutchman wasn't wrong; it really was, as he put it, the icing for Europol's cake. Now Operation Stormbringer would be seen by most as an unquestionable success. When the FBI's SAC in Tucson rang to say Vincent Dubois had been shot and killed in Glendale, Arizona, Koeman couldn't have been happier. And whilst the circumstances surrounding the Monsignor's bloody demise at a car rental outlet were still unclear, it didn't matter, it was official: the mastermind behind The Divinity's vile trade, the man who had orchestrated the whole elaborate charade, the man who had milked it for everything he could, was dead, and that was the result that would have the biggest impact.

"Dead is good," Koeman had said to the SAC. "It's going to save the US taxpayers a lot of money, a lot of money indeed."

Now, thirty-five minutes after the call, he was back behind his desk and was quick to ensure the news of Dubois's shooting was briefed to all. He fired emails off to his superiors and the already ecstatic agency chiefs were even happier with the overall result. When the fifth floor team heard the news, its full forty-member contingent gave a rousing cheer. As Koeman stood on top of a hastily cleared desk in the centre of the office, he praised the efforts of his staff. As he told them that in his eyes it was simply not possible to assemble a better team than the one he had before him, he nearly shed a tear.

After the clapping, cheering, and back slapping had died down, the bespectacled Dutchman returned to his office to make a call. He needed to share this final vital snippet of information with the men from Ebro. Ultimately, it was the stand-up Spaniards who brought The Divinity down. They were the men who had held their nerve for eighteen months, the men who could have said no but didn't.

"Hello, Pedro, it's Virgil," he purred as he was put through. "I have some news you may like."

Pedro Grillo was intrigued. "Tell all," he replied. "Is it more good news?"

"It is done, my friend," the Europol chief said triumphantly. "It is finally over; we have closure...Dubois is dead."

There was a long pause as the Spaniard took in what he'd just been told, relief flooding over him. "It is like the Americans say, Virgil, my friend," he replied eventually. "Ding dong, the Witch is dead!"

***

Landing back in the UK, the HSG team were greatly relieved to be on home soil but after a long weekend off to acclimatise was over, it was time to return to work. When Lucas and Rick finally arrived back at HSG headquarters they weren't quite sure what was waiting for them. Undeterred, Rick bounded up the steps and through the front door like a bull elephant on speed.

"Come on, Sarge," he barked as he held the heavy wooden door open for his less enthusiastic colleague. "We haven't got all day, you know. The meeting's in ten."

As Lucas stepped into the dimly lit reception area, the main lights came on. Then suddenly the sound of clapping and cheering erupted and staff members appeared from doorways. "Ladies and Gentlemen, the Wanderers return," a voice boomed before a grinning Ray Stuart walked out from the front of the waiting crowd. "It's been a while, boys," he said, "but welcome home." Holding his smile firmly in place, he shook hands with both men like his life depended on it.

Lucas and Rick were gobsmacked; they stared at their CEO for a moment then past him at the sea of smiling faces gathered behind. Suddenly Lucas laughed and pointed upward. "Is that for us?" he asked as he looked at a banner suspended above the reception desk that read *Welcome Home, Boys!*

"Of course," Ray said. "To say we're bloody glad to have you two back alive would be an understatement."

Then, as if by magic, Gerry Hanlon materialised out of nowhere. "I second that," he said with a grin even wider than Ray's, "but I tell you, boys, there will be no more trips to the US for a while and that's a bloody promise, OK?" Everyone laughed, then Ray held his hands aloft and announced that a special breakfast was about to be served in the canteen. The gathering cheered in appreciation.

"Is it FOC, Mr Stuart?" Lucas asked cheekily. "Or we still got to pay?"

Ray looked at Lucas then glanced at his heavily strapped shoulder. "For the walking wounded," he said, "and all their hard-working colleagues, well, today it's on the house, Roxy." With that good news officially confirmed, everyone clapped. Ray then instructed the throng to form an orderly queue behind the returning duo and follow them down to the canteen for a celebratory welcome home feast.

Lucas and Rick had been away for a full three weeks. Since leaving the Warrington HQ in the early hours of August 21st to their return on this misty September morning, they'd had a roller coaster twenty-one-day ride. And, whilst from a company point of view the mission had been classed as an abject failure, judging by the fuss being made over their return it seemed their colleagues weren't bothered about the poor result.

Lucas got served quickly and, once he'd settled at a table, Sarah was first to join him. "How you feeling?" she asked. "How's the shoulder?"

The ex-sapper looked up and smiled. "It bloody kills," he said. "But don't tell anyone I told you, OK?"

Sarah sat down opposite him, and, as she expertly dispensed a jet of brown sauce over her scrambled eggs, she looked thoughtful.

"So, what was this Marion Armstrong like?" she asked. "I only spoke to her the once but from that she sounded nice and obviously knew her stuff. Was she as nice in real life?"

Lucas thought for a moment. "She was an absolute star," he said with a twinkle in his eye. "One of the sweetest women I have ever had the pleasure of meeting."

Sarah stared in disbelief. "My God, Lucas," she said. "Have you gone soft in your old age? I never thought I'd hear you say anything as generous as that about anyone."

He grinned then took a long slow slug of coffee. "Well, it just goes to show you, then, doesn't it?" he said as he put his mug down. "You should never say never."

Just as Sarah opened her mouth to respond, Rick arrived at the table. "Can't believe all this, Sarge," he said, beaming at his partner. "We need to fail more often!" Then, grinning wildly added, "And you need to get shot on a regular basis."

As Rick plonked himself down next to Sarah she turned toward him. "Lucas was just telling me about Marion," she said. "Seems she was a top drawer find."

Rick finished chomping on his first mouthful, then laughed. "Well, let's just say that without her we wouldn't have found your chapel," he said, "and without her little sister we'd both be six foot under."

Sarah sat wide eyed. "Yeah, from what Dad told me," she said, "it sounds like it was a close call. So, what exactly happened then?"

Lucas looked at Rick then back to Sarah. "How long you got?" he asked.

"As long as it takes," came an honest reply.

***

Sarah stayed in the canteen chatting with Rick and Lucas for what seemed like hours. Ray and Gerry joined the group for a while as did other colleagues who came over in dribs and drabs to pass on their regards and welcome them back. The returnees enjoyed the attention and answered everyone's questions as honestly and as fully as they could - but some were a little too probing for Lucas's liking.

"Did you and this Marion get it on?" Steve Harrison asked, obviously eager for some dirt. "From what I gather she was a bit of alright, wasn't she?"

Lucas laughed. "Jesus, Steve," he said, "that's a bit close to the bone, isn't it?"

The ex-DI looked round the table for support but got nothing but blank stares. "Well, you've gotta ask, haven't you?" he said not feeling in the least bit embarrassed. "I mean; it would be rude not too."

"OK, for all you cheeky bastards out there," Lucas said, "what I will say is that me and Ricky are now classed as fully paid up members of the Armstrong family and that's more than enough for me." He looked across at Rick. "That's how it is, isn't it Ricky? Me, you, Marion, and Babb: best mates for life!"

Rick looked around the expectant faces. "That's exactly how it is," he said with a beaming smile. "Fully Loaded and Library Lady will be forever in our hearts. A finer duo of travelling companions you will never find, and that's the God's honest truth."

All eyes looked in puzzlement at the South African. "I get the Library Lady tag," Sarah said, "but Fully Loaded, what the hell's that all about?"

Rick looked across at Lucas. "Over to you, Sarge," he said, "I think you best explain that one."

Lucas smiled. "It's a long story, but, in a nutshell, Marion's sister Babb, known in some circles as the ex-Mrs Teller, turned out to be a very well prepared and tenacious lady." He looked round at his listening colleagues. "And she had this top of the range Wrangler Jeep, right…and it had all sorts on it. She called it Ruby, and in her words Ruby was 'fully loaded' – and I can tell you, she wasn't bloody lying."

"Loaded with what kind of stuff?" Steve asked.

"Everything you could imagine," Lucas answered. "From winches to spotlights, from camping gear to tequila, from torches to first aid kits, from binoculars to wet wipes, you name it, the woman had it on, or in, that Jeep."

"Tell them the best bit, Sarge," Ricky said with a little smirk, "explain the surprise hidden extra."

Lucas looked at the South African blankly for a second. "Oh yeah," he said as the penny dropped, "Rick's right, the thing we couldn't have anticipated, well that's easy ..." he paused for dramatic effect, looked from the ex-DI to Rick and then back again, "because, Mr Harrison, unbeknownst to us, Fully Loaded was *truly* fully-loaded, and that's how she managed to save our lives."

***

Everyone was happy to have Lucas and Rick back in the fold. Due to her intimate involvement with their job, Sarah was probably happier than most. She'd thoroughly enjoyed the morning's coffee-fuelled Q & A session and was now looking forward to what the rest of the week would bring. More stories, more theories, and the chance of recriminations were all distinct possibilities. But for now, she'd heard enough; it was Monday afternoon, she had things to do and she needed to finish early.

***

David Stuart was 85 years old, a widower and although seeming a little frail at times was generally in good health. Despite numerous offers for him to move in with relatives close by, he lived alone in the end terrace he'd shared with his wife for more years than he could remember. His family were not overly worried, in fact they were impressed with the old man's self-reliant, can do attitude, and simply kept a watchful eye on him without making it too obvious. They saw him regularly. Deep down, old man Stuart, known to many as Diamond Dave due to his abundant generosity, loved the fact that if he ever did have problem there were a lot of people he could rely on to sort it out for him.

Monday evenings were a favourite of his: at the beginning of every week without fail, his beloved granddaughter visited him for a catch up and a fish supper. Usually she'd come calling around 6.00pm, so by 5.45 he'd have the table set. Two places laid out, a pot of tea, four slices of bread and butter, a large bottle of his favourite Sainsbury's own brand ketchup and some sachets of vinegar.

"That'll do it," he said to himself as he looked at the neatly arranged table. "Now better get that kettle filled."

Sarah was rarely late; even if work demands were piling up, she'd manage to work round it. She always saw her grandfather a couple of times a week, but their Monday night get togethers were sacrosanct. They were cast in stone and she wouldn't miss one for the proverbial gold clock.

"Gramps!" she shouted as she opened the door with her key. "It's only me. You got that table set?"

The old man shuffled to his kitchen door and looked down the hall at his adoring granddaughter. "As if you need to ask, child," he said with a wily grin. "That table is always set before you get here, you know that."

"I know," she said. "It must just be habit to ask."

He smiled. "You didn't forget the mushy peas, did you?"

Sarah laughed. "Now who's asking stupid questions?" She waved the bulging plastic bag in front of her.

Quickly she dished out battered haddock, chips and mushy peas she'd bought from granddad's local chippy, then, as the pair settled down to tuck into their weekly feast, old Dave looked up.

"So how was work today, young lady?" he asked. "How's your dad, is he behaving himself?" He paused to nudge his glasses back up his nose, then added, "Any more developments on this book thing?"

Granddad Stuart loved his progress updates and was always fascinated to hear how things were going at work. The HSG was his eldest son's life and for a long while now his granddaughter had played a significant part in the business too.

"The lads came back to work today," she said referring to Lucas and Rick's much heralded return. "It's been three weeks since any of us last saw them and I tell you, Gramps, they've been through it."

"How's the fella that got shot?" the old man enquired. "Is he on the mend?"

Sarah shrugged. "I think so, although he did admit it was still painful," she said. "But, hey, they both looked good, both seemed upbeat," she paused. "I think they're relieved to be back."

"Of course, they are," he said. "Three weeks away from home is a long time for anyone."

She smiled. "Yeah, you're right," she said as she prepared to pour the tea, "and Dad's OK, I suppose. He's glad they got back in one piece, but I think he's still pissed off they didn't get the book." She leant over and topped up her granddad's cup. "As you know, he doesn't take failure well, does he?"

Diamond Dave looked at his guest. "None of us do, my dear," he said slowly. "Can't say I've ever met a man who admitted to liking failure, so don't be too hard on him."

"Oh, I'm not," she said, "and I'm as bad. It pisses me off as well. It's such a shame they went all that way, went through all that grief, only to come home empty-handed."

"So, what's the story on the book then?" he probed, "Or is that it – is the case closed?"

Sarah drained the dregs of her tea and put the cup down. "We don't call it a case, gramps," she said with an impish grin, "but in reality the job's been a dud and there's little else we can do, so, yes, in essence it's closed." She sat back in her chair and sighed. "No one knows where that book is, even the American authorities are clueless, so for now Gerry's put Lucas on light duties in the yard and sent Rick to help a team in Ireland for a few days." She looked her grandfather in the eye. "I reckon even Dad's given up hope now."

Dave nodded his understanding then the two of them continued to natter about Arizona and the book saga in general. They talked at length about her role, about the research she'd done, and about her father's annoyance that all the company's hard work had come to nothing.

"Oh, by the way, did he solve his other little puzzle?" Dave asked as he recalled a previous conversation. "The issue about why this Reid chap kept quiet about the link with the Campbell's and Culloden?"

Sarah looked closely at her grandfather. Eighty-five he might be, but there was nothing wrong with his memory, still sharp as a pin. "No, sadly not," she replied. "Dad still can't fathom that one out, in fact nobody can…and no one dares ask."

The old man raised his hand. "Well, I have a theory," he said as he waggled his bony fingers jokingly, like some demented old wizard. "Do you want to hear it?"

She was intrigued. "Of course I do, Gramps," she said. "Fire away."

Dave smiled, then stroked his chin and looked even more wizard like. "Could've been the name, maybe," he said. "Might have got them spooked, see, could be why they didn't let on…but it's just a thought, mind."

Sarah was confused. "What do you mean 'the name'?" she asked.

He raised an eyebrow. "Well, what's your name?" he said.

"Sarah," she replied, now bemused by her grandfather's line of questioning, "but why ask?"

"No, silly, what's your full name?" he repeated in mock exasperation.

"Sarah Jane Stuart," she said.

"Right answer," he said. "Now what's your Dad's full name?"

She pulled a face. "Raymond Edward Stuart," she said, mystified, "but you know all this, what the hell are you trying to say?"

Diamond Dave wasn't giving up. "Bear with me," he said. "One more question, OK?" She didn't say a word but nodded slowly once, so he continued. "What was Bonnie Prince Charlie's full name?" he asked.

Sarah stared at her grandfather as she wracked her brains, then, as a frown as deep as a snow drift crept across her face, she whispered. "It was Charles Edward Stuart, wasn't it?" The old man smiled but said nothing. She answered her own question. "Yes, it was Charles Edward Stuart," she said as she sat back shaking her head in bewilderment. "But surely that's just pure unadulterated coincidence, isn't it?"

The old man sat up straight and folded his arms across his chest. "I think you should check your family history, my dear," he said with a mischievous wink. "A connection with that infamous House of Stuart may not be as far away as you think."

Sarah sat in stunned silence. "I'm sure you're wrong," she said, after mulling over the likelihood of a family connection, "but I'm back in the office in the morning so I'll start digging." She mimicked her grandad's hand waggling gesture. "If your crack-pot theory really is right, Gramps," she was beaming with excitement, "well, I can't wait to explain it to Dad!"

EPILOGUE

A Promise is a Promise

The email was completely unexpected. It was curt, concise and clear. But still, Ray had to read it three times before it sank in. And once it had, he reached for the phone.

"Gerry," he bellowed as his partner answered, "I think you need to get down here as fast as your fat hairy legs will carry you."

"What you on about?" came a bemused reply. "What's suddenly so important?"

"Just got some news from the States," Ray said, "and I think you'll want to hear it."

"From who?"

"The US authorities," he replied. "The Federal Bureau of Investigation, to be exact."

Gerry was now intrigued. "Saying what?" he asked.

Ray thought about winding his partner up for a second but then decided against it, "Just come down here. It's better explained face to face."

***

It was now two weeks since the field team had returned from Arizona. They'd come back battered, bruised, pissed off and empty handed, and things hadn't improved much. The job was still classed as a write-off but thankfully there were some positives: Lucas was on the mend and the doctors were confident he'd make a full recovery; Rick was back from a brief foray in Ireland and was now eagerly preparing for a job on the South coast; Gerry, well, good old Gerry had travelled to Glasgow for the unenviable task of appeasing Doctor Reid and his distraught Synod. During this second visit to the weird and wonderful citadel of St. James, the HSG Ops Director had gone to great lengths to explain the circumstances surrounding the final stages of the operation and had ultimately apologised for the company's failure to locate the PCOS's cherished book. The Elders were far from impressed with what they were told but begrudgingly accepted the situation; although they appeared understanding, Gerry knew the climb-down was a sympathy vote based on Lucas and Rick's near-death experience.

Ray wasn't the only one that didn't cope well with failure; it was a collective company response. It was obvious every member of the team involved with the Arizona operation was feeling aggrieved. But now Ray was confident that in one fell swoop he could lift the gloom; this latest news was just the tonic they needed. So, before Gerry even had the chance to make himself comfortable, Ray let loose.

"They've found it!" he announced triumphantly. "The bloody FBI have bloody recovered our bloody book."

Gerry stopped in his tracks and stood staring in wide-eyed disbelief at his grinning partner. "You've gotta be kidding me," he squawked. "What have they said? Where was it?"

Ray smiled. "The teaching place in Colorado," he said. "According to the email it was in a safety deposit box in the building's strong room."

"Would you Adam and Eve it!" Gerry eased himself into an armchair. "Big Ronnie's tip-off was on target after all!" He chuckled and scratched his head, "And there was me thinking it was just another wild goose chase."

"That's not the best of it," Ray grinned. "The FBI confirm the book's been assessed by the investigation team and despite some blood staining," he pulled a face and shrugged, "it's been deemed irrelevant to the case and can be returned to its rightful owners." He glanced at his laptop screen, "The only thing is, we've got to arrange collection and shipping ourselves."

"That's fair enough," Gerry muttered. "So, OK, then, when can we get our hands on it?"

"That's the drawback," Ray said. "The book is with US customs. It's in a clearing house in Tucson and has to be rubber-stamped by them before it can leave US soil. Here's the only rub: the FBI are saying that process could take at least six months, possibly even more."

Gerry pushed back in his chair. "Better than no book at all, though. isn't it?" he said. "So, it's still great news all round, in fact. Raymond. it's absolutely fantastic fuckin' news."

The two men sat congratulating themselves in the office for a while then started to think about the next course of action. "What about asking the big man?" Gerry asked. "Your pal Ronnie said he was well up on US customs regulations, didn't he? I'm sure he said Excel shipped a lot stuff back and forth from the States or am I making that bit up?"

Ray looked at his partner. "No… he did say that," he said. "So maybe he is the man to look into the return for us - might be right up his street. mightn't it?"

"Hopefully this time," Gerry said, "we can just get it shipped direct to here. No need for a collection team…probably cost an arm and a leg, mind, but it would make life so much easier, wouldn't it?"

Ray reached for the phone. "Let's give him a bell," he said. "See what the man says. Might as well get the ball rolling now we're in the swing of it."

***

Ronnie Stafford was positively ecstatic to hear from his new friend. After Ray thanked him profusely again for the Colorado tip-off he explained the latest situation. Then he asked his advice about shipping the book back to the UK.

"Sure," Ronnie said. "If you've got the depot address and contact details plus an item reference number, then, yes, I can make some enquires for you."

Ray was impressed with the big man's willingness to help. "That's great, Ronnie," he said. "Yeah, we've got all the details, so I'll send them over now if you like."

"Get them to me, Raymond," he said. "I'll get straight on the case – and let's see what I can do."

Ray said his goodbyes to Man Mountain then looked across the desk at his expectant partner. "Well, Gerry," he said, "he's up for it… says he'll see what he can do and get back to us."

The Irishman looked relieved. "Good," he said. "Might take months before it's back but I reckon we tell the troops it's been found. Might go a long way to restoring morale."

"Absolutely," Ray said as he leapt up from behind his desk. "In fact, let's do it now" and with that he charged out of the office towards the stairs…

***

The news went down a storm. And, exactly as they'd predicted, the mood of the entire team lifted. Sarah was ecstatic about the announcement and felt both relieved and vindicated in equal measure. "Well there you go, Steve," she said as she sat back in her chair and looked across the office. "From the jaws of defeat, we snatch victory. What a turnaround, eh?"

"Almost worth getting shot for," the ex-DI said. "It's like you've said before, though, isn't it…when you think of all the blood that's been spilt over that book it breaks your heart." He thought about his own comment, then shrugged. "Maybe Lucas Roxby's will be the last."

Sarah shook her head. "I'd love to think that was the case," she said, "but you know what, Steve, there's more chance of getting a Nandos in North Korea than that."

***

Ray was surprised Ronnie Stafford rang back so quickly. It was less than 24 hours since he'd called so, eager for an update, he hit the flashing red button hard.

"Hi, Ronnie. that was quick," he said. "You got something already?"

Stafford took a deep breath. "Well, Raymond. you know I like questions," he said, "so let's start with one: what do you want first - the good news or the bad news?"

Ray thought for a second. "Well. let's go for the bad news first," he said, happy to play along. "I've always preferred it that way."

Ronnie chuckled. "OK, then," he said. "The bad news is your book hasn't even been officially logged in Tucson yet; there's an eight month back-log of impounded items awaiting inspection and clearance and your little treasure is at the end of the queue."

Ray sighed and shook his head. "Oh, right," he said. "That does sound like bad news…so what's the good news then?"

"Well, here's the thing," Ronnie said. "We know a man who knows a man, if you get my drift…a man who's always on hand to help ease problems for people in the business."

"The import and export business you mean?" Ray interrupted. "Like Excel?"

"I suppose you could say that," he said, "but you don't need to worry about the detail, the point is he can help us."

"Us being you and me right?"

"Correct, Raymond," Stafford replied. "You and me together, and here's the deal, right," he paused, "our man can fast track the system – but only if the price is right."

Ray fell silent as he considered the offer. "OK, so this guy," he said eventually, "what money are we talking and what timescales?"

"Excellent question," Ronnie said, knowing Ray would ask that exact question. "How's the back end of next week grab you?"

"Back end of next week?" the CEO repeated. "Are you fucking joking?"

"No, Raymond, I am not joking," came the reply. "Like I said, this man can fast track the process."

"There's a difference between fast tracking and miracle working," Ray replied, "and that offer definitely falls into the latter category."

Ronnie laughed. "Oh, very droll, Raymond," he said, "but you are right; it does sound too good to be true. He *can* do it," he chuckled to himself, "of that I can assure you."

"OK, say he can," Ray replied, before thinking about how to phrase his next question, "if he can guarantee that our book will clear US customs and be shipped back to the UK by the end of next week how much is that going to cost me?"

The line fell silent for a second. "A steak dinner," Ronnie said, "plus a few bottles of decent claret."

Ray took the phone away from his ear, looked at it in disbelief then returned it. "Did I hear you right?" he asked. "A steak dinner and a couple of bottles of wine – are you mental?"

"Possibly," came the reply, "but that's the deal, Raymond. I'll sort getting your book back for next week, then you take me out for a slap-up, then we're both happy.... take it or leave it."

"But how...why?" Ray stammered.

Ronnie drew another deep breath. "Because, Raymond, like I've said to you before, my friend, I look after those who look after me." Then the big man sighed a deep sigh, "Surely you remember? I told you, I'm a man of my word and I did promise to make it up to you."

Ray didn't answer...he couldn't; he had a lump in his throat.

The End

Printed in Great Britain
by Amazon

42935274R00303